Medusa

Clive Cussler is the author or co-author of thirty-seven previous books, including twenty Dirk Pitt® novels, seven NUMA® Files adventures, six *Oregon* Files books, three works of non-fiction, and his historical adventure, *The Chase*. He lives in Arizona.

Paul Kemprecos has co-authored all seven previous NUMA® Files novels with Cussler and is a Shamus Award-winning author of six underwater detective thrillers. A certified scuba diver and a former newspaper reporter, he lives in Massachusetts.

Find out more about the world of Clive Cussler by visiting: *www.clivecussler.co.uk*

MEDUSA

CLIVE CUSSLER

WITH PAUL KEMPRECOS

MICHAEL JOSEPH
an imprint of
PENGUIN BOOKS

MICHAEL JOSEPH

Published by the Penguin Group

Penguin Group (Australia), 250 Camberwell Road, Camberwell, Victoria 3124, Australia
(a division of Pearson Australia Group Pty Ltd)

Penguin Group (USA) Inc., 375 Hudson Street, New York, New York 10014, USA

Penguin Group (Canada), 90 Eglinton Avenue East, Suite 700, Toronto ON M4P 2Y3, Canada
(a division of Pearson Penguin Canada Inc.)

Penguin Books Ltd, 80 Strand, London WC2R 0RL, England

Penguin Ireland, 25 St Stephen's Green, Dublin 2, Ireland
(a division of Penguin Books Ltd)

Penguin Books India Pvt Ltd, 11 Community Centre, Panchsheel Park, New Delhi – 110 017, India

Penguin Books (NZ) Ltd, 67 Apollo Drive, Rosedale, North Shore 0632, New Zealand
(a division of Pearson New Zealand Ltd)

Penguin Books (South Africa) (Pty) Ltd, 24 Sturdee Avenue,
Rosebank, Johannesburg 2196, South Africa

Penguin Books Ltd, Registered Offices: 80 Strand, London, WC2R 0RL, England

First published in the United States of America by G. P. Putnam's Sons 2009
First published in Great Britain by Michael Joseph 2009
This edition published by Penguin Group (Australia), 2009

1   3   5   7   9   10   8   6   4   2

Copyright © Sandecker, RLLLP, 2009

Printed and bound in Australia by McPherson's Printing Group, Maryborough, Victoria

A CIP catalogue record for this book is available from the British Library

This is a work of fiction. Names, characters, places and incidents either are the product of
the author's imagination or are used fictitiously, and any resemblance to actual persons,
living or dead, businesses, companies, events or locales is entirely coincidental.

While the author has made every effort to provide accurate telephone numbers and internet
addresses at the time of publication, neither the publisher nor the author assumes any
responsibility for errors, or for changes that occur after publication. Further, the publisher
does not have any control over and does not assume any responsibility for author
or third-party websites or their content.

ISBN: 978-0-718-15469-1

penguin.com.au

'If the epidemic continues its mathematical rate of acceleration, civilization could easily disappear from the earth.'

– Dr. Victor Vaughn,
The American Experience, *'Influenza 1918'*

'Wash inside of nose with soap and water each night and morning; force yourself to sneeze night and morning, then breathe deeply; do not wear a muffler; take sharp walks regularly and walk home from work; eat plenty of porridge.'

– *Influenza prevention advice in
the* News of the World *newspaper, 1918*

PROLOGUE

THE PACIFIC OCEAN, 1848

IN ALL HIS YEARS SAILING THE WORLD'S OCEANS, CAPTAIN Horatio Dobbs had never known the sea to be so barren. The captain paced the quarterdeck of the New Bedford whaling ship *Princess,* gray eyes darting like twin lighthouse beams to every point of the compass. The Pacific was a disk-shaped blue desert. No spouts feathered the horizon. No grinning porpoises danced off the bow. No flying fish skittered above the wave tops. It was as if life in the sea had ceased to exist.

Dobbs was considered a prince in the New Bedford whaling hierarchy. In the waterfront bars where hard-eyed harpooners gathered, or in the parlors of the rich Quaker shipowners on Johnny Cake Hill, it was said that Dobbs could sniff out a sperm whale at fifty miles. But only the rank smell of a simmering mutiny had filled the captain's nostrils of late.

Dobbs had come to dread having to record each day of failure in the ship's logbook. The entry he had penned in his log the night before summed up the troubles he faced. He had written:

March 27, 1848. Fresh breeze, SW. Not a whale in sight. Hard luck hangs over voyage like a stinking fog. No oil in all of Pacific Ocean for poor ship Princess. *Trouble brewing in the fo'c'sle.*

Dobbs had a clear view of the length of the ship from the elevated quarterdeck, and he would have had to be blind not to see the averted gazes and the furtive glances from his crewmen. The ship's officers had reported with alarm that the usual grumbling among the forecastle crew had become more frequent and vehement. The captain had instructed his mates to keep pistols ready and never to leave the deck unattended. No hand had yet been lifted in mutiny, but in the dark and dingy forecastle, the cramped living quarters located where the bow narrowed, men were heard to whisper that the ship's luck might change if the captain were to meet with an accident.

Dobbs was six foot four and had a profile like a cliff. He was confident he could put down a mutiny, but that was the least of his worries. A captain who returned to port without a profitable cargo of oil had committed the unpardonable sin of costing the ship's owners their investment. No crew worth its salt would ever ship out with him. Reputation, career, and fortune could rise or fall on a single voyage.

The longer a ship spent at sea, the greater the chance of failure. Supplies ran short. Scurvy and disease became more likely. The ship's physical condition deteriorated and the crew lost its edge. Putting into port for repairs and supplies was risky. Men might jump ship to sign on to a more successful vessel.

The whaling expedition had gone downhill since the crisp autumn day when the gleaming new ship had pulled away from the bustling wharf to a roaring send-off. Dobbs was bewildered by the change in the ship's fortunes. No ship could have been better prepared for its maiden voyage. The *Princess* carried an experienced captain, a handpicked crew, and newly forged, razor-sharp harpoons.

The three-hundred-ton *Princess* was built by one of the most reputable shipyards in New Bedford. Just over a hundred feet long, the ship had a beam of nearly thirty feet that gave her room to store three thousand casks that could hold ninety thousand gallons of oil in her hold. She was built of sturdy live oak that could withstand the toughest seas. Four whaleboats rested in wooden davits that overhung the deck rails. Other mariners scorned the wide-bodied and square-ended New England whaling ships, but the rugged craft could sail for years through nasty conditions that would have had their sleeker counterparts leaking at the seams.

As the *Princess* left the dock, a spanking breeze had filled the great square sails that hung from the three masts, and the helmsman steered a course east out of the Acushnet River and into the Atlantic Ocean. Pushed by steady winds, the *Princess* had made a fast ocean crossing to the Azores. After a brief stop in Fayal to load up on fruit that would ward off scurvy, the vessel had pointed its bow toward the southern tip of Africa, rounding the Cape of Good Hope with no mishaps.

But in the weeks that followed, the *Princess* had zigzagged across the Pacific without seeing a single whale. Dobbs knew that finding whales had more to do with a solid knowledge of weather and migratory patterns than luck, but as he scanned the distant skyline in desperation, he began to wonder if his ship was cursed. He pushed the dangerous thought from his mind, strode over to the ship's cook, who was cleaning his stove, and said, "Play us a song with your fiddle."

Hoping to lift morale, the captain had urged the cook to play his fiddle at sunset every day, but the jolly music only seemed to highlight the sour mood aboard ship.

"I usually wait 'til sundown," the cook said glumly.

"Not today, cook. See if you can fiddle up a whale."

The cook put his cleaning rag aside and reluctantly unwrapped the cloth protecting his weather-beaten violin. Tucking the fiddle under his jowls, he took up the frayed bow and sawed away without tuning the instrument. He knew from their sullen looks that the crew thought his fiddling scared the whales away, and each time the cook played he feared, with good reason, that someone might toss him overboard. On top of that, he was down to two strings and his repertoire was limited, so he played the same songs the crew had heard a dozen times before.

As the cook sawed away, the captain ordered the first mate to take charge of the quarterdeck. He climbed down the narrow companionway to his cabin, tossed his weathered top hat onto his bunk, and sat down at his desk. He scanned his charts, but he had tried all the usual whaling grounds with nothing to show for his efforts. He sat back in his chair, closed his eyes, and let his chin drop to his chest. He had only dozed off for a few minutes before the wonderful words he hadn't heard in months penetrated his veil of sleep.

"She *blows*!" a voice repeated. "Thar she blows."

The captain's eyes snapped wide open, and he came out of his chair like a catapulted projectile, grabbed his hat, and vaulted up the ladder to the deck. He squinted against the bright sunlight at the main masthead a hundred feet above the deck. Three mastheads were manned in two-hour shifts, with the lookouts standing inside iron hoops on small platforms.

"Where away?" the captain shouted to the mainmast lookout.

"Starboard quarter, sir." The lookout pointed off the bow. "*There*. She breaches."

A huge hammer-shaped head rose from the sea a quarter of a mile away and splashed down in an explosion of spray. *Sperm whale*. Dobbs barked at the helmsman to steer for the breaching whale. Deckhands scrambled into the rigging with the agility of monkeys and unfurled every square inch of canvas.

As the ship came slowly around, a second lookout shouted down from his perch.

"*Another*, Captain!" The lookout's voice was hoarse with excitement. "By God, *another*."

Dobbs peered through his spyglass at a shiny gray back mounding from the sea. The spout was low and bushy, angled forward forty-five degrees. He moved the telescope to the right and then to the left. *More* spouts. A whole pod of whales. He let forth with a deep whooping laugh. He was looking at a potential fortune in oil.

The cook had stopped playing at the first sighting. He stood on the deck dumbfounded, his fiddle hanging limply at his side.

"You *did* it, cook!" the captain shouted. "You fiddled up enough *spermaceti* to fill our hold to the decks. Keep on playing, damnit."

The cook gave the captain a gap-toothed grin and drew his bow across the violin strings, playing a jaunty sea chantey, as the helmsman brought the ship up into the wind. The sails were trimmed. The ship plowed to a stop.

"Clear away the larboard boats!" the captain roared with a gusto that had been pent up during the long whale drought. "Move smartly, men, if you like money."

Dobbs ordered three boats launched. Each thirty-foot-long whaleboat was under the command of a mate who acted as boat officer and steersman. A skeleton crew stayed on board the *Princess* to sail the ship, if necessary. The captain held the fourth whaleboat in reserve.

The entire launch took slightly longer than a minute. The slender boats splashed into the sea almost simultaneously. The boat crews clambered down the side of the ship, took their places on the benches, and dug their oars in. As soon as each whaleboat cleared the ship, its crew quickly hoisted a sail to gain another few knots of speed.

Dobbs watched the boats fly like a flight of arrows toward their targets.

"Easy does it, boys," he murmured. "Give 'er another pull, steady as she goes."

"How many, Captain?" the cook called out.

"More than enough for you to burn a ten-pound steak for every man on board. You can heave the salt pork over the side," Dobbs yelled.

The captain's laughter roared across the deck like a full gale.

CALEB NYE ROWED FOR all he was worth in the lead boat. His palms were raw and bleeding and his shoulders ached. Sweat poured down his forehead, but he didn't dare lift his hand off his oar to wipe his eyes.

Caleb was eighteen, a wiry, good-natured farm youth from Concord, Massachusetts, on his first sea voyage. His 1/210 share, or "lay," put him at the bottom of the pay scale. He knew he'd be lucky to break even, but he had signed on anyhow, drawn by the prospect of adventure and the lure of exotic lands.

The eager lad reminded the captain of his own first whaling voyage. Dobbs had told the young farmer that he would do well if he jumped to orders, worked hard, and kept his nose clean. His willingness to bend to every task and to shrug off jibes had gained him the respect of the tough whalemen who treated him as a mascot.

The boat was under the command of the first mate, a scarred veteran of many whaling voyages. Rowers were constantly reminded to stay focused on the mate, but, as the ship's green hand, Caleb bore the brunt of the officer's nonstop patter.

"Come be lively, Caleb me boy," the mate cajoled. "Put your back into it, lad, you're not pulling a cow's teat. And keep your eyes on my pretty face—I'll look out for mermaids."

The mate, who was the only one allowed to face forward, was watching a big bull whale swimming on a collision course with the boat. Sunlight glinted off the shiny black skin. The mate issued a quiet order to the harpooner.

"Stand and face."

Two seven-foot-long harpoons rested in bow cradles. Their razor-sharp barbs were made to swivel at right angles to the shank. The deadly feature made it almost impossible for a harpoon to come free once it had been embedded in the whale's flesh.

The bowman stood and shipped his oar, then grabbed a harpoon from its cradle. He removed the sheath that covered the barb. He unsheathed the second harpoon as well.

Eighteen hundred feet of line ran from each harpoon through a V-shaped groove in the bow to a box where the rope had been coiled with exquisite care. From there the line ran down the length of the boat to the stern, where it was given a turn or two around a short post called a loggerhead, then was run forward to a tub.

The mate swung the tiller and pointed the bow at the whale's left side, placing the right-handed harpooner in position to make the throw. When the whale was about twenty feet away from the boat, the mate yelled an order at the harpooner.

"*Give* it to him!"

Bracing his knee against the inside of the boat, the harpooner pitched the spear like a javelin and the barb sunk into the whale's side several inches behind its eye. Then he snatched up the second harpoon and planted it a foot behind the first.

"Stern away!" the mate shouted.

The oars dug into the water, and the boat shot back several yards.

The whale huffed steam through its blowhole, raised its great flukes high in the air, and brought them down with a thunderous clap, slapping the water where the boat had been seconds before. The whale lifted its tail in the air a second time, buried its head in the sea, and dove. A diving sperm whale can descend to a thousand feet at a speed of twenty-five knots. The line flew out of its tub in a blur. The tubman splashed seawater on the rope to cool it down, but the harpoon line smoked from friction as it rounded the loggerhead despite his best efforts.

The boat skimmed over the wave tops in a mad dash that whalers called a Nantucket sleigh ride. A cheer burst from the oarsmen, but they tensed when the boat stopped moving; the whale was on its way back up. Then the huge mammal surfaced in a tremendous explosion of foam and thrashed around like a trout caught on a lure, only to plunge once more to the depths, surfacing again after twenty minutes. The routine was repeated over and over. With each cycle, more line was hauled in and the distance shortened, until only a hundred feet or so separated the whale and boat.

The whale's great blunt head swung around toward its tormenter. The mate saw the aggressive behavior and knew it was the prelude to an attack. He yelled at the harpooner to move aft.

The two men exchanged places in the rocking boat, tripping over oars, oarsmen, and lines in a scramble that would have been comical if not for the potentially fatal consequences.

The mate grabbed the lance, a long wooden shaft tipped with a sharp-edged, spoon-shaped point, and stood in the bow like a matador ready to dispatch a fighting bull. The mate expected the creature to roll on its side, a maneuver that would allow the whale to use the sharp teeth lining its tubular lower jaw to their best advantage.

The harpooner swung the tiller over. Whale and boat passed each other only yards apart. The whale began its roll, exposing its vulnerable side. The mate plunged the lance into the whale with all his strength. He churned the shaft until the point was six feet into the animal's flesh, penetrating its heart. He yelled at the crew to reverse direction. *Too late.* In its death throes, the whale clamped the midsection of the slow-moving boat between its jaws.

The panicked rowers fell over each other trying to escape the sharp teeth. The whale shook the boat like a dog with a bone, then the jaws opened, the mammal pulled away, and the great tail thrashed the water. A geyser of blood-tinged steam issued from the spout.

"Fire in the hole!" an oarsman shouted.

The lance had done its deadly work. The whale thrashed for another minute before it disappeared below the surface, leaving behind a scarlet pool of blood.

The rowers lashed their oars across the gunwales to stabilize the sinking craft and plugged the holes with their shirts. Despite their efforts, the boat was barely afloat by the time the dead whale surfaced and rolled onto its side with a fin in the air.

"Good work, boys!" the mate roared. "Settled his hash. One more fish like this and we'll be heading for New Bedford to buy candy for our sweethearts." He pointed to the approaching *Princess*. "See, boys, the old man's coming to pick us up and tuck you into bed. Everyone's all right, I see."

"Not *everyone*," the harpooner called out in a hoarse voice. "Caleb's gone."

THE SHIP DROPPED ANCHOR a short distance away and launched the reserve boat. After the rescue crew conducted a fruitless search for Caleb in the bloodstained water, the damaged whaleboat was towed back to the ship.

"Where's the green hand?" the captain asked as the bedraggled crew climbed back on board the *Princess*.

The first mate shook his head. "The poor lad went over when the whale struck."

The captain's eyes were shadowed in sadness, but death and whaling were no strangers. He turned his attention to the task at hand. He ordered his men to maneuver the whale's body until it was under a staging on the ship's starboard side. Using hooks, they rolled the carcass over and hoisted it to a vertical position. They cut the head off, and, before starting to strip off the blubber, used an iron hook to extract the whale's innards and haul them onto the deck to examine them for ambergris, the valuable perfume base that can form in the stomach of a sick whale.

Something was moving inside the big stomach pouch. A deckhand assumed it was a giant squid, a favorite meal of sperm whales. He used his sharp spade to cut into the pouch, but, instead of tentacles, a human leg flopped out through the opening. He peeled back the stomach walls to reveal a man curled up in a fetal position. The cutter and another deckhand grabbed the man's ankles and pulled the limp form out onto the deck. An opaque, slimy substance enveloped the man's head. The first mate came over and washed away the slime with a bucket of water.

"It's *Caleb*!" the mate shouted. "It's the green hand."

Caleb's lips moved, but they made no sound.

Dobbs had been supervising the removal of blubber from the whale. He strode over and stared at Caleb for a moment before he ordered the mates to carry the green hand to his cabin. They stretched the youth out on the captain's bunk, stripped off his slime-coated clothes, and wrapped him in blankets.

"Lord, I've never seen anything like it," the first mate muttered.

The handsome farm boy of eighteen had been transformed into a wizened old man of eighty. His skin was bleached ghostly white. A lacework of wrinkles puckered the skin of his hands and face as if they had been soaked in water for days. His hair was like strands on a cottonweed.

Dobbs laid a hand on Caleb's arm, expecting him to be as icy cold as the corpse he resembled.

"He's on fire," he murmured.

Assuming his role as the ship's doctor, Dobbs placed wet towels over Caleb's body to bring down the fever. From a black leather medicine case he produced a vial of patent medicine containing a heavy dose of opium and got a few drops down Caleb's throat. The youth rambled for a few minutes before slipping into a deep sleep. He slept for more than twenty-four hours. When Caleb's eyelids finally fluttered open, he saw the captain sitting at his desk writing in the log.

"Where am I?" he mumbled through dry, crusted lips.

"In my bunk," Dobbs growled. "And I'm getting damned sick of it."

"Sorry, sir." Caleb furrowed his brow. "I dreamed I died and went to hell."

"No such luck, lad. Seems the *spermaceti* had a taste for farm boys. We pulled you out of his belly."

Caleb remembered the whale's round eye, then being tossed into the air, arms and legs spinning like a pinwheel, and the shock of hitting the water. He recalled moving along a dark, yielding passage, gagging for breath in the heavy, moist air. The heat had been almost unbearable. He had quickly passed out.

A horrified look came to his pale, wrinkled face. "The whale *et* me!"

The captain nodded. "I'll get cook to fetch you some soup. Then it's back to the fo'c'sle with you."

The captain relented and let Caleb stay in his cabin until all the blubber had been rendered into oil and stored in barrels, then he summoned the forecastle hands on deck. He praised them for their hard work, and said:

"You all know that a whale ate the green hand like Jonah in the Bible. I'm happy to say that young Caleb will soon be back at his work. I'm cutting his pay for time lost. The only one on this ship who's allowed to shirk his job is a dead man."

The comment brought a few ayes and grins from the assembled hands.

Dobbs continued. "Now, men, I must tell you that young Caleb looks different than you remember him. The foul juices of the whale's innards have bleached him whiter than a boiled turnip." He cast a stern eye on the crew. "I'll allow no one on this ship to make light of another man's misfortune. That's all."

The ship's officers helped Caleb climb onto the deck. The captain asked Caleb to remove a square of cloth that covered his head, shadowing his face like a monk's cowl. A collective gasp came from the crew.

"Take a good look at our Jonah and you'll have something to tell your grandchildren," the captain said. "He's no different from the rest of us under that white skin. Now, let's get us some whales."

The captain had purposely called Caleb a *Jonah,* a seaman's name for a sailor who attracted bad luck. Maybe if he made light of it he'd suck the wind out of the sails of unfavorable comparisons to the biblical character who'd been swallowed by a great fish. A few hands quietly suggested heaving Caleb over the side. Fortunately, everyone was too busy for mischief. The sea that had been so barren now teemed with whales. There was no doubt that the ship's fortunes had changed for the better. It was as if the *Princess* had become a magnet for every whale in the ocean.

Every day, the boats were launched after cries from the lookout. The cast-iron try-pots bubbled like witches' cauldrons. An oily pall of black smoke hid the stars and sun and turned the sails a dark gray. The cook sawed away on his fiddle. Within months of Caleb's encounter with the whale, the ship's hold was filled to capacity.

Before the long voyage home, the ship had to be resupplied and the weary crew given shore leave. Dobbs put into Pohnpei, a lush island known for its handsome men, beautiful women, and their willingness to provide services and goods to visiting whalemen. Whaling vessels from every part of the world crowded the harbor.

Dobbs was Quaker by upbringing and didn't indulge in spirits or native women, but his religious beliefs took second place to his sailing orders: maintain harmony among his men and bring home a shipload of oil. How he accomplished these tasks was left up to him. He laughed heartily as boatloads of drunken and raucous crewmen stumbled back on board or were fished out of the water into which they'd fallen.

Caleb stayed on board and watched the comings and goings of his fellow hands with a benign smile. The captain was relieved that Caleb showed no interest in shore leave. The natives were friendly enough, but Caleb's bleached hair and skin might cause problems with the superstitious islanders.

Dobbs paid a courtesy call to the American consul, a fellow New Englander. During the visit the consul was notified that a tropical sickness had struck the island. Dobbs cut his men's shore leave short. In his log he wrote:

Last day of shore leave. Captain visits U.S. Consul A. Markham, who conducted tour of ancient city named Nan Madol. Upon return, Consul advised of sickness on island. Ended liberty and left island in a hurry.

The remnants of the crew stumbled back onto the ship and promptly fell into a rum-soaked snooze. The captain ordered the sobered-up hands to raise the anchor and set sail. By the time the cherry-eyed men were roused from their bunks and ordered back to work, the ship was well at sea. With a steady breeze, Dobbs and his men would be sleeping in their own beds in a few months time.

The sickness struck the *Princess* less than twenty-four hours after it left the port.

A forecastle hand named Stokes awakened around two in the morning and raced to the rail to purge his stomach. Several hours later, he developed a fever and a vivid rash over much of his body. Brownish red spots appeared on his face and grew in size until his features looked as if they were carved in mahogany.

The captain treated Stokes with wet towels and sips of bottled medicine. Dobbs had him moved to the foredeck and placed under a makeshift tent. The forecastle was a pesthole in the best of circumstances. Fresh air and sunlight might help the man, and isolation could possibly prevent the spread of his illness.

But the disease spread through the foremast hands like a windblown brush fire. Men crumpled to the deck. A rigger fell from a yardarm onto a pile of sails, which fortunately broke his fall. An impromptu infirmary was set up on the foredeck. The captain emptied his medicine kit. He feared that it would only be a matter of hours before he and the officers fell ill. The *Princess* would become a phantom ship, drifting at the mercy of wind and currents until it rotted.

The captain checked his chart. The nearest landfall was called Trouble Island. Whalers normally shunned the place. A whaling crew had burned a village and killed some natives there after an argument over a stolen cask of nails, and the inhabitants had attacked several whalers since the incident. There was no choice. Dobbs took the helm and put the ship on a straight course for the island.

The *Princess* soon limped into a cove lined with white sand beaches, and the ship's anchor splashed into the clear green water with a rattle of chain. The island was dominated by a volcanic peak. Wisps of smoke could be seen playing around its summit. Dobbs and the first mate took a small boat ashore to replenish freshwater while they could. They found a spring a short distance inland and were on their way back to the ship when they came across a ruined temple. The captain gazed at the temple's walls, overgrown with vines, and said, "This place reminds me of Nan Madol."

"Pardon me, sir?" the first mate said.

The captain shook his head. "Never mind. We'd best get back to the ship while we can still walk."

Not long after dusk, the mates fell sick, and Dobbs, too, succumbed to the disease. With Caleb's help, the captain dragged his mattress onto the quarterdeck. He told the green hand to carry on as best he could.

Caleb somehow remained untouched by the plague. He carried buckets of water to the foredeck to cure the terrible thirst of his crewmates and kept an eye on Dobbs and the officers. Dobbs alternated between shivers and sweats. He lost consciousness, and, when he awakened, he saw torches moving about the deck. One torch came closer, and its flickering flame illuminated the garishly tattooed face of a man, one of a dozen or so natives armed with spears and cutting tools used to strip blubber.

"Hello?" said the islander, who had high cheekbones and long black hair.

"You speak English?" Dobbs managed.

The man lifted his spear. "Good harpoon man."

Dobbs saw a ray of hope. In spite of his savage appearance, the native was a fellow whaler. "My men are sick. Can you help?"

"*Sure,*" the native said. "We got good medicine. Fix you up. You from New Bedford?"

Dobbs nodded.

"Too bad," the native said. "New Bedford men take me. I jump ship. Come home." He smiled, showing pointed teeth. "No medicine. We watch you burn up from fire sickness."

A quiet voice said, "Are you all right, Captain?"

Caleb had emerged from the shadows and now stood on the deck in the glare of torchlight.

The native leader's eyes widened and he spat out a single word.

"*'Atua!*"

The captain had picked up a smattering of Oceanic and knew that *'atua* was the islanders' word for "a bad ghost." Rising onto his elbows, Dobbs said, "Yes. This is my *'atua*. Do what he says or he will curse you and everyone on your island."

Caleb had sized up the situation and went along with the captain's bluff.

Lifting his arms wide above his head for dramatic effect, he said, "Put your weapons down or I will use my power."

The native leader said something in his language and the other men dropped their killing tools to the deck.

"You said you could do something about the fire sickness," the captain said. "You have medicine. Help my men or the 'atua will be angry."

The islander seemed unsure of what to do, but his doubts vanished when Caleb removed his hat and the silky white hair caught the tropical breeze. The islander issued a curt order to the others.

The captain blacked out again. His slumber was filled with weird dreams, including one in which he felt a cold, wet sensation and a sting on his chest. When he blinked his eyes open, it was daytime, and crewmen were moving around the deck. The ship was rigged with full sail against a clear blue sky, and waves slapped the hull. White-plumed birds wheeled overhead.

The first mate saw Dobbs struggling to sit up and came over with a jug of water. "Feeling better, Captain?"

"Aye," the captain croaked between sips of water. The fever had gone, and his stomach felt normal except for a gnawing hunger. "Help me to my feet."

The captain stood on wobbly legs, with the mate holding an arm to steady him. The ship was on the open sea with no island in view.

"How long have we been under way?"

"Five hours," the mate said. "It's a miracle. The men came out of their fever. Rashes disappeared. Cook made soup, and they got the ship moving."

The captain felt an itch on his chest and lifted his shirt. The rash was gone, replaced by a small red spot and a circle of irritation a few inches above his navel.

"What about the natives?" Dobbs said.

"*Natives?* We saw no natives."

Dobbs shook his head. Did he dream it all in his delirium? He told the mate to fetch Caleb. The green hand made his way to the quarterdeck. He wore a straw hat to protect his bleached skin from the sunlight. A smile crossed his pale, wrinkled face when he saw the captain had recovered.

"What happened last night?" Dobbs said.

Caleb told the captain that after Dobbs had passed out, the natives had left the ship and returned carrying wooden buckets that emitted a pale blue luminescence. The natives went from man to man. He couldn't see what they were doing. Then the natives left. Soon after, the crew started waking up. The captain asked Caleb to help him down to his cabin. He eased into his chair and opened the ship's log.

"*A strange business,*" the captain started. Although his hands were still shaking, he wrote down every detail as he remembered it. Then he gazed with longing at a miniature portrait of his pretty young wife, and he finished his entry with a single declaration: "*Going home!*"

FAIRHAVEN, MASSACHUSETTS, 1878

The French mansard-roofed mansion known to the townspeople as the Ghost House stood back from a secluded street behind a screen of dark-leafed beech trees. Guarding the long driveway were the bleached jawbones of a sperm whale, placed upright in the ground so their tapering tips met in a Gothic arch.

On a golden October day, two boys stood under the whale-bone arch, daring each other to sneak up the driveway and look in the windows. Neither youngster would take the first step; they were still trading taunts when a shiny black horse-drawn carriage clattered up to the gate.

The driver was a heavyset man whose expensive russet suit and matching derby hat failed to cloak his villainous looks. His rough-hewn features had been sculpted by the hard knuckles of the opponents he had faced back in his prizefighting days. Age had not been kind to the misshapen nose, the cauliflower ears, and the eyes squeezed to nailheads by scar tissue.

The man leaned over the reins and glared down at the boys. "What're you lads doing here?" he growled like the old pit bull he resembled. "Up to no good, I suppose."

"Nothin'," one boy said with averted eyes.

"Is that a fact?" the man sneered. "Well, I wouldn't be hanging around here if I was you. There's a mean ghost lives in that house."

"*See,*" said the other boy. "*Told* you so."

"Listen to your friend. Ghost is seven feet tall. Hands like pitchforks," the man said, injecting a tremor into his voice. "Got fangs that could rip boys like you in half just so he could suck out your guts." He pointed his whip toward the house and his mouth dropped open in horror. "He's *coming*! By God, he's coming. *Run!* Run for your lives!"

The man roared with laughter as the boys raced off like startled rabbits. He gave the reins a flick and urged the horse through the whalebone gate. He tied up in front of the big house, which resembled an octagonal wedding cake layered with red and yellow frosting. He was still chuckling to himself as he climbed the porch steps and announced his arrival using the brass door knocker shaped like a whale's tail.

Footsteps approached. A man opened the door, and a smile crossed his pallid face.

"*Strater,* what a pleasant surprise," Caleb Nye said.

"Good to see you too, Caleb. Been meaning to stop by, but you know how it is."

"Of course," Caleb said. He stepped aside. "Come in, come in."

Caleb's skin had grown even whiter over the years. Age had added wrinkles to skin that looked like parchment to begin with, but, despite his premature aging, he still retained the boyish smile and puppy-dog eagerness that had endeared him to his whaling colleagues.

He led the way to a spacious library lined with floor-to-ceiling bookcases. The wall sections not devoted to books on the subject of whaling were decorated with large, colorful posters that had the same motif: a man caught in the jaws of a sperm whale.

Strater went up to one particularly lurid poster. The artist had made liberal use of crimson paint to depict blood flowing from the harpoon shafts into the water. "We made a bundle of money out of that Philadelphia show."

Caleb nodded. "Standing room only, night after night, thanks to your skills as a showman."

"I'd be nothing without my star attraction," Strater said, turning.

"And I have you to thank for this house and everything I own," Caleb said.

Strater flashed a gap-toothed grin. "If there's one thing I'm good at, it's putting on a show. The minute I laid eyes on you, I saw the potential for fame and fortune."

Their partnership had begun a few nights after the *Princess* docked in New Bedford. The oil barrels had been off-loaded, and the owners tallied the take and calculated the lays. Crewmen who didn't have wives or sweethearts to go home to went off in a raucous mob to celebrate in the waterfront bars that were more than willing to relieve the whalers of their hard-won earnings.

Caleb had stayed on the ship. He was there when the captain came back onto the *Princess* with Caleb's pay and asked if he was going home to his family farm.

"Not like this," Caleb had replied with a sad smile.

The captain handed the young man the pitifully small amount of money he had earned for his years at sea. "You have my permission to stay on board until the ship sails again."

As he walked down the ramp, the captain felt a heavy sorrow for the young man's misfortune, but he soon put it out of his mind as his thoughts shifted to his own promising future.

About the same time, Strater had been contemplating a much bleaker outlook as he sat in a seedy bar a few blocks from the ship. The former carnival pitchman was down on his luck and almost broke. He was nursing a mug of ale when the crewmen from the *Princess* burst into the bar and proceeded to get drunk with all the energy they had devoted to killing whales. Strater perked up his ears and listened with interest to the story of Caleb Nye, the green hand who was swallowed by a whale. The bar patrons greeted the tale with loud skepticism.

"Where's your Jonah now?" a barfly shouted above the din.

"Back at the ship, sittin' in the dark," he was told. "See for yourself."

"The only thing I want to see is another ale," the barfly said.

Strater slipped out of the noisy bar into the quiet night and made his way along a narrow street to the waterfront. He climbed the ramp to the lantern-lit deck of the *Princess*. Caleb had been standing by the rail, staring at the sparkling lights of New Bedford. The young man's features were indistinct, but they seemed to glow with a pale luminosity. Strater's showman juices started flowing.

"I have a proposition for you," Strater told the young man. "If you accept it, I can make you a rich man."

Caleb listened to Strater's proposal and saw the possibilities. Within weeks, flyers and posters were plastered around New Bedford with a blaring headline in circus typeface:

SWALLOWED BY A WHALE.
A Living Jonah Tells His Tale.

Strater hired a hall for the first show and had to turn away hundreds. For two hours, Caleb told his thrilling story, standing with harpoon in hand in front of a moving diorama.

With Caleb's whaling earnings, Strater had hired an artist who had painted reasonably accurate pictures on a long strip of canvas several feet high. The backlit canvas was slowly unrolled to reveal pictures of Caleb in the whaleboat, the attack by the whale, and a fanciful depiction of his legs sticking out from between the mammal's jaws. There were images of exotic, palm-studded locales, and their inhabitants as well.

The show played to enthralled audiences, especially in churches and halls in cities and towns along the eastern seaboard. Strater sold story booklets, adding pictures of half-nude dancing native girls to spice up the narrative. After a few years, Strater and Caleb retired from public life as rich as the wealthiest whaling captains.

Strater bought a mansion in New Bedford, and Caleb built his wedding-cake house in the village of Fairhaven across the harbor from the whaling city. From the roof turret, he watched the whaling ships come and go. He rarely went out in daylight.

When he did leave his mansion, he covered his head and shaded his face with a hood.

He became known to his neighbors as the Ghost, and he became a generous benefactor who used his fortune to build schools and libraries for the community. In return, the townspeople protected the privacy of their homegrown Jonah.

Caleb guided Strater into a large chamber that was empty except for a comfortable revolving chair in the center. The diorama from Caleb's show wrapped around the walls. Anyone sitting in the chair could pivot and see the "Living Jonah" story from beginning to end.

"Well, what do you think?" Caleb asked his friend.

Strater shook his head. "It almost makes me want to go on the road with the show again."

"Let's talk about it over a glass of wine," Caleb said.

"I'm afraid we don't have time," Strater said. "I carry a message to you from Nathan Dobbs."

"The captain's oldest son?"

"That's right. His father is dying and would like to see you."

"*Dying!* That's not possible! You have told me yourself that the captain looks as hale and hearty as a young bull."

"It's not an ailment that brought him down, Caleb. There was an accident at one of his mills. A loom fell over and crushed his ribs."

Caleb's old man's face lost its last faint traces of color. "When can I see him?" he asked.

"We must go *now,*" Strater replied. "His time is short."

Caleb rose from his chair. "I'll get my coat and hat."

THE ROAD TO THE Dobbs mansion wound around New Bedford Harbor and climbed to County Street. Carriages lined the driveway and street in front of the Greek Revival mansion. Nathan Dobbs greeted Strater and Caleb at the door and thanked them profusely for coming. He was tall and lanky, the younger image of his father.

"I'm sorry to hear about your father," Caleb said. "How is Captain Dobbs?"

"Not long for this world, I'm afraid. I'll take you to him."

The mansion's spacious parlor and adjoining hallways overflowed with the captain's ten children and countless grandchildren. There was a murmur as Nathan Dobbs entered the parlor with Strater and the strange hooded figure. Nathan asked Strater to make himself comfortable and escorted Caleb to the captain's room.

Captain Dobbs lay in his bed, tended by his wife and family doctor. They had wanted to keep the sickroom dark, as was the medical practice then, but he insisted that the curtains be opened to let in sunlight.

A shaft of honeyed autumn sunlight fell on the captain's craggy face. Although his leonine mane had gone silver-gray, his features were more youthful than would have been expected for a man in his sixties. But his eyes had a far-off look, as if he could see death creeping closer. The captain's wife and doctor withdrew, and Nathan lingered by the door.

Dobbs saw Caleb and managed to crack a smile.

"Thank you for coming, Caleb," the captain said. The voice that once boomed across a ship's decks was a hoarse whisper.

Caleb pushed the hood back from his face. "You told me never to question the captain's orders."

"Aye," Dobbs wheezed. "And I'll give you more good advice, green hand. Don't stick your nose where it doesn't belong. Tried to fix a balky loom. Didn't move fast enough when it keeled over."

"I'm sorry for your misfortune, Captain."

"*Don't* be. I have a faithful wife, handsome children, and grandchildren who will carry on my name."

"I wish I could say the same," Caleb said in a wounded voice.

"You've done well, Caleb. I know all about your generosity."

"Generosity is easy when there's no one to share your fortune with."

"You have shared it with your neighbors. And I have heard of your wonderful library of books on the old trade."

"I don't smoke or drink. Books are my only vice. Whaling gave me the life I have. I collect every volume I can on the old trade."

The captain closed his eyes and seemed to drift away, but after a moment his eyelids fluttered open. "I have something I want to share with you."

The captain's son stepped forward and presented Caleb with a mahogany box. Caleb opened the lid. Inside the box was a book. Caleb recognized the worn blue binding.

"The log of the *Princess,* Captain?"

"Aye, and it's yours," the captain said. "For your great library."

Caleb drew back. "I can't take this from you, sir."

"You'll do as your captain says," Dobbs growled. "My family agrees that you should have it. Isn't that right, Nathan?"

The captain's son nodded. "It's the family's wish as well, Mr. Nye. We can think of no person more worthy."

Unexpectedly, the captain raised his hand and placed it on the log. "A strange business," he said. "Something happened on that island of wild men. To this day, I don't know if it was God's work or the Devil's."

The captain closed his eyes. His breathing became labored,

and a rattling sound came from his throat. He called his wife's name.

Nathan gently took Caleb's arm and escorted him from the room. He thanked him again for coming, and then told his mother that the captain's time had come. The loyal family streamed into the bedroom and adjacent hallway, leaving Strater and Caleb alone in the parlor.

"Gone?" Strater said.

"Not yet but soon." Caleb showed Strater the logbook.

"I'd prefer some of the Dobbs fortune," Strater snorted.

"*This* is a treasure to me," Caleb said. "Besides, you have more money than you could spend in a lifetime, my friend."

"Then I'll have to live longer," Strater said with a glance toward the bedroom.

They left the house and climbed into Strater's carriage. Caleb clutched the logbook closer and his mind went back to the remote island and its savage inhabitants, his masquerade as an *'atua,* the sickness, and the strange blue lights. He turned around for a last look at the mansion and recalled the captain's dying words.

Dobbs was right. It had been a strange business indeed.

CHAPTER 1

MURMANSK, RUSSIA, PRESENT DAY

As THE COMMANDER OF ONE OF THE MOST FEARSOME KILL-ing machines ever devised, Andrei Vasilevich once held in his hands the power to wipe out entire cities and millions of people. If war had ever broken out between the Soviet Union and the United States, the Typhoon-class submarine Vasilevich had commanded would have launched twenty long-range ballistic missiles at the U.S. and sent two hundred nuclear warheads raining down on American soil.

In the years since he had retired from the navy, Vasilevich had often breathed a sigh of relief that he had never been told to unleash a salvo of nuclear death and destruction. As a captain second rank, he would have carried out the orders of his government without question. An order was an order, no matter how evil it was. A nuclear sub commander was an instrument of the state and could have no room for emotions. But as the tough old undersea Cold Warrior said good-bye to his former command, the submarine unofficially known as *Bear,* he could not hold back the sentimental tears that rolled down his plump cheeks.

He stood on the dock overlooking the port of Murmansk, his eyes following the sub as it glided toward the harbor entrance. He raised a silver flask of vodka high in the air in toast before taking a slug, and his thoughts drifted back to those years prowling the North Atlantic in the monster vessel.

With a length of five hundred seventy feet and a seventy-five-foot beam, the Typhoon was the biggest submarine ever built. The long forward deck stretched out from the massive, forty-two-foot-tall conning tower, or *sail,* to make room for twenty large missile tubes arranged in two rows. The design gave the Typhoon a distinctive profile.

The unique hull design extended past its metal exterior. Instead of one pressure hull, as in most submarines, the Typhoon had two parallel ones. This arrangement gave the Typhoon a cargo capacity of fifteen thousand tons and room in the starboard hull for a small gym and a sauna. Escape chambers were located above each hull. The submarine's control room and attack center were both in compartments located under the sail.

The *Bear* was one of six 941 Typhoons commissioned in the 1980s and introduced into the Northern fleet as part of the first flotilla of nuclear submarines based at Nerpichya. Leonid Brezhnev called the new model "the Typhoon" in a speech, and the name stuck. They were deployed as the Russian Akula class, meaning "shark," which was the name the U.S. Navy used for them.

Despite its huge size, the Typhoon clipped along at more than twenty-five knots underwater and around half that speed on the surface. It could turn on a ruble, dive to the ocean depths, and stay down a hundred eighty days, accomplishing these maneuvers with one of the quietest power systems ever designed. The sub carried a crew of more than one hundred sixty. Each hull had a reactor plant that powered a steam turbine which produced fifty thousand horsepower to drive the two huge propellers. Two propulsion pods allowed the sub to hover and maneuver.

The Typhoon subs eventually outlived their military and political usefulness and were taken out of service in the late 1990s. Someone had suggested that they might be converted to carry cargo under the arctic ice by replacing the missile tubes with cargo space. The word went out that the Typhoons were for sale to the highest bidder.

The captain would have preferred to see the subs scrapped rather than have them turned into undersea cargo scows. What an ignoble end for a fine war machine! In its day, the terrible Typhoon was the subject of books and movies. He had forgotten how many times he had seen *The Hunt for Red October.*

Vasilevich had been hired by the Central Design Bureau for Marine Engineering to oversee the conversion. The nuclear missiles had long been removed as part of a joint treaty with the U.S., which had agreed to scrap its own city busters.

Vasilevich had supervised the removal of the missile silos to create a vast cargo hold. The silos were plugged and modifications were made that would allow easier loading and off-loading of cargo. A crew half the size of the original would deliver the sub to its new owners.

The captain took another shot of vodka and tucked his flask into a pocket. Before leaving the dock, he couldn't resist turning back for one last look. The submarine had cleared the harbor and was on the open sea headed to its unknown fate. The captain pulled his coat closer around him to ward off the damp breeze coming off the water and headed back to his car.

Vasilevich had been around too long to accept things at face value. The submarine supposedly had been sold to an international freight company based in Hong Kong, but the details were vague, and the deal was structured like a set of matryoshka nesting dolls.

The captain had his own theories about the sub's future. An undersea vessel with the long range and huge cargo capacity of the Typhoon would be perfect for smuggling goods of every kind. But Vasilevich kept his thoughts to himself. Modern-day Russia could be dangerous for those who knew too much. What the new owners did after taking possession of the Cold War relic was none of his business. This deal had warning signs posted all over it, but the captain knew it was wise not to ask about such things, and even wiser not to know.

CHAPTER 2

ANHUI PROVINCE, PEOPLE'S REPUBLIC OF CHINA

THE HELICOPTER DARTED IN FROM NOWHERE AND CIRCLED above the village like a noisy dragonfly. Dr. Song Lee looked up from the bandage she was applying to a cut on the young boy's arm and watched as the helicopter hovered and then started its vertical descent to a field at the edge of the settlement.

The doctor gave the boy a pat on the head and accepted her payment of half a dozen fresh eggs from his grateful parents. She had treated the wound with soap, hot water, and an herbal poultice, and it was healing nicely. With little in the way of medicine and equipment, the young doctor did the best she could with what she had.

Dr. Lee brought the eggs into the hut and then joined the noisy throng rushing to the field. Excited villagers, including many who had never seen an aircraft up close, completely surrounded the helicopter. Lee saw the government markings on the fuselage and wondered who from the Ministry of Health would be coming to her remote village.

The helicopter door opened and a short, portly man wearing

a business suit and tie stepped out. He took one look at the chattering crowd of villagers and an expression of terror crossed his broad face. He would have retreated into the helicopter if Lee had not eased her way through the mob to greet him.

"Good afternoon, Dr. Huang," she called out in a strong enough voice to be heard above the babble. "This is quite the surprise."

The man cast a wary eye over the crowd. "I hadn't expected such a large reception."

Dr. Lee laughed. "Don't worry, Doctor. Most of these people are related to me." She pointed to a couple whose weathered brown faces were wreathed in smiles. "Those are my parents. As you can see, they're quite harmless."

She took Dr. Huang by the hand and led him through the swarm of onlookers. The villagers started to follow, but she waved them off and gently explained that she wished to speak to the gentleman alone.

Back at her hut, she offered her visitor the battered folding chair she sat in to treat patients. Huang mopped the sweat off his bald pate with a handkerchief and scraped the mud from his polished leather shoes. She boiled water for tea on a camp stove and poured a cup for her visitor. Huang took a tentative sip, as if he were unsure it was sanitary.

Lee sat down in the patched-up old dining-room chair that the patients used. "How do you like my open-air treatment room? I see my more modest patients inside the hut. Farm animals, I treat on their own territory."

"This is a far cry from Harvard Medical School," Huang said, gazing in fascination at the hut, with its walls of mud and thatched roof.

"This is a far cry from *anywhere*," Lee said. "There are some advantages. My patients pay me in vegetables and eggs, so I never go hungry. The traffic is not as bad as in Harvard Square, but it's next to impossible to find a good caramel caffe latte."

Huang and Lee had met years before at a mixer for Asian students and faculty at Harvard University. He was a visiting professor from China's National Laboratory of Medical Molecular Biology. She was finishing her graduate studies in virology. The young woman's quick wit and intelligence had impressed Huang immediately, and they had continued their friendship after returning to China, where he had risen to a high position in the ministry.

"It has been a long time since we talked. You must be wondering why I'm here," Huang said.

Dr. Lee liked and respected Huang, but he had been among a number of highly placed colleagues who were conspicuously absent when she needed someone to speak out on her behalf.

"Not at all," Lee said with a note of haughtiness. "I expect that you are probably carrying the apology of the authorities for their heavy-handed treatment of me."

"The state will never admit that it is wrong, Dr. Lee, but you have no idea how many times I have regretted not standing up in your defense."

"I understand the government's tendency to blame everyone but itself, Dr. Huang, but *you* have no idea how many times *I* have regretted that my colleagues failed to come to my defense."

Huang wrung his hands.

"I don't blame you," he said. "My silence was a clear act of cowardice. I cannot speak for my colleagues. I can only offer my most humble apologies for not defending you in public. At the same time, I did work behind the scenes to keep you out of jail."

Dr. Lee resisted the temptation to show the doctor the harsh conditions in the impoverished village. He would soon learn that a jail didn't need bars. She decided that it would be unfair to pick on Huang. Nothing he could have done would have changed the outcome.

She forced a smile.

"Your apology is accepted, Dr. Huang. I am truly pleased to see you. Since you do not bear the thanks of a grateful nation for my service, what *are* you doing here?"

"I come as the bearer of bad news, I'm afraid." Although they were alone, he lowered his voice. "It has returned," he said in a near whisper.

Lee felt an icy coldness in the pit of her stomach.

"Where?" she asked.

"To the north of here." He rattled off the name of a remote province.

"Have there been any other outbreaks?"

"None so far. It is an isolated area, thank goodness."

"Have you isolated the virus to confirm its identity?"

He nodded. "It's a coronavirus, as before."

"When was it first detected? And have you found its source?"

"About three weeks ago. No source yet. The government immediately isolated the victims and quarantined the villages to prevent its spread. They are taking no chances this time. We are working with the World Health Organization and the U.S. Centers for Disease Control."

"That's quite different from the last response."

"Our government learned its lesson," Huang said. "Their secrecy regarding the SARS epidemic damaged China's reputation as an emerging world power. Our leaders know that secrecy is not an option this time."

The Chinese government had come under international fire because it kept the first SARS epidemic secret from the world, causing a delay and slowing treatment that could have prevented a number of deaths. Song Lee was working as a teaching physician in a Beijing hospital when the epidemic broke out. She suspected it was serious and assembled the facts to make her case. When she urged her superiors to take action, they warned her to stay silent. But the World Health Organization's outbreak-alert system issued a global warning. Travel came to a halt and quarantines were enforced. An international lab network isolated a virus never before found in humans. The disease was called SARS, short for severe acute respiratory syndrome.

The virus spread to more than two dozen countries on several continents, infecting more than eight thousand people. Almost a thousand died, and a pandemic of worldwide proportions was narrowly averted. The Chinese government imprisoned the doctor who had told the world that the cases were being under-reported and that patients were being driven around in ambulances to keep them away from the World Health Organization. Others who had tried to expose the cover-up also became targets. One of them was Dr. Song Lee.

"Secrecy wasn't an option then, either," she reminded Huang, making no attempt to keep the heat out of her voice. "You still haven't told me what this has to do with me."

"We are assembling a research team and want you to be on it," Huang said.

Lee's anger spilled out.

"What can *I* do?" she asked. "I am simply a country doctor who treats life-threatening diseases with herbs and voodoo."

"I implore you to put your personal feelings aside," Huang said. "You were one of the first to detect the SARS epidemic. We need you in Beijing. Your combined expertise in virology and epidemiology will be invaluable in developing a response." Huang folded his hands together as if in prayer. "I will get down on my knees to beg, if you wish."

She gazed at his anguished face. Huang was brilliant. She could not expect him to be valiant as well. Softening her voice, she said, "It won't be necessary to beg, Dr. Huang. I will do what I can."

His round face lit up.

"Mark my words," he said, "you won't be sorry for your decision."

"I *know* I won't," Lee said, "especially after you meet my conditions."

"What do you mean?" Huang asked in a guarded tone.

"I want enough medical supplies to take care of this village for six months . . . No, make that a year, and expand it to encompass the villages around this one."

"Done," Huang said.

"I have established a network of midwives, but they need a trained professional to oversee them. I want a family-practice physician flown in here this week to take over my practice."

"Done," Huang repeated.

Lee chided herself for not demanding more.

"How soon do you need me?" she asked.

"Now," Huang said. "The helicopter is waiting for you. I would like you to speak at a symposium in Beijing"

She did a quick mental inventory. The hut was on loan. Her belongings could fit into a small valise. She would have to inform only the village elders and bid her aged parents and her patients a quick good-bye. Standing, she extended her hand to seal the bargain.

"Done," she said.

✦ ✦ ✦

THREE DAYS LATER, Dr. Lee stood on a podium behind a lectern at the Ministry of Health in Beijing, steeling herself to address more than two hundred experts from around the world. The woman on the podium bore no resemblance to the country doctor who had delivered babies and piglets by candlelight. She wore a pin-striped business suit over a blouse of Chinese-flag red, a rose silk scarf encircling her neck. A touch of makeup had lightened the amber complexion that had been darkened by outdoor life. She was grateful that no one could see her callous palms.

Soon after she had arrived in Beijing, Lee had gone on a shopping spree, courtesy of the People's Republic of China. At the first shop, she tossed her cotton jacket and slacks in the trash. With each subsequent purchase, in some of Beijing's most fashionable boutiques, she redeemed a bit of her lost self-respect.

Song Lee was in her mid-thirties, but she looked younger. She was slender, with small hips and breasts, and long legs. While her figure was adequate but unremarkable, it was her face that inevitably turned heads for a second look. Long dark lashes shaded alert, questing eyes, and full lips alternated between a friendly smile and a slight, more serious pucker when she was deep in thought. Working in the country, she had tied her long jet-black hair in a loose ponytail and tucked it under a cap that may have belonged to a foot soldier on Mao's Long March. But now it was styled and cut short.

Since arriving in Beijing, Lee had attended a dizzying schedule of briefings and had been impressed at the swift reaction to the latest outbreak. In contrast to the slow response several years before, hundreds of investigators and support staff had been mobilized around the world.

China was taking the leading role in the fight against the outbreak and had invited experts to Beijing to demonstrate its robust reaction. The speedy response had revealed a silver lining to a serious situation: everyone she talked to seemed confident that basic health practices could contain the SARS outbreak while researchers continued to look for the source and develop a diagnostic test and an appropriate vaccine.

But while the mood was upbeat, Dr. Lee was unable to share their confidence. She was worried that no source of the virus had been found. The civets that had carried the original SARS strain had been wiped out, so maybe the virus had jumped to another host—dogs, chickens, insects—who knew? Also, the Chinese government's uncharacteristic transparency bothered her as well. Bitter experience had taught her that the authorities did not easily give up their secrets. Even so, she might have dismissed these qualms had not the government refused to let her visit the province that had been infected. Too dangerous, she was told, the province was under the strictest quarantine possible.

Dr. Lee had set her suspicions aside for now to focus on the daunting prospect of appearing before an audience of sharp-minded experts. Her heart thumped madly in her chest. She was nervous about speaking in public after spending years among people whose greatest concern was the rice yield. The computer programs now available to chart an epidemic not only baffled her, she was unsure of her own expertise as well. She felt like a Stone Age holdover thawed from a glacier after ten thousand years.

On the other hand, practicing medicine at its most basic level had given her a gut instinct that was more valuable than all the charts and tables in the world. Her intuition was telling her that it was too early to celebrate. As a virologist, she had respect for how fast a virus could adapt to change. As an epidemiologist, she knew from painful experience how an outbreak could quickly get out of control. But maybe she was just gun-shy. She had gone over the statistics Huang had given her, and the epidemic seemed to be on the road to being contained.

Dr. Lee cleared her throat and looked out at the audience. Some of the people waiting for her to speak were aware of and possibly responsible for her exile, but she swallowed her bitterness.

"To paraphrase the American writer Mark Twain, rumors of my professional demise have been greatly exaggerated," she said with a straight face.

She let the ripple of laughter roll over her.

"I must admit, I come to you humbled," she continued. "Since I established my rural practice, great strides have been made in the world of epidemiology. I am impressed at the way the nations of the world have come together to fight this new outbreak. I am proud of the role my country has taken in leading the effort."

She smiled at the applause. She was learning to play the game. Those wanting angry denunciations of past policy would be disappointed.

"At the same time, I must warn against complacency. Any epidemic contains the seeds of a pandemic. These pandemics have come to us in the past, and human beings have *always* come out the worse for it."

She talked about the great plagues in history, starting with the first recorded pandemic that struck Athens during its war with Sparta. The Roman pandemic of 251 A.D. had killed five thousand people a day, the Constantinople epidemic of 452 ten thousand a day. Around twenty-five million died in Europe of the Black Death during the 1340s, and forty to fifty million worldwide in the great influenza epidemic of 1918. She repeated her warning against complacency, and repeated how pleased she was at the multinational response to the current epidemic.

Dr. Lee was stunned at the applause that her presentation received. Her acceptance back into the medical community after years of exile was unexpected, and she was overcome with emotion. She left the stage, but instead of returning to her seat she strode to the exit. Tears welled in her eyes, and she needed to compose herself. She walked along the corridor, not sure where she was going.

Someone called her name. It was Dr. Huang, hurrying to catch up to her.

"That was a fine presentation," he said, breathless from the chase.

"Thank you, Dr. Huang. I'll return to the auditorium in a few minutes. It was quite an emotional experience for me, as you can imagine. But it was reassuring to hear that a worldwide pandemic is unlikely."

"On the contrary, Dr. Lee, a pandemic is a *certainty*. And it will kill millions before it runs out of victims."

Song Lee glanced at the door to the auditorium. "That's not what I heard in there. Everyone seemed quite optimistic that this epidemic can be contained."

"That's because the speakers don't know all the facts."

"What *are* the facts, Dr. Huang? Why is this SARS epidemic any different from the last?"

"There is something I must tell you . . . this business about SARS . . . well, it's a fraud."

Lee glared at Huang.

"What are you saying?"

"The epidemic we are concerned about is caused by *another* pathogen, a variation of the influenza virus."

"Why didn't you tell me this? Why did you let me blather on about SARS?"

"It pained me to do so, but the presentation was intended as a smoke screen to hide the fact that the pathogen we are dealing with is much more dangerous than SARS."

"The experts speaking in the auditorium may beg to differ . . ."

"That's because we have been feeding them misleading information. When they have asked for specimens of the strain to help with their research, we have given them the old SARS virus. We are trying to prevent a panic."

She felt a dryness in her mouth.

"What is this new pathogen?"

"It is a mutated form of the old influenza strain. It spreads faster, and the mortality rate is much higher. Death comes more quickly and more often. It's incredibly adaptable."

Dr. Lee stared in disbelief. "Hasn't this country learned its lesson about secrecy?"

"We have learned it very well," Dr. Huang said. "China is working with the United States. We and the Americans have agreed to keep the existence of this new pathogen a secret for now."

"We saw before that delay in releasing information costs lives," Lee said.

"We also saw forced quarantine," Huang said. "Hospitals shuttered, travel and commerce interrupted, people attacked in Chinatowns around the world. We can't tell the truth now. There's no way to stop this pathogen until we've developed a vaccine."

"You're sure of this?"

"Don't take my word for it. The Americans have far more sophisticated computers. They have created models suggesting we can temporarily contain pockets of the disease, but it will eventually break out and we *will* have a worldwide pandemic."

"Why didn't you tell me all this back in the province?" Lee asked.

"I was afraid you might still think I had betrayed you before and wouldn't believe me," Huang said.

"Why should I believe you now?"

"Because I am telling the truth . . . I swear it."

Dr. Lee was confused and angry, but there was no doubt in her mind that Dr. Huang was being forthright.

"You mentioned a vaccine," she said.

"A number of labs are working on it," he said. "The most promising drug is being developed in the U.S. at the Bonefish Key lab in Florida. They believe a substance derived from ocean bio-medicine will produce a vaccine that will stop this pathogen."

"You are saying that *one* lab has the only viable preventative?" Lee almost laughed at the absurdity despite the direness of the situation.

The auditorium doors opened, and people were starting to spill into the corridor. Huang lowered his voice.

"It's still in development," he said, "but, yes, our hopes are high. It might go even faster if you were there as the representative from the People's Republic."

"The government wants me to go to Bonefish Key?" she said. "It seems that I have been 'rehabilitated.' I'm willing to do anything I can. But you are putting everything on this one vaccine. What if it doesn't work?"

A haunted look came to Huang's eyes, and his voice dropped to a whisper.

"Then only divine intervention can help us."

CHAPTER 3

THE INFLUENZA EPIDEMIC OF 1918 APPEARED SUDDENLY, striking the world as it was trying to stitch itself back together after the devastating war that had ripped it apart. The epidemic raged through Spain, killing eight million people, and for that accomplishment was dubbed the Spanish flu, though it hit many other countries including America as well. Within months, it had spread around the world. There was no known cure. Victims would sicken in the morning, breaking out in the telltale mahogany-colored rash within hours, and die before nightfall. Millions died; a billion were infected. Before it petered out in 1919, influenza had killed more people than five years of brutal war had. It was worse than the Black Death.

The grim statistics raced through Dr. Song Lee's mind as she covered the last leg before setting foot on Bonefish Key. She had flown into Fort Myers and caught a limo to the Pine Island Marina, where she met a colorful local character named Dooley Greene. He had taken her on his boat through the mangroves to the island. A man was waiting on the dock to greet her.

"Hi, Dr. Lee," the man said, extending his hand. "My name is Max Kane. Welcome to Fantasy Island. I'm the director of this little speck of paradise."

In his faded Hawaiian shirt and tattered denim shorts, Kane looked more like a beach bum than the respected ocean micro-biologist whose impressive résumé she had perused. A Chinese scientist of his stature would not have been caught dead without his white lab coat.

"I'm pleased to meet you, Dr. Kane," Lee said, glancing around at the rippling palm trees and a whitewashed building perched on a low, grassy rise a few hundred feet back from the dock. "I've never seen a research lab in such a picturesque setting."

Kane gave her a lopsided grin. "Not half as picturesque as the island's current inhabitants." He grabbed her suitcase and headed inland. "C'mon, I'll show you to your quarters."

They climbed a stairway cut into the side of the hill and then followed a crushed-shell pathway to a row of neat cabins painted flamingo pink with white trim. Kane opened the door of one cabin and ushered Lee inside. A bed, chair, dresser, and desk had been tucked into the snug space.

"It's not the Ritz, but it has everything you need," Kane said.

Lee thought about her one-room shack in the rural country-side. "I'm sure I'll be very comfortable here."

Kane placed the suitcase on the bed.

"Glad to hear that, Dr. Lee," he said. "How was your trip?"

"Long!" she said, punctuating her reply with an exaggerated sigh. "But it's good to be back in the U.S."

"I understand you spent some time at Harvard," Kane said. "We appreciate your returning to this country to help us out."

"How could I *not* come, Dr. Kane?" Lee said. "The world has been lucky up to now. Despite all our medical advances, we've never developed a vaccine for the original 1918 influenza. We're dealing with a mutant strain of that virus. Very complicated. The outcome will depend on our work here. How soon can I start?"

Max Kane smiled at Song Lee's eagerness.

"Let's get you something cold to drink," he said, "and I'll show you around, if you're up to it."

"I may fall asleep on my feet when the jet lag hits, but I'm fine for now," she said.

They walked back to the patio in front of the resort-style building. While Song rested in an Adirondack chair, Kane went into the building and brought out two glasses of mango and orange juice on ice. Sipping the delicious drink, she let her eyes wander along the shoreline. She had expected that the epicenter of secret research that had worldwide implications would be surrounded by fences and guards, and she couldn't contain her surprise that it didn't.

"It's hard to imagine that there is a lab doing vital work here," she said. "It's so tranquil."

"People would wonder if we put up barbed wire and guard towers. We've worked hard to project the image of a sleepy little research center. We decided that hiding in plain sight was the best strategy. Our website says that this is a private facility and suggests that our work is so boring to most people that no one would want to visit. You probably noticed the PRIVATE signs scattered around the island that say the same thing. We've only had a few requests to visit the center and we managed to put them off."

"Where are the lab buildings?"

"We had to get a little sneakier when it came to the research space. There are three labs farther inland. The labs are pretty well camouflaged. Google Earth would see only trees."

"What about security? I didn't see any guards."

"Oh, they're there, all right," Kane said with a tight smile. "The kitchen and maintenance staffs are all security people. There's an electronic-surveillance center that keeps track of any-one coming too close to the island twenty-four/seven. They've got cameras all over the place."

"What about the water-taxi man, Mr. Greene? Is he in on the deception?"

Kane smiled. "Dooley provides a useful cover. He worked for the old resort before Hurricane Charlie drove it into bankruptcy. We transported equipment and personnel here in our own boats when we were setting things up, but we needed someone to run people and supplies between the island and the mainland. Doo-ley's never been farther inland than the dock. He's a bit of a wind-bag, so if he does spout off about something he's seen out here the people who know him will figure that he's making it up."

"He was curious about me. I put him off as best I could."

"I'm sure everyone on Pine Island will know within hours about your visit, but I doubt anyone will care."

"That's good. I must confess that I'm nervous enough at the enormity of the task confronting us and the consequences if we fail."

He considered her answer and then said, "I'm optimistic from what we have done so far that we will *not* fail."

"I don't mean to be disrespectful, but I would feel more at ease if I knew the scientific basis for your optimism."

"Skepticism is the lifeblood of scientific inquiry," Kane said, spreading his hands. "I'll do my best. Our work is complex but not complicated. We know what we have to do. The toughest part is *doing* it. As you know, nothing is ever certain when you're dealing with viruses."

Song Lee nodded.

"With the exception of the human race," she said, "I don't think there is a more fascinating entity on the planet. What has your strategy been?"

"Are you up for a leisurely walk? I think better on my feet."

They struck off along one of the shell paths that laced the island, a holdover from the nature trails cut for guests at the old resort.

"I understand you worked at Harbor Branch," Lee said. Harbor Branch was a marine lab on Florida's east coast.

"I was at Harbor Branch for several years," Kane said. "The ocean biomed field is in its infancy, but they were among the first to recognize the vast potential for pharmaceuticals from marine organisms. They saw that ocean creatures had to develop ingenious natural mechanisms to cope with an extreme environment."

"How did you end up at Bonefish Key?"

"Harbor Branch was researching a number of different compounds from the sea, but I wanted to concentrate exclusively on antiviral agents, so I left and, with foundation money, established a new lab. Bonefish Key came up at auction after Hurricane Charlie. The foundation bought the island and fixed up the buildings that were left standing."

"You've apparently been successful," Lee said.

"We were doing pretty well scientifically," Kane said, "but last year the lab's funding dried up. The heirs of our prime benefactor challenged the legality of the foundation in court and won their case. I managed to hold things together, but it would have been only a matter of time before we closed. Sorry to say it, but the developments in China saved our butts."

"No need to apologize," she said. "We Chinese invented yin

and yang. Opposing forces can create a favorable balance. Tell me, how did Bonefish Key become the center of research on the newest epidemic? I've only heard bits and pieces of the story."

"Pretty much by chance," he said. "I'm chairman of a board that advises the feds about scientific discoveries that have defense or political implications. I had routinely passed along news of a possible breakthrough in antiviral research to the Centers for Disease Control. When the new virus strain was discovered in China, we were recruited to come find a way to fight it. The funds put us on the fast track in our research."

"You said you were optimistic about your progress," Lee said.

"*Guardedly* so. As a virologist, you know the hurdles in developing an antiviral agent."

Lee nodded.

"I am still amazed," she said, "at the complexity of the mechanisms stuffed into what is essentially a submicroscopic bit of nucleic acid wrapped in protein."

Now Kane nodded.

"I've always believed that the lack of fossilized records of viruses was circumstantial evidence that they are an alien life-form from another planet."

"You're not the only one who has posed the theory of an alien invasion," she said, "but we have to fight them with the tools we have available on earth." Lee smiled. "Or, in your case, what you find in the sea. How can I be of help during my time here?"

"We're honing in on a single antiviral chemical. We could use your expertise in virology as we put the stuff through the tests. At the same time," he added, "I'd like you to develop an epidemiological plan on how best to use the vaccine once we have synthesized it."

"How close are you to synthesis?" she asked.

"I wish we were closer, but we're almost there," he answered.

Kane turned down a well-worn path that branched off from the main walking trail. After about a hundred feet, the path ended at a cinder-block building. A man was standing there in front of a door of reinforced steel. He wore tan shorts and a blue T-shirt and could have passed for a maintenance man, but instead of tools a sidearm hung from his wide leather belt. The man didn't look surprised to see them. Song Lee recalled Max Kane saying that there were cameras everywhere on the island.

The man opened the door and stepped aside to allow his visitors in. The interior of the building was cool and dark except for the light coming from dozens of glass tanks that held various types of sea life. There was a low hum from the water-circulation pumps.

As they strolled past the rows of tanks, Kane said, "We had been conducting research on all these organisms but put the work on the back burner after we got the call from the CDC."

He led Lee to a side door and punched some numbers in the combination lock. The door opened into a smaller chamber that was completely dark except for the cold blue light coming from a vertical, tube-shaped water tank. The glow emanated from a number of undulating circular forms that rose and fell in the tank in a slow-motion dance.

Song Lee was mesmerized by the ghostly figures.

"They're beautiful," she said.

"Meet the blue medusa, Dr. Lee," Kane said. "All our research efforts have been concentrated on this lovely creature. Its venom is one of the most complex chemical compounds I've ever come across."

"Are you saying this jellyfish is the source of the compound you're trying to synthesize?"

"Uh-huh. The tiniest amount of the medusa's venom is fatal to humans, but the entire fate of millions of people could rest on the lowly creature in that tank. I can fill you in after you've had a chance to rest."

Dr. Lee's scientific mind was hungry for details.

"I don't *need* any rest," she insisted. "I want to start now."

Song Lee's roselike delicateness hid thorns that had been sharpened by her dealings with a stonehearted Chinese bureaucracy. Despite the seriousness of their conversation, Kane couldn't prevent the faint smile that came to his lips.

"I'll introduce you to the staff," he said.

Kane guided Lee through the labs, introducing her to the other talented scientists who were working on the blue medusa project. She was particularly impressed with Lois Mitchell, Kane's first assistant and project manager. But jet lag eventually caught up with Lee, and she caught a good night's sleep in her comfortable cabin. When she awoke the next day, she threw herself into her work.

In the days that followed, Dr. Lee rose early and worked late. Her daily kayak paddle through the mangroves was the only recreational break in her ferocious schedule. Then, one day, she and the rest of the scientific staff were asked to attend a meeting in the dining room. To applause, Dr. Kane announced that the compound they had been looking for had been identified. He and a handpicked team of volunteers would go into seclusion to put the final touches on the synthesis at a new lab. He could not say where the lab was located, only that it was nearer to the resource. Lee agreed to stay on at Bonefish Key with a skeleton crew so she could finish her epidemiological analysis and lay out an immunization production and distribution plan.

The quarantine was holding, but Lee knew that it was only a matter of time before the virus got loose. As she analyzed the clusters of the virus outbreak, she kept China's experience with the SARS virus in the back of her mind. All suspected or probable cases had been placed in negative-pressure rooms, shut off from the outside world by two airtight doors, every breath they took filtered. But the disease still managed to spread, demonstrating the difficulty in sealing off the virus.

In the weeks that followed the exodus of the key scientific staff, reports filtered back to Bonefish Key from the secret lab. The most exciting news was the report that the toxin had been synthesized, the prelude to developing a vaccine.

Spurred on by the successful research, Lee had hurried to develop a plan to administer the antidote and to contain the epidemic before it developed into a pandemic.

Dr. Huang had asked to be kept informed of Dr. Lee's progress. The only place on the island where cell-phone service was available was at the top of an old water tower. Every day after her work, Lee climbed the tower and summarized the progress of the project for her old friend and mentor.

There was no way she could have known that her every word was being relayed to unfriendly ears.

CHAPTER 4

BERMUDA, THREE MONTHS LATER

THE TAXI DRIVER WARILY EYEBALLED THE MAN STANDING on the curb outside the arrival gate at Bermuda's L. F. Wade Airport. His potential fare had an unruly ginger beard, and hair pulled back in a short pigtail that was tied with a rubber band. In addition, he wore faded jeans, high-top red sneakers, Elton John sunglasses with white plastic frames, and a rumpled tan linen suit jacket over a T-shirt with a picture on it of Jerry Garcia from the Grateful Dead.

"Please take me to the ship harbor," Max Kane said. He opened the door, threw his duffel bag in the backseat, and then slid in beside it. The driver shrugged and put the taxi in gear. A fare was a fare.

Kane sat back and closed his eyes. His brain was about to explode. His impatience had ballooned with each mile traveled over the past twenty-four hours. The long flight from the Pacific Ocean to North America and the two-hour trip from New York were nothing compared to the dragging minutes it took for the taxi to get to the waterfront.

Kane directed the driver to stop near the gangway of a turquoise-hulled ship. The distinctive color and the letters NUMA emblazoned on the hull below the ship's name, WILLIAM BEEBE, identified the vessel as belonging to the National Underwater and Marine Agency, the largest ocean-study organization in the world.

Kane exited the cab and shoved a wad of bills at the driver, then slung the duffel over his shoulder and briskly climbed up the gangway. A pleasant-faced young woman wearing the uniform of a ship's officer greeted Kane with a warm smile.

"Good afternoon," the woman said. "My name is Marla Hayes. I'm the third mate. May I have your name?"

"Max Kane."

She consulted a clipboard and put a check mark next to Kane's name.

"Welcome to the *Beebe,* Dr. Kane. I'll show you to your cabin and give you a tour of the ship."

"If you don't mind, I've come a long way and I'm anxious to see the B3."

"No problem," Marla said, leading Kane toward the ship's fantail.

The two-hundred-fifty-foot-long search-and-survey ship was the marine equivalent of a professional weight lifter. With its stern-ramp A-frame crane and wide deck, the fantail was the business end of the ship. It bristled with the winches and derricks that scientists used to launch underwater vehicles and devices that probed the depths. Kane's eyes went to a large tangerine-colored globe resting in a steel cradle beneath a tall crane. Three portholes that resembled short-range cannons protruded from the sphere's surface.

"There it is," Marla said. "I'll come by in a little while to see how you're doing."

Kane thanked the young woman and cautiously approached the globe, treading softly as if he expected the strange object to bolt on the four legs attached to the bottom. He walked around to the other side of the sphere and saw a man in a Hawaiian shirt and cargo shorts standing in front of a circular opening slightly more than a foot in diameter. The man's head was inside the globe, his right shoulder angled through the hatch as if he were being devoured by a bug-eyed monster. The string of salty curses that echoed from inside the globe sounded as if they were coming from a pirate cave.

Kane set his duffel bag down, and asked, "Tight quarters?"

The man bumped his head as he backed out of the opening, prompting a few more colorful oaths, and brushed away a shock of steel-gray hair from eyes that were the blue of coral under flat water. He had a broad-shouldered frame that was an inch over six feet, and he must have weighed two hundred pounds. He grinned, showing perfect white teeth against features that had been bronzed by years at sea.

"*Very* tight. I'd need a shoehorn and a can of grease to get me into this antiquated refugee from a marine-salvage dump," he said.

A dark-complexioned face poked from the hatch, and its owner said, "Give it up, Kurt. They'd have to baste you with WD-40 and pound you in with a sledgehammer."

The broad-shouldered man made a face at the unpleasant image. He extended his hand in introduction. "I'm Kurt Austin, project director for the Bathysphere 3 expedition."

The man in the sphere wriggled out feetfirst and introduced himself. "Joe Zavala," he said. "I'm the engineer for the B3 project."

"Nice to meet you both. My name is Max Kane." He jerked his thumb at the sphere. "And I'm scheduled to dive a half mile into the ocean in this antiquated refugee from a marine-salvage dump."

Austin exchanged a bemused glance with Zavala. "Pleased to meet you, Dr. Kane. Sorry to cast doubt on your sanity."

"It wouldn't be the first time someone accused me of being one beer short of a six-pack. You get used to it when you're doing pure research." Kane removed his sunglasses, revealing eyes of Kris Kringle blue. "And please call me Doc."

Austin gestured toward the orange globe. "Don't pay any attention to my earlier comment, Doc. I'm nursing a serious case of sour grapes. I'd make the dive in a heartbeat if the bathysphere came in a bigger size. Joe is the best deep-sea guy in the business. He's made the diving bell as safe as any NUMA submersible."

Zavala cast an appraising eye on the sphere. "I used technology that wasn't available back in the thirties, but otherwise it's the original Beebe-Barton design that set the record by diving 3,028 feet in 1934. The bathysphere was beautiful in its simplicity."

"The sphere design seems so obvious to us now," Kane said. "At first, William Beebe thought that a cylinder-shaped bell might work. He was chatting with his friend Teddy Roosevelt years before the actual dive and sketched his idea out on a napkin. Roosevelt disagreed and drew a circle instead, representing his preference for a globe-shaped bell. Later, when Beebe saw the Otis Barton design based on a sphere, he realized that was the only way to deal with the pressure at great depth."

Zavala had heard the story before. "Beebe saw that the cylinder's flat ends would cave in," he picked up the story, "but a sphere would distribute the pressure more evenly around its entire surface." He squatted next to the globe and ran his hand over the thick skids that the legs rested upon. "I've added emergency flotation bags in the runners. There's more than a little self-preservation involved, Doc. I'll be making the dive with you."

Kane rubbed his palms together like a hungry man savoring a juicy steak. "This is a dream come true," he said. "I pulled every string I could to get on the dive list. William Beebe is responsible for my career in marine microbiology. When I was a kid, I read about the glowing, deep-ocean fish that he found. I wanted to share Beebe's adventures."

"My biggest adventure has been trying to stuff myself through that fourteen-inch door," Austin said. "Try it on for size, Doc."

Kane, who was about five foot eight, hung his jacket on the bathysphere's frame, then poured himself headfirst into the sphere, doubled his body with the skill of a contortionist, and poked his head out the circular opening.

"It's roomier in here than it appears from the outside."

"The original bathysphere was four feet nine inches in diameter, and had walls one and a half inches thick made of fine-grade, open-hearth steel," Zavala said. "The divers shared their space with oxygen tanks, filter trays, a searchlight, and telephone wires. We've cheated a little. The portholes are polymer instead of fused quartz. The tether is Kevlar rather than steel, and we've replaced the copper communications link with photo-optic fiber. We miniaturized the bulkier instruments. I would have preferred a titanium sphere, but the costs were higher."

Kane easily exited the sphere and stared at it with near reverence. "You've done an amazing job, Joe. Beebe and Barton were aware they were risking their lives, but their boyish enthusiasm overcame their fears."

"That enthusiasm must have rubbed off on you to come all this distance," Austin said. "I understand you were in the Pacific Ocean."

"Yeah. Contract work for Uncle Sam. Pretty routine stuff. We're about to wrap it up, which is fortunate because there was no way I would have missed this opportunity."

The third mate was making her way across the deck toward the bathysphere accompanied by two men and a woman carrying video cameras, lights, and sound equipment.

"That's the NUMA film crew," Austin said to Kane. "They'll want to interview the intrepid divers on camera."

A look of horror came over Max Kane's face. "I must look like crap. *Smell* like it too. Can they wait until I hop into the shower and trim the porcupine quills on my chin?"

"Joe will fill them in while you clean up. I'll see you in the bridge after you're done with the interview," Austin said. "We'll go over the plans for tomorrow."

As he headed for the bridge, Austin reflected on how Beebe's books had stirred his own imagination when he was a boy growing up in Seattle. He recalled one story in particular. Beebe described standing at the edge of an underwater precipice at the limit of his surface air supply, looking down with yearning into the deep water beyond his reach. The scene crystallized Austin's own tendency to push to his limits.

Born and raised in Seattle, Austin had followed his boyhood dreams, studying systems management at the University of Washington. He also attended a prestigious deepwater diving school, specializing in salvage. He worked a few years on North Sea oil rigs and put in a stint with his father's ocean-salvage company, but his spirit of adventure needed freer rein. He joined a clandestine underwater-surveillance unit of the CIA that he led until it was disbanded at the end of the Cold War. His father hoped he would return to ocean salvage, but Austin moved over to NUMA to head up a unique team that included Zavala and Paul and Gamay Trout. Admiral Sandecker had seen the need to create the Special Assignments Team to investigate out-of-the-ordinary events above and below the world's oceans.

After completing the team's last assignment, the search for a long-lost Phoenician statue known as the *Navigator,* Austin had heard that the National Geographic Society and the New York Zoological Society were sponsoring a docudrama on Beebe's historic half-mile bathysphere dive of 1934. Actors would play Beebe and Barton, using a prop bathysphere, with much of the action simulated.

Austin persuaded the NUMA brass to let Zavala design a state-of-the-art bathysphere. The diving bell would be launched from the agency's research vessel, *William Beebe,* in conjunction with the docudrama. Like all government agencies, NUMA had to fight for its share of the federal funding pie, and favorable publicity never hurt.

Dirk Pitt had taken over from Sandecker as NUMA's director after Sandecker became the Vice President of the United States, and Pitt was equally interested in creating favorable public awareness of the agency's work. The bathysphere's pressure sphere would be recycled after the expedition as the heart of a new deep-sea submersible. The diving bell was nicknamed the B3 because it was the third pressure hull using the Beebe-Barton design.

Trailed by a cameraman and sound technician, Zavala and a freshly scrubbed Kane climbed to the bridge after being interviewed in front of the bathysphere. Austin introduced Kane to the captain, an experienced NUMA hand named Mike Gannon, who spread a chart out on a table and pointed to Nonsuch Island off the northeast tip of Bermuda.

"We'll anchor as close as possible to Beebe's original position," the captain said. "We'll be about eight miles from land with just over a half mile of water under the ship's keel."

"We decided on a shallower location than the original so we could film the sea bottom," Austin said. "How's the weather looking?"

"There's a gale expected tonight, but it should blow out before morning," Gannon said.

Austin turned to Kane. "We've been doing all the talking, Doc. What do you hope to get out of this expedition?"

Kane gave the question a moment's thought.

"Miracles," he said with a mysterious smile.

"How so?"

"When Beebe reported hauling phosphorescent fish in his trawl nets, his fellow scientists didn't believe him. Beebe hoped the bathysphere would vindicate his research. He compared it to a paleontologist who could annihilate time and see his fossils alive. Like Beebe, my hope is to dramatize the miracles that lie beneath the surface of the ocean."

"Biomedicine miracles?" Austin asked.

Kane's dreamy expression vanished, and he seemed to catch himself.

"What do you mean, biomeds?" Kane's voice had an unexpected edge to it. He glanced at the video camera.

"I Googled Bonefish Key. Your website mentioned a morphine substitute your lab developed from snail venom. I simply wondered if you had come across anything similar in the Pacific Ocean."

Kane broke into a smile. "I was speaking as an ocean microbiologist . . . *metaphorically*."

Austin nodded. "Let's talk miracles and metaphors over dinner, Doc."

Kane opened his mouth in a yawn.

"I'm about to hit the wall," he said. "Sorry to be a bother, Captain, but I wonder if I could have a sandwich sent to my cabin. I'd better get some sleep so I can be fresh for tomorrow's dive."

Austin said he would see Kane in the morning. He watched

Kane thoughtfully as he left the bridge, wondering at his edgy response to a routine question. Then he turned back to confer with the captain.

THE NEXT MORNING, the NUMA ship followed the course Beebe's expedition had taken, heading out to sea through Castle Roads, passing between high, jagged cliffs and old forts, past Gurnet Rock and into the open sea.

The gale had petered out, leaving a long, heaving swell in its wake. Plowing through low mounding water, the ship traveled for another hour before dropping anchor.

The diving bell had been put through dozens of tank tests, but Zavala wanted an unmanned launch before the main dive. A crane lifted the sealed bathysphere over the water and allowed it to sink to the fifty-foot mark. After fifteen minutes, the B3 was winched back onto the deck, and Zavala inspected the interior.

"Drier than an eye at a miser's funeral," Zavala said.

"Ready to take the plunge, Doc?" Austin asked.

"I've been ready for nearly forty years," Kane said.

Zavala tossed two inflatable cushions and a couple of blankets through the door. "Beebe and Barton sat on cold hard steel," he announced. "I've decided a minimum of comfort will be necessary."

In turn, Kane produced two skullcaps from a bag and handed one to Zavala. "Barton refused to dive unless he wore his lucky hat."

Zavala pulled the cap down on his head. Then he crawled through the bathysphere's hatch, taking care not to snag his fleece-lined jacket and pants on the steel bolts that surrounded it. He curled up next to a control panel. Kane got in next and sat on the window side. Zavala turned the air supply on and called out to Austin, "Close the door, Kurt, it's drafty in here."

"See you for margaritas in a few hours," Austin gave the order to seal the bathysphere.

A crane lifted the four-hundred-pound hatch cover into place. The launch crew used a torque wrench to screw ten large nuts over the bolts. Kane shook hands with Austin through a four-inch circular opening in the center of the door that allowed instruments to be passed in and out without having to move the cumbersome cover. Then the crew screwed a nut into the hole to seal it.

Austin picked up a microphone connected to the bathysphere's communications system and warned the divers they were about to become airborne. The winch growled and the crane hoisted the B3 off the deck as if the fifty-four-hundred-pound steel globe and its human cargo were made of feathers, swung it over the side, and kept it suspended twenty feet above the heaving ocean surface.

Austin called the bathysphere on the radio and got Zavala's go-ahead to launch.

Through the B3's windows, the divers caught a glimpse of the upturned faces of the launch and film crews and slices of ship and sky before the portholes were awash in green bubbles and froth. The B3 splashed into the crystal clear waters and slipped beneath the surface in the valley between two rolling swells.

The crane lowered the diving bell until it was just under the surface.

Zavala's metallic-sounding voice came over a speaker mounted on a deck stand. "Thanks for the soft landing," he said.

"This crane crew could dunk this doughnut in a cup of coffee," Austin said.

"Don't mention coffee and other liquids," Zavala said. "The *baño* is located on the outside of the bathysphere."

"Sorry. We'll book you a first-class cabin next time."

"I appreciate the offer, but my main concern is making sure our feet stay dry. Next stop . . ."

The winch let out fifty feet of cable, and the bathysphere stopped for the final safety inspection. Zavala and Kane checked the bathysphere for moisture, paying close attention to the watertight seals around the door.

Finding no leaks, Zavala made a quick run-through of the B3's air-supply, circulation, and communications systems. The indicator lights showed that all the bathysphere's electronic nerves and lungs were working fine. He called up to the support ship.

"Tight as a tick, Kurt. All systems go. Ready, Doc?"

"Lower away!" Kane said.

The sea's foamy arms embraced the bathysphere like a long-lost denizen, and with only a mound of bubbles to mark its descent the hollow sphere and its two passengers began the half-mile trip to King Neptune's realm.

CHAPTER 5

THE B3'S PASSENGERS WERE SEALED OFF IN A STEEL PRISON that would have defied Harry Houdini, but their images freely roamed the globe. A pair of miniature cameras mounted on the interior wall transmitted pictures of the bathysphere cabin up a fiber-optic cable to the *Beebe*'s mast antenna, where the signals were bounced off a roving communications satellite and instantaneously beamed to laboratories and classrooms around the world.

Thousands of miles from Bermuda, a red-and-white communications buoy bobbing in a remote section of the Pacific Ocean relayed the pictures to a dimly lit room three hundred feet below the surface. A row of glowing television screens set into the wall of the semicircular chamber displayed green-hued pictures showing schools of fish darting past the cameras like windblown confetti.

A dozen or so men and women were gathered around the only screen that did not display the sea bottom. All had their eyes glued to a blue-and-black depiction of the globe and the letters

NUMA. While they watched, the logo vanished to be replaced by a shot of the B3's cramped interior and its two passengers.

"*Ya-hoo!*" Lois Mitchell yelled, pumping her arm in the air. "Doc's on his way. And he's wearing his lucky hat."

The others joined in her applause, then the room went silent as Max Kane began to talk, his words and mouth slightly out of synchronization. He leaned toward the camera, his eyes and cheeks bulging from lens distortion.

"Hello, everyone. My name is Dr. Max Kane, director of the Bonefish Key Marine Center, broadcasting from a replica of the Beebe-Barton bathysphere."

"Leave it to Doc to get in a plug for the lab," said a gray-haired man seated to Lois's right.

Kane continued. "We are in Bermudan waters, where we're about to re-create the historical half-mile Beebe-Barton bathysphere dive made in 1934. This is the third bathysphere, so we've shortened its name to B3. The bathysphere's pilot is Joe Zavala, a submersible pilot and marine engineer with the National Underwater and Marine Agency. Joe is responsible for designing the bathysphere replica."

Zavala had rigged voice-activated controls that allowed the divers to switch camera views. His face replaced Kane's on the screen, and he began to describe the B3's technical innovations. Lois was only half listening, more interested in the NUMA engineer's dark good looks than his shoptalk.

"I envy Doc," she said without removing her gaze from Zavala's face.

"Me too," said the gray-haired man, a marine biologist named Frank Logan. "What a great scientific opportunity!"

Lois smiled slightly as if enjoying a private joke. Her desire to spend time in the close confines of the bathysphere with the handsome Zavala had nothing to do with science. Well, maybe *biology.*

The camera went back to Kane.

"Great job, Joe," Kane said. "At this time, I'd like to say a hello and offer personal thanks to everyone who has helped make this project possible. *National Geographic,* the New York Zoological Society, the government of Bermuda . . . and NUMA, of course." He put his face closer to the camera, a move that made him look like a grinning grouper. "I'd also like to give my best to all the denizens at Davy Jones's Locker."

The room echoed with loud whoops and applause.

Logan was a soft-spoken Midwesterner and was normally reserved, but he slapped his thigh in his excitement. "Wow!" he exclaimed. "Nice of Doc to recognize us denizens still slaving away down here in the Locker. Too bad we can't return the favor."

Lois said, "Technically, it's possible but not advisable. As far as the rest of the world is concerned, this undersea lab doesn't even exist! We're probably just a line item in a congressional budget cleverly disguised as an order of five-hundred-dollar toilet seats for the Navy."

A smile came to Logan's face. "Yes, I know, but it's *still* too bad we can't offer Doc our congratulations. I can't think of anyone who deserves it more, after all he's done." He sensed from the blank expression on Lois's face that he had made a verbal gaffe, and said, "You deserve a great deal of credit, Lois. After all, your work bringing the medusa project to its near conclusion allowed Max to get away for the bathysphere dive."

"Thanks, Frank. We *all* gave up our normal lives to be here."

A soft gong echoed throughout the room, and a green light blinked over a television monitor that showed what looked like a diamond diadem against dark velvet.

"Speaking of administrative duties," Logan said with a wry grin, "your company is about to arrive."

Lois wrinkled her nose. "*Damn*. I wanted to watch the rest of Doc's dive."

"Bring your guest back here to watch the show," Logan suggested.

"Oh, *no*! I'm getting rid of him as quickly as I can," Lois said, rising from her chair.

Lois Mitchell was nearly six feet tall, and in her late forties she had packed a few more pounds on her frame than she would have preferred. The voluptuous figure under the baggy sweat suit didn't live up to contemporary ideals of beauty, but artists of a bygone day would have drooled over her curves and creamy skin, and the way her thick raven hair fell to her shoulders.

She bustled from the room and descended a spiral staircase to a brightly lit passageway. The tubelike corridor connected to a small chamber occupied by two men who stood at an instrument panel facing a heavy-duty double door.

One man said, "Hi, Lois. Touchdown is in forty-five seconds." He pointed to a television screen set into the instrument panel.

The cluster of sparkling lights displayed on the control-room monitor had materialized into a submersible vehicle slowly descending through the murk. It resembled a large utility helicopter that had been stripped of its main rotor and was powered by variable-thrust turbines on the fuselage. Two figures were silhouetted in the bubble cockpit.

The room reverberated with the hum of motors. A diagram of the lab on the control panel began to blink, indicating that the airlock doors were open. After a few moments, the display stopped blinking, signifying that the doors had closed. The floor vibrated with the thrash of powerful pumps. When the water had been expelled from the airlock, the pumps went silent, and a green light flashed over the doors. At the push of a button on the control panel, the doors opened, and a briny smell rushed out. The submersible rested in a circular domed chamber. Curtains of seawater rolled off the fuselage and swirled down gurgling drains.

A hatch slid open in the side of the submersible, and the pilot got out. The men at the control panel went to help unload cartons of supplies from a cargo space behind the cockpit.

Lois strode over and greeted the man emerging from the passenger's side. He was a couple of inches taller than she was and wore blue jeans, sneakers, and a windbreaker and baseball cap both emblazoned with the logo of the company that provided security for the lab.

She extended her hand. "Welcome to Davy Jones's Locker. I'm Dr. Lois Mitchell, assistant director of the lab while Dr. Kane is away."

"Pleased to meet you, ma'am," the man said in a deep-voiced Southern drawl. "My name is Phelps."

Lois had expected to see a quasi-military type like the tough-looking guards she had glimpsed on trips to the surface ship, where lab staff could take a break from the seafloor, but Phelps looked as if he had been assembled from spare parts. His arms were too long for his body, his hands too big for his arms, his head too big for his shoulders. With his sad-looking dark eyes and large mouth accented by drooping mustache, he had a hound-dog quality about him. He wore his dark brown hair in unfashionably long sideburns.

"Did you have a pleasant shuttle ride, Mr. Phelps?"

"Couldn't have been better, ma'am. The best part was seeing the lights on the ocean bottom. Kept thinking this must be Atlantis."

Lois cringed inwardly at the overblown comparison to the lost city.

"Glad to hear that," she said. "Come to my office and we'll chat about how we can help you."

She led the way from the airlock along another tubular passageway, then up a spiral staircase to a low-lit, circular room. Fish nosed against the room's transparent domed ceiling, creating the illusion that the sea was pressing in.

Phelps swiveled his head in wonder. "Talk about a water view! This is unbelievable, ma'am."

"People find it hypnotic at first, but you get used to it. This is actually Dr. Kane's office. I'm using it while he's away. Have a seat. And please stop calling me *ma'am*. It makes me feel a hundred years old. I prefer Dr. Mitchell."

"You sure look pretty good for a hundred years old, ma'am . . . I mean, Dr. Mitchell."

Lois cringed again, and turned up the lights in the room so that the marine life was less visible and distracting. She opened a small office refrigerator, extracted two cold bottles of springwater, and gave one to Phelps. She settled herself behind a plastic-and-chrome desk of starkly simple design.

Phelps pulled up a chair. "I'd like to thank you for your valuable time, Dr. Mitchell. You must have lots better things to do besides talking to a boring old security guy."

If you only knew, Lois thought. She gave her visitor a polite smile. "How can I help you, Mr. Phelps?"

"My company sent me to probe for weaknesses in the sea-lab security."

Lois wondered what kind of an idiot had sent Phelps to waste her time. She leaned back in her chair and pointed toward the transparent ceiling.

"We've got three hundred feet of ocean separating us from the surface, and it's better than any castle moat. There's a patrol ship up there with heavily armed guards from your company, backed up, if necessary, by the on-call resources of the U.S. Navy. How could we be any more secure than that?"

Phelps furrowed his brow. "With all due respect, Dr. Mitchell, the first thing you learn in this business is that there is *no* security system in the world that can't be breached."

Lois ignored the condescending tone. "Very well, then, let's start with a virtual tour of the facility," she said.

She swiveled her chair and tapped a computer keyboard. A three-dimensional diagram that looked like a series of globes and connecting tubes appeared on the monitor.

"The lab consists of four large spheres, arranged in a diamond shape and connected by tubular corridors," Lois began. "We're at the top of the administrative pod . . . here. Below us is the crew's quarters and mess hall." She manipulated the cursor to highlight another globe. "There's a control room and some labs and storage in this pod. This pod contains the small nuclear plant. Air is supplied through a water-to-oxygen setup, with backup tanks for emergencies. We're a few hundred yards from the edge of a deepwater canyon."

Phelps pointed to a hemispheric shape in the center of the rectangle. "Is this where the surface shuttle came in?"

"That's right," Lois said. "The minisubs attached to the underside of the transit module are used for specimen collection in the canyon, but they can be used to evacuate the lab, and there are escape pods available as a last resort. The shuttle airlock is connected by reinforced passageways that give the staff access from any module and contribute to the structural strength of the complex."

"What about the fourth module?" Phelps said.

"Top secret."

"How many folks work in the complex?"

"Sorry, top secret again. I don't make the rules."

"That's okay," Phelps said with a nod. "This is one hell of a job of engineering."

"We're fortunate that the Navy had the facility readily available. The lab was originally planned as an undersea observatory. The components were built on land, fully equipped, and towed out here in special barges. The barges were then rafted together, and the setup was fitted together like an old-fashioned Tinkertoy and lowered into the sea in one piece. Luckily, we're not at great depth, and the sea bottom is fairly level. It's what they call a turn-key operation. The complex was not meant to be permanent, so it has compressed-air capabilities that allow it to attain negative buoyancy. It could be retrieved and moved to another location."

Phelps said, "If it's not too much trouble, I'd like to see the nonrestricted areas."

Lois Mitchell frowned, signaling that she was doing this under protest. She picked up the intercom phone and called the control room. "Hello, Frank," she said. "This is going to take a little longer than I expected. Anything new with Doc? No? Okay, I'll keep in touch."

She replaced the phone with more force than was necessary, and stood to her full height. "C'mon, Mr. Phelps. This is going to be fast and furious."

FIFTY MILES FROM Davy Jones's Locker, the rolling surface of the dark sea erupted in an explosion of foam and spray. A twenty-foot-long aluminum tube burst from the center of the churning geyser, sped skyward at a sharp angle, leaving a white fan-shaped trail behind it, and quickly dove back toward the waves in a curving trajectory.

Within seconds, the cruise missile had leveled out, until it was traveling twenty-five feet above the wave tops, so low that its passing left a wake in the water. Powered by its solid-fuel rocket booster, the missile quickly accelerated, and by the time it had shed its rocket and the fan-jet engines had kicked in it had achieved its cruising speed of five hundred miles per hour.

A series of sophisticated guidance systems kept the cruise missile on track as unerringly as if it were being steered by a skilled pilot.

The speeding missile's unsuspecting target was a large, gray-hulled ship anchored near the red-and-white buoy that marked the location of the undersea lab. The name on the hull was PROUD MARY, and it was registered in the Marshall Islands as a survey ship. The *Proud Mary* was anchored near the buoy waiting for the shuttle sub to return with Phelps.

The ship's owner was a shadowy corporation that provided vessels to international security companies in need of naval services. They supplied everything from small, fast, and heavily armed speedboats to ships large enough to land an army of mercenaries anywhere in the world.

Assigned to protect the undersea laboratory, the *Proud Mary* carried two dozen guards proficient in the use of every type of small arms as well as an array of electronic sensing gear that could pick up vessels or planes approaching the lab. The ship also served as a parking garage for the shuttle that ferried supplies and people to and from the lab.

In its leap from the ocean, the cruise missile had blipped on the ship's radar screen for only a few seconds. Inactivity had dulled the operator's edge, and he was engrossed in a motorcycle magazine when the missile made its brief appearance, before dropping from surveillance's view. The ship also had infrared sensors, but even if the missile had been flying at altitude they would have failed to pick up the low-temperature heat from its engines.

Undetected, the missile streaked toward the *Proud Mary* carrying a half ton of high explosives in its warhead.

Lois Mitchell and Gordon Phelps were making their way along the connecting tube to the control room when they heard a loud *whump* that seemed to come from far over their heads. She stopped in her tracks and pivoted slowly, ears cocked, concerned that it indicated a systems failure.

"I've never heard anything like *that* before," she said. "It sounded like a truck slamming into a wall. I'd better check to make sure all the lab systems are operating as they should be."

Phelps glanced at his watch. "From the sound of it, things seem to be moving a little ahead of schedule."

"I'd better check the situation in the control room."

"Good idea," Phelps said amiably.

They started walking toward the door at the end of the passageway. A few steps from the control-room module, the door hissed open, and Frank Logan burst through. His pale face was flushed with excitement, and he was grinning.

"Lois! I was coming to get you. Did you hear that weird noise—"

Logan stopped short, his grin vanishing. Lois turned to see what he was staring at.

Phelps was holding a pistol in his hand, dangling it loosely next to his thigh.

"What's going on?" she said. "We don't allow weapons in the lab."

Phelps gave her a hangdog look. "Like I said, no security system is totally foolproof. Lab's under new management, Dr. Mitchell."

He was still soft-spoken, but his voice had lost the obsequious quality that Lois had found so irritating and now had an edge that hadn't been there before. Phelps told Logan to stand next to Lois so he could keep an eye on him. As Logan complied, the control-room door hissed open again, and a lab technician stepped through. Phelps instinctively brought his gun around to deal with the interruption. The lab tech froze, but Logan, seeing Phelps's momentary distraction, tried to grab his gun.

They struggled, but Phelps was younger and stronger and would have gotten the upper hand even if the gun had not gone off. The noise was muffled to a soft *putt* by a silencer on the pistol barrel, but a red stain blossomed on the front of Logan's white lab coat. His legs gave out, and he crumpled to the floor.

The lab tech bolted back into the control room. Lois ran over and knelt by Logan's motionless body. She opened her mouth in a scream but nothing came out. "You killed him!" she finally said.

"Aw, hell," Phelps said. "Didn't mean to do that."

"What *did* you mean to do?" Lois said.

"No time to talk about that now, ma'am."

Lois stood up and confronted Phelps. "Are you going to shoot me too?"

"Not unless I have to, Dr. Mitchell. Don't do anything crazy like your friend. We'd hate to lose you."

Lois Mitchell stared defiantly at Phelps for a few seconds before she wilted under his unrelenting gaze. "What do you want?"

"For now, I want you to round up all the lab folks."

"*Then* what?" she said.

Phelps shrugged. "Then we're going for a little ride."

CHAPTER 6

THE B3 PASSENGERS HAD DECIDED TO REPORT THEIR OBSER-
vations like sportscasters. Joe Zavala would do the play-by-play,
Max Kane would provide the color using William Beebe's
writings.

At two hundred eighty-six feet down, Kane announced, "The
torpedoed ocean liner *Lusitania* is resting at this level."

At three hundred fifty-three feet, he noted, "This was the
deepest any submarine had ever gone when Beebe made his
bathysphere dives."

When the bathysphere reached six hundred feet, Kane slipped
the lucky skullcap from his head and held it in his hands.

"We've entered what Beebe called the Land of the Lost," he
said in a hushed tone. "This is the realm that belongs to the human
beings who have been lost at sea. Going back to the Phoenicians,
millions of human beings have descended this far, but all of
them have been dead, the drowned victims of war, tempest, or act
of God."

"Cheery thought," Zavala said. "Is that why you said hello to Davy Jones's Locker . . . where drowned sailors go?"

Zavala had rigged a switch to turn off the TV camera and microphone. Kane reached out and said, "Joe and I are taking a short break. We'll be back with more observations in a few minutes." He pushed the button. "I need a breather," he said with a smile. "You asked about the Locker . . . It's the nickname my colleagues gave to the lab."

"The marine center at Bonefish Key?" Zavala said.

Kane glanced at the camera. "That's right, Bonefish Key."

Zavala wondered why anyone would compare a sunny Florida island on the Gulf of Mexico with the grim domain of the drowned. He gave a mental shrug. Scientists were strange birds.

"Beebe sounds morbid, but he had a relatively benign view of the ocean," Kane said. "He knew the dangers were real, but he thought the hazards of the deep overblown."

"The millions of drowning victims you mentioned might disagree," Zavala said. "I respect everything Beebe and Barton did, Doc, but from an engineer's point of view I'd say they were just plain lucky they didn't become part of that Land of the Lost. The original bathysphere was an accident waiting to happen."

Kane greeted the blunt assessment with a chuckle.

"Beebe was a realist as well as a dreamer," he said. "He compared the bathysphere to a hollow pea swaying on a cobweb a quarter of a mile below the deck of a ship rolling in midocean."

"Poetic but not inaccurate," Zavala replied. "That's exactly why I built safety features into the new diving bell."

"Glad you did," Kane said. He switched the microphone back on and turned his attention to the scene visible through the porthole.

The B3 rocked slightly from time to time, but its descent was signaled more by changes in the light coming in through the portholes than by any sense of motion. The most drastic color change comes at the start of a dive. Red and yellow are wrung from the spectrum as if from a sponge. Green and blue dominate. Deeper still, the water color shifts to navy and finally becomes an intense black.

In the early stages of the dive, pilot fish, silver eels, motelike clouds of copepods, and strings of lacelike siphonophores drifted past the windows like tiny ghosts, along with shrimp, translucent squid, and snails so tiny that they resembled brown bubbles. Long, dark shapes could be glimpsed at the extreme range of the B3's searchlight beam.

At seven hundred feet, Zavala switched the searchlight off. He looked out the window and murmured an appreciative exclamation in Spanish. Zavala had grown up in Santa Fe, and the view through the porthole looked like a New Mexico sky on a clear winter's night. The darkness sparkled with stars, some alone, others in groups, some continuously flashing, others just once. There were floating threads of luminescence, and glowing smudges that could have been novas or nebulas in a celestial setting.

The cabin was as hushed as a cathedral; the loudest sound was the low hum of the air-circulation motor, so when Kane saw an undulating form float by the porthole his response was like a gunshot.

"*Wow!*" Kane exclaimed. "An Aurelia jellyfish."

Zavala smiled at Kane's excitement. Although there was no denying the beauty in the jellyfish's undulating motion, the creature outside the bathysphere's porthole was only a few inches across.

"Had me for a second there, Doc. Thought you'd seen the Loch Ness Monster," Zavala said.

"This is so much better than Nessie. The medusae are among the most fascinating and complex animals on the face of the earth or under the sea. Look at that school of fish lit up like the Las Vegas Strip . . . lantern fish . . . Hey," Kane said, "what was that?"

"You see a mermaid, Doc?" Zavala asked.

Kane pressed his face against the porthole. "I'm not sure *what* I saw," he said, "but I know it was *big*."

Zavala flicked on the searchlight, a green shaft of light edged with purple-blue stabbing the darkness, and he peered through the porthole.

"Gone," he said, "whatever it was."

"Beebe spotted a big fish he thought might have been a whale shark," Kane said to the camera. "Until the bathysphere's dive, his fellow scientists never believed that he had seen fish with glowing teeth and neon skin. He got the last laugh when he proved the abyss abounded with such strange creatures."

"They're getting stranger all the time," Zavala said, pointing at himself. "The locals swimming around out there must think that you and I are pretty unsavory-looking additions to their neighborhood."

Kane's loud guffaw echoed off the bathysphere's curving walls.

"My apologies to the listening audience out there, hope I didn't blow out your speakers. But Joe is right: humans have no right being where we are at this moment. The pressure on the outside of this sphere is half a ton per square inch. We'd look like jellyfish ourselves if it weren't for the steel shell protecting us . . . Hey, there's some more lantern fish. Man, they're beautiful. Look, there's— *Whoops!*"

The bathysphere's descent had been smooth and without deviation, but suddenly a strong vibration passed through the sphere as Kane was talking. The B3 first lifted up, then dropped, in slow motion. Wide-eyed, Kane glanced around, as if expecting the sea to come pouring in through the sphere's shell.

Zavala called up to the support vessel. "Please stop yo-yoing the B3, Kurt."

An unusually mounding sea had rolled under the ship, and the cable suddenly had gone limp. The operator of the crane noticed the change and goosed the winch motor.

"Sorry for the rough ride," Austin said. "The cable went slack in the cross swell, and we moved too fast when we tried to adjust."

"Not surprising, with the length of cable you're handling."

"Now that you bring up the subject, you might want to check your depth finder."

Zavala glanced at the display screen and tapped Kane on the shoulder. Kane turned away from the window and saw Zavala's finger pointing at the gauge.

Three thousand thirty feet.

They had exceeded the original bathysphere's historic dive by two feet.

Max Kane's mouth dropped down practically to his Adam's apple. "We're *here*!" he announced, "more than half a mile down."

"And almost out of cable," Kurt Austin said. "The sea bottom is around fifty feet below you."

Kane slapped Joe Zavala's palm a high five. "I can't believe it," he said. His face was flushed with excitement. "I'd like to take this moment to thank the intrepid William Beebe and Otis Barton," he continued, "for blazing the trail for all who have followed. What we have done today is a tribute to their courage . . . We're going to be busy for a while shooting pictures of the sea bottom, so we're signing off for a few minutes. We'll get back to you when we're riding to the surface."

They cut television transmission, positioned themselves next to the portholes with still cameras, and shot dozens of pictures of the strange glowing creatures that the bathysphere's lights had attracted. Eventually, Zavala checked their time on the bottom, and said the bathysphere would have time to head back up.

Kane grinned and pointed toward the surface. "Haul away."

Zavala called Austin on the radio and told him they were ready to make the ascent.

The B3 swayed slightly, vibrated, then jerked from side to side.

Zavala pulled himself back up to a sitting position. "Getting bounced around down here, Kurt. Sea picking up again?" he inquired.

"It's like a mirror. Wind's died down and the swells have flattened out."

"Joe," Kane shouted, "there it is again . . . the monster fish!" He jabbed his index finger at the window.

A shadow passed near the edge of the searchlight beam and turned toward the bathysphere.

As Zavala pressed his face against a porthole, every hair on his scalp stood up and saluted. He was looking into three glowing eyes, one of them over the other two.

He had little time to analyze his impressions. The sphere jerked again.

"We're seeing cable oscillations near the surface," Kurt's voice came over the speaker. "What's going on?"

There was another jerking movement.

"There's something out there," Zavala said.

"What are you talking about?" Austin asked.

Zavala wasn't sure himself, so he simply said, "Haul us up."

"Hang tight," Austin said. "We're starting the winch."

The bathysphere seemed to stabilize. The numbers on the fathometer blinked, showing that the sphere was moving up toward the surface. Kane broke into a relieved grin, but the expression on his face froze as the bathysphere jerked once more. A second later, the men in the B3 were levitating as if plunging on a runaway elevator.

The bathysphere had gone into free fall.

CHAPTER 7

AUSTIN LEANED AGAINST THE SHIP'S RAILING AND SAW THE B3's tether cable oscillating like a plucked violin string. He spoke into the headset microphone that connected him with the bathysphere. "What's going on, Joe? The cable is going crazy."

Austin heard garbled voices, the words inaudible against a background of metallic clanging. Then the cable abruptly stopped its wild gyrations, and the line went dead.

Austin strained his ears. *Nothing.* Not even a whisper of static. He removed the headset and examined the connections. Everything was in place. He unclipped his belt radio and called the captain in the ship's bridge.

"I've lost voice communication with the B3. Is the video transmission coming through?"

"Not since it was cut off," the captain reported.

"Have you checked the redundant systems?" Austin asked.

Unlike the original bathysphere, which was connected to the surface with a single telephone line, the B3's hauling cable incorporated several different communications routes in case one went out in the hostile deep-sea environment.

"Ditto, Kurt, *nothing*. All systems are out."

A frown crossed Austin's tanned face. It made no sense. If one system failed, another system should have taken over. Zavala had bragged that the instrumentation he'd designed for the B3 equaled that of a jetliner.

Austin instructed the crane operator to reel the cable in. As it slithered out of the water and around the drum, the operator's voice came over Austin's headset.

"Hey, Kurt, something's wrong. There's no weight resistance at the other end. The cable's coming up too fast and easy. It's like cranking a spinning reel after you've lost your fish."

Austin asked the crane man to speed up the retrieval of the bathysphere, and the cable slinked from the sea at an even faster rate. The launch crew was pressed against the railing, silently watching the streaming cable. The NUMA film crew, sensing the tension in the air, had stopped filming.

"Almost at the surface," the crane operator warned. "Heads up!"

The operator slowed the winch, but still the cable snapped like a bullwhip when it came out of the water, the bathysphere no longer attached. He swung the dangling cable over the ship and put the winch in reverse, letting several yards of the cable coil on the deck. Austin went over to the coil and picked up the end of the cable.

A cameraman standing nearby saw Austin holding the free end of the cable. "Damned thing snapped!" he said.

Austin knew that the cable could hold ten times the weight of the B3. He examined it closely. The strands were as even edged as the bristles of a paintbrush. He turned to the NUMA oceanographer who had chosen the dive site.

"Is there any feature down there, a coral ridge or overhang, that could have snagged the cable?" he asked.

"The bottom is as flat as an ironing board," the oceanographer said, almost insulted at the question. "There's a carpet of marine growth, but that's it. Nothing but mud. That's why we selected this spot. We did intensive bottom profiling before we made our recommendation."

Watching from the bridge, Captain Gannon had seen Austin examining the cable. He hustled down to the deck, and he swore lustily when Austin showed him the sheared-off end. "What the hell happened?"

Austin shook his head. "I wish I knew."

"The press boats have been calling in," the captain said. "They want to know what happened to the video transmission."

Austin scanned the cordon of encircling boats being kept away from the area by a Coast Guard patrol. "Tell them that there was a problem with the fiber-optic cable. We need time to figure this thing out."

The captain called the bridge, relayed Austin's suggestion, and snapped the radio back onto his belt.

"It's going to be all right, isn't it, Kurt?" Gannon asked with worry in his eyes. "The B3's flotation bags will bring them to the surface, right?"

Austin squinted against the glare coming off the surface of the water. "The bathysphere is a long way down; let's give it a while. But we should ready an ROV in case we need to take a look."

Despite his apparent serenity, Austin knew that each passing minute diminished the possibility of a flotation-bag ascent. The bathysphere could rely on battery power for light, but its air would eventually peter out. He waited a few more minutes, then called the captain and recommended that they launch the ROV.

The remotely operated vehicle, or ROV, has become the workhorse of undersea exploration. Controlled by means of a tether, an ROV can dive deep, maneuver into the tightest spaces, and transmit television images, allowing the operator to travel to the depths without leaving the dry comfort of the ship.

The captain had chosen a medium-sized vehicle, about the size and shape of an old steamer trunk, that could operate at a depth of six thousand feet. Six thrusters positioned the vehicle with pinpoint accuracy; it was equipped with two manipulators for collecting samples, and several cameras, including high-resolution color video.

A telescoping starboard boom swung the ROV off its cradle and lowered it into the sea. Austin watched it sink under a mound of pale green bubbles, trailing its tether behind it, then stepped into the remote-sensing control center located in a cargo container on the main deck.

The video feed through the ROV's tether was connected to a console from which the remote's movement was controlled by a pilot with a joystick. Images from the feed were transmitted to a big screen above the console. The ROV's heading and speed were displayed in combination letters and numbers at the top of the screen, along with elapsed time.

Moving in a descending spiral, the ROV traveled in minutes the same distance it had taken the bathysphere hours. The remote blasted through schools of fish, scattering them like leaves, as it corkscrewed into the sea.

"Leveling out," the pilot said.

She put the remote into a shallow-angled dive like an airplane preparing to land. Its twin searchlights picked out brownish green bottom vegetation that looked like leaves of spinach undulating in the current. There was no sign of the Bathysphere 3.

Austin said, "Start searching, in parallel passes, a hundred feet long."

The ROV cruised about twenty feet over the vegetation. It finished its first hundred-foot pass, then traveled back with fifteen feet separating it from the first pass. The speed indicator showed the ROV was doing five knots.

Austin clenched and unclenched his fists, impatient with the glacially slow pace. Other crew members now gathered around the screen, but no one spoke except for the quick communication between Austin and the ROV pilot. Austin mentally excluded everything in the room, pouring himself into the monitor as if he were riding atop the ROV.

Five more minutes passed.

The ROV's methodical back-and-forth movement was similar to that of a lawn mower. The picture transmitted by its electronic eye was the same unchanging monotonous carpet of brownish green.

"Wait," Austin said. He had seen something. "Go to the left."

With a jiggle of the joystick, the pilot pivoted the vehicle so that it was perpendicular to its original path. The twin searchlights picked up mud splatter around the rim of a crater. A mud-covered, domelike shape protruded from the center of the crater. Now Austin saw why the B3 hadn't surfaced; its flotation bags were buried deep in the mud. He asked the pilot to blow mud away from the bathysphere. The ROV's thrusters kicked up a thick brown cloud that hardly made a dent in the heavy muck.

At Austin's request, the pilot put the ROV on the bottom and pointed its searchlights at the sphere. Austin stared at the image, plumbing his training and experience.

He was pondering the technical challenge involved in freeing the B3 from the clutches of the sea when a shadow appeared on the right-hand side of the monitor. Something was moving. It was there for an instant, then gone.

"What was that?" the pilot asked.

Before Austin could venture a guess, the screen went blank.

CHAPTER 8

ZAVALA LAY ON HIS SIDE, HIS RIGHT ARM PINNED UNDER his hipbone, his left curled up to his chest. His legs were immobilized by a soft weight. Ignoring the jagged shards of pain stabbing under his ear, he lifted his head and saw Kane stretched belly down across his knees.

In the dim, battery-powered light, Zavala saw that the cabin was littered with papers, ditty bags, clothing, bottles of water, seat cushions, and other loose items. Zavala reached for his headset and held it to his ear. *Silence.* He tested Kane's headset. Not even a hint of static.

The loss of communication was ominous, but Zavala's optimistic nature would not let him dwell on such bad luck. He wiggled one leg, freed his foot, and used it to shove Kane's body off the other leg. Kane rolled onto his back, and a low groan escaped his lips.

The painful exertion triggered waves of nausea in Zavala. He unclipped the first-aid kit from the wall and broke open an am-

poule, waving it under his nostrils. The acrid odor snapped him
to alertness.

He removed the good-luck cap. Gingerly probing his scalp
with his fingertips, he found a lump that felt as big as an egg. He
poured water from a canteen on a compress bandage and held it
lightly against his head. Even the slight pressure was painful, but
the throbbing eased.

Zavala tucked a seat cushion under Kane's head. He removed
Kane's skullcap and applied the compress. Kane winced, and his
eyes blinked wide open.

"*Ow!*" he said. A good sign.

Zavala lightened the pressure but kept the compress in
place.

"Sorry, Doc, Florence Nightingale couldn't make it, so
you're stuck with me," Zavala said. "Try moving your toes and
fingers."

Kane flexed his hand and foot joints, then bent his legs at the
knees, grimacing in pain. "Nothing seems broken."

Zavala helped Kane sit up and handed him the canteen. He
waited until Kane had slugged down a couple of gulps, then said,
"What do you remember, Doc?"

Kane pursed his lips in thought. "I was looking out the window, broadcasting my observations." He glanced at his headset.

"Don't bother," Zavala said. "The headsets don't work."

Kane's face turned the color of oatmeal. "We're not connected
to the surface?"

"Temporarily . . . Keep talking."

Kane took a deep breath. "We saw some kind of weird big
fish or whale. Next, I remember heading for the moon. Then
blotto. What about you?"

Zavala jerked a thumb upward. "Same scenario. I went airborne and slammed against the roof. I put my hand out to soften

the blow, but all I got for the effort was a sore arm. Good thing I've got a hard head."

"From the sounds of it, the cable probably slipped on the winch drum."

Zavala said nothing.

"I don't get it," Kane said. "Why haven't they winched us up by now?" He noticed that the bathysphere was perfectly still, and he seemed to catch his breath. "We're not moving, Joe. What's happened to us?"

Zavala wanted to avoid panic, but there was no sugarcoating their situation. "We seem to be sitting on the bottom, Doc."

Kane looked at the instrument panel and saw that the systems were operating on batteries. "If we were still attached, we'd have power. Oh, hell! The cable must have snapped."

"That's almost impossible. And there could be other reasons for the breakdown. We're talking about maintaining contact over a cable through more than a half mile of ocean. Remember Beebe comparing the bathysphere to a pea on a cobweb? No man-made system is flawless, but this isn't the *Titanic*. Even if we were no longer connected to the surface, we've got other options."

Kane brightened. "Duh, of *course*! Your flotation system."

Zavala managed a smile. "What do you say we pop up to the Beebe lounge and mix a pitcher of margaritas?"

"What are we waiting for?" Kane was as ebullient as a condemned man given an eleventh-hour reprieve.

Zavala unclipped a nylon bag from the wall and asked Kane to clean up the cabin. Busywork would lift Kane's spirits as well.

"The compressed-air tanks are in the center of the platform, and they feed into flotation bags that are stuffed into the skids," Zavala explained. "When the GO switch is activated, doors open in the sides of skids, compressed air fills the bags instantly, and they lift us to the surface, where the ship can snag us."

Kane rubbed his palms together in anticipation. "Margaritaville, here we come."

Zavala slid over to the instrument panel. "Funny, isn't it? We go through all sorts of trouble to get to the bottom of the sea, and, when we finally make it, we want to go home."

"We can discuss the philosophical implications on the deck of the *Beebe,*" Kane said. "I'd be happy just to be able to stretch out my legs."

Zavala turned his attention to a plastic box attached to the wall next to the instrument panel. He unsnapped the box's cover to reveal a red button emblazoned with an arrow pointing up.

"This is a two-step process," he explained. "This button arms the system, and that identical button on the control panel activates it. When I say *go,* you hit the switch, and I'll do the same with mine. Then hold on. There's a ten-second delay."

Kane put his finger to the button Zavala had indicated. "Ready."

"Go," Zavala said.

Zavala had tested the escape system in a water tank and prepared himself for a muted bang and a whoosh, but nothing happened at the end of ten seconds. He told Kane to try again. Again, nothing happened. Zavala checked a troubleshooting display that would have indicated a system malfunction but saw nothing amiss.

"Why won't it work?" Kane asked.

"Something must have gotten banged around when we hit bottom. Don't worry, I programmed in a backup system."

Zavala tapped a keypad to reroute the signal and told Kane to try again. Again, there was a failure to inflate. They would have to go with the manual switch. Zavala opened another plastic-covered panel and looped his fingers through a handle attached to a cable. Pulling the cable, he explained, would produce a small electrical current that would trigger the flotation mechanism.

He clenched his teeth and yanked. Nothing happened. He tried several more times, but it was no use. The manual trigger failed to activate.

Kane watched these fruitless attempts with growing apprehension. "What's wrong?" he asked.

Zavala's hand dropped from the manual switch. He stared into space, letting his mind's eye travel through the workings of the flotation system. His gaze wandered to the window.

He flicked the searchlight on and was puzzled when he didn't see a glimmer. He moved closer to the window. Sliding a flashlight from its wall rack, he pointed the light out the window, cupping his eyes to prevent reflection. The light failed to penetrate the darkness.

He passed the flashlight to Kane. "Take a look."

Kane peered through the porthole. "Hell, there's black mud against the windows."

"We came down hard. There's nothing wrong with the system. The mud is blocking the flotation doors."

Kane was silent for a time. When he did speak, it was almost in a whisper. "We're screwed, aren't we?"

Zavala reached out and gripped one of Kane's wrists tightly. "Calm down, Doc," he said evenly.

Their eyes locked for a second, and Kane said, "Sorry, Joe, your call."

Zavala loosened his grip. "I don't mean to sound casual. We're in a tough spot, yes, but it's far from hopeless. The folks on the *Beebe* must know something has happened, and they've got our position."

"What good will *that* do if the cable is broken? They still have to haul us up somehow."

"I'm sure Kurt will figure it out."

Kane snorted. "Austin's an impressive guy, but he's not a miracle man."

Zavala thought about the countless times Austin's courage and resourcefulness had snatched them back from the edge of disaster.

"I've worked with Kurt for years, and he's as close to a miracle worker as I've ever seen. If anyone can get us out of here, he can. We've got more than three hours of air and enough power to give us light and heat. Our biggest problems will be boredom and *el baño*." He picked up a plastic bag. "This should take care of our sanitary needs. Since we've been thrown together by the fates, maybe we should know more about each other. Tell me about your work," Zavala said.

Kane's face lit up, and he seemed to forget his claustrophobic surroundings. "My specialty is the phylum Cnidaria, which includes the class commonly known as jellyfish. Many people don't find jellyfish terribly exciting."

"I think jellyfish are *very* exciting," Zavala said. "I was zapped once by a Portuguese man-of-war. The encounter was extremely painful."

"The man-of-war is not considered a 'true' jellyfish but rather a colony of different organisms living in symbiosis. The tentacles are equipped with thousands of nematocysts—the venom apparatus—and grow as long as sixty-five feet. Size isn't everything, though. You're lucky you didn't encounter the little sea wasp. That critter's string could have landed you in the morgue."

"I didn't consider myself lucky at the time," Zavala said as he recalled the burning sting. "What's the focus of your research?"

"My lab has been looking into ocean biomedicine. We think the ocean will be the most important future source of pharmaceutical compounds."

"Like the Amazon rain forest?"

"There's been a lot of interest in the Amazon, but we think the ocean will far surpass anything that's been found in the jungle."

"You're talking jellyfish instead of jaguars?"

"There are more similarities than differences between the land and the sea. Take curare, for instance. The Amazon Indians used it as a paralyzing poison on their arrow tips, but its muscle-relaxant properties make it useful as a medicine."

"And you see similar potential for jellyfish?"

"That and *more*. Jellyfish, squid, octopi, snails—seemingly simple creatures with complex systems for feeding and defense."

"What sort of work were you doing in the Pacific Ocean?" Zavala asked.

"I was working on a project that could affect every man, woman, and child on this planet."

"Now you've *really* got my attention. Tell me more."

"Can't," Kane said, "top secret. I've already said too much. If I told you more, I'd have to kill you."

He realized the absurdity of his threat, given their dire circumstances, and began to giggle uncontrollably. Zavala choked back his laughter. "Laughing uses up too much oxygen."

Kane became serious again. "Do you really think Austin is going to come to our rescue?"

"He's never failed before."

Kane pretended he was zipping his mouth shut. "Then the nature of our work will have to remain classified in case there is a slim chance that we'll get out of this damned hollow steel ball."

Zavala laughed softly. "I guess your romance with Beebe's world is over."

Kane managed to eke out a smile. "Your turn, Joe. Tell me how you came to NUMA."

"Admiral Sandecker hired me right out of college. He needed a good mechanic."

Zavala was being typically modest. The son of Mexican immigrants, he had graduated from New York Maritime College with a degree in marine engineering. He had a brilliant mechanical mind and expertise in every known kind of propulsion, able to repair, modify, or restore any engine—automobile, ship, aircraft—be it steam, diesel, or electric.

Sandecker had heard reports about the bright young student and recruited him before he received his diploma. He was NUMA's top submersible designer of manned and unmanned vehicles. And he was a skilled aircraft pilot as well.

"You make it sound like NUMA hired you to change tires in the agency's motor pool," Kane said. He glanced around the interior of the bathysphere. "We wouldn't be alive if it hadn't been for the modifications you installed in the B3."

Zavala shrugged. Despite his reassurances, he knew that their rescue was problematic. Using less air would only prolong the inevitable. He glanced at the display panel: slightly more than two hours of air left. Sleepy from the effects of stale atmosphere, he closed his eyes and tried not to think about the air supply ebbing away.

CHAPTER 9

ONCE AGAIN, AUSTIN WATCHED, TIGHT-LIPPED, AS THE dripping tether snaked from the ocean without its payload. He swore a sailor's oath at the loss of the ROV, and called the captain in the bridge.

"The ROV cable's been sheared off just like the bathysphere's," Austin said. "Looks like someone worked it over with a pair of hedge clippers."

"This is *crazy*!" Captain Gannon said. He calmed down, and asked, "Should I send down another ROV?"

"Hold off for now," Austin said. "I need a couple of minutes to think this through."

Austin stared at the heaving sapphire surface of the sea. He pushed aside thoughts of the two men locked into a steel ball half a mile below the ship's hull and focused on the retrieval of the bathysphere as a salvage problem. His nimble mind began to formulate a rescue plan and assemble the equipment he would need to carry it out.

He called the captain back. "I've got an idea, but I'll need your help."

"Tell me what you want and it's yours, Kurt."

"Thanks, Captain. I'll meet you in the machine shop."

The *Beebe*'s machine shop, below the main deck, was a vital component of the ship's operation. A research vessel is basically a platform that allows scientists to plumb the depths with instruments or underwater vehicles. Powerful ocean forces constantly battered the vessel. The *Beebe*'s shop kept the ship operational with a crew of only three, including the chief mechanic, and an array of tools to cut, grind, turn, mold, mill, and press.

Austin had until then kept the shop busy tending to the specialized needs posed by the bathysphere's launch. As project director, he had developed a close professional relationship with the chief machinist, a burly, troll-like man named Hank, who liked to wrap up a project with the words, "Good enough for government work."

Hank must have heard about the B3 because he greeted Austin with a somber face. "What can I do to help, Kurt?"

Austin unfolded the diagram of the B3 and spread it out on a table. He pointed to the horseshoe-shaped metal swivel that joined the cable to the top of the sphere.

"I need to snag the bathysphere here." Austin sketched out a hook attached to the end of a cable and showed it to Hank. "Can you put this setup together in less than an hour?"

"Forty-five minutes, tops," Hank said. "I'll splice the cable to a spare hook. But, I'll be honest, I can't give you something that is likely to last for the half-mile haul back up to the surface."

"I'm only interested in the first ten or twenty feet," Austin said. "Once the B3 is clear of the muck, it can trigger its own flotation system."

"Getting the hook attached to the swivel is going to be tough at this depth," Gannon said. "The gap between the swivel and the top of the B3 is only a few inches." He held his thumb and forefinger up. "Like trying to snag something this size from a helicopter half a mile in the air. It would be almost impossible, in my opinion."

"I disagree," Austin said. "It would be *absolutely* impossible. That's why I'm not going to do it from the surface."

"How are you . . . ?" A thoughtful look came to the captain's face. *"Bubbles?"*

"Why not? She's been tested to five thousand feet."

"But . . ."

"Let's talk about it in the control van," Austin said.

The box-shaped, twenty-foot-long atmospheric-diving-suit control van was next to the ship's garage, where the ship's underwater vehicles and other deep-ocean hardware were housed. The van had a console that was separate from the controls for the ship's submersibles, and it had a workshop where Bubbles was stored.

Austin and Gannon stood in front of a puffy-limbed, anthropomorphic metal figure that resembled the Michelin man. The transparent dome capping the figure could have come from a bubblegum dispenser.

Bubbles's technical name was atmospheric diving suit, or ADS, but it was considered an anthropomorphic submersible. A diver using the ADS could go to great depths without having to worry about the killing water pressure or the need to decompress. The bulky life-support system on the back of the aluminum body, or hull as it was known, could sustain the pilot for six to eight hours, or for more time in an emergency.

Bubbles was an experimental ADS owned by the U.S. Navy. It was a successor to the Hardsuit 2000, which had been developed for submarine rescue. The research vessel was transporting

Bubbles as a courtesy, then rendezvousing with a Navy ship near Bermuda after the B3 expedition.

Gannon stood with his hands on his hips, vigorously shaking his head.

"I can't let you do this, Kurt," said the captain. "Bubbles is a *prototype*. She hasn't been field-tested yet. Last I heard, she's got a for-sure depth limit of only twenty-five hundred feet."

"Joe would tell you that any engineer worth his salt builds in a huge safety factor," Austin said. "The Hardsuit 2000 made it to three thousand feet in test dives."

"Those were *test* dives, not operational dives. That's a fact."

Austin pinioned the captain with his coral-blue eyes. "It's *also* a fact that Joe and Kane will freeze to death or die from lack of air if we don't do something about it."

"*Damnit,* Kurt, I know that! I just don't want someone else dying senselessly."

Austin realized he had come down too hard and backed off.

"Neither do I," he said. "So here's my offer: you get Bubbles gussied up for a dive, I'll get an opinion on dive limits from the Navy and abide by whatever they tell me."

Gannon had learned a long time ago that Austin was a primal force, as unstoppable as the east wind.

"What the hell," the captain said with a lopsided grin. "I'll get Bubbles ready to go."

Austin gave him a thumbs-up, and hurried to the bridge. A satellite phone connected him with the Navy's Deep Submergence Unit in California. He listened with mounting impatience to a recorded directory and spoke with several people before he landed on a junior officer in the unit's Diving Systems Support Detachment. Austin quickly laid out his predicament.

The officer let out a low whistle.

"I sympathize with your problem, sir, but I can't give you permission to use the Hardsuit. That would have to come from higher up. I'll connect you."

"I'll deal with the Navy brass," Austin said with thinly veiled annoyance. "I just want to know if the new Hardsuit can dive a half mile."

"That's what the tests were supposed to determine," the officer said. "The weak spots in an ADS have always been the joints. With the new joint design, theoretically it's possible to go deeper, maybe to five thousand feet. But if there is one tiny flaw, you could have a massive failure."

Austin thanked the officer and said he would clear the dive with the officer's superiors, although he didn't say *when*. He hoped to be unavailable by the time the Navy bureaucracy reacted.

While Austin had been discussing the Hardsuit with the officer, a nagging thought had been buzzing around in his head like a hungry mosquito. Heading back down to the ROV control center, he found the young woman who had tracked the ROV still sitting at her station. He asked her to rerun the last sixty seconds of its video. She clicked her mouse and the sea bottom a half mile down appeared on the screen. Once again, Austin watched the ROV soar like a bird over the undulating vegetation covering the seafloor. Its camera soon picked up the splatter from the B3's impact, then the bathysphere's dome protruding from the crater.

"Freeze the image right there," Austin said. He pointed to a dark area in the upper-left-hand corner of the screen. "Now, run it in slow motion."

The shadow moved off the screen.

The ROV operator stared at the screen, jutting out her lower lip. "I don't remember seeing that."

"It was easy to miss," Austin said. "We were all focused on finding the bathysphere."

She sat back, folded her arms, and focused on the oblong shape that was barely visible at the edge of the searchlight beam.

"Might be a fish or whale," she said, "but something about it isn't quite right."

Austin asked the operator to enlarge the image. It broke apart as it was blown up, but Austin nonetheless detected a vague manta-ray shape to the shadow. He asked her to print the image, and to play back the final transmission from the bathysphere.

The operator ran off a printout, then reduced the shadow image and tucked it in the upper-right-hand corner of the screen, which now displayed a picture of Kane. He was rattling off an excited description of the luminescent fish swimming around the bathysphere when suddenly he stopped short and pressed his face against the window.

"What was that?" Kane said.

The voice-activated camera switched to Zavala.

"You see a mermaid, Doc?"

Back to Kane.

"I'm not sure what *I saw, but I know one thing: it was* big*!"*

Austin snatched up the printout and headed for the aft deck. The big double doors on the garage were wide open, and the Hardsuit had been wheeled out under the crane that would lift it off the deck.

Austin showed Gannon the ROV printout.

"This object was nosing around the B3 when both cables were cut," he said.

The captain shook his head. "What *is* that thing?"

"Got me," Austin said. He glanced at his watch. "What I *do* know is that the B3 will soon run short of power and air."

"We'll be ready in a few minutes," the captain said. "Did you contact the Navy?"

"A Navy engineer told me that, theoretically, Bubbles could dive to five thousand feet."

"Wow!" the captain said. "Did you get an okay to use the ADS?"

"I'll work on it later," Austin said with a quick smile.

"Why did I even ask?" the captain said. "Hope you realize that you're making me your accomplice in hijacking Navy property."

"Look on the bright side. We can be cell mates at a federal country-club prison. Where do things stand?"

Gannon turned to the head machinist, who was standing by.

"Hank and his crew did a hell of a job," the captain said.

Austin inspected the machine shop's work and gave Hank a pat on the back.

"Good enough for government work," he said.

The severed end of the bathysphere's cable had been looped through a hook and then laid back along itself in a classic sailor's eye splice and wound dozens of times with thin steel wire. Austin thanked the rest of the shop crew for their good work, then asked them to attach the hook to the ADS frame.

While the crew tended to his request, Austin hurried to his cabin and exchanged his shorts and T-shirt for thermal underwear, a wool sweater, and wool socks. He zipped himself into a crew coverall and pulled a knit cap down over his thick mane of hair. Although the Hardsuit had a heating system, the temperature inside could drop to forty degrees or less at depth.

Back up on deck, Austin quickly explained the rescue plan. Making a silent plea to the gods of dumb luck to look approvingly on this venture, he climbed up a stepladder and eased his muscular body into the lower half of the Hardsuit, which separated into two parts at the waist. Once the top half of the suit was on, he tested the power, communications link, and air supply. Then he gave the order to launch.

The frame and Hardsuit were lifted from the deck and lowered into the water. Austin called for a halt at thirty feet down to retest the systems. While everything was in working order, he was sobered by the fact that the Navy's record-breaking two-thousand-foot dive had taken years of planning and teams of specialists to pull off. It was a far cry from the mad dash to the bottom he was about to undertake.

The Hardsuit helmet's digital time display told him that the bathysphere had less than an hour's supply of air left.

He reached out with his hand-pod clamp and detached the hook from the frame. First making sure the hook was clamped tightly, he gave the order to send him to the bottom of the sea.

The cable winches for the suit and hook worked in tandem to lower Austin. The quick descent kicked up bubbles that obscured his view of his surroundings. As the minutes ticked away on the digital clock, he kept a close eye on the depth gauge.

After passing two thousand feet, Austin was aware that the suit now had entered uncharted territory, but his mind was too busy with other things to contemplate the possibility that it might have been pushed beyond its limits. At twenty-eight hundred feet, still with no discernible problem, he felt a change in the speed of his descent.

Gannon's voice came on the intercom.

"We're slowing you down so you don't drill a hole through the bottom, Kurt."

"Appreciate that. Hold at three thousand."

The winch soon slowed to a stop.

The curtain of bubbles cleared around the dome that encased

his head. Austin switched on lights that would have been useless during descent. Their pale yellow shafts accentuated blackness so devoid of color that any attempt to describe it in words would be doomed to fail.

All systems were working, and the joints were still water-tight. Austin called for more slack on the cable. The winch slowly lowered him more until he was fifty feet off the bottom.

"You're on your own from here on," the captain said. "We'll let out cable as you move."

Scattered groupings and pinpoints of phosphorescence could be seen beyond the range of the searchlights, and odd-looking luminescent fish nosed up to the faceplate of Austin's helmet.

He pressed down with his left foot and two vertical thrusters whirred, raising him up a yard or so. He next used his right foot to activate the horizontal thrusters, moving him forward several feet.

Austin tried moving his arms and legs and found that, even with the tremendous water pressure, the suit's sixteen well-oiled joints allowed for an amazing range of movement.

He activated the suit's camera zoom and focused on an anglerfish attracted by the light.

"Picture's coming through," the captain reported. "Good definition."

"I'll see if I can find something for the family album. Moving out."

Skillfully handling the thruster controls, Austin piloted the Hardsuit horizontally, tilting forward slightly, cable trailing behind.

The seven-hundred-pound ADS lost its clumsiness and moved through the water as if on wings. Austin focused on a small sonar screen glowing wheat-colored yellow. Employing a range of fifty feet to either side of the suit, it cut a swath a hundred feet wide. It tracked his position, heading, speed, and depth as it read the bottom.

A dark object appeared on the screen, approximately twenty-five feet to his right and down.

Austin maneuvered the Hardsuit into a sharp right turn and descended until the searchlights reflected off the gleaming plastic-and-metal surface of the ROV. It was lying on its back like a dead beetle.

Gannon also saw it. "Thanks for finding our ROV," his voice came over the communicator.

"My pleasure!" replied Austin. "B3 should be within spitting distance."

He extended the range of his search a hundred feet, then spun around slowly. The sonar picked up another object close by. Accelerating too quickly, he overshot the bathysphere and, turning sharply, had to come around again.

Austin hovered some twenty feet over the B3. The temperature inside the Hardsuit had dropped, yet sweat beaded his forehead. The difficulty of the task in this hostile environment having dawned on him, he knew that a mistake made in haste could be fatal. He took a deep breath, pressed the vertical-control pedal, and began his descent to the bathysphere entombed in mud below.

CHAPTER 10

THE B3 WAS QUICKLY BECOMING A GLOBE-SHAPED FREEZER as its battery-operated heating system fought a losing battle against the deep-ocean chill. Joe Zavala and Max Kane had wrapped blankets around themselves like Navajo Indians and sat back-to-back to conserve heat. Their numb lips proved useless for speech, and their lungs labored to extract an ever-diminishing amount of oxygen from the rapidly thinning air.

Zavala dreaded the moment when the power would fail completely. He didn't want to die in the dark. The bathysphere had an auxiliary air tank, but he wondered if it would be worth prolonging the misery. At the same time, he stubbornly fought the urge to give up, and he filled his mind with visions of the mountains around Santa Fe. Closing his eyes, he imagined he was resting after a hike in the winter, not trapped in a hollow steel ball at the bottom of the cold sea.

Clunk!

Something had thumped against the bathysphere. Zavala pressed his head against the wall, ignoring the coldness that seeped through the metal skin. He could hear a gritty, scraping sound, then another clunk, followed by several more.

Morse code for *k*, he realized.

Then, after an agonizing pause, he heard *a*.

Kurt Austin.

Kane had been sitting with his head down and hunched over his knees. Raising his chin off his chest, he glanced toward Zavala with rheumy, unfocused eyes.

"Wha'sat?" he said, his words drunkenly slurred from the cold and lack of oxygen.

Zavala's cracked lips widened in a ghost of a smile.

"The *cavalry* has arrived."

AUSTIN CROUCHED ON TOP of the bathysphere like a spider, using his manipulator claw to tap out letters. A deepwater suit's size and shape makes it susceptible to currents, and a bottom eddy threatened to push him off his perch. He hooked the cable to the top of the sphere, clamped a manipulator onto the cable to keep himself from floating off, and maneuvered the suit's thrusters so that they were facing down into the mud surrounding the sphere.

He depressed a foot pedal and was immediately enveloped in a blinding cloud of stirred-up silt that settled after a moment. He turned the Hardsuit's searchlights off. The faint glow coming through the B3's previously buried windows indicated that systems were still operating. Austin blinked the suit's lights on and off to get Zavala's attention.

Zavala saw the flashing lights, and his mind lost some of its cold-induced sluggishness.

Kane had seen the lights as well.

"What should we do?" he asked.

Zavala hungered for the opportunity to do something, *anything,* to get out of this mess, but he knew they would have to be patient.

"We *wait,*" he said.

AUSTIN UNCLAMPED HIS MANIPULATOR from the cable and began to tap out a new message on the bathysphere's skin. He got out only a few letters before the current suddenly caught his suit and pushed him several feet away from the sphere. Regaining control, he returned to tap out more letters.

The Hardsuit's camera had been transmitting his struggles to the surface ship.

"What's going on down there?" Gannon's voice called. "Picture went dark, and now it's back all jumbled."

"Stand by," Austin said, then finished tapping out his message.

"Standing by," the captain replied.

Austin's efforts had sapped his strength. Sweat was dripping into his eyes, and he was gulping for air like a beached flounder.

"Haul away!" he shouted breathlessly into the suit's microphone.

ZAVALA HAD LISTENED CAREFULLY to the measured tapping coming through the skin of the B3. He'd caught the first few letters. After a pause, he'd caught the rest.

Float.

Hell, Kurt, if I could float, I would float.

The bathysphere still stuck in the mud, and Zavala vacillated

between anger and despair. Maybe this was all a dream brought
on by lack of oxygen. Maybe he was imagining all this, playing
out a rescue that existed only in his mind.

A buzzer yanked him back to reality.

A red light blinked madly on the control panel. He realized
that the light had been going on and off for some time, but his
slow-moving mind had not realized it was warning that the air
supply was about to end.

He reached out for the spare tank, barely got it off the wall,
and turned on the valve.

Air hissed into the cabin and blew the fog from his brain. He
flipped back the panel covering the manual switch for the flotation system and waited for something to happen.

AUSTIN HOVERED ABOVE the bottom of the ocean with the
Hardsuit's lights trained on the top of the B3. The cable went
taut as, a half mile above his head, the winch began to turn, but
the bathysphere didn't budge. Dire scenarios marched through
Austin's head: the jury-rigged hook would break immediately
and the sphere would remain trapped in the suction created by
the mud; Zavala would forget to deploy the flotation system or
the system wouldn't work when he did; worse of all, both men
were unconscious.

"Cable's tight to the winch," Gannon called down. "Anything
happening at your end?"

Austin saw that the cable splice was unraveling.

"Just keep hauling," he said.

He gritted his teeth as if he could lift the B3 through sheer
willpower. The bathysphere remained where it was. The cable
unraveled some more.

"*Move,* damnit!" he yelled.

Plumes of mud billowed around the bathysphere. Then the sphere pulled free, popping from the mud like a cork from a bottle, and righted itself. A thick cloud of silt hid the sphere for an instant before it rose into the glare of the Hardsuit's searchlights.

Austin's triumphant yell blasted through the ship's public-address system.

The B3 was ten feet from the bottom, mud streaming off its sides, then twenty feet, and still there was no sign of air-bag deployment. What was Joe waiting for? Maybe the flotation doors were clogged with mud.

Austin kept pace, rising slowly with the bathysphere, his eyes glued to the hook and cable.

As the last strand of cable splice gave way, doors along the sides of the sphere suddenly blew open and six air bags blossomed and rapidly filled. The bathysphere rocked back and forth, stabilized, then began to ascend.

Austin watched the B3 until it was out of sight.

"They're on their way," he notified Gannon.

"You're next," the captain said. "How are you?"

"I'll be a lot better topside."

Austin steadied the thrusters so that he was in a more or less vertical position, and was ready when the Hardsuit jerked at the end of the cable. As the suit began its long trip, Austin turned off his lights and saw that he was not alone.

The blackness was speckled with dozens of constellations. He was surrounded by luminescent sea creatures that hung in place like stars. Occasionally, he saw something moving like the lights of an airplane across the night sky. Then his eye caught movement off to the left. The constellation hanging there at the edge of his peripheral vision seemed to be growing larger. Turning his head, he saw what looked like a trio of glowing amber eyes moving closer.

An alarm went off in Austin's brain. He'd been focusing on the rescue and forgotten about the sinister shadow loitering nearby when the cables were cut on the B3 and the ROV.

The Hardsuit's searchlights reflected off the smooth, dark surface of something shaped like a flattened teardrop. It was a submersible of some kind, most likely an automated underwater vehicle, or AUV, because he couldn't see a tether. The glowing eyes on the leading edge were apparently sensors, but Austin was more interested in the sharp-edged metal mandibles protruding from the front of the vehicle.

The vehicle moved fast, gliding at a depth where the mandibles would intersect the cable pulling him to the surface. Austin stomped on his vertical-thrust pedal. There was a second's delay before the thrusters overcame the Hardsuit's inertia, then he shot up several feet, his attacker passing below him, the mandibles snapping at empty water.

The vehicle made a wide banking turn, rose to keep pace, and circled back for another attack.

Gannon was watching the encounter on the ship's monitor.

"What the hell was *that*?" the captain yelled.

"Something that wants me for dinner!" Austin yelled back. "Haul faster!"

The nimble AUV was quick to adjust its strategy and speed. Coming in for its second attack, it slowed to a walk, stalking its target with the wariness of a predator whose prey showed unexpected behavior.

Austin waited until the thing was just yards away and then tapped his foot pedal. The Hardsuit rose a few feet, but not fast enough to escape the attacker. He raised his arms defensively, holding them out straight and close together. He crashed into the AUV's extended manipulators glancingly, but not before his claw stabbed the AUV in its middle eye.

Austin's head slammed against the inside of the Plexiglas helmet. The impact knocked him sideways, and he swung at the end of his cable like soap on a rope. Pain shot up his left arm from the wrist.

The AUV went for another pass, but it was moving slowly, and it jerked erratically from side to side like a hound sniffing out prey. Rather than coming straight for Austin, it feinted a frontal attack, then angled upward toward the cable. Because Austin was still dazed from the last attack, he was slow to give the vertical thrusters juice. The AUV's pincers caught his raised right arm at the elbow and closed around it.

With his left manipulator, he grabbed onto a thruster mandible and powered himself down, then up, operating like a yo-yo. The thrusters were designed for horizontal rather than vertical movement, and the weight of the vehicle worked against it, bending the mandible so that it was useless. Then the blade snapped at the base. The AUV thrashed wildly, peeled off, and disappeared into the darkness.

"Kurt, are you okay?" the captain's voice rang in Austin's earphones. "For God's sake, answer me!"

"Finestkind, Cap," Austin managed to croak. "Haul me up."

"Hauling away," the captain said with relief in his voice. "What kind of music do you want for the ride to the top?"

"I'll leave that up to you," Austin said. He was too tired to think.

A moment later, the strains of a Strauss waltz came through his earphones, and he began his long trip to the surface to "Tales from the Vienna Wood."

As Austin was hauled toward the ship, he was vaguely aware that he still clutched the AUV's blade in his metal claw as if it were a hunting trophy.

CHAPTER 11

THOUSANDS OF MILES FROM THE *WILLIAM BEEBE,* LOIS Mitchell was trying to quell a riot in the mess hall, where Gordon Phelps had herded the staff at gunpoint. Someone had noticed that Dr. Logan was missing, and when Lois said that the marine biologist had been shot dead the news had prompted a chorus of anger and fear.

Lois tried to shout down the cacophony. When that didn't work, she lined up several mugs on the counter and filled them from a coffeepot. The simple ritual had a calming effect. After the uproar had quieted down and she could be heard, Lois flashed a sweet smile.

"Sorry this isn't a Starbucks Grande, but it will have to do for now."

Her attempt at humor triggered an outburst from a young female lab tech whose pale face and tearful eyes indicated that she was on the verge of hysteria. Lacing into Lois in a voice choked with sobs, the tech demanded: "How can you be so calm *knowing* Dr. Logan was murdered?"

Stubbornly refusing the urge to break into tears herself, Lois said, "Dr. Logan is lying in the passageway outside the control room with a bullet in his heart. He tried to fight back and was killed by the man who locked us in here. If you want to avoid the same fate, I suggest you take several deep breaths and calm down."

With a trembling hand, Lois pushed a mug across the counter. The young lab tech hesitated, then reached out for it and took a noisy slurp. Lois then gathered everyone around a large table and described her encounter with Phelps and the murder of Logan. A biologist who had been Logan's closest friend rose from his chair and picked up a kitchen knife from the counter. He summed up his rage in a single word.

"Bastard!"

Lois remained in her seat and regarded the biologist with a calm gaze.

"You're absolutely correct," Lois said. "In fact, the man who shot Dr. Logan is *worse* than a bastard, he's a *murderer,* but his moral character is not at issue here. You might get him with that knife, although I doubt it, but what then? Phelps obviously is not the only one involved. We are dealing with ruthless people who have the resources to gain entry into a heavily guarded facility three hundred feet below the ocean's surface. I don't know how they learned about the Locker, who they are, or how many are involved, but we are completely at their mercy."

The knife clattered on the counter, and the biologist sat down.

"You're right, Lois," he said in defeat. "I just wish I knew what they wanted."

"I'm sure they'll let us know," she replied. "In the meantime, let's have something to eat. It's important we keep our strength up. *MiGod!*" she said with her rollicking laugh. "I sound like an actor in one of those disaster movies telling everyone to remain calm after the ocean liner turns upside down or the plane crashes in the jungle."

The comment produced nervous smiles. A couple of people headed for the kitchen and, in short order, returned with a tray stacked with ham, turkey, and peanut-butter-and-jelly sandwiches. Fear must have sharpened the scientists' hunger because they devoured the sandwiches like victims of a famine.

They were cleaning up when the mess hall reverberated with loud humming. Everyone stopped working and listened. After a few moments, the humming stopped, and the floor jolted as if jarred by an earthquake. There was a second jolt, and the room shuddered and swayed.

Those still standing fought to keep their balance, and there was an outcry of alarm, but the room went silent when the door burst open and two armed men stepped into the mess hall to clear the way for Phelps. The two strangers were wearing black diver's suits still wet with seawater and carried short-barreled machine pistols.

Phelps grinned and said, "Looks like we arrived too late for lunch."

"What's happening to the lab?" Lois asked, holding on to the edge of a counter to keep from falling.

"Don't you remember what I said about going for a little ride? The lab's being moved to a new neighborhood."

Lois thought she must be going mad. "That's *impossible*."

"Not really, Dr. Mitchell. All we had to do was hitch the lab to a tow truck, so to speak."

"What happened to our support ship?"

"It's out of action," Phelps said. He issued an order to the gunmen: "Take these folks to their quarters."

The gunmen stepped aside to allow the scientists to pass.

"Thank you for allowing my staff to leave," Lois said. She went to follow her colleagues through the door, but Phelps reached out and held her arm. He shut the door, pulled up a chair, and asked Lois to sit down. Then he sat in another chair and leaned on the backrest.

"I've been looking at your bio, Dr. Mitchell. Pretty impressive background. Bachelor's degree in marine biology from the University of Florida, master's from Virginia Institute of Marine Science, topped off with a Ph.D. in marine biotechnology and biomedicine from Scripps."

"Is this a job interview?" Lois said in an icy voice.

"I guess you could call it that," Phelps said. "You've been doing some work that my bosses are interested in."

"Who are your bosses?"

"They're kinda shy. Just think of them as the folks that sign my paycheck."

"Did they pay you to kill Dr. Logan?"

He frowned. "That wasn't in the plans, Dr. Mitchell. That was an accident, pure and simple."

"An accident like hijacking the lab, I suppose."

"Guess you could say that. Look, Dr. Mitchell, you may not like me, probably hate my guts, and I don't blame you, but it's best for you and your staff if we try to get along because we're going to be working together."

"What do you mean?"

"My bosses didn't tell me exactly what you're doing here in the lab, but I heard it's got something to do with jellyfish."

Lois saw no reason to hold back. "That's right. We're using a chemical found in a rare species of jellyfish to develop a vaccine for an influenza-type virus that has a lot of people worried."

"My bosses said that you're about ready to wrap things up here."

So much for secrecy, Lois thought.

"That's correct," she said. "We're within days of synthesizing the chemical used as the basis of the vaccine. You still haven't answered my question about working together."

"When we get to the new location, you'll continue your research. You'll have free run of the lab except for the control room. You'll report your results to me on a regular basis. I'll pass the reports along to my bosses. Otherwise, it's business as usual."

"And if we refuse to work for you?"

"We know we can't make scientists do their jobs by beating them with truncheons. We'll just leave you down here on your own and withhold food and oxygen until you feel like working again. The rules are simple: If you go on strike, you will die. Not my idea, but that's the way it is."

"Thank you for your kind advice. I'll pass it along to my colleagues as soon as you allow me to rejoin them."

He stood up and opened the door.

"You can go along now, if you want to."

Lois stayed where she was.

"One question," she said. "What happens after we complete our research? Are you going to kill us or leave us to rot on the bottom?"

Phelps was a hard man and seasoned professional. He considered his job as a mercenary a link in a proud profession that stretched back hundreds, probably thousands, of years. Older than prostitution, he often joked. He had his own peculiar sense of honor that would not allow him to harm a woman, especially one as attractive as Lois Mitchell. He pushed the dangerous thoughts aside. There was no room in his business for personal attachments, but he vowed to keep a close eye on Lois.

"They hired me to hijack this nifty little hideaway and to make sure you keep on working. My contract doesn't say anything about killing you or your friends. They know that when the work is done, I plan to take you from the lab and drop you somewhere close to civilization. We'll probably run into each other in a bar in Paris or Rome someday and have a big laugh over this thing."

Lois had no desire to see Phelps ever again. More important, she had no idea whether Phelps was telling the truth or not. The strength seemed to flow out of her body. She felt as if she were being smothered even though her lungs were hyperventilating. She concentrated on her breathing, taking breaths deep into her diaphragm, and after a moment the hammering of her heart began to subside. She became aware that Phelps was watching her reaction closely.

"You okay, Dr. Mitchell?"

Lois stared into space for a moment, reordering her jumbled thoughts, then rose from her chair. "I'd like to go to my quarters now, if you don't mind."

He nodded. "I'll be in the control room if you need me."

Lois made her way to her room. The floor still swayed, and she had to walk wide-leggedly to keep from losing her footing. Somehow, she made it to her quarters. She crawled into her bunk and pulled the covers over her head, as if she could shut out the world she had found herself in, but to no effect. Thankfully, after a few minutes, she fell into a fitful slumber.

CHAPTER 12

CAPTAIN GANNON FURROWED HIS BROW AS HE GAZED OUT the bridge windows at the restless sea. The weather had changed for the worse in the hours since the B3 had dropped into the depths. Gray slabs had replaced the puffy white clouds of morning. The easy breeze that had greeted the ship's arrival had freshened, puckering the heaving sea. The water gained a dark, leaden cast as the sun lowered, and foam crested the corrugated wave tops.

The rugged research vessel had been built to take the worst kind of weather imaginable, but retrieving the bathysphere and an exhausted Hardsuit diver would have been delicate operations even without dicey conditions.

Gannon had moved the ship back from the bathysphere's last known position to give the B3 room to surface. The starboard crane was still hauling up the Hardsuit, and Austin would not appreciate being dragged all over the ocean, so the ship could only move a short distance.

If anyone can survive this ordeal, the captain thought, *it would be Austin. Hell, the man's a perpetual-motion machine!*

Having dived a half mile to the bottom of the ocean to free the bathysphere, Austin was keeping in constant touch with the ship, reporting his ascent to the bridge at regular intervals, relaying vivid descriptions of the sea life he observed.

Lookouts lined the railings or were gathered on the bow and fantail. A Zodiac inflatable boat sat on the slanting stern ramp under the A-frame. Two divers in neoprene wetsuits were perched on the pontoons waiting for the signal to push the Zodiac into the water.

The diesels rumbled in the engine room, waves slapped against the hull, and the rising wind thrummed through the rigging. But otherwise, an eerie stillness had descended over the ship.

The quiet was broken by a lookout yelling over the bridge intercom.

"She's *up!*"

Keeping his eyes glued to the newly formed patch of foam a hundred yards to port, Gannon picked up his microphone and gave the command to launch.

The divers pushed the Zodiac down the stern ramp and clambered in. It leaped over the waves as its powerful outboard motor kicked in, curving around to the side of the ship, slip-sliding over the seas, trailing the retrieval line behind it like a prehensile tail.

The Zodiac slowed to a wallowing stop near six wave-slicked orange mounds that had bobbed to the surface. The cabled hook at the end of the line was lowered into the water, and one of the divers slid off the Zodiac and disappeared beneath the waves.

Every eye on the ship watched the drama play out. When the

diver popped to the surface and pumped his fist in the air, a loud cheer went up. The B3 was hooked. Winches pulled the bathysphere and its flotation air bags slowly to the surface.

The recovery crew cut the air bags away, and the crane lifted the dripping bathysphere from the sea and onto the deck of the ship. A power wrench burped, the lug nuts were quickly unscrewed, and the hatch cover clanged to the deck.

The ship's medic stuck her head through the hatch opening and saw a rumpled pile of blankets surrounded by a loose assortment of equipment.

"Hello," she said in a tentative voice.

Zavala pulled back the corner of the blanket and blinked his eyes against the light. He smiled.

"Hello yourself," he said.

AUSTIN WAS STILL ON his way to the surface when Gannon called and said the bathysphere was back on board. Austin asked how Joe and Doc were doing.

"I've seen dead eels with more life to them," the captain said. "But the medic says they're suffering from the *-shuns*: dehydra*shun,* air depriva*shun,* and exhaust*shun.*"

Austin let out a groan that the captain could have heard without the need for a fiber-optic connection.

"Captain, you're a cruel man."

"They'll be fine," Gannon said with a chuckle. "They just need water and rest. I've notified the press that the B3 recovery was a success. No details for now, but someone on one of their boats or in a chopper must have figured out we were having problems. I'm going to have to explain what happened eventually. I'll deal with that later . . . How about you?"

"Anxious to get out of this tin suit, but feeling good otherwise. One request, though: the classical music you're piping down here is putting me to sleep. Got anything livelier?"

Minutes later, Austin was listening to Mick Jagger belting out "You Can't Always Get What You Want."

He smiled in full agreement with the sentiment of the Rolling Stones song, that if you try some time, you can get what you need . . . especially if you have friends.

THE B3'S PASSENGERS had been rushed into sick bay, laid out on examination tables, stripped of their evil-smelling clothes, treated for bumps and bruises, and given a rubdown to get their circulation going again. Then the medic buried them under piles of blankets and let them sleep.

When Joe Zavala awoke, the first thing he saw was Kurt Austin's face.

"Guess I'm not in heaven," Zavala croaked.

Austin held up a round, brown glass bottle with a wooden screw cap.

Tequila!

"Maybe you *are,*" he said.

Zavala's lips parted in a cracked smile.

"A sight for sore eyes," he said. "When did you get back on board?"

"They peeled me out of my suit around a half an hour ago," Austin said. "Feel like telling me what happened?"

Zavala nodded.

"Let me warm my outside first," he said, "then I'll warm my inside."

It took fifteen minutes under the hottest shower he could

stand before warmth finally seeped into Zavala's bones. Austin handed him a plastic cup of tequila through the shower-stall door, then went to his cabin, showered, and changed.

By the time Austin returned, Zavala had put on some clothes that Austin had left for him and was sitting in a chair sipping tequila. Austin helped him walk to the mess hall and ordered two pastramis on rye.

They devoured their sandwiches, then Zavala closed his eyes and sat back in his chair.

"That may be the best meal I've ever had," he said.

"I'll refill your cup if you tell me what happened with the bathysphere," Austin said.

Zavala held his cup out. The tequila helped loosen his tongue, and he described the harrowing plunge to the bottom of the ocean and the problem activating the flotation bags.

"I still can't figure out how that cable snapped," Zavala said with a shake of the head.

"It *didn't* snap," Austin said.

Austin opened the case he'd brought with him and extracted a laptop, which he set on the table. He showed Zavala the video the Hardsuit camera had filmed of his encounter with the AUV.

Zavala uttered an appreciative *Olé!* as Austin dodged the deadly pincers. When the video ended with Austin disabling the AUV, Zavala said, "Nice work, but don't quit your day job to become a matador."

"I don't intend to," Austin said. "Bullfighting technique aside, how hard would it be to program an AUV to cut the bathysphere's cable?"

"Not hard at all, Kurt, but it would take some sophistication to build the AUV in the first place. It's a slick piece of engineering. Very agile. Learns from its mistakes and is quick to adjust. Too bad you had to mess it up."

"You're right, Joe. I should have let it kill me, but I was having a bad-hair day."

"Happens to the best of us," Zavala said.

"Any idea where it might have come from?" Austin asked.

"There were at least two dozen boats watching the bathysphere dive. That hungry critter could have been launched from any one of them. Why do you think it attacked you after scuttling the B3?"

"Nothing personal. I think I was what the military likes to call collateral damage." He pointed at the screen. "Someone sicced Fido there on the bathysphere. It went for me because I happened to be in the neighborhood."

"Who would want to torpedo the B3 project?" Zavala said.

"I've been wondering the same thing," Austin said. "Let's see if Doc is awake."

KANE WAS NOT ONLY awake but quite chipper. He had showered, wrapped his body in a terry-cloth robe, and was sitting in a chair chatting with the medic.

"Now I know what it feels like to be a canned sardine," he said. "Thanks for the rescue, Kurt. I can't believe the cable broke."

"It didn't break," Zavala said. "Kurt says that it was cut."

"*Cut?*" Kane's lower jaw dropped open. "I don't understand."

Austin showed Kane the video of the AUV, and said, "Can you think of anyone who would go through all this trouble to put the bathysphere on the bottom?"

Kane shook his head. "Nope. What about you?"

"Joe and I are as much in the dark as you are," Austin said. "There's no reason we can think of to scuttle a scientific and educational project."

Gannon's voice came over the ship's intercom.

"Call coming in for Dr. Kane," the captain said. "Can he take it?"

Austin plucked the intercom's receiver from the wall and handed it to Kane.

Kane listened to someone on the line, and said, "That's impossible! . . . Yes, of course . . . I'll be ready."

When Kane had clicked off, Austin asked, "Is everything all right?"

"Not really," Kane said. His face had turned the color of cold ashes. "If you'll excuse me, I've got to talk to the captain."

Kane asked the medic to help him get to the bridge.

Austin stared at the door for a moment, then shrugged and said to Zavala, "Come to the machine shop with me. I've got something to show you."

The mandible Austin had wrested from the AUV had been wrapped in cloth and clamped in a padded bench vise. Using a set of thick work gloves, he removed the blade from the vise. It was about four feet long and six inches wide, curved along the inner edge and tapering to a point. He found the metal surprisingly light, and he estimated its weight at less then twenty pounds.

Zavala whistled softly. "Beautiful," he murmured, "a metal alloy of some kind. Whoever built it didn't expect it to be twisted where it joined the AUV. That was the weak spot. The edge on this thing is as sharp as a samurai sword."

"You can see how a pair of these butter knives could ruin your day."

"Too bad Beebe isn't around," Zavala said. "It might change his mind about the dangers of the deep ocean being exaggerated."

"The ocean didn't produce this thing. It's decidedly man-made." Austin carefully turned it over. The metal had been perfectly forged except for a single flaw the size of a pinhead a few inches from where the blade had snapped off the AUV.

Austin rewrapped the blade and clamped it back in the vise.

"You spent quality time with Doc . . . Did he say anything that might shed some light on this mystery?"

"He talked about jellyfish a lot, but one other thing stood out." Zavala dug into his memory. "While we were stuck in the mud, I asked him about his research. He said he was working on some research that could affect every man, woman, and child on the planet."

"Did he elaborate?"

Zavala shook his head.

"I asked him about specifics. He said that if he told me what he'd been working on he would have to kill me."

The right side of Austin's mouth turned up in a lopsided grin.

"He actually *said* that? Seems ironic, considering that you were minutes away from what the tabloids call a grisly death."

"We had a good laugh about it, but I think he was sincere."

Austin pondered Zavala's reply, and said, "What do you make of that call Doc got a few minutes ago?"

"Doc looked as if a horse had kicked him in the stomach."

"He was upset, no doubt about that."

Austin suggested that they talk to Kane again. As they stepped out onto the deck, they saw Kane and the captain. Kane was still somewhat stiff-legged as he walked in their direction with Gannon by his side and he was carrying his duffel bag.

"We were on our way to see you folks," said the captain,

pointing to the lights of the approaching vessel. "That's a U.S. Coast Guard cutter coming in for Dr. Kane."

The cutter stopped around a hundred yards from the ship. Austin helped Kane put his flotation vest on and walked him to the ramp at the stern, where the Zodiac crew was waiting. He thanked Austin, Joe, and the captain for all their help.

"Sorry you have to leave, Doc," Austin said.

"Not as sorry as I am to go." He smiled, and added, "Beebe's adventures pale by comparison to our dive."

"Going back to Bonefish Key?"

"No, not for a while . . . I'll be in touch."

Kane got into the Zodiac. The inflatable pushed off into the chop and bounced over to the Coast Guard vessel, Kane was helped aboard, and it started to move away even before the inflatable made it back to the ship.

Austin, Gannon, and Zavala watched the cutter until it was out of sight, then Gannon turned to Austin and asked if he wanted to head back to port in the morning. Austin suggested that they try to retrieve the lost ROV. Gannon said the forecast called for fair weather after the gale blew itself out. He'd plan a salvage operation using the ship's largest ROV, a mechanical monster nicknamed Humongous.

"We don't really know very much about Doc," Zavala said after the captain had left.

"It's time we remedy that situation. I'll ask the Trouts to check into Bonefish Key. In the meantime, British Navy regulations allow a second shot of grog."

"This is NUMA, not the British Navy," Zavala said. "And, technically speaking, tequila is not grog."

"May I point out that we are in Bermudan waters and thus in British territory."

Zavala slapped Austin on the back and said something in Spanish.

"My *Español* is a bit rusty, pal," Austin said. "Please translate."

Zavala lifted his chin and sniffed the air, as if he had smelled something unpleasant.

"I said, 'Jolly good show, old chap.'"

CHAPTER 13

THE COAST GUARD CUTTER BROUGHT KANE TO THE MAIN-
land, where a car drove him to a business jet waiting at the
airport. Kane watched the lights of Bermuda fade in the distance, then turned away from the plane's window and tried to
make sense of the past twenty-four hours. His undersea ordeal
had worn him out. His thoughts tripped over one another until,
finally, he closed his eyes and dozed off. The jounce of the plane's
landing woke him up, and the pilot's voice over the intercom
informed him that they had touched down at Washington's Reagan National Airport.

The plane taxied to an off-limits section reserved for VIPs. A
strapping young man sporting a military brush cut greeted Kane
as he stepped onto the tarmac. Aviator sunglasses shaded the
man's eyes, even though it was nighttime, and his black suit
would have sent a conspiracy theorist into a swoon.

"Dr. Kane?" the man asked, as if there were some doubt.

The question irritated Kane, since he was the only passenger
on the six-seat plane.

"Yes," he said, "that's me. How about you?"

"Jones," the man said without a change in his expression. "Follow me."

Jones led the way to a black Humvee, opened the rear door for Kane, then got in front next to the driver, who was also dressed like an undertaker. After leaving the airport, they raced along the George Washington Memorial Parkway as if there was no speed limit, skirted the city, and headed toward Maryland.

Jones had been silent during the drive, but as they entered Rockville he spoke briefly into a hand radio. Kane overheard something about a package being delivered. Minutes later, the Humvee pulled up to a large office building. The sign out front identified the building as the Food and Drug Administration's headquarters. The windows of the FDA were dark except for a few offices lit for cleaning crews.

Jones escorted Kane to a side entrance. They rode an elevator down one level and walked along a hushed corridor to an unmarked door. Jones knocked softly, then opened the door for Kane, who stepped into a nondescript conference room similar to hundreds of other sterile spaces scattered in government edifices around the capital. The room had pale green wall-to-wall carpeting, beige walls decorated with generic artwork, a lectern, and a projection screen. A dozen or so people were seated around a long oak table.

Kane went around the table shaking hands and was greeted with hellos or smiles from everyone except a stranger who identified himself as William Coombs, representing the White House.

Kane sat down in the only unoccupied seat next to a firm-jawed man wearing the uniform of a lieutenant in the U.S. Navy.

"Hello, Max," he said. "How was your trip from Bermuda?" His name was Charley Casey.

"Fast," Kane said. "Hard for me to believe that a few hours ago I was a half mile under the ocean."

"I watched the dive on TV," Casey said. "Too bad you lost contact with the surface just when things started to get really interesting."

"Interesting isn't the word for it," Kane said. "But it's nothing compared to the craziness about the lab. Any news?"

The lieutenant shook his head.

"We're still trying to make contact," he said, "but there has been no response."

"Could it simply be a foul-up in the communications system?"

Casey glanced over at Coombs.

"We have reason to believe that there is more involved than a systems failure," Casey said.

"You might want to bring Dr. Kane up to date on the details as we know them, Lieutenant Casey," Coombs said.

The lieutenant nodded, opened a folder, and pulled out several sheets of paper.

"We've pieced together a scenario based on witness statements. The situation has been confused, and reports are still coming in, but here's what we have so far. Yesterday, at approximately 1400 hours our time, a cruise missile was launched against the *Proud Mary,* the lab's support-and-security ship."

Kane shook his head in disbelief.

"A *missile?* That can't be true!"

"I'm afraid it is true, Max. The missile hit the ship on the port side. No one was killed, but at least a dozen were injured. The *Mary* is a tough old gal. She stayed afloat and got off a Mayday. The Navy cruiser *Concord* showed up within hours and rescued the survivors. Repeated attempts were made to contact the Locker. No reply."

"Maybe the blast damaged the communications buoy," Kane suggested.

"Negative. The cruiser checked out the buoy and found it undamaged."

"Where was the lab's service shuttle when all this happened?"

"A short while before the attack, the submersible had made a run down to the lab to deliver a representative from the company in charge of the Locker's security. The sub was still on the lab when the missile came in."

"What about the Locker's minisubs?" Kane said. "They could be used to evacuate the lab in an emergency. The lab also has escape pods it can use as a last resort."

"No subs or pods, Max. Our guess is that what happened to the lab was sudden and catastrophic."

Kane's head was spinning. He slumped in his chair as he tried to digest the implications of Casey's last statement. He thought about Lois Mitchell and the other members of the Bonefish Key lab staff who had gathered to send him off on the B3 dive. He rallied after a moment, reminding himself that he was a scientist who dealt with facts, not suppositions.

Straightening up in his chair, Kane said, "How long before we can check out the lab itself?"

"The *Concord* is sending down a remote-operated vehicle," Casey said. "All we can do at this point is to wait for them to report in."

"I hope the Navy is doing more than sitting on its hands," Coombs said. "Have you tracked the source of the missile?"

The lieutenant raised an eyebrow. Coombs was one of those ubiquitous young staff aides who looked as if he had been punched out of white dough with a cookie cutter. He was as clean-cut as a West Point grad, although his closest brush with a uniform had been as an Eagle Scout. He had cultivated an all-purpose facial expression of quiet competence that failed to hide a barely restrained arrogance. During his naval career, Casey had frequently encountered clones of the White House man, with their inflated sense of power, and had learned to cloak his disdain under a polite veneer.

He prefaced his answer with a pleasant smile.

"The Navy can walk and chew gum at the same time, Mr. Coombs. We've reconstructed the probable trajectory of the missile, and we've got planes and ships vectoring in on the launch position."

"The White House isn't interested in trajectories or vectors, Lieutenant. Has the source of the launch been tracked? If it was launched by a foreign power, this could have serious international repercussions."

"The missile could have come from a ship, a sub, or a plane, sir, that's all we know. Pretty much a crapshoot at this time. We'd welcome suggestions as to how to proceed, sir."

Coombs was too well practiced in the art of passing the buck to take the bait.

"I'll leave that up to the Navy," he said, "but I can tell you one thing: this has all the earmarks of a well-organized and well-financed plan."

"You won't get any argument from me on that score," Kane said. "About the same time the *Proud Mary* was being attacked, an attempt was made to sabotage the bathysphere dive."

Kane waited for the noisy reaction to subside and then laid out the details of the attack on the sphere.

When Coombs heard about Austin's rescue dive, he said, "I've heard Vice President Sandecker talk about Kurt Austin. He's some sort of NUMA troubleshooter. From the little I know of the man's exploits, you would still be at the bottom of the ocean if he had not been on board the *Beebe*. This thing with the lab is starting to make sense now. Someone wants to destroy our project."

"That's my take on it too," Kane said. "The people behind the attack on the lab must have figured that I'd be ripe for the picking in the bathysphere."

Dr. Sophie Pappas, the sole female member of the scientific board, asked, "Why didn't the people behind these events wait until you were back on the lab? Instead of two simultaneous attacks, they only would have had to mount one."

"Good question." Coombs turned to Kane. "Could the work of the lab go on without you?"

Kane nodded.

"*Sure,*" he said. "As director, my job is to ride herd on the project. I'm a scientific coordinator now rather than a researcher. Lois Mitchell, my assistant, knows more about the actual nuts and bolts of the project."

"You're saying that the project could continue without you, but not without her," Coombs said.

Kane said, "I have more experience working with the government bureaucracy, but she could easily wrap up this project in days without me. On the other hand, I know enough to reconstitute the work with the scientists remaining at Bonefish Key. It would take time, but I could get things moving again."

"Not if you're dead," Coombs said. "But the lab's work could continue without you, which means that it may *not* have been destroyed."

"Your theory makes sense in a nutty sort of way," Kane said.

"Thank you. A devious mind is essential at the higher levels of government. Have we informed the Chinese government of the attacks?"

"After the meeting, I'll contact Colonel Ming, who is my Chinese counterpart on this project," Lieutenant Casey said. "He's corrupt as hell, I hear, but well connected. Perhaps he knows something that can help."

"I hope so. This incident with the lab couldn't have come at a worse time," Coombs said. "The other shoe is about to drop."

Coombs snapped his fingers, and his assistant went over to a large-screen computer at the end of the table and brought up a map of China.

"This red spot shows the village where the original outbreak occurred. These other three dots show that the epidemic has broken the quarantine and is spreading beyond the original source. We think the virus may be moving through the water table. The bug is leaping from village to village. Eventually, it will hit the big cities. Once it gets into the populations of Hong Kong, Beijing, and Shanghai, there will be no stopping it from spreading to the rest of the world. It will be in North America within weeks."

There was silence around the table for a moment, then Casey said, "How long before it strikes an urban area?"

"The computers say seventy-two hours from midnight."

"That still gives us time to stop it with the vaccine," Casey said. "Presumably, we'll be able to reestablish contact with the lab. Once we have the cultures, we hope to produce the vaccine in quantity."

"We're whistling in the dark," Coombs said. "We won't know what happened to the lab until the Navy does its job." Coombs leaned back in his chair and tented his fingers. "Let's back up. Who would benefit from scuttling the work of the lab?"

"I'll pass on that one until we know more," Kane said, and the others at the table nodded their heads in agreement.

"Okay, then," Coombs said with a shrug of his shoulders. "Maybe somebody can answer the question about how the attackers knew about the existence *and* location of a top secret facility."

"Leaks may have been inevitable," Kane said. "When this committee first approached the government with our findings and Uncle Sam set up Bonefish Key as a front, we were pretty inexperienced at this whole spook thing. The instinct of a scientist is to make information public, not withhold it."

"Which is why the research was removed from Bonefish Key to the Locker," Coombs said, "so we could keep a tight lid on it and be closer to the resource."

"There were safety reasons as well," Kane said. "We were working with a waterborne pathogen and tinkering with altered life-forms. The Bonefish Key lab is near populated areas that could have been impacted in the advanced stages of research."

Coombs frowned.

"The Locker's existence was under tighter security than the Manhattan Project," he said. "What about that woman at your lab? The scientist the Chinese sent over as a liaison?"

"Dr. Song Lee? I'll vouch for her. She was a whistle-blower during the SARS epidemic. She risked prison by speaking out. Her contributions to the project have been vital."

"So were Oppenheimer's during the original Manhattan Project," Coombs said. "That didn't keep his loyalty from being compromised."

"Before you indict Dr. Lee, I'd like to point out that I was the only one at Bonefish Key who knew the exact location of the lab. That information could have come from an outside source. What about the security company?"

Lieutenant Casey said, "The security people didn't know what the lab was for, but they knew *where* it was. And they might not have been as tight-lipped as government operatives."

The lieutenant had made no secret of his opposition to outsourc-
ing the security arrangements for the lab to a civilian company.

"The use of civilian contractors has been widespread," Coombs
said, "especially since the Iraq War."

"Where it was proven time after time that the government
had limited oversight-and-control capabilities," Casey said. "The
taxpayers pay for a professional Navy, not a bunch of oceangoing
cowboys."

"You're out of line, Lieutenant," Coombs said. He had lost his
cool demeanor, and his face was flushed with anger.

The lieutenant's phone trilled, heading off a heated argument
over the use of private warriors. He had a brief conversation with
the caller and hung up.

"The ROV is on the lab site," he announced with a cutting
glance at Coombs. "It's transmitting photos of the bottom."

He rose from his chair and went over to a computer at one
end of the table, which was connected to a PowerPoint setup. He
clicked the mouse and an image of the ocean bottom appeared
on the projection screen. There was no trace of the lab, no wreckage to suggest that the Locker had been destroyed.

"Are you sure you've got the correct location?" Coombs asked
with irritation in his voice.

"*Absolutely,*" Casey said. "Look closer. You can see the big
circular indentations in the sand. That's where the lab's support
legs rested."

"What's this all mean?" Coombs demanded.

Casey gave him a bleak smile.

"Taking a wild guess, Mr. Coombs, I'd say this means that
Davy Jones's Locker has been *hijacked.*"

Kane still didn't believe it.

"How could anything that big simply disappear?" he asked.

"You fellows figure out how this facility was hijacked under the nose of the U.S. Navy," Coombs said. "I'm going to see that Dr. Kane does a similar vanishing act."

Coombs raised his hand to cut Kane's next question off, reached into his suit jacket for a cell phone, and hastily punched in a number.

"We've got a problem," he said into the phone.

After a quick conversation, he hung up.

"You're going to a safe house, Dr. Kane," he announced.

When Kane protested, Coombs again cut him off.

"Sorry for the temporary inconvenience," he said, "but someone wants you out of the picture. These attacks show that unauthorized people have found out about the lab even though we have gone to a great deal of trouble to keep it a secret. Even without the natural disaster you suggested, the political repercussions would be staggering if word of this research gets out."

"I can't see that happening," Kane said. "Whoever tried to torpedo our research seems to like secrets too."

"The difference is, we were prepared to go public once we had a vaccine," Coombs said.

There was a quick knock at the door, and Jones stepped into the room. He was still wearing sunglasses. Kane felt as if he were being placed under house arrest. He said good-bye, then followed Jones out into the hall.

After Kane was gone, Coombs turned to the others.

"I'm going to recommend to the President that he prepare the country for a state of emergency," he said. "We'll contact the CDC and tell them this is the big one."

"I'll inform Vice President Sandecker directly," Casey said. "He maintains contacts at NUMA and will enlist them in the search for the lab."

"Good idea," Coombs said. "Maybe their guy Austin can give the Navy some help doing its job."

This parting comment was intended as another dig at the Navy, but Casey didn't come back at Coombs as he had at the earlier jibes from the White House aide. He merely smiled.

"Maybe he can," he said.

KANE TRIED TO GET a rise out of the man in black.

"Guess we're going to the mattresses," he said as they walked to the elevator.

"Huh?" Jones said.

"From *The Godfather* . . . Mafia talk."

"We're not the Mafia, sir."

No, you're not, Kane thought as he followed Jones from the room, *but you might as well be.* He couldn't resist using another borrowed line from the movie.

"Don't forget the *cannoli,*" he said.

CHAPTER 14

A FEW MINUTES AFTER ONE O'CLOCK IN THE MORNING, AN inflatable pontoon boat softly bumped against the hull of the *William Beebe* and four figures dressed in black-and-green camouflage suits clambered up the side of the ship on rope ladders suspended from padded grapnel hooks. They vaulted over the rail one by one and dashed across the deck as silently as the shadows they resembled.

Except for the night-shift watch on the bridge, the crew was sound asleep in their cabins, recovering from the exertions of the bathysphere launch and rescue. Austin was awake, however, and after staring at the ceiling, his mind churning, he got up and got dressed and made his way to the machine shop.

He switched on the lights, and went over to examine the blade clamped in a table vise. He found a magnifying glass, placed a desk lamp directly over the blade, and examined the tiny ding near the hilt. Through the lens he saw that the flaw was actually a mark in the shape of an equilateral triangle with a dot at each point.

Austin drew the design on a pad of paper. He stared at it for a few moments but nothing jumped out at him. He set the pad down and went out onto the deck, thinking the cool air might blow away the cobwebs of sleep. He took a deep breath, but the sudden influx of oxygen produced a yawn instead. His synapses needed a stronger jolt.

He looked up at the bridge lights glowing in the window of the pilothouse. The night watch always kept a coffeepot brewing. He climbed the exterior stairs to the starboard bridge wing. A man's voice came through the partially open door. The words were growled rather than spoken, and had an accent Austin couldn't place, but one word stood out from the others.

Kane.

Austin's well-honed instincts came into play. He moved away from the door, plastered his back against the outside wall of the bridge, and edged up to a window. He saw Third Mate Marla Hayes, a male crewman, and Captain Gannon standing together in the pilothouse. The captain must have been rousted from his bunk because he had a jacket on over his pajamas and slippers on his feet.

Four figures wearing commando outfits were gathered around the captain, the third mate, and the crewman. Hoods covered the faces of three of the commandos, the fourth having removed his to reveal an Asian face with jade-green eyes and a clean-shaven head. All four cradled short-barreled automatic weapons carried sidearms, and had long-bladed knives hanging at their waists.

"I'll tell you again: Dr. Kane is no longer on this ship," Gannon was saying. "He left hours ago on a seaplane."

The unhooded commando reacted with the swiftness of a striking rattlesnake, his free hand shooting out in a short, stabbing blow to the captain's solar plexus.

"Do not lie to me!" he snapped.

The captain doubled over, but he managed to gasp out a reply.

"Kane is not here," he wheezed. "Search the whole damned ship, if you don't believe me."

"No, Captain," his assailant said. "*You* will search the ship. Tell everyone to come up to the deck."

Still bent over in pain, Gannon reluctantly picked up a receiver connected to the *Beebe*'s public-address system. When he hesitated with the receiver at his mouth, his assailant forcefully jabbed a gun barrel into the captain's side to show his impatience.

Gannon winced, but he stubbornly resisted the impulse to cry out. He took a deep breath and spoke into the receiver.

"This is the captain. All hands on deck. All officers and crew assemble on the fantail."

Gannon's assailant barked out an order, and then he and two of his accomplices herded their three prisoners toward the door leading out onto the wing. Austin saw the move and climbed up a ladder that provided access to the radio tower on the pilothouse roof. From his perch, he watched the group descend to the main deck. He climbed back down and peered in a window. One attacker had been left to guard the ship's control center.

Austin descended the stairs to a lower deck, quietly opened the door to Zavala's cabin, stepped inside, and poked the mound beneath the blankets. Zavala groaned, then pushed the covers aside and sat up on the edge of his bed.

"Oh, hi, Kurt," he said with a yawn. "What's up?"

"Didn't you hear the captain tell the crew to gather on deck?" Austin asked.

Zavala rubbed the sleep out of his eyes.

"I heard him," he said, "but I'm not crew, so I stayed in the sack."

"Your skill at splitting hairs may have saved your butt," Austin said.

Zavala suddenly came to life.

"What's going on, Kurt?"

"Uninvited company. A bunch of heavily armed gentlemen in ninja suits."

"How many?"

"Four that I know of, but there may be others. They're looking for Kane. Gannon told them Doc's not on the ship, but they didn't believe him. He was forced to round up the crew."

Zavala muttered something in Spanish, then bounded out of bed and pulled on a pair of jeans and a windbreaker. He yanked his lucky skullcap down over his ears.

"What sort of firepower are we dealing with?" he asked.

Austin told him about the machine guns and pistols the commandos carried. Zavala frowned. Neither man had thought to bring along a weapon on a peaceful scientific expedition.

"We'll have to improvise for now," Austin said.

Zavala shrugged.

"What else is new?" he said.

Austin checked the passageway. Seeing it was clear, he led the way to the bridge, with Zavala a few steps behind. The commando was still inside. He was lighting a cigarette. Austin pointed to his own chest, then to the roof ladder. Zavala curled his forefinger and thumb into an *OK* gesture. As soon as Austin was on the roof, Zavala tapped on the window and waved at the commando, who burst onto the wing with his machine gun at waist level.

"*Buenas noches,*" Zavala said, brandishing his friendliest smile.

Zavala's Latin charm fell on deaf ears. The man pointed his gun at Zavala's midsection. Zavala raised his hands. The man was reaching for a radio at his belt when Austin called down from the roof.

"Yoo-hoo," Austin said, "I'm up here."

The man looked up and saw a steel-haired gargoyle grinning down at him. He brought his gun up, but Austin leaped off the roof and landed with his full weight on the man's shoulders. The man folded like a rag doll under the impact of more than two hundred pounds of muscle and bone and crashed to the deck.

The machine gun flew from the man's hand. Zavala dove for the weapon and deftly snatched it up before it skittered over the edge. He held the gun on the man, who lay on the deck without stirring.

"Did you really say, 'Yoo-hoo'?" he asked Austin.

"There wasn't time for a full introduction."

Austin prodded the man with his toe and told him to get up. When there was no response, he rolled the limp man over onto his back and pulled the mask back to reveal broad-faced Asian features. Blood drooled from the man's mouth.

"He's going to need a good orthodontist when he wakes up," Zavala said.

Austin felt for a pulse in the man's neck.

"That's the least of his worries," he said. "He'd be better off seeing the undertaker."

Zavala stepped on the cigarette that had flown from the man's mouth.

"Someone should have told him that smoking is bad for his health," he said.

They dragged the body inside the bridge. Austin radioed a quick Mayday while Zavala picked up the man's gun. They descended to the deck. Crouching low and taking advantage of the shadows, they made their way to the fantail. The powerful flood-lights used to illuminate night operations had been turned on, bathing the deck in bright light. The crew and officers were huddled in a tight knot guarded by two of the commandos. The clean-shaven man had his machine gun trained on Gannon with one hand while with the other hand he brandished a photo of Kane in Gannon's face.

The captain shook his head and pointed skyward. He looked more exasperated than frightened.

The man angrily pushed Gannon aside and turned to the Beebe's crew. He held the photo high.

"Tell me where this man is hiding," he announced, "and we will let you go."

When no one took him up on the offer, he strode over to the crewmen, studied their frightened faces, then reached out and grabbed an arm that belonged to Marla. He forced her to her knees, glanced at his watch, and said, "If Kane does not appear in five minutes, I will kill this woman. Then we will kill one of your crew every minute until Kane comes out of hiding."

Austin lay belly-down on the deck next to Zavala, trying to train his sights on the commando. Even if he took the man out with the first shot, he might not get the other two, who could sweep the deck clean with a few bursts from their automatic weapons. He lowered his gun and signaled to Zavala. They crawled backward until they were in the shadows of the ship's garage.

"I can't nail Bullethead," Austin said. "Even if I do, his pals could go on a shooting spree."

"What we need is a *tank*," Zavala agreed.

Austin stared at his friend and punched him in the shoulder.

"You're a *genius,* Joe. That's *exactly* what we need."

"I am? Oh, hell," he said as if something had occurred to him. "The Humongous? That's an ROV, Kurt, not an Army tank."

"It's better than nothing, which is what we've got," Austin said.

He quickly outlined a plan.

Zavala saluted to show that he understood, then turned and sprinted off to the remote-control center. Austin slipped through a door to the ship's garage and turned the lights on. The Humongous had been pulled up close to the doors in preparation for the search for the sunken ROV the next morning.

The Humongous was about the size of a Land Rover. It was built with treads that allowed it to crawl along the sea bottom. It had a flotation pack full of foam that held the instruments, lights, and ballast tanks. Six thrusters allowed for agile, precise maneuvering in the water, and it carried a battery of still and television cameras, magnetometers, sonar, water samplers, and instruments that measured water clarity, light penetration, and temperature.

The pair of now-folded mechanical manipulators that extended from the forward end could be operated with surgical precision. Their claws could pluck the tiniest of samples from the bottom and store them in a collection cage slung under the front of the vehicle.

A couple hundred feet of umbilical tether had been coiled behind the ROV. Austin stood in front of it, waiting, as precious seconds went by. Then the vehicle's searchlights snapped on, and the electric motors began to hum.

Austin waved his arms at the camera. Zavala saw him on the monitor and waggled the manipulator arms to signal that he was at the controls.

Austin went around behind the ROV and climbed on top. Zavala gave the vehicle power. The Humongous lurched forward and crashed into the double doors, pushing them wide open. As it emerged onto the deck on grinding treads, Zavala waved the manipulators around and worked the claws, adding to the dramatic effect.

Marla's would-be executioner whirled around to face the garage doors and saw what looked like a giant crustacean heading directly for him. Marla took advantage of the distraction, scrambled to her feet, and made a run for safety. One of the other commandos saw the third mate trying to escape and aimed his weapon at her fleeing figure.

Austin snapped off a stuttering fusillade that stitched a row of holes across the man's midsection. The clean-shaven man and the other commando took cover behind a crane and peppered the oncoming Humongous with hundreds of rounds. The unrelenting gunfire blasted away its searchlights, then a lucky shot found its camera.

Inside the control room, the screen went blank. Zavala kept the vehicle moving at full speed, but without electronic eyes he was having trouble controlling it. The Humongous veered drunkenly to the right, came to a jerking stop, then shot off to the left. It went through the same moves again, peppered all the while by the hail of bullets. Fragments of plastic, foam, and metal filled the air until, finally, the shooting triggered an electrical fire.

Austin gagged on the acrid smoke filling his nostrils. He could feel the Humongous disintegrating beneath him. He dropped off the back of the erratically moving ROV and ran to one side of the ship, dove behind a tall air vent, hit the deck, and rolled several feet. He stopped and fired a blast directly above the stroboscopic muzzle flashes in front of him. It was his turn for a lucky hit. One of the guns went silent. Austin kept on shooting until he emptied his gun of bullets.

A moment later, the clean-shaven man took advantage of the lull and ran for the side of the ship.

Austin stepped out into the open, pointed his empty gun at the fleeing man, and yelled, "Hey, Bullethead! Don't leave so soon. Fun's just starting." Austin raised the gun to his shoulder.

The man stopped and turned to face Austin from twenty feet or so away. The Humongous was now ablaze, and the man's face and strange green eyes were visible in the light of the flickering flames. A smile came to his evil features.

"You're bluffing," he said. "You would have shot me if you had the chance."

"*Try* me," Austin said, squinting with one eye as if taking aim.

Either the man didn't buy Austin's bluff or he didn't care. He raised his own gun, and Austin thought he was going to shoot, but instead the man let out a snarl and dashed toward the railing, firing from the hip as he ran. Austin ducked for cover, and when he dared look again, the man had disappeared. He heard the sound of an outboard motor starting and ran to the railing. The boat was already up on plane, and within seconds it had disappeared into the darkness.

He stared at the pale wake foaming the water and was listening to the motor fading into the night when there was a new sound on the deck behind him.

Footfalls.

Austin pivoted into a crouch, only to relax when he saw why the man had decided to bolt. Zavala had emerged from the control center and was trotting toward him. They both grabbed fire extinguishers from a bulkhead and sprayed the Humongous with foam.

"It sounded like World War Three out here," Zavala said after they had the blaze under control. "Glad to see you're still in one piece."

"Thanks to your timely appearance," Austin replied. "Wish I

could say the same for the Humongous," he added with a tinge of guilt in his voice.

Zavala gazed in wonder at the smoldering ROV, its components scattered around the deck.

"I can see now why the video died," Zavala said.

"That's not the *only* thing that died," Austin said.

He went over to the bodies lying on deck. He removed the mask from the man who had tried to kill Marla, revealing a cruel face with Asian features. The second man was Asian as well. Austin surveyed the deck, which was covered with cartridge shells. The smell of cordite hung in the smoke-filled air.

"Now we know why the B3 was attacked," he said. "Doc Kane . . . We've got to talk to him."

"Good luck!" Zavala said. "Doc made it pretty clear that his work was none of our business."

Austin's lips tightened in the smile that, in Zavala's experience, had always presaged trouble.

"That's too bad," Austin said in an even tone. "Because I'm *making* it our business."

CHAPTER 15

THE LICENSE PLATE ON THE SILVER MERCEDES S65 AMG sedan that emerged from the parking garage under Pyramid Trading Company's fifty-story building displayed only the number 2, suggesting that the car's owner enjoyed extreme wealth. Vanity plates were auctioned off for millions of dollars to affluent and superstitious bidders who believed that the low numbers would bring good luck.

To reinforce that good luck, the car's skin was fashioned from rocketproof armor plate and its tinted-glass windows were bulletproof. The underside was fortified against street bombs. The six-hundred-horsepower V-12 engine under the hood could push the car's speed up to two hundred miles an hour.

An armed guard wearing denim fatigues sat in the front seat next to the driver. For added security, the Mercedes was sandwiched between two four-hundred-ninety-three-horsepower Mercedes G55 AMG SUVs. Each SUV carried a driver and five guards armed with Chinese-made, lightweight Type 79 submachine guns that had firing capabilities of five hundred rounds per minute.

The three-vehicle motorcade followed a route that took it away from the high-rise apartment complexes and glitzy clubs around the Oriental Pearl Tower, the tallest building of its kind in the world. The car and its escorts sped along the banks of the Yangtze River, then turned off the highway and headed toward the destitute neighborhoods that are the embarrassing underside of the largest and wealthiest city in the People's Republic of China.

The procession plunged deep into the warren of slums, entering a hellish landscape of a no-man's-land that was so burned out and devoid of human life even the most desperate slum dwellers avoided it. The vehicles turned onto a narrow, unlit street and went through a gate, pulling up next to an abandoned brick warehouse. Weathered plywood covered the widows, broken glass and boards from packing crates littered the oil-soaked dirt parking lot, but the razor wire topping the electrified chain-link fence that gleamed in the headlights was brand-new.

The guards poured out of the SUVs and formed a cordon between the Mercedes sedan and a loading platform. The man riding shotgun in the sedan's front seat got out and opened the rear door. The lone passenger emerged and walked briskly toward the platform, accompanied by his bodyguard. As the men climbed the platform stairs, a door on well-greased rollers slid silently open.

They entered the warehouse and the door slid shut. The illumination from fluorescent overhead lights revealed that the passenger from the Mercedes was a small man dressed in a medium blue suit that had been hand-tailored in London, a neatly knotted silk tie, and Testoni shoes that sold for two thousand dollars a pair. He had a rigid, almost military posture about him.

Silver hair, neatly parted on the left, and black-plastic-framed glasses gave Wen Lo an avuncular air of bland respectability more befitting a desk clerk in a three-star hotel than the head of a giant real-estate and financial consortium that was the cover for extensive prostitution, gambling, and drug operations on a global scale.

Wen Lo's face was asymmetrical, not from left to right but from top to bottom. The lower part of his face featured plump cheeks and a boyish smile while the upper part had a wide forehead, heavy furrowing brows, and soulless jade-green eyes that showed no more emotion than an abacus.

Waiting inside the warehouse door were three men in blue-green hospital gowns and a pair of heavily armed guards wearing generic tan security uniforms. The hard-faced guards carried Tasers, sidearms, and clubs that hung from their wide leather belts.

A balding, weasel-faced man dressed as if for the operating room stepped forward.

"An honor to have you visit us, sir," he said, giving a quick bow of the head.

Wen Lo responded with a barely perceptible nod.

"Tell me how your work is coming, Dr. Wu," he said.

"We are making progress," Wu said with cheerful optimism.

Although the lower part of Wen Lo's face smiled, his eyes didn't mirror the same pleasant expression.

"Please show me your progress, Dr. Wu."

"I'd be glad to, sir."

Wu led Wen Lo and his personal bodyguard through two sets of airtight chambers and along a short corridor that ended in a thick glass door. Responding to a gesture from Wu, a guard pressed an electrical switch that unlocked the door. Wu, Wen Lo, and the bodyguard stepped into a cellblock. Steel doors, solid except for small rectangular openings, enclosed a dozen cells.

As they walked between the cells, Dr. Wu said, "The men and women are segregated, four to a cell. We maintain full occupancy at all times."

A few inmates pushed their faces close to the barred openings and called out to Wu and his guests to help them. Wen Lo, his face devoid of pity, turned to Wu.

"What is the source of these lab rats?" he asked.

Dr. Wu was rewarded handsomely enough for his work to afford a large apartment in a new high-rise overlooking the Yangtze and to keep his wife and his mistress clothed in the latest fashions, but he had convinced himself that his research was for the good of mankind. Although his work required that he suppress his humanity under a thin veneer of medical noninvolvement, the coldness of Wen Lo's question stunned him. He was, after all, still a physician.

"As medical professionals, we prefer to call them *subjects*," he said.

"Very well, Dr. Wu, I'm sure these *subjects* appreciate your professionalism. But you haven't answered my question."

"My apologies, sir," Wu said. "This lab is surrounded by teeming slums, and it's easy to lure the subjects in with promises of food and money. We choose only those in relatively good physical shape. People in the slums rarely report the missing, and the police never follow up."

Wen Lo said, "Show me the next phase. I have seen prisons before."

Wu escorted the two men out of the cellblock to a black-walled room. One wall was half glass, like the viewing area for a maternity ward. Visible through the glass were a number of full-sized beds, each occupied and enclosed in a transparent cylinder.

The occupants of the beds were quiet for the most part, but occasionally someone stirred restlessly under a tightly tucked sheet. Figures in white body-encasing protective suits moved like ghosts among the beds, checking electronic monitors and IV tubes.

"This is one of several sick rooms," Wu said. "The subjects in each have been injected with the new pathogen and are proceeding through the stages of the virus. Although the virus is water-borne, it can be spread through contact as well. You can see by the way the technicians are dressed, and the separately vented enclosures for each subject, that we take every precaution to keep the disease contained to the rooms."

"If the subjects were left on their own, they would die?" Wen Lo asked.

"That's correct, sir, within twenty-four hours. The disease would take its course by then, and it is always fatal."

Wen Lo asked to see the next phase.

They set off down another corridor, through more airtight doors, and entered a second observation area similar to the first. The room on the other side of the glass held eight gurneys enclosed by cylinders. On the gurneys were four men and four women. Their faces looked like they had been carved from mahogany. Their eyes were closed, and it was difficult to tell if they were alive or dead.

"This is phase three," Wu said. "These subjects show the dark rash that is typical of the virus, but they are still alive."

"You call these ripe vegetables in your little garden *alive,* Dr. Wu?"

"Admittedly, it would be preferable if they were up and about, but they are still breathing, and their vitals are sound. The experimental cure is helping."

"Would you like to be infected and helped by your cure, Dr. Wu?"

Wu couldn't miss the implied threat. Sweat trickled down his back between his shoulder blades.

"No, I would not, sir. The cure is imperfect at this time. The virus is amazing! Its ability to adapt quickly to any treatment we try has made our task difficult but not impossible."

"In other words, you have failed."

Wen Lo's smile could not counteract the coldness in his eyes.

"Success is possible," Wu said. "But it will take time. I don't know how long."

"Time is the thing we have in little supply, Wu."

Dr. Wu couldn't help but notice that Wen Lo had dropped his title. He was doomed. He started to croak something about one more chance, but Wen Lo wagged a finger at him.

Wu was about to faint, but Wen Lo clapped him on the back.

"Don't worry, Dr. Wu," he said. "We appreciate your hard work here. We are near to developing a highly promising cure at our offshore facility. You will go there to make sure the work is satisfactory."

"I'm grateful for another chance," Wu said. "When might I expect to start new tests?"

"There won't be time," Wen Lo said. "The testing will be done using computer simulation." He turned back to stare at the forms on the gurneys. "Dispose of this material. The subjects in the cellblock too. We will find our way out."

After Wen Lo and the bodyguard left, Dr. Wu glanced through the glass at the supine forms on the gurneys and sighed heavily. He had fifty subjects going through tests and most of them would die, so it was simply a question of disposing of the remains. But those in the cellblock would pose a particular problem, and it was going to be a messy job getting rid of this batch. He hurried back to the main lab to fill his staff in on the task that lay ahead.

✦ ✦ ✦

AN HOUR LATER, Wen Lo got off the elevator on the top floor of the Pyramid Trading Company building, where he had his luxurious penthouse office suite. He was alone as he made his way across an enormous room decorated in French Empire style.

Floor-to-ceiling windows lined one long wall, but he paid no attention to Shanghai's tapestry of lights. He stood in front of a tall wall cabinet and barked a password. A microphone hidden in the cabinet filtered the password through a voice-identification device, and the cabinet rolled aside to reveal a metal door.

Wen Lo pressed his hand against a panel that examined the whorls of his fingertips and the lines of his palm and the door opened with a click, admitting him into a room of about twenty feet square. The room was perfectly circular in shape, and the only furniture was a plastic-and-aluminum table and three chairs. Cones that looked like oversize swag lamps hung from the ceiling. The deceptive blandness of the room obscured its function as a sophisticated communications center, its walls and ceiling containing a complicated system of microphones, projectors, transmitters, and receivers.

Wen Lo settled into a cushioned chair, looked across the table at the other two chairs, and uttered a single word.

"Begin."

The LED lighting in the ceiling dimmed except for a cone-shaped shaft of light that illuminated each chair. The air in one shaft seemed to shimmer as if superheated, becoming wavy, then darkening with tiny swirling motes, until a fuzzy silhouette formed, amorphous at first, then more solid, outlining first shoulders and then a head. Details filled in: eyes and nose, flesh and clothing. In short order, Wen Lo was looking at a three-

dimensional laser projection of a man so real that he could almost touch it.

The man's face was the mirror image of Wen Lo's, which was
not surprising, because they were two of a set of triplets. They
both had the same high forehead, beetled brow, and unfathom-
able eyes, but the projected man's scalp was clean-shaven. Where
the menace in Wen Lo's face was quietly understated, the projected face had an unvarnished, street-thug toughness around the
mouth and chin that suggested barely restrained violence.

"Good evening, Brother Chang," Wen Lo said.

"And good evening to you, Brother Wen Lo. Number One is
about to join us."

The air under the third light went through the same wavy
sequence. The hologram that appeared in the chair was of a man
dressed in a red silk robe and wearing a round, high-brimmed
hat. The face was long and lean, with arched brows over a prominent forehead, cunning cat-green eyes, and a long, thin mustache that draped down below his chin.

Wen Lo clapped his hands upon recognizing the apparition.

"Bravo!" he said. "Dr. Fu Manchu, if I am not mistaken."

The hologram responded with a knife-edged chuckle.

"Congratulations, Wen Lo," Fu Manchu said. "You are looking at the master criminal who is preparing to unleash the Yellow
Peril against the civilized nations of the world."

The silken embodiment of evil was a clever illusion carved in
light by the latest in computer and laser technology. Although the
figure of the Chinese archvillain seemed solid, it had no more substance than the literary character created in the Sax Rohmer series.
The system that brought the triplets together for their meetings
could be manipulated, using data on figures real or imagined, to
create any image desired. Past meetings had been presided over by
such monumental figures as Mao or Genghis Khan.

Although Fu Manchu was an illusion created by electronic ectoplasm that defined the smallest detail, the voice behind the leering archfiend belonged to a flesh-and-blood person who ran a criminal empire that Rohmer's villain could only have dreamed of.

In the tradition of the age-old crime cults know as Triads, the triplets who ran the far-flung organization were ranked by numbers rather than names, given them according to their order of birth. Wen Lo was *Two,* and he directed the Triad's criminal enterprises behind a thin screen of respectability. Chang was *Three,* and he was in charge of the global network's security, including the gangs that infested Chinatowns in every major city. The triplet behind the Fu Manchu mask served as CEO, overseeing criminal and legitimate operations, a responsibility that went with the name *One.*

"I enjoyed the hatchet man from the tong wars," said Chang.

"I'm not surprised, given your efficient stewardship of our *own* hatchet men," Fu Manchu said. "However, I understand that this efficiency did not extend to your expedition in Bermuda. Dr. Kane escaped from the bottom of the ocean."

"Our machine cut the bathysphere's cable. There was no way anyone could have saved it at that depth."

"Apparently, *someone* did. His name is Kurt Austin. The television reports say he is an engineer with NUMA. Also, how do you explain your botched attack on the NUMA ship?"

Chang scowled.

"We met unexpected resistance," he said.

"We cannot afford any more slipups. We would not be dealing with this situation if you had kept a closer eye on things at your testing lab, Wen Lo."

The third triplet had been enjoying the discomfiture of his

brother, but now it was his turn to squirm in his chair under the cold gaze of the archvillain.

"I accept full responsibility. The laboratory guard who brought the virus to his home province did not follow the proper decontamination safeguards. I have tightened them and prohibited travel by any of our security people."

"Has the virus spread further?" Fu Manchu asked.

"It has broken past the quarantine. The government is trying to contain it."

"Not good," Fu Manchu said. "Our plan was to release the virus selectively when we had a vaccine to control it. We are trying to destabilize the government and profit from the spread of the disease. Wiping out the human race would be rather counterproductive, don't you think?"

"It would solve our country's problem with population control," said Wen Lo in a weak attempt at humor.

"I'm sure it would. Unfortunately, *we* are part of the population. Is there any word of Dr. Kane?"

"We checked Bonefish Key," Chang said. "He never returned. We still have our feelers out, but he seems to have disappeared."

"His disappearance doesn't concern me as much as the possibility that he now is aware that he is a target. And that he may have conveyed that concern to others. Fortunately, he is no longer vital to the completion of the project. But the work cannot be allowed to regerminate at Bonefish Key."

"The only one who can reconstitute the project, other than Kane, is Dr. Song Lee, the representative that the People's Republic sent to work with U.S. scientists," Chang said. "She is about to be removed and disposed of."

"See that it is accomplished quickly and cleanly," Fu Manchu said. "And you, Brother Wen Lo, what is the status of the vaccine?"

"The vaccine will soon be a reality, and we can proceed with the next phase. I have ordered our land lab closed and its contents liquidated."

"Very good. Is that all?"

"For now," Wen Lo said.

Fu Manchu bowed his head, folded his hands. His evil face began to disintegrate, falling apart into whirling motes that grew from dark to light and then vanished. Moments later, the second hologram vanished

Wen Lo rose from his seat and left the now-empty room. There was much to do.

CHANG REMAINED in his chair, brooding. After his attack on the NUMA ship had been rebuffed, he had boarded a fast powerboat that took him to the mainland. From there, he booked a private jet that flew him to the United States. He entered the country carrying the credentials of a trade representative and joined the holographic meeting with his siblings from a Virginia warehouse the Triad used as a cover.

After a moment of thought, Chang turned to a computer and typed in Kurt Austin's name. The computer took him to the NUMA website and provided him with a short blurb that identified Austin as a project engineer. Austin's photo also was posted.

Chang stared at the coral-blue eyes, and the smile that seemed to mock him, until he could stand it no longer. He pressed the OFF button and Austin's face vanished. Chang glared at the blank screen.

The next time I encounter Kurt Austin, he vowed, *I will make him vanish forever.*

CHAPTER 16

THE BERMUDA COAST GUARD CUTTER HAD RESPONDED quickly to Captain Gannon's Mayday. After a quick look at the bodies and empty bullet casings littering the aft deck, the guardsmen hurriedly called in the Marine Police Service. Within hours, a boat carrying a crime-scene investigation team arrived at the NUMA ship.

The six-man CSI team that stepped on board the research vessel's deck looked like the car valets at a Nassau resort hotel. With the exception of Detective-Superintendent Colin Randolph, they were dressed identically in navy blue Bermuda shorts, light blue shirts, and kneesocks. As an officer, Randolph was allowed to wear a white shirt.

The men, in their spit-and-polish uniforms, stood in sharp contrast to Gannon, who was still wearing his pajamas when he welcomed Randolph and his team aboard. The captain led the way to the aft deck and introduced Randolph to Austin and Zavala, who had been talking to crew members about the night's events. The inspector gave the NUMA men each a quick hand-shake, then turned his wide-eyed gaze to the bodies lying on the cartridge-littered deck.

The detective-superintendent was a round-faced man in his mid-forties who spoke with a lilt that hinted at his origins in Barbados, where he had been born.

He blew out his prominent cheeks like a puffer fish.

"Good Lord!" he said in astonishment. "Looks like a bloody war zone." Then glancing at the bullet-riddled wreck of the Humongous, he said, "What's *that* thing?"

"It *was* a remote-operated submersible vehicle designed to move along the ocean bottom," Zavala said.

"Well, from the looks of it, that pile of junk won't be moving anywhere soon." He shook his head. "What happened to it?"

"Austin here was using the vehicle for cover, and the gunmen shot it out from under him," Zavala said.

Randolph glanced at Austin, then gave Zavala a hard stare. Seeing nothing in either man's face that suggested Zavala was joking, the detective-superintendent ordered his team to cordon off the crime scene with yellow police tape.

He turned to the captain.

"I'd be very pleased if you could tell me what happened on your ship last night."

"Glad to," Gannon said. "Around three in the morning, four armed men boarded the ship from a small boat and rousted me out of my bunk." He plucked the front of his ratty-looking pajamas. "As you can see, I wasn't expecting company. They were looking for Dr. Max Kane, a scientist who had been involved with the bathysphere project."

"Did they say why they wanted Dr. Kane?"

Gannon shrugged.

"Their leader was a creepy guy with a shaved head. When I told him that Kane had left the ship, he rounded up my crew and threatened to kill them. He would have followed up on his threat if Kurt and Joe hadn't intervened."

Randolph turned back to Austin and Zavala.

"So *you're* the ones responsible for this mess?"

"We didn't have a lot of choice at the time," Austin said.

"Do all NUMA research vessels carry armed security men?"

"Joe and I weren't armed at first. We borrowed weapons from the gunmen. And we're not security men, we're NUMA engineers running the Bathysphere 3 project."

Austin might just as well have said he was from France, like the Coneheads in the old *Saturday Night Live* skit.

Randolph's eyes swept the scene, taking in the bodies, the weapons next to them, and the wrecked ROV. He was chewing his lower lip, and it was obvious that he was having a difficult time reconciling the blood-soaked deck with Austin's explanation.

"Engineers," Randolph repeated in a flat voice. Clearing his throat, he then said, "What *kind* of engineers?"

"I specialize in deep-sea diving and salvage," Austin said. "Joe designs and pilots submersibles. He built the bathysphere."

"And it was you two *engineers* who, against overwhelming odds, routed an armed band, using their own weapons to kill two of them in the process?"

"*Three,*" Austin corrected. "There's another body on the bridge."

"We were lucky," Zavala pitched in, as if it explained everything.

"What happened to the fourth man, with the shaved head?" Randolph asked.

"*He* was lucky," Austin said. "He got away."

Randolph held a degree in police studies and was a veteran

policeman, but even an untrained observer would have sensed something different about these two NUMA engineers. Relaxed and genial as he appeared to be, the broad-shouldered Austin had a commanding presence that went beyond his strikingly coral-blue gaze, thick gray mane of hair, and chiseled profile. And the handsome Zavala looked as if he just stepped out of some swashbuckling Hollywood epic.

"Is there any chance the men were pirates?" Randolph asked. "Bermuda does a big cruise-ship business, and rumors of piracy could be very damaging."

"Piracy is possible but not probable," Austin replied. "This isn't Somalia, and these guys weren't interested in the scientific equipment that pirates normally go after when they hit a research vessel. They knew Dr. Kane had been aboard and they were looking for him."

"Thank goodness! I'll put this down as an isolated attack, then."

"Has the Coast Guard come up with any leads?" Austin asked.

"They surveyed the area around the ship, and will continue to keep an eye out. I suspect that the boat carrying the men who attacked your ship is long gone. I'd like full statements from you gentlemen and every crew member on board. Any way I can reach Dr. Kane?"

"We don't know his present whereabouts," Gannon said. "We can try to contact him."

"Please do that, Captain. Could you also prepare a list of everyone on board?"

"I'll get right to it, Detective-Superintendent. You can conduct your interviews in the mess hall."

"Thank you very much for your cooperation, Captain."

As Gannon hurried off to carry out Randolph's request, Ran-

dolph said, "Now, gentlemen, since you were so intimately ac-
quainted with the events of last night, perhaps you wouldn't
mind being interviewed first."

"We'd be happy to tell you the whole story," Austin said.

They shook hands all around. As Randolph walked off to
supervise his team, he snorted like a horse.

"Engineers," he muttered.

Austin suggested that Zavala take the first interview while
he tried to reach Kane. He walked a short distance from the
activity on the aft deck, and called directory assistance on his cell
phone, asking for the number of Bonefish Key Marine Center.
A computer-generated voice informed him that the lab was not
open to the public and referred callers to the center's website.

After a moment's thought, he punched in another number
from his phone list.

A low, cool female voice answered his call.

"Hi, Kurt," said Gamay Morgan-Trout, "congratulations.
Paul and I watched the bathysphere dive on TV until the transmission got cut off. How was the briny deep?"

"Briny and deep. I'll tell you about it later. Sorry to interrupt
your sabbatical at Scripps, but I need a favor. I'd like you or Paul
to wrangle an invitation to the Bonefish Key marine lab in Florida. They discourage visitors, but if anyone can get in it's you."

"Didn't the director of Bonefish Key make the B3 dive with
Joe?"

"His name is Max Kane. But don't expect any help from
him."

"I'll give it a try, Kurt. What exactly should I be looking for?"

"I don't know. Just keep your eyes open for anything that
strikes you as funny."

Gamay responded with a soft chuckle.

"I love the crisp specificity of your directive, Kurt."

"It's a management course they teach called Cover Your Ass 101. The first lesson in CYA is that if anything goes wrong, it's not your fault. Call me when you or Paul get to Bonefish Key. Joe and I will be on the *Beebe* for another day or two."

Austin clicked off, then walked to the ship's railing. He was burning with impatience. He didn't like interrupting the sabbatical Paul and Gamay Trout were taking from the Special Assignments Team, but until he and Zavala managed to extricate themselves from the police investigation they would have to be the team's eyes and ears.

He gazed at the sparkle of the morning sun on the water. He sometimes joked that he was afflicted with what he called the King Neptune syndrome. He had spent so much of his life on or under the ocean that he had developed a proprietary attitude toward the two-thirds of the globe covered by water.

Austin had conceived the Bathysphere 3 project as a way to instill respect for the sea in the young people who would someday become its caretakers.

The faceless entity behind the attacks had almost ruined that.

He knew his mortal limitations. Unlike Neptune, Austin couldn't raise a storm at the touch of a trident.

A cold glint came to his eyes, and he compressed his lips in a tight, humorless smile.

But he had shown numerous times that he could raise *hell*. He couldn't wait to get off the ship so he could rattle the walls of Hades.

CHAPTER 17

PAUL TROUT WAS NEAR THE END OF THE SEMINAR HE WAS leading on global warming when his cell phone began to vibrate. Without missing a beat, he reached into his sports jacket pocket, shut off the phone, and threw the next graph up on the projection screen, only to hear a soft ripple of laughter behind his back. He turned, curious at what could be so humorous about an ocean-salinity pie chart.

No one was looking at the chart. Every eye in the room was staring out the window at an attractive red-haired woman in a two-piece bathing suit who was on the lawn outside the building. She was doing jumping jacks and waving a cell phone in the air at the same time.

Trout's head dipped down, as if looking over his glasses in deep thought, and he tugged at the large, colorful bow tie at his neck.

A seminar participant snickered.

"Who *is* that crazy woman?"

A faint smile came to Trout's lips.

"I'm afraid that crazy woman is my wife. Please excuse me."

A quiet gasp of disbelief followed Trout's exit from the room, but he was used to such reactions. He was a good-looking young man with large hazel-colored eyes and light brown hair neatly parted down the middle and combed back at the temples Gatsby style. In a tailored suit that draped his six-foot-eight physique perfectly, he was impeccably dressed as usual. But while he displayed a sly sense of humor, people often found his serious demeanor at odds with that of his more vivacious wife.

Trout stepped out into the hall and glanced at his phone. A text message appeared.

CAN U TALK?

Trout hit the MEMORY button to return the call.

"Quite the show you put on for my seminar on climate change," Trout said in his dry New England tone. "Are you auditioning for the Rockettes?"

Rich feminine laughter cascaded from the phone.

"I tried to call you but you didn't answer, Herr Professor," said Gamay. "Then I waved my hands outside your window until I was blue in the face. I had on my bathing suit from this morning's dive, so in desperation I slipped my shift off and put on a skin show. Apparently, it worked."

Paul broke into an easy grin.

"Oh, it *worked,* all right," he said. "The body temperature of every male in the room rose twenty degrees. Your little striptease may have set off a new round of global warming."

"Sorry," Gamay said lightly, "but Kurt called. He and Joe are still on the *Beebe.*"

"*Kurt?* Why didn't you say so? How'd the bathysphere dive go?"

"I told him we had watched until the transmission got cut short. He said the dive was *memorable.*"

"Odd choice of words. What did he mean?"

"He said he'd explain later. But it appears our attempt to re-
live our courting days here at Scripps is over. Kurt needs somebody to go to Florida to look into the Bonefish Key Marine
Center."

"Why the interest in Bonefish?"

"He again said he'd explain later. He'd like us to snoop around
the center and let him know if anything there strikes us as
funny . . . As in *peculiar.*"

"It's going to be awkward trying to get out of my schedule,"
Paul said. "I'm committed to two more days of panels and lec-
tures."

"I've finished my research dives," Gamay said. "While you
wrap up your seminar, I'll head off to Florida. You can follow
when you're done."

Paul glanced at his watch.

"Let's discuss it over lunch," he said. "I'll meet you in the
cafeteria after I cool down my seminar group."

He had been amused but not surprised at his wife's effective,
if unorthodox, attention-getting technique. It was typical of her
resourcefulness and her fearlessness. Her open personality was
the opposite of Trout's New England reserve, but they had been
immediately attracted to each other from the time they first met
at the Scripps Institution of Oceanography in La Jolla, California. Paul was studying for his Ph.D. in ocean science, while
Gamay had changed her field of interest from marine archae-
ology to marine biology and was working toward her doctor-
ate also.

They had met on a Scripps field trip to La Paz, Mexico, and
were married after graduation the following year. NUMA's former director, James Sandecker, had recognized their unique tal-
ents and asked them to join the Special Assignments Team under

Austin's leadership. After their last assignment, they had been invited to come back to Scripps and had jumped at the chance. Between their seminars and dives, they had spent their time revisiting familiar haunts and hooking up with old friends.

Trout ignored the grins that greeted his return to the seminar room and ran through the rest of his presentation. Gamay was waiting for him in the cafeteria when he was done. He was relieved to see that she had put her shift back on.

Gamay was a fitness nut and a fanatic about eating nutritious foods, but she had given up trying to fight the high-starch diet found on campus. She dipped a long French fry into a puddle of ketchup and popped it in her mouth.

"It's a good thing I'm leaving this place," she complained. "I must have put on twenty pounds since we got here. I'm blowing up like a tick."

Paul rolled his eyes. Gamay was up at six every day for her five-mile run that burned off any possible trace of culinary excess. Although she was only two inches short of six feet tall, she carried no more than one hundred thirty pounds on her small-hipped frame, most of it muscle from her active lifestyle.

Paul eyed a tall glass that contained a frothy strawberry concoction.

"Maybe you shouldn't have the frappe," he said.

Gamay brushed a strand of dark red hair out of her eyes and flashed a dazzling smile that showed the slight gap between her two front teeth.

"Last one . . . promise."

Her eyes had a dreamy expression as she took a long sip.

"Easy promise to keep, now that you're leaving town. What do you know about Bonefish Key?"

Gamay dabbed the pink mustache off her upper lip with a napkin.

"Only what I've read in scientific journals or come across on the Internet. It's on the west coast of Florida. They've made some discoveries that have led to patents in the field of biomedicine. There's a great deal of interest in finding something in the wild that could be used to cure disease."

"I remember the bioprospectors we met a while back in the Amazon rain forest."

Gamay nodded.

"Same concept, but there's a growing consensus that the ocean's potential for pharmaceuticals and medicines dwarfs that of the rain forest. The organisms that grow in the ocean are far more dynamic, biologically speaking, than anything on land."

Furrowing his brow, Paul said, "If Kurt is interested in the marine center, why not go through Kane?"

"I asked him the same question. He said not to expect help from Kane. That we're on our own and that—"

"He'll explain later," Paul finished the sentence.

Gamay feigned a look of astonishment.

"You're positively psychic at times."

He put his index finger to his temple.

"My mystic powers are telling me that you are about to offer me the rest of your strawberry frappe."

Gamay pushed the glass across the table.

"How do you think we should approach this thing with Kane out of the picture?"

"You could try using your NUMA bona fides to leverage a tour of the place."

"I thought of that. The NUMA connection might get me in the front door, but I don't know if I'd get the kind of access that would do us any good."

Paul nodded in agreement.

"You'd get the VIP treatment, a quick tour by a PR flack, a

ham sandwich, and a fond good-bye. Kurt apparently wants us to take a look behind the scenes."

"That was my impression. I need an edge, and I think I know where I can find one."

"While you work on that edge, I'll see if I can get you on a flight to Florida."

Paul stopped by his office to make travel arrangements. Gamay went to the boat dock to tell her dive crew that she was leaving Scripps. She hauled her scuba gear to the dormitory room that had been provided for their stay. She called an ocean chemist colleague at the Scripps Center for Marine Biotechnology and Biomedicine. In her usual Gamay fashion, she got right to the point.

"I'm trying to wrangle an overnight stay at Bonefish Key. I remember you saying that your center has worked with them on oceanborne treatments for asthma and arthritis."

"That's right," said Stu Simpson, an ocean biologist. "Most of the institutions working on this stuff share information. Bonefish Key is pretty tight, though. Have you contacted the director, Dr. Kane?"

"He's a hard guy to track down."

"Out in the field a lot, I've heard, and the place is being run by a Dr. Mayhew. I've met him at conferences. Not exactly Mr. Personality, but I may be able to help. Kane used to be with the Harbor Branch Oceanographic Institute, in Fort Pierce, Florida, before he got some money and set up the lab at Bonefish Key. I've got a friend at Harbor Branch who's a pal of Mayhew's. He owes me. I'll see if I can call in that marker for you."

While Gamay waited for Simpson to call back, she turned her laptop on and called up all the information she could find on Bonefish Key. She had been reading for only a few minutes when Dr. Mayhew called. Gamay explained her interest in Bonefish

Key, said she was at Scripps but would be in Florida visiting friends and wondered if she could visit the lab. He said he appreciated the interest of someone from NUMA in the marine center's work, but their visitor schedule was full up.

"That's too bad," Gamay said. "NUMA had no problem finding accommodations for your director on the B3 project. Why don't you talk to Dr. Kane? I'm sure he would love to reciprocate NUMA's hospitality if you asked him."

"That's not possible." Pause. "We have a guest room free, but only for tomorrow night. Too bad you're on the other side of the country."

Gamay saw the opening and struck with the speed of a cobra.

"I'll be there tomorrow," she said.

"I wouldn't want you to come all this way for just one night."

"No problem, I can revise my schedule. So let's make it *two* nights, then. How do I get out to the key?"

There was a stunned silence at the other end of the line.

"When you get to Fort Myers, call a man named Dooley Greene. He works for the center and has a boat."

Mayhew almost hung up without giving her Greene's phone number. *Cute,* she thought as she jotted down the information. When Paul returned a few minutes later, she already was packing her duffel bag.

"Are you in?" he asked.

"Just barely."

She told him how she arm-twisted Mayhew.

"*Slick,*" Paul said. "You'd make a deadly telemarketer. You're in luck, by the way. The travel bureau at NUMA has booked you on an early-morning flight to Fort Myers. I'll come out after I wrap up my seminar."

They spent the rest of the afternoon walking and riding around the campus, visiting spots from their grad-student days. After a late dinner, Gamay finished packing her bag, and they got to bed early. The next morning, Paul drove Gamay to the airport, gave her a good-bye kiss, and said he would see her in a couple of days.

THE PLANE LIFTED OFF the ground and leveled out at thirty-five thousand feet. Gamay settled back in her seat and read about Bonefish Key on her laptop. It was a narrow strip of land near Pine Island on the Gulf of Mexico. Indians inhabited the island before the Spaniards turned it into a combination fort and trading post. Later, it became a fishing center named after the bonefish that abounded in nearby waters.

Around 1900, an enterprising New Yorker built a hotel, but it was wrecked in a hurricane. The island then passed through a series of owners. After another hurricane stymied an attempt to operate an inn, the owner sold Bonefish Key to a nonprofit foundation and it became a center for the study of marine organisms with pharmaceutical potential.

The flight was smooth, and Gamay used some of the time to work on a report about her work at Scripps. When the plane landed at Fort Myers Airport late in the afternoon, the efficient NUMA travel bureau had arranged for a van to deliver her to the Pine Island ferry landing.

A twin-hulled powerboat was tied up at the dock. The grizzled man at the wheel had a nut-brown tan that only partly hid the creases in his genial face.

"I guess you're going out to Bonefish," he said. "I'm Dooley Greene. I make runs for the marine center, which kinda makes me the official greeter."

Gamay tossed her duffel bag in the double-hull and stepped on board with the sureness of someone who spent a lot of time on boats.

"I'm Dr. Morgan-Trout," she said, shaking his hand with a grip that surprised Dooley with its firmness. "Please call me Gamay."

"Thanks, Dr. Gamay," he said, unable to avoid the honorific. Despite her informality, her almost-regal self-confidence could be intimidating. Emboldened by her friendliness, he added, "Pretty name. Unusual too."

"My father was a wine nut. He named me after his favorite grape."

"My father's favorite booze was cheap gin," Dooley said. "Guess I should be grateful he didn't name me *Juniper.*"

Dooley uncleated the line and pushed the boat away from the dock. As they headed out into the bay, he seemed in no hurry.

"How long have you worked for the center?" Gamay asked.

"I was the dockmaster for the Bonefish Key Inn back when every fisherman and boater on the waterway used to hang out at the bar. After the hotel got beat up by Hurricane Charlie, the owner went bankrupt. When the marine center bought the property, they fixed up the inn. Dr. Kane asked me to run the water taxi and carry supplies. I used to be pretty busy running staff people back and forth, but that's all quieted down some."

"Aside from staff, do you bring many visitors out here?"

"Nope. The folks at the lab aren't the friendliest people . . . *Scientists.*" He shook his head. Then, realizing his faux pas, he added, "Oh, hell, you a scientist?"

"Yes, Dooley, but I'm a *friendly* scientist," she said with her engaging smile. "And I know what you mean. I talked to Dr. Mayhew on the phone."

"Preachin' to the choir," Dooley said with a grin like an old picket fence.

He reached into his work-shirt pocket and pulled out a worn business card that he handed to Gamay.

"I don't live on the island," he said. "Call me if you want to get off it. Phones don't work there unless you climb up the water tower."

"Dr. Mayhew called me from the island."

"They got a radiotelephone setup for emergencies and for the mucky-mucks to use."

The boat left the open water and wound its way through a green maze of mangroves. Gamay felt as if she were heading into Joseph Conrad's *Heart of Darkness*. Eventually, they rounded a turn and headed to an island that was mounded higher and appeared more solid than its surroundings. The pointed top of the white water tower Dooley had mentioned rose above the trees like a coolie hat. He tied the boat to the small dock and turned off the motor.

A grassy slope rose up to a patio and the veranda of a white-stucco building. It was practically hidden in the sun-baked palmettos, the light breeze carrying their damp perfume to Gamay's nostrils. A snowy egret waded along the shore. It was a picture-postcard perfect Florida scene, but the place gave her an uneasy feeling. Maybe it was the remoteness, the burned-up look of the vegetation, or simply the unearthly stillness.

"It's so quiet," she said, unintentionally speaking in almost a whisper. "Almost spooky."

Dooley chuckled.

"The lodge's built on an Indian mound. The island belonged to the Calusa before the white man killed them off or made them sick with disease. People still pick up on the bad stuff."

"Are you saying the island is haunted, Dooley?"

"No Indian ghosts, if that's what you mean. But everything that's been built here seems to have come to a bad end."

Gamay picked up her duffel bag and climbed up on the dock.

"Let's hope that doesn't include *my* short visit, Dooley."

She had tried to leaven the gloomy mood with her joke, but Dooley wasn't smiling when he followed her up on the dock.

"Welcome to paradise, Dr. Gamay."

CHAPTER 18

As Dooley escorted Gamay down the dock to the island, they encountered a young Asian woman coming their way.

"Afternoon, Dr. Song Lee," Dooley said. "I got your kayak all
ready for you before I made my run to Pine Island."

"Thank you, Dooley."

Lee's eyes darted to Gamay, who assessed her expression as
neither friendly nor unfriendly. Neutral, maybe.

"This is Dr. Morgan-Trout," Dooley said. "She's visiting the
island for a couple of days. Maybe you two could go kayaking
together."

"Yes, of course," Lee answered without enthusiasm. "Pleased
to meet you, Doctor. Enjoy your stay."

Lee brushed Gamay's extended hand with hers, and continued along the dock.

"Has Dr. Lee been here long?" Gamay asked.

"A few months," Dooley said. "She doesn't talk much about
what she's doing, and I don't ask."

He stopped at the end of the dock.

"This is as far as I'm allowed to go," he said. "Give me a call if you need me. Remember, the only phone service from the island is from the top of the water tower."

Gamay thanked Dooley, and watched his boat until it was out of sight. Then she picked up her duffel bag and climbed the stairs to the patio. The front door of the lodge burst open just then, and a man in a white lab coat came springing down the stairs from the veranda to the patio. He had the painfully thin physique of a runner. The stiffly extended handshake he gave Gamay was as limp and damp as a dead fish.

"Dr. Morgan-Trout, I presume," he said, flashing a quick, precise smile. "I'm Dr. Charles Mayhew, the acting keeper of this madhouse while Dr. Kane is away."

Gamay guessed that Mayhew had been watching for her arrival from the lodge. She smiled. "Thank you for having me as a guest on the island."

"Our pleasure," Mayhew oozed. "You have no idea how thrilled we were to learn that NUMA had invited Dr. Kane to dive in the bathysphere. I watched him make the dive. Too bad the television broadcast was cut short."

"Will I get a chance to meet Dr. Kane?" Gamay asked.

"He's involved with a field project," Mayhew said. "I'll show you your room."

They climbed to the veranda and passed through wide double doors to the wood-paneled lobby. Beyond the lobby was a large, sunny dining room furnished with rattan chairs and tables of dark wood. Screened-in windows wrapped around the room on three sides. A smaller room off the dining room was called the Dollar Bar, harkening back to the days when guests signed dollar bills and stuck them on the wall. The bills got blasted off in the hurricane, Mayhew explained.

Gamay's room was off a hallway a few steps from the bar.

Despite Mayhew's earlier claim to having a full house, she was the only guest staying in the lodge. Her simple room had natural wood walls, an old metal-frame bed, and a dresser, and it projected a look of seedy comfort. A second door opened onto a screened-in porch that offered a view of the water through the palmettos. Gamay put her duffel on the bed.

"Happy hour starts in the Dollar Bar at five," Mayhew said. "Make yourself at home. If you'd like to take a stroll, there are nature trails all over the island. A few areas have been restricted to avoid contamination from the outside world, but they are clearly marked."

Mayhew bounded off with his bouncy Reebok stride. Gamay flipped open her cell phone, to let Paul know she had arrived, only to remember that Dooley said the only place with service was the water tower.

She followed a crushed-shell pathway past a row of neat cabins to the foot of the tower. After climbing to a platform at the top, she got a signal, but then she hesitated. Paul was most likely in a seminar, and she didn't dare interrupt him again. She tucked the phone in her pocket.

She took in the view from the tower. The long, narrow island was shaped like a deformed pear. It was one of a group of mangrove islands whose rough texture looked like scatter rugs when seen from the air.

Gamay climbed down from the tower, working up a good sweat in the humidity with little exertion, and walked until she came to a tangle of mangroves where the trail ended. Turning around, she explored the island's network of trails before returning to her room. After a refreshing catnap, she took a shower, and was patting her body dry when she heard laughter. Happy hour had started.

Slipping into white shorts and a pale green cotton blouse that complemented her dark red hair, now twisted up on the back of her head, she made her way to the Dollar Bar. About a dozen people in lab coats were sitting at the bar or around tables. The conversation came to a near stop as she entered, like a scene in an old Western where the gunslinger pushes through the swinging doors into the saloon.

Dr. Mayhew got up from a corner table, came over to the bar, and greeted Gamay with his quick smile.

"What can I get you to drink, Dr. Trout?" he asked.

"A Gibson would be fine," she replied.

"Straight up or on the rocks?"

"Straight up, please."

Mayhew relayed the order to the bartender, a well-muscled young man with a military-style brush cut. He shook the gin, poured, and put three onions on a toothpick, making it a Gibson martini instead of a martini with olives.

Mayhew guided Gamay and her drink back to a corner table. Pulling out a chair, he introduced her to the four people seated around the table, explaining that they were all part of the center's development team.

The lone female at the table had short hair, and her pretty face was more boyish than feminine. Dory Bennett introduced herself, and said she was a toxicologist. She was drinking a tall mai tai.

"What brings you to the Island of Dr. Moreau?" asked the woman.

"I heard about this wonderful bar." Gamay glanced around at the practically bare walls, and with a straight face added, "It seems that a dollar doesn't go as far as it used to."

There was a ripple of laughter around the table.

"Ah, a woman scientist with a sense of humor," said Isaac Klein, a chemist.

"Dr. Klein, are you saying I don't have a sense of humor?" Dr. Bennett asked. "I find your scientific papers *very* funny."

The good-natured ribbing drew another round of laughter.

Dr. Mayhew said, "Dr. Bennett forgot to mention that the center's assistant director is a woman as well: Lois Mitchell."

"Will I get to meet her?" Gamay asked.

"Not until she gets back from—" Dr. Bennett caught herself midsentence. "She's away . . . in the field."

"Lois is working with Dr. Kane," Mayhew said. "When she's here, the island is not as male dominated as might appear at first glance."

Gamay pretended she hadn't seen Mayhew gently nudge Bennett's arm and looked around at the other tables in the room.

"Is this the lab's entire staff?" she asked.

"This is a skeleton crew," Mayhew said. "Most of our colleagues are working in the field."

"It must be a very large field," she said in a lame attempt at humor.

There was deafening silence.

Finally, Mayhew showed his teeth.

"Yes, I suppose it is," he said.

He glanced around at the others, who took his comment as a signal to force grins on their faces.

Gamay had the feeling that they were all connected to one another with wires and that Mayhew had the switch in his hand.

"I met another woman on the dock," she said. "I believe her name was Dr. Lee."

"Oh, yes, Dr. Song Lee," Mayhew said. "I didn't count her because she's a visiting scientist and not regular staff. She's extremely shy, and even dines in her cabin by herself."

Chuck Hallum, who headed the immunology section, said,

"She's Harvard educated, and one of the most brilliant immunologists I've ever met. Speaking of off islanders, what *really* brings you to Bonefish Key?"

"My interest in marine biology," Gamay said. "I've read in the scientific journals about the groundbreaking work you've been doing in biomedicine. I was planning to visit friends in Tampa and couldn't pass up the opportunity to take a firsthand look."

"Are you familiar with the history of the marine center?" asked Mayhew.

"I understand that you're a nonprofit funded by a foundation, but I don't know much beyond that," Gamay said.

Mayhew nodded. "When Dr. Kane started the lab, his initial funding came from the bequest of a University of Florida alumna who had lost a close relative to disease. There were some legal challenges to the will from disgruntled family members, and the funding was about to dry up when he formed a foundation and started attracting money from other sources. Dr. Kane envisioned Bonefish Key as the ideal research center because it would be away from the hubbub of a busy university."

A bell rang to announce dinner, and they moved into the dining room, the bartender taking over as waiter. The meal prepared by the chef was fresh-caught redfish, with a pecan crust and seared to perfection, washed down with a delicate French sauvignon blanc. Conversation around the table was on the light side, with little talk about the work being done on the island.

After dinner, the scientists moved out onto the veranda and the patio. There was more chatter, almost none of it having to do with the lab. As darkness deepened, most drifted off to their cabins.

"We hit the sack early here," Mayhew explained, "and we're up with the sun. We close the bar, so there's not much action after ten o'clock."

Mayhew asked Gamay a few more polite questions about her work at NUMA, then excused himself and said he would see her at breakfast. Any remaining staff followed, leaving Gamay alone on the veranda to absorb the sights and sounds of the subtropical night.

Gamay decided to call Paul, and she followed the same path to the water tower that she had taken earlier. The crushed white shells glowed under the brilliant moon. She started up the tower, only to stop in midstep. A female voice was coming from the platform. Speaking in what sounded like Chinese.

The conversation ended after a minute or two, and Gamay heard soft footfalls descending. Gamay backed down the ladder and hid behind a palmetto. She watched Dr. Lee descend the ladder, then hurry off down the path.

Gamay followed the path to the cabins. All were dark except for one, and, as she watched, the light in its window went out. She stood there looking at the darkened cabin, wondering what Nancy Drew would do in a case like this.

She decided to go back to the water tower. There, she left a voice mail on Paul's phone, saying she had arrived safely, then headed back to her room.

She sat on her screened-in porch and tallied up the impressions of the few short hours she had spent on the island. Her natural powers of intuition had been honed by years as a scientific observer, first as a nautical archaeologist, then as a marine biologist.

She had picked up on Dooley's suggestion that there was more than meets the eye on Bonefish Key. The man who had mixed her drinks looked as if he had stepped out of the pages of *Soldier of Fortune* magazine. Then Mayhew and his people were laughingly clumsy in their attempts to be evasive whenever talk touched on Dr. Kane, the center's mysterious field project, and the whereabouts of the rest of the staff. She was intrigued, too, by the young Asian scientist who had given her the cold shoulder at the dock, and how Mayhew had conveniently forgotten to mention Dr. Song Lee. And how the other scientists avoided Gamay as if she were a leper.

Austin told her to look for anything *funny* on the island.

"How about *weird,* Kurt old boy?" she muttered to herself.

Based on Austin's standard, Bonefish Key should be a barrel of laughs. But as she sat in the darkness listening to the sounds of the night, Gamay was beginning to understand why Dooley hadn't smiled when he welcomed her to paradise.

CHAPTER 19

DETECTIVE-SUPERINTENDENT RANDOLPH'S GOOD-NATURED nonchalance was misleading. He seemed to be everywhere at once. He hovered over the forensic experts who photographed the crime scene and collected evidence, listened to the witness interviews for discrepancies, and went over the *Beebe* with a very large fine-tooth comb.

All he needed to complete the picture was a deerstalker hat and meerschaum pipe.

The detective-superintendent and his team worked late into the night before they took advantage of the temporary sleeping quarters that Gannon had arranged for them. The next day, at Randolph's request, the captain moved the ship closer to the Marine Police Service station on the mainland. The bodies were transported to the pathology lab for autopsies.

After Austin and Zavala gave their interviews, they cleaned up the bathysphere and inspected it for damage. Except for places where the paint had been scraped away from the unexpected plunge to the bottom of the sea, the doughty little diving bell had come through its ordeal in fine fashion.

Austin wished the same could be said for the Humongous. He supervised the removal of the wreckage by crane from the deck of the *Beebe* to a flatbed truck, then to a garage on the mainland.

Satisfied that this last piece of major physical evidence was in police hands, Detective-Superintendent Randolph thanked Gannon and his crew for their cooperation and said the ship was free to leave. He said he would handle the questions from the dozens of reporters who were swarming around the station now that word of the attack had leaked out.

Randolph gave Austin and Zavala a ride in his police car to the airport, where the NUMA jet they would travel on to Washington was parked. Zavala was an experienced pilot certified to fly small jets, and by late afternoon he was taxiing the plane up to a hangar at Reagan National Airport reserved for NUMA aircraft. Austin and Zavala then went their separate ways, agreeing to touch base the following day.

AUSTIN LIVED IN A converted Victorian boathouse, part of a larger estate that he bought when he commuted to CIA headquarters in nearby Langley. At the time, it was what the real-estate agents called a fixer-upper. It had reeked of mildew and old age, but its location on the banks of the Potomac River persuaded Austin to open his wallet and spend countless hours of his own fixing it up.

Following his usual ritual, Austin dropped his duffel bag in the front hall, went in the kitchen and grabbed a cold bottle of beer from the refrigerator, then walked out on the deck to fill his lungs with the damp-mud fragrance of the Potomac.

He tossed back the beer, then went into his study and plunked himself down in front of his computer. The study was an oasis for Austin. He likened himself to ship captains who grow sick of the sea and retire to Kansas or anyplace other than the ocean when their careers are over. The sea was a demanding mistress, and it was good to get away from her strong embrace. Except for a few paintings of ships by primitive artists and photos of his small fleet of boats, there was little in his house that would indicate his connection to the world's premier ocean-study agency.

The walls were taken up by bookshelves housing his collection of philosophy books. While he liked to read the old philosophers for their wisdom, their writings also provided the moral anchor that kept him from going adrift. The men on the *Beebe* were not the first he had killed. Nor, unfortunately, would they be the last.

Over the fireplace was a matched pair of dueling pistols, part of an extensive collection that he considered his main vice. While he admired the pistols for their technical innovations, they also reminded him of the role that chance plays in life-or-death situations.

He plucked a Miles Davis record from his equally extensive jazz collection and put it on the turntable. He sat back in his chair, listening to a couple of cuts from the seminal *Birth of the Cool,* then flexed his fingers and began typing. While the details were still fresh in his mind, he wanted to pound out a first draft of his report on the attack on the B3.

Shortly before midnight, Austin crawled into his bed high in the boathouse turret. He awoke refreshed around seven the next morning. He made a pot of Jamaican coffee and toasted a frozen bagel found in his pitifully empty refrigerator. Thus fortified, he returned to his report.

He made surprisingly few changes to it. After a quick review, he sent his words off on electronic wings to NUMA director Dirk Pitt.

Austin decided to reward his hard work with a row on the Potomac. Rowing was his main form of exercise when he was home and was largely responsible for packing even more muscle onto his broad shoulders. He dragged his lightweight racing shell from its rack under the boathouse.

As the slender shell skimmed over the river, his measured scull strokes and the beauty of the river quieted his mind. When he had cleared away the mental clutter—the sabotage of the B3, his fight with the AUV, the night raid on the *Beebe*—he was still left with an undeniable conclusion: somebody wanted Max Kane dead and would go to extreme lengths to make it happen.

After his row, Austin stowed the shell, showered off the sweat from his exertions, shaved, and called Paul Trout.

Trout told Austin that Gamay had left for Bonefish Key the day before. He had received a voice mail confirming her arrival but had yet to talk to her.

Austin then gave Trout a condensed version of his report of the attacks on the bathysphere.

"Now I know why you told Gamay that the dive was *memorable*," Trout said. "Where do we go from here?"

"I'm hopeful Gamay will turn up something on Doc Kane. He's our major lead right now. Joe and I will compare notes and figure out our next move."

Austin said he would keep Trout posted, and then he thawed out another bagel to make a tuna-fish sandwich. He ate the sandwich in his kitchen, wistfully reminiscing about the wonderful meals he had eaten in the world's capitals, when the phone trilled.

He checked the caller ID. Then he pushed the SPEAKER button, and said, "Hello, Joe, I was just about to call you."

Zavala got right to the point.

"Can you come over right away?" he asked.

"The Zavala black book has more women listed in it than the D.C. directory, so I know you're not lonely. What's going on?"

"I've got something I want to show you."

Austin couldn't miss the unmistakable note of excitement in Zavala's soft-spoken voice.

"I'll be over in an hour," Austin said.

At sea, Austin's typical work outfit was a Hawaiian shirt, shorts, and sandals. The switch from oceangoing to land creature always came as a shock. Shoes felt like vises attached to his feet, legs seemed imprisoned in tan cotton slacks, the collar of his blue dress shirt chafed. While he would slip on his navy blue linen blazer, he refused to wear a tie. It felt like a noose around his muscular neck.

Unlike Dirk Pitt, who collected cars and seemed to have one for every occasion, Austin put his passion into his antique dueling pistols and instead drove a turquoise-colored Jeep Cherokee from the NUMA motor pool.

Suburban traffic was piling up, but Austin knew the shortcuts, and slightly less than an hour after Joe's call he pulled up in front of a small building in Arlington.

At the front door of the former library, he punched the entry code into a keypad and stepped into the main living level. The space, which once had housed stacks, now looked like the interior of an adobe building in Santa Fe. The floors were dark red Mexican tile, the doorways arched, and niches in the whitewashed walls displayed colorful folk art that Zavala had collected on trips to his ancestral home in Morales. His father, a skilled carpenter, had made the beautifully carved furniture.

Austin called out Zavala's name.

"I'm down in Frankenstein's lab," Zavala yelled up from his

basement, where he spent his spare time when he wasn't tinkering with his Corvette.

Austin descended the stairs to the brightly lit workshop. Zavala had utilized every square inch of the former book-storage room for his gleaming collection of lathes, drills, and milling machines. Odd-shaped metal parts whose functions were known only to Zavala hung from the walls next to black-and-white poster engravings of old engines.

Mounted in glass cases were scale models of the cutting-edge underwater vehicles Zavala had designed for NUMA. A Stuart model steam engine he was restoring sat on a table. Zavala never hesitated to get his hands greasy when it came to tinkering with mechanical contrivances or creating new ones, but today he was facing a computer screen with his back to Austin.

Austin glanced around at the bewildering shrine Zavala had established to moving parts.

"Ever think of continuing where Dr. Frankenstein left off?" he asked.

Zavala spun in his chair, his lips cracked in their usual slight smile.

"Making monsters out of junk parts is ancient history, Kurt. Robotics is where it's at. Isn't that right, Juri?"

A Tyrannosaurus rex, around ten inches high, with plastic skin the color and texture of an avocado, stood next to the computer. It waggled its head, shuffled its feet, rolled its eyes, opened its toothy mouth, and said, *"Sí, Señor Zavala."*

Austin pulled up a stool.

"Who's your green friend?"

"Juri, short for Jurassic Park. Got the little guy over the Internet. He's programmed for about twenty functions. I tinkered with his innards to make him speak Spanish."

"A bilingual T-Rex," Austin said. "I'm impressed."

"It wasn't that difficult," Zavala said. "His circuits are relatively simple. He can move and bite, and he can respond to external stimuli. Give him a little more muscle, bigger teeth, optical sensors, put him in a waterproof jacket, and you have something like the mechanical shark that thought an Austinburger would make a tasty snack."

Zavala wheeled his chair aside to give Austin a clear view of his monitor. Floating in a slow rotation against a black background was a three-dimensional neon-blue image of the manta-ray AUV that had cut the bathysphere cable and attacked Austin.

Austin let out a low whistle.

"That's *it*. Where did you find this thing?"

"I went back to the original video from the Hardsuit camera."

Zavala clicked his mouse to replay the skirmish with the AUV. There was a quick succession of images, a confusion of bubbles, and glimpses of the vehicle.

"I didn't give you much to go on," Austin said.

"You gave me enough. I slowed the action and culled details here and there. I used those bits to create a rough outline of the AUV and then compared it with the automated underwater vehicles in my database. I've got info on practically everything self-propelled ever made, but at first I couldn't find this one anywhere."

"My first impression was that it resembled the Manta, the sub that the Navy developed for mine detection and destruction."

"Not a bad call," Zavala said. "Here's the Manta. There are some of the same features that you get when you have a computer-generated design. But your guy didn't have the launching pads for mini mine sniffers and torpedoes like the Navy's model."

"Good thing. Neither one of us would be here if our little friend had been armed with the hard stuff."

"After I breezed through military models, I went to scientific applications. Most of the AUVs I found are torpedo-shaped, like Woods Hole Oceanographic's ABE or Scripps's Rover. After ruling out military and scientific, I looked to industry. But oil, gas, and communications didn't pan out, so I tried commercial fishing."

He called up an article from a commercial-fishing magazine.

Austin looked at the photos with the article and smiled.

"Jackpot," he said.

"The vehicle in the magazine piece is used to film experimental fishnet designs," Zavala said.

"That would account for the manta shape," Austin noted. "You'd need something flat and smooth to get under the nets, no projecting fins that might catch."

"The pincers allow the AUV to cut its way through tangled nets," Zavala said. "It was used by a Chinese company, Pyramid Seafood Exports."

"Chinese? That's significant. The men who attacked the ship were Asian. The weapons they carried were Chinese."

"I Googled the name," Zavala said. "Pyramid is headquartered in Shanghai, but they're a global company."

Austin said, "Why would a legitimate fishing company be involved in the attacks on the *Beebe* and the bathysphere?"

"I may be able to answer that question after seeing my friend Caitlin Lyons at the FBI's Asian Crime Unit later today," Zavala said.

Austin had to admit that Zavala's wide network of women friends sometimes came in handy.

"Have you figured out how the attack on the B3 may have been set up?" Austin said.

"The vehicle could have been launched from any of the press and party boats watching the dive," Zavala said.

"Maybe someone saw the launch," Austin said. "We could get Detective-Superintendent Randolph and the Bermuda Coast Guard to ask around."

"That's not a bad idea, but my guess is that the vehicle went into the water hours before the bathysphere dive and was put into a sleep mode, programmed to wake up after a certain time to begin the hunt. It could have been directed from the surface, in the general area of the *Beebe*."

"How would it have picked its target?"

"Sonar combined with the optical sensors would look for a vertical line. The AUV homes in on the B3's tether. *Snip-snip*. There goes the bathysphere."

"And there goes Doc Kane and the mysterious research project that was going to affect everybody on the planet."

"Any word from Kane since he took off into the wide blue yonder?" Zavala asked.

"I've tried a number of official and nonofficial channels," Austin answered. "Bonefish Key may be our only lead."

"Doubt he's there. Somebody wanted him to die a horrible death at the bottom. Bonefish Key would be the first place to look after finding out he wasn't on the *Beebe*."

A look of alarm crossed Austin's tanned face.

He dug his cell phone out of a pocket and called Paul Trout.

"Have you heard from Gamay?" he asked.

"I've been trying to reach her but my calls won't go through," Trout said.

"Keep trying," Austin said. "I'm at Zavala's place. I may have been too casual when I asked you to poke around Kane's lab. Gamay should be alerted to possible danger from the people who wanted to take down Kane."

Trout said, "Don't worry, Kurt, Gamay can take care of herself."

"I know she can," Austin said. "Just tell her to be careful and not take any chances."

HAVING DONE ALL HE could to warn the Trouts, Austin put in a call to NUMA and asked for a dossier on the Pyramid Trading Company. The agency's computer center, under the supervision of cybergenius Hiram Yeager, was one of the greatest repositories of specialized information in the world. The powerful computers at NUMA were linked with databases around the world and in an instant could churn out reams of information on any subject having to do with the world's oceans.

Austin said he would talk to Zavala after he'd studied the results of the computer search. He got back in his Jeep and drove to the thirty-story green-glass tower, overlooking the Potomac, that housed NUMA's headquarters. He parked in the underground garage and took the elevator up to his Spartanly furnished office.

A thick file was sitting on his desk with a note from Yeager telling him to "Enjoy!"

He opened the file, but had only made it past the first page when his telephone buzzed. Caller ID couldn't identify the number.

He realized why after he picked up the receiver and heard the crisp voice of James Sandecker, the founder and longtime director of NUMA before being appointed Vice President of the

United States when the elected second-in-command died. As was his usual style, Sandecker got right to the point.

"Pitt forwarded your report on the B3 incident to me. What in blazes is going on, Kurt?"

Austin could imagine Sandecker's crackling blue eyes and flaming red Vandyke beard, fixtures around NUMA for years.

"I wish I knew, Admiral," Austin said, using Sandecker's hard-earned Navy title over his more recent political one.

"How is Zavala faring after his ordeal?"

"Joe's fine, Admiral."

"That's fortunate. If Zavala had bought the farm, half the female population of Washington would go into mourning and we'd have to shut down the whole damned town . . . Then this attack on the *Beebe* . . . *Shocking*. It was a miracle no one was hurt. Are you making any progress?"

"We think there's a Chinese connection," Austin said. "The AUV that went after me and the B3 is the same model used by a Chinese fishing company that's part of a multinational called Pyramid Trading. The men who attacked the ship carried Chinese weapons and were Asian. Joe will chase down any possible criminal connection. I'll check with the Bermuda police to see if their forensics turned up anything we can use. We think Doc Kane's research may hold the key to everything. Gamay is on Bonefish Key checking out the lab."

Sandecker chuckled.

"I don't know how Gamay wangled her way in, but she's not likely to learn a thing. The work they're doing is highly classified."

"Sounds like you know what the lab is up to."

"More than I'd like. This is part of something very big, Kurt, and we'll have to move quickly. The situation is reaching critical mass. I'm setting up a meeting that will explain things. I'll call you in about an hour, so stand by. In the meantime, pack your bags for a trip."

"I still haven't unpacked from my last assignment."

"That's good. You and Joe will have to move out on short notice. I'm still working out the details, don't have time to get into it now. Don't ever let anyone tell you the job of Veep is as worthless as a bucket of warm spit."

Sandecker hung up without another word. Austin stared at the phone in his hand.

He pushed speculative thoughts aside and soon was engrossed in the file on his desk. It didn't take him very long to learn that Pyramid was no ordinary corporation.

CHAPTER 20

GAMAY HAD BEEN AWAKENED EARLIER THAT DAY BY THE thin shafts of sunlight filtering through the louvered windows. She slipped out of bed and pulled on her running shorts, sport top, and shoes. Quietly exiting through the screened-in porch, she did a series of warm-up exercises, walked around the back of the lodge to the start of a trail, and began a slow jog that gradually accelerated into a steady rhythm.

Feet crunching on the shell pathway, Gamay ran with an athletic grace, using a loose-boned economy of motion that assured that, if she were ever reincarnated, she'd come back as a cheetah. She ran every morning, a habit that went back to her tomboy days, hanging out on the streets of Racine with a gang of boys.

Gamay heard footfalls and turned to see Dr. Mayhew coming up from behind.

He caught up with Gamay and ran beside her.

"Good morning, Dr. Trout!" he exhaled. "Enjoying your run?"

"Yes, very much, thank you."

"Good." He clicked on his quick smile. "See you at break-fast."

Mayhew stepped up his pace and continued past Gamay until he disappeared around a corner.

The legendary Florida humidity soon nudged the coolness of early morning aside, and Gamay returned to her room drenched in perspiration. She showered and dressed in a fresh pair of shorts, a tank top, and sandals, and she followed the sound of voices to the dining room.

Dr. Mayhew waved Gamay over to join the group she had met the previous night and pointed to an empty chair. The consensus at the table was in favor of the brie-and-tomato omelet. It was cooked to perfection, and served with homemade oatmeal bread.

Noting Gamay's gusto, Mayhew said, "The cooking here is one of the perks we insisted upon before marooning ourselves on Bonefish Key."

He drained the rest of his coffee mug and dabbed his mouth with a napkin. Then he reached under his chair and handed Gamay a plastic bag with a clean lab coat in it.

"Ready for the tour, Dr. Trout?"

Gamay rose and buttoned herself into the coat.

"Anytime you are, Dr. Mayhew."

He replied with the inevitable switched-on smile.

"Follow me," he said.

They took an unmarked shell path in a direction opposite that of the nature trail and came upon a one-story cinder-block building painted a light mossy green. The air vibrated with the hum of unseen electric motors.

"Resource cultivation is done in this building," Mayhew said. "It may look like a garage, but this lab is on the leading edge of biomedical research."

The dimly lit building housed dozens of large, lighted fish tanks. A couple of white-coated technicians armed with clipboards moved from tank to tank. They paid no attention to the newcomers, except for a casual wave. The air was heavy with a wet, fishy smell.

"These seawater tanks are precisely maintained to duplicate exactly the habitat of the marine organisms they contain," Mayhew explained.

"How many different organisms are you researching?" Gamay asked.

"Dozens of species and subspecies. Let me show you the current reigning star of the show."

Mayhew went over to a tank that housed several vibrantly colored red blobs, each about the size of a grapefruit. Short, pointed tentacles surrounded their mouths. They festooned the rocks inside the tanks.

"Lovely," she said. "This must be the sea flower that I read about it in the scientific journals."

"The staff likes to give common names to the creatures," Mayhew said. "Saves wrapping our tongues around Latin locutions. There's the sea star and the sea blossom, and so on. Ironic, when you realize that these exquisite creatures are efficient killing machines superbly engineered to attract small fish close enough to sting and devour."

"There's another irony," Gamay said. "Despite being poisonous, they may be able to cure disease."

"Killing and curing aren't mutually exclusive. Curare is a good poison that's used in medicine. Botox too."

"Tell me about the sea star, Dr. Mayhew."

"*Gladly.* That little beauty is related to another sponge discovered in 1984. Harbor Branch Oceanographic was diving off Bermuda in the Sea-Link submersible. They found a piece of sponge in the sub's suction tube. The sponge contained a chemical that in lab tests killed cancer cells."

"I read about that in the scientific journals. An exciting discovery," she said.

Mayhew nodded.

"And frustrating as well," he said.

"In what way, Dr. Mayhew?"

"Scientists searched for another twenty years for a whole sponge without success. Then someone had a brainstorm: why not dive deeper and find the sponge's true habitat? On the first dive, they found enough sponges to support *years* of research. The scientists had been looking for the sponge in places where other stuff was growing. Their sponge grew at a depth of a thousand feet, where the bottom was practically bare."

"Did you use the same search procedure for the sea star?" Gamay asked.

"Essentially. We found fragments of an unknown specimen not far from the Harbor Branch dives, did a habitat profile, and, as that TV chef says, *Bam!* We found whole sponges that also contained the cancer-killing chemical."

"Does the star's potential live up to its beauty?" she asked.

"The Harbor Branch specimen produced a chemical dozens of times more potent than the most powerful drug. The star is almost twice that strong."

"Do I detect a note of smugness in your voice, Dr. Mayhew?"

The scientist widened his mouth in a smile that for once did not look pasted on his face.

"We've got a long slog ahead of us before we can license the chemical to a pharmaceutical company, which would take the compound through clinical tests. We have to find a way to produce the chemical in quantity. Harvesting sponges in the wild isn't feasible economically or ecologically."

"I'm sure you've looked into raising sponges through aquaculture," Gamay said.

"We're researching that possibility. Better still would be culturing the microorganisms that produce the chemical. That would support our ultimate goal of synthesizing the chemical for wider distribution." He shrugged. "First, we have to figure out how it works."

"You have your job cut out for you, Dr. Mayhew."

"True, but the potential rewards are mind-boggling. Ocean biomedicine is expected to be the greatest source of pharmaceuticals in the future."

Gamay cast her eyes around the lab.

"What's in the other tanks?" she asked.

"More sponges, different varieties. Each specimen has its own chemical characteristics. We're looking at cures for a host of human ailments. For instance, we've got corals that produce potential antibacterial and antiviral agents, and painkillers many times more powerful than morphine but without addictive qualities. The possibilities are endless."

Mayhew attempted to move the tour along.

"I'm a bit puzzled," Gamay said, subtly resisting the push of his guiding hand. "I'm sure I read on your website that you were doing research on other invertebrates. I haven't seen any species of Cnidaria."

The question seemed to catch Mayhew by surprise. He dropped his hand from her elbow and glanced reflexively at the door to a walled-off section of the lab.

"Jellyfish? Well . . ."

Mayhew may have been an accomplished scientist, but he was

an amateur at cloak-and-dagger. Gamay's eyes followed the direction of his revealing glance, and she gave him her most charming smile. Taking him by the arm, she urged him toward the door.

"I'll bet you forgot," she said.

"It's not that," he said. "It's . . . We don't like to disturb them." He was folding under her unrelenting gaze. "Well, I suppose it won't do any harm."

He opened the door and ushered Gamay into a room that was dark except for the light emanating from a tall, cylindrical transparent plastic tank four feet across and eight feet high.

The light came from a dozen or so jellyfish, each about the size of a cabbage, that glowed with pulsating blue lights. They were in constant motion, moving from the bottom to the top of the tank in a graceful, hypnotic underwater dance.

A figure on a ladder, bending over the top of the tank, turned toward their interruption. The unearthly light revealed the face of Dr. Bennett, the toxicologist. She opened her mouth in surprise.

"Dr. Mayhew, I didn't expect—"

"I leaned on Dr. Mayhew to show me this part of the lab," Gamay explained. "I hope I'm not disturbing you."

Bennett glanced at Mayhew, who gave her a nod.

"Not at all," Bennett said with a halfhearted smile. She brandished the long-handled dip net in her hands. "This procedure can be a little tricky at times."

Gamay's eyes took in Bennett's protective gloves and clear plastic face mask and coverall, and then she shifted her gaze back to the undulating, vaguely cube-shaped forms and their strange acrobatic ballet. Threadlike tentacles were attached to lacy fringe that rimmed each diaphanous creature. Their bioluminescence was almost bright enough to read a book by.

"In all my years of diving," Gamay said, "I don't think I have ever seen anything this beautiful."

"Or as deadly," added Mayhew, who had come up behind her. "The medusae in this tank produce a toxin that would put a cobra to shame."

Gamay dug into her memory.

"This is a box jellyfish, isn't it?" she asked.

"That's right. Chironex fleckeri, the sea wasp. There have been almost one hundred recorded deaths from its sting, which can kill a human being in under three minutes. I suggest that we stand back and give Dr. Bennett some room."

Dr. Bennett pulled the mask over her face and dipped the net in the tank.

To Gamay's surprise, the jellyfish didn't shy away from the net but clustered closer to it, making it easy to snag one and transfer it to a beaker. In the process, the color of the jellyfish deepened and the pulsating became more frequent, as if they were agitated.

"I've never seen jellyfish act in that fashion before," she said. "They'll usually try to avoid any threat they perceive."

"Jellyfish are predators," Mayhew said, "but most species simply drift around, encountering their meals quite by chance. The eye in jellyfish is more acutely developed, which means it can *see* rather than sense its prey. Combined with its jet-propulsion capabilities, a jellyfish actually can chase down its intended meal."

Slowly shaking her head, Gamay said, "I'm not sure I understand. You said 'most species.' Didn't you say these were box jellyfish?"

Dr. Mayhew realized that he had said more than he had intended.

"I misspoke a moment ago," he said. "Actually, it's closely related to the sea wasp, but more highly developed and aggressive."

"I've never seen a sea wasp quite that color," she said.

"Nor I. We came up with all sorts of fanciful names before settling on blue medusa."

"What is their potential pharmaceutically?"

"We're in the early stages of study, but the chemical it produces is far more complex than anything we've encountered. Experimenting with this delicate creature is like riding an untamed stallion."

"Fascinating," Gamay said.

Mayhew glanced at his watch.

"Thank you, Dr. Bennett," he said. "We'll leave you alone now with your poisonous friends."

Gamay offered no resistance as Mayhew guided her out of the room and back into the main lab. He showed her some other species under study, then they left the resource-cultivation building and walked a short distance to another cinder-block structure.

This lab had fewer tanks than the first one. Ocean scientists like to distinguish between *wet* labs, where specimens are housed and prepared, and *dry* labs, where computers and sensitive analytical instruments are kept. This was both, Mayhew explained. The wet part was where chemicals were extracted and placed with bacteria or viruses to see what the reaction might be.

They spent more time in this lab than the first one, and by the time Gamay was out of questions it was nearly midday.

"I'm as hungry as a horse," Mayhew said. "Let's break for lunch."

The kitchen served up gourmet-quality hamburgers. Mayhew chatted nonstop about nothing in particular, and Gamay figured he was just stretching things out. After their long break, the tour continued to a third building, which contained almost all computers and no tanks.

Mayhew said the computers were matching chemicals to diseases faster than could be done by human beings. Gamay glimpsed Dr. Song Lee. Her eyes were glued to a computer.

The tour was over by midafternoon. Mayhew seemed relaxed for the first time since Gamay had met him. He excused himself, and asked if Gamay would mind if he didn't accompany her back to the lodge.

"Not at all," she said. "See you at happy hour."

As she left the lab building area, Gamay felt as if she had been given the bum's rush. Since setting foot on the island, she had been wined, dined, zipped through a packaged tour, and prepped to be sent on her way in the morning.

Mayhew had been correct to fear the attention of a trained observer. She might have passed off his close attention to her every move as a clumsy attempt at hospitality, but there was no doubt that he had tried a verbal bait and switch concerning the jellyfish tank's occupants.

Gamay had easily seen through Mayhew's smoke screen. The collegial little research group was a façade. No amount of barroom cheer could hide the fact that the island was a secretive, hermetically sealed, pressurized environment. People laughed too hard, or, in the case of Mayhew, switched on his phony jawbreaker smile.

GAMAY MADE HER WAY to the dock to get some fresh air. Dooley Greene was painting a skiff. He saw her approaching and removed the cigar stub from his mouth.

"'Afternoon, Dr. Gamay. Dr. Mayhew give you a good tour of the labs?"

"It was short but interesting," she said, keeping a poker face.

Dooley picked up on the unenthusiastic response.

"Thought so," he said with his jack-o'-lantern grin.

"I saw Dr. Song Lee in one of the labs," she said. "Doesn't she go kayaking every afternoon about this time?"

Dooley nodded. "Like clockwork. She'll go out later on."

Gamay pointed to the kayak rack.

"Could I borrow one of those, Dooley? I've got a few hours, and thought it might be nice to explore the mangroves."

Dooley plunked his paintbrush into a can of turpentine.

"I'd be glad to show you around in my boat, Dr. Gamay. You'll see a lot more and save yourself some paddling."

Having nothing else to occupy her time, Gamay got into Dooley's boat. He headed away from the dock, and, once clear of the island, goosed the throttle. The double hulls cut through the flat water like scissors through silk. Within minutes, they entered a small bay enclosed by mangroves.

Dooley stood at the steering console, dead cigar clenched between his teeth. Squinting because of the sun's reflection off the calm waters, he kept the boat pointed toward an old wooden cabin cruiser that lay off the tip of a mangrove island. The cruiser sat at an angle, with its stern in the water. The glass in the windows was missing, and there was a hole in the rotting wooden hull at the waterline that was big enough for a man to swim through.

"Hurricane pushed that wreck up onto an oyster bar," Dooley said, slowing the boat to a fast walk. "Makes a good navigation point when you're cruising around the mangroves. It can get confusing out here at times, even with a GPS and compass."

The boat had gone past the tip of Bonefish Key, a long, tapering point shaped like a shirttail. The marine center dock was no longer visible, and palmettos obscured the water tower. The low, monotonous islands offered no outstanding features that could be used as reference points, and perspective constantly changed.

"You must know these waters like the back of your hand," Gamay said.

Dooley squinted at the sun-dappled water.

"It all looks the same, but you get so you can pick out little details that most people wouldn't see." He opened a storage box and pointed to a pair of goggles. "I cheat when I go out fishing at night," he said with a smirk. "Got these night vision gogs over the Internet. Got some spare ones back at the boathouse."

"Where does Dr. Lee go kayaking?"

"She paddles down the back side of the barrier beach. Lots of birds there. I'll show you."

Dooley headed between two mangroves. The passage narrowed, funneling them to a dead end. Dooley brought the boat to a halt and handed Gamay a pair of binoculars. She raised them to her eyes and saw dozens of snowy egrets and great blue herons wading in the shallows, looking for food.

Dooley pointed to a wooden stake that stuck out of the water a few feet from the shore.

"That marks a path that leads across the island. Only a few hundred yards, and there's good surf fishing on the other side."

Dooley powered up the outboard motor, and they sped out of the V-shaped cove and toward the wrecked boat. He made a sharp turn and headed back toward Bonefish Key. The water tower popped into view, and minutes later Dooley cut speed and expertly brought them alongside the dock. Gamay tied the boat off with a few turns of the bow and stern lines. She thanked Dooley and borrowed a chart of local waters, saying she wanted to see where they had been.

She passed Dr. Lee, who was on her way for her daily kayak paddle. Gamay said hello, and got the same polite reception as the first time they met.

She then stood at the top of the hill overlooking the marina and watched Lee until she paddled around a bend.

When Gamay looked past the superficial beauty of the island, she saw that it had a beaten aspect to it. The mangroves were half dead, and even the high ground had never dried out after the hurricane, producing rank decay that overpowered the flowers and hung over the island in an invisible miasma.

She wrinkled her nose.

This place stinks in more ways than one, she thought.

CHAPTER 21

JOE ZAVALA SAT BEHIND THE WHEEL OF HIS 1961 CHEVRO-let Corvette, cruising along Interstate 95 to Quantico, Virginia, at a safe ten miles over the speed limit. The convertible top was down, the powerful V-8 engine under the hood purred like a contented tiger, a CD of Ana Gabriel was playing, the wind was blowing in his dark brown hair, he was on the NUMA payroll, and he was about to meet a beautiful woman. Life was sweet.

Around forty miles southwest of Washington, he turned off the highway onto a tree-shaded road and drove through coun-tryside that first offered glimpses of military vehicles and struc-tures, then led to a checkpoint manned by an armed guard. He showed the guard his NUMA credentials, had his name matched against a visitors' list, and followed the signs to the main building of the FBI Academy.

Surrounded by three hundred eighty-five acres of woods, the Academy was built on the Marine Corps base in the 1970s under the reign of J. Edgar Hoover. The campus-style complex consisted of twenty-one buildings of a soothing honey color connected by a network of glass-enclosed corridors.

Zavala went through the front entrance of the main building and walked past a bubbling fountain into the atrium lobby. He checked in at the reception desk, and said he had an appointment with Agent Caitlin Lyons. He was given a security badge with his name on it to wear. A young woman was assigned to guide him through the maze of buildings and corridors.

He heard a commotion that sounded like a gunfight at the O.K. Corral and knew that he was near the shooting range. The guide ushered him in and pointed to a row of booths.

"Number ten," she said. "I'll wait outside for you. Gets a little noisy in here. Take your time."

Zavala nodded his thanks, and took some ear protectors from an attendant. Then he went over to a booth and stood behind a woman who was firing at a silhouette of a man. She stood with her pistol in both hands, slowly and methodically pumping bullets into the target, hitting it in spots that would have proved fatal had the bullets been perforating human flesh instead of paper.

Zavala had no desire to startle a trained FBI agent while she had a gun in her hand. He stood behind her patiently until she turned and saw him. She beckoned for him to step into the booth. She replaced the spent magazine with a full one, handed him the pistol, and pointed toward the target.

The Walther PPK was a favorite of Zavala's, and the grip felt comfortable in his hand. He raised it to eye level, flicked the safety off, and let off six shots in rapid succession. Every squeeze of the trigger found the center circle of the bull's-eye over the heart.

He flicked the safety back on and handed the gun back to the woman. She pressed a button that brought the target to the front of the booth. She stuck her finger through one of the holes Zavala's bullets had made and said something he couldn't hear. He removed his ear protectors, and she said it again.

"*Show-off.*"

She placed the pistol in a hip holster and pointed to her wristwatch. They made their way to the door, first dropping off their ear protectors. The guide was waiting in the hallway, but Caitlin said she would show Zavala to the lobby when their meeting was over.

"Let's go for a walk," she said.

They strolled along a shady path that was a world away from the sound of gunfire and the smell of cordite in the shooting range.

Caitlin Lyons was an attractive woman in her thirties, and if she hadn't been wearing black, short-sleeved coveralls with a sidearm on her belt she could have passed for a member of Celtic Women, the musical ensemble. She had a peaches-and-cream complexion, and the brows over her remarkable blue-green eyes were high and arched. Her dark blond hair was tucked under a black baseball cap with FBI on the front.

"Not bad shooting, Joe. Ever think of joining the FBI?"

"As soon as they have a navy," Zavala said.

Caitlin laughed. "You were very brave to come up to me when I had a gun in my hand."

"Should I have been worried?"

"You know what they say about a woman scorned . . ."

Zavala winced. His dark good looks and unassuming manner made him popular with many women around Washington. He had gone out with Caitlin, but their budding romance was interrupted by a mission for the Special Assignments Team. He had not gotten back to her until now.

"*Scorned* is an ugly word, Cate. I was planning to get in touch with you after my last job."

"How about *abandoned*, then? Jilted? Left in the lurch. Forsaken." She saw the distress on his face. "Don't worry, Joe," she said with a smile, "I'm not angry at you for leaving me to run off on another NUMA mission. I'm a cop, I might have done the same. And I wasn't looking for anything permanent anyhow. The FBI is as demanding as NUMA. Besides, if I need you, all I have to do is turn on the TV and I'll see those Latin good looks. I watched the bathysphere dive. Very exciting."

"The most exciting part was what you *didn't* see."

Caitlin gave him a quizzical look, and he pointed to a park bench alongside the walkway. They sat down, and Zavala told her about the attack on the bathysphere, Austin's close call, and the connection to the Pyramid Trading Company. When he was done talking, she took his hand and squeezed it.

"You're a cad and a bounder, Joe, but I would have been devastated if anything had happened to you." She gave him a peck on the cheek. "Now, how can I be of help in solving an ocean crime? As you pointed out, I'm a landlubber."

"You're also an expert on Asian crime, which I'm not."

Zavala described the triangular mark Austin had discovered on the AUV's blade and the connection between the underwater robot that attacked the bathysphere and the fishing company owned by Pyramid Trading.

She let out a low whistle.

"*Pyramid.* The baddest of the bad. You couldn't have chosen a worse bunch to tangle with, if that's the case. You and Kurt are damned lucky to be alive."

"What do you know about Pyramid?"

"Let me give you some perspective," Caitlin said. "My job is to keep Asian crime as far from U.S. shores as possible and to solve crimes when they do occur. It's a losing battle. We've had

Asian criminal enterprises in this country since the early 1900s, starting with the Chinese tongs."

"Didn't the tongs originate the term *hatchet man*?" Zavala asked.

"The hatchet men were the Chinese thugs who fought one another during the tong wars. The tongs started as social clubs but then became gangs. They are still thriving today as part of an international network that's dominated by the big criminal organizations known as Triads. That's why the triangle you described is so interesting."

"In what way?"

"The term *Triad* was coined by the British, who saw that the Chinese symbol for secret society was a triangle."

Zavala's eyes narrowed.

"You're right," he said, "that *is* interesting."

"The triangle symbolized the unity of heaven, earth, and man," Caitlin said. "Pyramid uses it as a trademark for its legitimate enterprises. But it's still involved with extortion, murder, prostitution, drugs, loan-sharking, and money laundering."

"The tried and true," Zavala said.

"It's also got a worldwide network of gangs in every city. The names all start with *Ghost*: the Ghost Devils, the Ghost Shadows, the Ghost Dragons. You get the picture. They do the dirty work: intimidation, enforcement, murder. They're ready to go at a moment's notice."

"What about the legal side?"

"The criminal stuff is the bedrock, but it has evolved into a nontraditional organization with foreign affiliates and legitimate businesses: manufacturing, real estate, movies, phamaceuticals. And, as you discovered, commercial fishing. Some of its divisions have gotten into trouble for producing contaminated, dangerous products."

"Does the Pyramid leadership have a human face?"

"Yes, as a matter of fact, it has *three*. The company is said to be run by a set of triplets."

"That's an unusual arrangement."

"Not when you consider the extent of their empire. Pyramid is like a country unto itself. It has a huge treasury, an army of thugs at its command, and a diplomatic corps that interacts with the Chinese government, which traditionally has supported the Triads. It has gangs in every major country, including the U.S. It's the biggest criminal organization in China, possibly in the world."

"How do you fight something like that?" Zavala asked.

"With great difficulty. Asian criminal groups are smart, rich, multilingual, and flexible. Advances in travel and communications have allowed them to operate on a global scale. We can make life tough for their street gangs and nibble around the edges of their financial empire, but they've been impervious up to now."

"What has changed?"

"They are up against the only enemy who could do them harm: the Chinese government. It's trying to put Pyramid out of business."

"Wait a second, didn't you say the government *supported* the Triads?"

"That's *history*. There's a huge gray area between what is legal and what is criminal in China. That's where the Triads operate. The government hadn't clamped down before this because the Triads produce money, keep order, and are patriotic."

"Why the sudden change of heart?"

"The Chinese military has been in business with the Triads

for years. Pyramid is particularly tight with the Army, giving it political muscle to defend its criminal interests, but the government is worried this cozy arrangement has given Pyramid too much power. They've put thousands of corrupt officials from the National People's Congress in jail, but they really began to push after the safety scandals. China lives on its exports. And anything that threatens them threatens the stability of the country and therefore its rulers.

"Tell me about the triplets," Zavala said.

"Not much *to* tell. Triads give their people numbers, according to rank rather than names. But they usually have someone to serve as their public face. Pyramid's front man is an immensely rich guy named Wen Lo. No one has ever seen the other two triplets. Triads are usually decentralized, but Pyramid has been strengthening its leadership, which also has the government worried." She paused. "Now it's my turn, Joe. Why would a Chinese Triad want to sabotage the bathysphere?"

"Kurt thinks they were after Dr. Kane because of a secret research project he was involved in. Does that sound plausible?"

"Anything is possible with this gang. What would you like me to do?"

"I was hoping you might poke around and see what you can dig up."

Caitlin cocked her head. "Not to be coy, but what can you offer me in return?"

"A ride in my 'Vette, a romantic dinner at an old inn in the Virginia countryside."

"Been there, done that, *señor.* Tell you what, Joe, if Pyramid is involved in *anything,* it's part of something very big. Pyramid doesn't do things in half measures."

"Would the government crackdown have anything to do with what we've talked about?"

"Possibly. Pyramid has reacted like a wounded snake since the purge began. They've killed cops, judges, and top officials as a warning to the government to keep its hands off, but I don't see the connection with your Dr. Kane."

"Neither do I. Can you help?"

"I'll put you in touch with Charlie Yoo. He's an agent that the Chinese security agency sent over to work with the FBI. He's a specialist in gangs. Pyramid made a mistake underestimating you and Kurt. But a few words of advice . . ."

"We always listen to advice from a pro, Cate."

Caitlin put her hand on her holster, a reflexive gesture, as if she sensed danger.

"That's good, Joe, because if I know Pyramid, you and Kurt are in their sights. And they won't miss a second time."

THOUSANDS OF MILES FROM Virginia, Pyramid Trading was also on the lips of Colonel Ming. The slender, soft-spoken man with the thick head of silver hair stood outside a dilapidated building in the slums of Shanghai. There had apparently been an attempt to burn the building, but the firefighters called in to keep the blaze from spreading to the nearby slums had nipped the fire in the bud.

The smoke still burned the colonel's eyes, even though he stood several hundred feet from the building. He didn't want the ash floating in the air to settle on his razor-creased Army uniform. Even if he had wished to get closer, he would have been prevented by the cordon of decontamination trucks and ring of armed police.

He turned to the Ministry of Health official, who had called him.

"I'm not sure why you asked me to come here," Ming said. "It appears that the city has the situation well in hand. There seems little need for crowd control by the military."

"This was no ordinary building and this was no ordinary fire," said the minister, whose name was Fong. "There were medical tests of some sort going on here."

"This seems an unlikely place for that sort of thing. Are you sure?"

Fong nodded.

"We found a number of people locked in cells," he said. "They had been left there to burn, but, fortunately, even though they were in poor condition, they were able to talk. They said they had been kidnapped, and that many people had been taken from their cells, never to return. We believe they were moved to labs, and, from the equipment we found, it seems they were the subjects of experiments."

"What kind of experiments, Fong?"

"We don't know specifically. But we did find traces of a virus strain that is of some concern to our ministry. It is the same virus that caused an outbreak in a village to the north. The person who caused that epidemic was from Shanghai."

"Quite the coincidence," said Ming.

"Even more, the person was employed in a security capacity by Pyramid Trading based here in the city. And, almost unbelievably, Pyramid owns this building."

"I think I know where you are going with this, Fong. It's well known that the Army operates a string of brothels in partnership with Pyramid. But there's no connection to this," he said with a wave of his hand.

"I understand that, Colonel, but perhaps you might want to reexamine your partnership when I tell you what else we found in the building: the remains of dozens of human beings, discovered in a crematory. We think they had been used in the experiments."

Ming's reaction was one of combined fear and revulsion, fear that his name had been linked to Pyramid, revulsion over the experiments.

He stared at the building, trying without success to imagine the horrors within its four walls.

"Thank you, Minister," he said. "I shall look into it and take the appropriate steps."

"I hope so," Fong said. "This is not good for China. Whoever is responsible must be brought to account, but it must be done quietly."

"I am in complete agreement with the need for discretion," Colonel Ming said. "And I think I know exactly where to begin."

CHAPTER 22

DOOLEY GREEN LOOKED UP FROM THE OUTBOARD MOTOR he'd been repairing at the end of the dock and his mouth widened in a gap-toothed grin when he saw the young Asian woman coming his way.

"Afternoon, Doctor," he said. "Going to take another crack at that pink bird?"

Dr. Lee tapped the zoom lens of the digital camera hanging from a strap around her neck.

"Yes, Dooley. You know how determined I am to get a photo of that beautiful roseate spoonbill."

"Spoonbills can be cagey all right," he said. "Kayak's waiting for you. I'll fetch your gear."

Dooley put his screwdriver down and got a kayak paddle and flotation vest from the boat shed. He and Lee walked along the beach to where a light blue fiberglass touring kayak sat on the sand with its bow partway in the water. Lee slipped her arms through the vest and snapped the buckles, then eased her slender body into the cockpit. Dooley handed her the paddle and pushed the craft into the water.

"I'll probably be back on the mainland by the time you get back, so just put your gear in the shed. Good luck with that spoonbill," Dooley called out. "And watch out for Granddaddy 'Gator."

Lee acknowledged the warning with an airy wave of the paddle.

"Thank you, Dooley. I'll keep an eye out for him."

The warning was a private joke. When Song Lee first arrived on Bonefish Key from China, Dooley told her about the monster alligator lurking in the mangroves. Seeing from her startled expression that she believed his tall tale, he had quickly explained that no alligator had been seen around Bonefish Key for decades.

Dooley watched Lee paddle the kayak to the mouth of the inlet and thought how fond he had become of the young Chinese scientist. He wasn't too old to appreciate her flowerlike beauty, but his interest was far from prurient. Lee was around thirty, the same age as a daughter who had disowned him years before. He had quit drinking, after running the family shrimp business aground on the shoals of gin, poker, and a series of wives, but he and his daughter were still estranged.

As Dooley went back to the outboard motor, Lee headed along the shore of the island and emerged from the mangroves into a small bay. She pointed the kayak's prow toward the stranded cabin cruiser, then left the bay and headed into the funnel-shaped cove Dooley had entered earlier that day on his tour with Gamay. Seeing a ripple on the water, Lee shipped her paddle and was rewarded a moment later when a shiny back scarred by propeller blades broke the surface.

Manatee!

She banged off some photos, until the lumbering mammal submerged to feed on the bottom. Lee took up her paddle again, heading farther into the cove. The distance between the mangroves diminished from a quarter of a mile to a couple hundred feet.

A great blue heron took off with a mighty flap of its long wings. Lee watched the big bird until it was out of sight, then she brought her binoculars to bear on a pair of snowy egrets wading in the shallows. Her heart skipped a beat at the flash of pink behind one of them.

The egrets moved, and she brought the camera up to her eye. Through the viewfinder, she saw a bird that looked like a flamingo with a duck bill. She snapped off several pictures of the roseate spoonbill, then reviewed the photos. They were all perfect. Lee was smiling when she took up her paddle again.

With a few strokes, she sent the kayak toward a weathered gray wooden post that stuck out of the water near the edge of a mangrove. It marked a narrow break in the otherwise impenetrable tangle of roots. The kayak's hull scraped an oyster bed and came to rest on shore.

Lee stepped into warm, knee-deep water. Although she knew that Dooley's giant alligator was a fable, she quickly hauled the kayak onto the narrow beach.

She grabbed a rucksack that held water and power bars and walked through a tunnel of trees for a hundred feet or so before she broke into an open area. A white sandy path wound through the cactus and shrub for a few hundred yards to the other side of the island.

A rush of air off the turquoise waters of the Gulf of Mexico cooled Lee's face as the path ended at a barrier beach. She strolled along the beach for a short distance and plunked down on the sand with her back against a sea-silvered driftwood log.

A blue-hulled fishing boat was anchored offshore just beyond the line of breakers. Otherwise, she had the beach to herself. She had seen the boat several times in the past week or so, but it had stayed a respectful distance away. She examined it through the zoom lens of her camera but saw no one on deck.

When she had first landed on Bonefish Key months before, Dr. Lee had been advised by Dr. Kane to find a distraction to take her mind off her work. Some scientists avoided burnout by fishing, others by playing chess or reading. A few spent too much time at the Dollar Bar. The daily kayak trips into the mangroves had been her salvation. The break she took each afternoon rejuvenated her, allowing her to work late into the night.

With the project nearly at an end, she would miss the remote beauty of the island when she returned to China. She wondered if her government would reward or even acknowledge her labors, or if she would just return to her country practice.

She gave in to her weariness and fell asleep. When she awoke, she glanced at her watch. She looked off along the beach and noticed that the blue-hulled boat had vanished. She frowned. She had regained her privacy, but it was time to go back to work. She got up, brushed the sand from her shorts, and headed across the island to her kayak.

When Lee broke through the tree canopy, she saw that the kayak was no longer where she had left it on the beach. She set her pack aside, waded out into the water, and visually searched the lagoon.

There was no sign of the kayak.

Lee turned back to the island, saw blue plastic gleaming in the grass, and let out a sigh of relief. The kayak had been pulled up into the tall grass on one side of the beach. She wondered why anyone would do such a thing and stepped into the grass to retrieve the kayak. It was a remote spot, and she felt uncomfortable knowing there was someone else on the island.

She was pulling the kayak back toward the water when she felt a prickling sensation that had nothing to do with the heat on the back of her neck. She turned and saw a man on the beach, his eyes hidden behind dark sunglasses.

He had soundlessly materialized from the scrub and now blocked Lee's way to the water. He was physically frightening. His hardened Asian features seemed to have been hammered on an anvil. His thin-lipped mouth looked as if it could not be pried into a smile with a crowbar. He wore shorts, and the muscles on his arms and legs appeared capable of driving his knuckles or clublike feet through a brick wall.

Making him even more formidable was the automatic weapon cradled in his arms. The muzzle was pointed at her heart.

Despite her fears, Song Lee managed to croak out a question.

"Who are you?" she said.

"I am the ghost who watches," he said with no change of expression.

What nonsense, Lee thought. The man was obviously deranged. She tried to assert control over the situation.

"Did you move my kayak?" she asked.

She thought she saw a slight nod of the chin.

"Then I'd appreciate your help in pulling it back to the water."

He smiled for the first time and lowered the gun. Thinking that maybe her bluff had worked, she turned to grab the kayak.

"Dr. Lee?"

Hearing her name called, she knew this was no random encounter. She saw a quick movement out of the corner of her eye as the man raised his gun above his head and brought it down stock first. She felt an explosion at the back of her skull, and saw a flash of white light before the darkness closed in, and she was unconscious before she crashed facedown into the mud.

CHAPTER 23

THE FBI's J. EDGAR HOOVER BUILDING HEADQUARTERS ON Pennsylvania Avenue is the antithesis of the bucolic, tree-shaded campus at Quantico. The hulking, seven-story structure was made of poured concrete, in the Brutalist architectural style made popular in the 1960s. The Hoover became even more fortresslike after the terrorist attack of 9/11. Tours for the public came to an end, and barriers were put up around the first floor.

Caitlin Lyons had called ahead, easing Zavala's entry into the FBI's inner sanctum. There was the visitor's badge, and the pleasant guide, a serious young man this time, who miraculously managed to navigate the labyrinth of the corridors without having to resort to map or GPS.

The guide stopped in front of an unmarked door and knocked softly. A voice on the other side of the door said to come in. Zavala thanked the guide, and opened it.

Inside was an office slightly bigger than the gray metal table and chairs it contained. There was nothing on the walls except a black-and-white photo of the Great Wall of China.

A man sat behind the desk talking on the phone in Chinese. He waved Zavala to a chair, continued chatting a minute, then ended the conversation and set the receiver back in its cradle. Popping up like a jack-in-the-box, he shook Zavala's hand as if trying to coax water from a reluctant pump, then settled back in his chair.

"Sorry to keep you waiting," he said. "I'm Charlie Yoo." He flashed a friendly smile. "Please, no jokes about the last name. I've heard enough '*Yoo*-hoo' and 'How's by *Yoo*' around here to last a lifetime."

Yoo was a pencil-thin man in his mid-thirties. He wore a stylishly cut shiny gray suit with a cobalt blue shirt and blue-and-red striped tie, a sartorial style more in keeping with a cocktail hour at the Willard Hotel than the bowels of the FBI, where conservative navy blue suits were the norm. Yoo spoke English with a New York accent, the sentences coming like bursts of photon energy.

"Nice to meet you, Agent Yoo. I'm Caitlin's friend, Joe Zavala."

"The man from NUMA . . . great organization, Joe. Please call me Charlie. Caitlin's a fantastic woman and a terrific cop. She said you were looking into the Pyramid Triad."

"That's right. She thought you might be able to help."

Yoo sat back in his chair and tented his fingers.

"Excuse me for asking, Joe, but NUMA is an underwater outfit, from what I've heard. Why would a guy from NUMA be interested in Chinese organized crime?"

"We wouldn't be, ordinarily. But someone tried to sabotage a NUMA operation, and we have circumstantial evidence that the seafood subsidiary of Pyramid Trading may have been involved."

Yoo hiked his eyebrows like Groucho Marx.

"Excuse me for being skeptical, Joe, but that doesn't seem like Pyramid's m.o. What's your evidence?"

"Let me fill in the background. A few days ago, NUMA launched the Bathysphere 3, a replica of a historical diving bell, in waters off Bermuda. The dive was broadcast all over the world . . . You may have seen it on television . . ."

Yoo spread his hands apart, his empty palms signifying no.

"I've been pretty busy, Joe. Haven't watched much TV. Is this the op that Pyramid supposedly tried to sabotage?"

Zavala nodded.

"I designed the diving bell," he said, "and Kurt Austin, my partner at NUMA, was the project leader. The most interesting part of the dive wasn't transmitted because an underwater robot cut the bathysphere's cable."

"*Whoa!*" Yoo said, a wide grin on his boyish face. "An underwater *robot*. That's pretty wild stuff, Joe."

"I thought so at the time. When the cable let go, the sphere was buried a half mile down in muck."

Yoo leaned forward across the desk. His grin had disappeared.

"You're not kidding, are you? That's an incredible story! How'd you get out of a situation like that?"

"Kurt made a rescue dive, and we were able to activate our flotation system. While we were on our way to the surface, the robot went after Austin. He beat the thing off of him and grabbed one of the pincers it had used to cut our cable. The pincer was stamped with a triangle identical to the Pyramid Trading logo."

Yoo shook his head.

"You had me going there for a minute. Sorry, Joe, but the triangle is a pretty common symbol. It could mean anything."

"I agree, Charlie, except for one thing. The robot is identical to one that Pyramid's seafood division uses to inspect nets."

"You know this for a fact?"

Zavala nodded.

"I know it for a fact, Charlie."

Zavala reached in his pocket and extracted a folded copy of the magazine article about the Pyramid seafood division's AUV, smoothing out the wrinkles on the desk. He put photos from Austin's Hardsuit camera next to it. Yoo read the article and studied the photos.

"*Wow!*" Yoo said. "Okay, you win . . . Pyramid tried to sabotage your dive. But why?"

"Haven't a clue. Which is why I went to see Caitlin. She said Pyramid Trading was the baddest of the bad when it came to Chinese Triads."

"Pyramid is definitely a major player. But it's one of hundreds of Triads based in cities around China. Did Caitlin tell you what I do?"

"She said you were a specialist in Chinese gangs around the world."

"I'm *more* than a specialist, I'm a former gang member. I'm from Hong Kong originally. My parents moved my family to New York."

"That accounts for the American accent," Zavala said.

"Learned English on the sidewalks of Mulberry Street. That's also where I joined the Ghost Shadows, one of the biggest gangs in the country."

"Caitlin said the Ghost Shadows is a Pyramid gang."

"That's right. My family saw what was going on and moved back to China to keep me out of the gangs. Pop had a bicycle-repair shop, and he kept me so busy I was too tired to get into trouble. I kept my nose clean, went to college. Now I'm part of a special unit from the Ministry of Security."

"How did you end up in Washington?" Zavala asked.

"Your guys needed my expertise. I'm over here for a few months sharing intel with the FBI. This is just a temporary office, as you've probably guessed."

"Caitlin said that Pyramid was bucking the old traditions, consolidating its power, and that's one of the reasons it's in hot water with the Chinese government. That, and the safety scandals over contaminated products."

"Caitlin's the expert on the Triads," Yoo said. "I'll go along with what she says."

"She also said that the front man for Pyramid is a guy named Wen Lo."

There was a slight tick, a second, when Yoo seemed to pause before answering.

"As I said," he began, "Caitlin knows more about the Triads. I'm familiar with organization and strong-arm stuff at the street level, but others can tell you about the leaders."

Yoo talked about gang ritual and power structure for another five minutes before glancing at his watch.

"Sorry to cut you short, Joe, I've got an appointment to keep."

"No problem," Zavala said. He rose from his chair. "Thanks very much for your time, Charlie. You've been a great help."

They shook hands, and Yoo called the security desk. They were standing out in the hallway when the guide arrived minutes later to take Zavala in tow.

Yoo flashed a smile.

"You've stirred up my curiosity about this thing with your robot stuff. Let me poke around and see if I can come up with anything else."

Yoo jotted down Zavala's cell-phone number and wished him good luck. He went back into his office and locked the door. He sat behind his desk, stone-faced, as he punched in a number on his cell. The cell's signal flashed around the world several times, passing through a series of filters and detours, until it was untraceable.

"Report, number thirty-nine," a gruff voice said.

"He just left," Yoo said.

"What does he know?"

"Far too much for comfort."

Yoo relayed the gist of his conversation with Zavala.

"This is a fortunate happenstance," the voice said. "Zavala is small fish. Use him as bait. I want you to take Austin alive and bring him to me."

"I'll get on it immediately," Yoo said.

"*Sooner,*" the voice said.

ZAVALA WAS in his Corvette on the way back to NUMA headquarters when his cell phone buzzed. It was Charlie Yoo.

"Hi, Joe, long time no talk. Look, I've got something for you on the Pyramid Triad."

"That was fast," Zavala said with genuine surprise. He had thought Yoo to be something of a lightweight when it came to police work.

"We lucked out. It's like pulling teeth with the guys at the Bureau. They'll pick your brains until there's nothing left, but I'm a foreigner so they still don't quite trust me. Anyhow, there's been an ongoing surveillance of a gang-connected alien-smuggling operation. After I told them about our little chat, they invited us to sit in. Might give you a chance to talk to some of the other Asian crime specialists. You could be in for some excitement if they make a bust."

"When and where?" Zavala asked.

"Later tonight, on the other side of the river. You interested? Your partner Austin is invited too, if he's not busy."

"I'll ask him and get back to you."

Zavala hung up and made a quick call to Austin and told him about Yoo's invitation.

"I'm expecting a call from Sandecker in a few minutes," Austin said. "I have no idea what the old sea fox has up his sleeve. I'll have to catch up with you later."

"Call me when you shake loose. And don't let Sandecker keep you too long."

"Not a chance, pal," Austin said, and, in words that would come back to haunt him later, added, "Hell, Joe, I wouldn't want you to have *all* the fun."

CHAPTER 24

THE SECOND HAPPY HOUR IN THE DOLLAR BAR WAS A RE-
peat of the first gabfest. The vacuous chitchat around the table
ground on Gamay's nerves, but she had to admit that the Gibson
was perfect and that the dinner that followed was superb, featur-
ing freshly caught shrimp in a savory jambalaya.

Mayhew waited politely until dessert was served before he
made his announcement.

"Dooley will pick you up promptly at nine-fifteen tomorrow
morning," he said. "You can leave right after breakfast. It's been
a pleasure to have you as our guest, Dr. Trout. We'll be sad to see
you go."

Mayhew's broad grin seemed at odds with his dismay over
Gamay's impending departure. She wondered how long he
would maintain his smiley face if she insisted on staying another
night.

"And I will be sad to leave," Gamay said in a performance
worthy of Ethel Barrymore. "Thank you for having me, and al-

lowing me to see the wonderful work that you and your staff are doing here in this slice of paradise."

Mayhew was too caught up in the moment to pick up on her veiled sarcasm. At his suggestion, they moved out onto the patio for a nightcap and to watch the sunset.

The scientists gathered in knots, keeping their voices low. Occasionally, Gamay heard a scientific term spoken, suggesting they were talking among themselves about their research.

By nine o'clock, all the staff people had gone to their cabins, leaving Gamay alone. She waited another half hour until everyone had settled in, then followed the shell path to Song Lee's cabin. The windows were dark.

Gamay climbed onto the small porch and knocked softly at first, then harder. There was no answer.

She was surprised to find the door unlocked. She went inside and switched on the lights. It only took a few seconds to see that the cabin was unoccupied. There was no sign that Lee had eaten dinner alone there. Gamay switched the lights off, and hurried along the path to the waterfront. Lee's kayak was not in the boat shed.

Gamay pondered what she should do. She could wake up Dr. Mayhew and the rest of the staff, but, given the penchant for oysterlike secrecy on the island, it was likely she'd be cut out of the action.

Impulsively, Gamay lifted the second kayak from its rack and set it on the beach.

Then she had another thought, and dashed back to the boathouse to grab Dooley's night vision goggles. She slipped them over her head, shoved the kayak in the water, got in, and paddled furiously.

She followed the perimeter of the island and headed out into the bay. The stranded cabin cruiser was greenish and grainy through the goggles. She paddled directly to it to get her bearings, then turned in to the funnel-shaped cove Dooley had shown her earlier that day.

The mangroves squeezed in on both sides. At the narrowest part of the cove, she found the post that marked the break in the mangroves. She paddled to shore, got out of the kayak, and was pulling it up onto the beach when she stumbled over Song Lee's rucksack, which was lying in the sand.

Gamay glanced around and saw something gleaming in the grass. It was Lee's kayak.

Gamay struck off inland, following the winding path through the thicket of trees, carrying her wooden kayak paddle in one hand. The path emerged from the trees into the open, meandering through cactus and scrub. The whisper of the waves washing the beach provided a backdrop to the insect chorus.

With the aid of the night vision goggles, Gamay moved quickly along the path. She paused where it broke out onto the beach and looked around. Two sets of footprints led off down the beach. Taking up the hunt like a hound on a scent, she followed the prints around a bend. She was trotting now, slowing only when she saw a yellow glow in the distance. There was a house up ahead, partially hidden by trees and bushes. She moved closer and saw that the light was spilling through a screen door and window.

She crept up to the house and put her back to the wall a few feet from the window. She could hear a man and a woman speaking excitedly in Chinese, their voices starting out low and then getting louder. The man now sounded angry, the woman hysterical.

Gamay edged up to the window, pushed the goggles up on her forehead, and peered through the glass panes at a sparsely furnished room illuminated with gas camp lanterns.

Song Lee was sitting at a kitchen table across from a brutish-looking Asian man who was dressed in shorts and T-shirt. An automatic weapon lay on the counter next to the stove. The man had apparently just run through his reserve of patience. He brought his hand back and slapped Lee across the face. The blow knocked her off her chair to the floor.

The man turned away from Lee to get his weapon, a big mistake on his part. She got to her knees and plucked a steak knife from a rack that was within arm's reach. There was a flash of blade as she plunged it into the man's thigh, then pulled it free. Letting out a scream of pain, he dropped the gun to the floor and grabbed his bleeding leg.

Lee stood up and dashed for the door. Bellowing with rage, the man lunged after her, but she was too quick for him. She burst through the screen door and ran down the beach.

The man picked his gun up off the floor and limped to the door. Standing in the doorway, he shouted in Chinese, then raised the gun up to shoulder level.

Gamay stepped from the shadows just then, raised the kayak paddle high, and brought it down on the man's head with all her strength. The handle snapped like a dry twig, and the man crashed to the ground, falling on top of his gun.

Gamay hoped the blow had knocked him out, but he soon groaned and began to stir.

She pulled the goggles down and sprinted along the beach. Seeing a figure running a hundred feet or so ahead, she called out Song Lee's name. The scientist stopped and wheeled around to face her pursuer. She clutched the steak knife defensively in her hand.

Gamay ripped the goggles from her head.

"It's me . . . Dr. Trout!"

"Doctor . . . What are you doing here?"

"I followed you."

Gamay glanced back toward the house.

"No time to talk," she said. "I slowed your friend down only for a second."

Gamay tossed away the useless paddle, and then she and Lee ran along the beach. In their haste, they missed the path that would take them across the island and had to go back, costing time. But Gamay took the lead, and within minutes they were on the other side of the island. She had Lee give her a hand getting the kayak out of the grass.

There was a soft footfall on the path, and seconds later a figure burst from the bushes. The man who had held Song Lee prisoner flicked on a flashlight and snarled in triumph. He was surprised to see Gamay, but only for an instant, and quickly swung his light and gun around and brought them to bear on her midsection for an easy gut shot.

Gamay put her head down and charged like a bull, butting the man in the stomach. He had abdominal muscles like a stone wall. He brought down the gun's stock on her head in a blow hard enough to knock her to the ground. Through a gray haze she punched his wounded leg and heard him scream in pain.

Lee leaped onto the man's back, clinging to him, but he shook her off and she fell to the ground. He stood there unmoving, staring at her, then the gun dropped from his hand and he crumpled to the ground as if all the air had gone out of him. The beam from his flashlight fell on the wooden handle of the steak knife protruding from his chest.

As Gamay helped Lee to her feet, Lee gazed at her deadly handiwork.

"I've never done anything like that," she said. *"Never."*

"You'll get used to it," Gamay said. "Who is he?"

"I don't know. He came up while I was getting my kayak and

struck me with his gun. He said he'd been watching me, and that others were coming in a boat to take me away."

Gamay suddenly put her hand on Lee's arm.

"Listen," she said.

Excited voices talking in Chinese could be heard coming along the path. The *others* had arrived.

Lee's kayak was righted and dragged to the water. She produced a spare plastic-and-aluminum paddle for Gamay to use. They both shoved their kayaks off the beach and paddled madly. They were about a hundred feet from the mangroves when flashlight beams probed the water around them.

The shafts of light reflected off the shiny fiberglass hulls. Gamay told Lee to hug the shore, where they'd make a more difficult target. She tensed, expecting gunfire, but the lights blinked out.

"They are going back to their boat," Lee said. "They will come around the other end of the island and intercept us."

"How long before they get there?" Gamay asked, without breaking the rhythm of her strokes.

"Five, ten minutes, maybe. What should we do?"

"Paddle as if our lives depended on it . . . because they *do*."

They put their backs into each stroke and made it out of the cove, but the sound of a boat engine soon shattered the quiet of the night. A spotlight moved slowly back and forth across the water. There was no place along the shore where they could put in and hide. Thick, gnarly roots extended out from mangroves, forming a formidable barrier.

A silhouette loomed ahead. They were coming up on the grounded cabin cruiser. Gamay paddled toward the old boat with Lee right behind. They climbed aboard the derelict, pulling their kayaks up behind them, and lay facedown on the rotting deck.

Through cracks in the hull, they saw the spotlight go past the cruiser. For a second, Gamay entertained a flash of optimism, but that faded as the search boat changed direction, circled the wreck, and came closer. The spotlight filtered through the cracks and fell on their faces.

The women's pursuers peppered the cabin cruiser with gunfire, starting with the elevated bow and working back toward the stern. They took their time, pumping round after round into the pilothouse. Splinters showered the two women. Gamay covered her head with her hands and cursed her own stupidity. The only thing they had accomplished by climbing on the old boat was to give these bozos some target practice. It would only be a matter of seconds before the bullets found them.

Then the firing stopped.

Gamay expected the attackers to swarm aboard, but instead a bottle filled with flaming gasoline arced through the air and landed on the deck. Crackling fire from the Molotov cocktail spread in a blazing puddle that lapped at their feet. The heat became unbearable. The two women stood up, preferring to be shot rather than be burned to death. But the boat carrying their assailants was moving away from them and picking up speed. By then, the cabin cruiser had become a blazing torch.

"*Jump!*" Gamay yelled.

They dove into the water and swam away from the burning wreck. They struck out for the nearest mangrove and had only gone a short distance before they heard a boat engine again and saw a spotlight coming their way.

Gamay's hopes were dashed. The shooters were coming back to finish them off.

The boat slowed and the spotlight played over the water, finally finding the pair of swimmers. Gamay expected that the rattle of gunfire would be the last thing she would ever hear, but instead a familiar voice rang out.

"*Gamay,*" Paul Trout called, "*is that you?*"

She stopped swimming and began to tread water. She stuck a hand in the air. The boat edged closer, looming over them, and she looked up to see Paul Trout's long arms reaching down to pull her to safety.

CHAPTER 25

ZAVALA SWUNG HIS CORVETTE INTO THE PARKING LOT OF the Eden Center shopping mall in Falls Church, Virginia, as Charlie Yoo had instructed. The Chinese agent was waiting for Zavala near the clock tower in a black government-issue Ford Crown Victoria. He rolled down the window.

"Where's your friend Austin?"

"Delayed," Zavala said. "He'll catch up with us later. Or we can wait."

Yoo frowned, raised an index finger indicating Zavala should wait, and rolled up the window. Zavala could see Yoo's lips moving and assumed he was talking on a wireless Bluetooth setup. Then the window came down.

"The guys on stakeout said to come along now. You can call Austin later and tell him where you are. Hop in."

Zavala didn't like the idea of leaving his prized Corvette in a public parking lot, but he raised the convertible top, locked the door, and slid into the passenger's seat of the Crown Victoria. Yoo drove out of the parking lot, through Seven Corners, and toward Wilson Boulevard, slowing after a few miles to take an off-ramp. After a short drive, they came to an industrial park consisting of large metal-sheathed buildings spread over several blocks. Except for the amber security lights over the loading-dock doors, the complex was dark and seemingly deserted.

Zavala expected Yoo to pull over and park before they got to the stakeout so that they would walk the rest of the way. Yoo slowed the car to a crawl, then, without stopping, hooked the steering wheel over to the right and accelerated through an open gate with a sign on it that read GOOD LUCK FORTUNE COOKIE COMPANY.

Yoo kept his foot on the gas pedal, swerved behind the building in a g-force turn, then pointed the car at a garage door. As the car headed for the big black square, Zavala braced himself for the impact, but then the headlights showed that the door was almost fully open. Yoo finally hit the brakes inside the warehouse, sending the car into a fishtail skid into a wall of cardboard cartons.

The car's grille slammed into the cardboard boxes with a loud crunching sound. The boxes split wide open, spilling dozens of plastic-wrapped fortune cookies over the hood.

The car's air bags exploded, cushioning the impact further.

Zavala caught his breath, then reached down and unclasped his seat belt. Pushing his air bag aside, he saw that Yoo was not in the driver's seat. Zavala's exit from the car was less than graceful, and he fell onto one knee. He was slow to anger, but as he got to his feet he wanted to rip Yoo's head off.

The overhead lights snapped on. Charlie Yoo was nowhere to be seen, but Zavala was not alone.

He was surrounded by several Asian men, all dressed in black running suits, and all carrying automatic weapons that were pointed at his midsection.

The closest man poked Zavala in the gut with the barrel of his gun.

"*Move,*" he ordered.

CHAPTER 26

AUSTIN FLIPPED OVER THE LAST PAGE OF THE VOLUMINOUS file on Pyramid Trading Company, leaned back in his chair, and rubbed his eyes. The picture that the file painted was of a vast corporation with no regard for human life. Pyramid had put out more than three hundred harmful products. It had exported tainted fish, killer pet food, unsafe tires, and poisoned toothpaste, candy, vitamins, and drugs. Under international pressure, the Chinese government had admitted that there was a problem with Pyramid and promised to remedy the situation. But nothing in what Austin had read would explain why Pyramid would go after Kane and his research project.

Austin went over to a window and gazed down at the lights of Washington as if they might coalesce into a crystal ball that could answer the questions whirling around in his mind. The phone buzzed, and he picked it up to hear the unmistakable voice of Admiral Sandecker in its full flower of authority and brevity.

"Kurt. Please be out front in five minutes."

Sandecker hung up without further explanation.

Austin put the Pyramid file in a desk drawer, then turned out the lights and headed for the elevator. Five minutes later to the second, he walked out the front door of NUMA headquarters as a dark blue Chevrolet Suburban SUV pulled up to the curb.

A young man in a naval officer's uniform got out of the back of the SUV and greeted Austin, who recognized Lieutenant Charley Casey, an up-and-coming officer Sandecker had introduced him to at a White House reception.

"Hello, Kurt," Casey said. "Climb aboard."

Austin got in the backseat with Casey, and the SUV swung out into Washington traffic.

"Nice to see you again, Lieutenant. What's going on?"

"Sorry to be evasive, Kurt, but the admiral has asked me to hold off answering any questions for now."

"Okay. Then how about telling me where we're headed?"

"Not *us*. It's where *you're* going." Casey pointed. "Right there."

The SUV had only gone a couple of bocks from NUMA headquarters before pulling over to the curb again. Austin thanked Casey for the ride, got out of the SUV, and walked up to the entrance of a restaurant. A neon sign spelled out the name AEGEAN GROTTO.

The restaurant's owner, an ebullient native of Naxos named Stavros, ambushed Austin as he stepped over the threshold.

"Good evening, Mr. Austin. How are things at the Fish House?"

Stavros used his nickname for NUMA headquarters, where many of his patrons worked as scientists or technicians.

"As fishy as ever," Austin said with a slight smile. "I'm meeting someone here."

"Your friend arrived a few minutes ago," Stavros said. "I've seated him at the admiral's table."

He led Austin to an alcove at the rear of the dining room. Admiral Sandecker had often dined at the restaurant when he was NUMA director. The table offered a modicum of privacy and a view of the dining room. The blue walls flanking the table were decorated with pictures of squid, octopi, and various other denizens of Stavros's kitchen.

The man seated at the table gave Austin a quick wave of recognition.

Austin pulled out a chair and sat down opposite Max Kane.

"Hello, Doc," he said. "This is a pleasant surprise."

"I'm shocked that you were able to see through my masquerade so easily."

"You had me for a second, Doc, then I noticed your hairline was listing to starboard."

Kane snatched the thick black wig from his head. With a flick of his wrist, he sent it gliding like a hairy Frisbee toward a nearby table where two men were seated. The wig almost landed in a bowl of avgolemono soup. They glared at Kane, and one man stuffed the hairpiece under the jacket of his dark suit, then went back to his dinner.

Kane burst into laughter.

"Don't look so worried, Kurt. Those guys are my babysitters. They're the ones who insisted that I wear the rug out in public."

Austin gave Kane a tight smile, but he was in no mood for idle talk. In the short time he had known the colorful microbiologist, Austin had almost lost one of his team, seen the B3 project scuttled, and fought an undersea robot a half mile down. He wanted answers, not wig tosses, however skillful. He signaled Stavros by holding two fingers in the air, then turned back to Kane and skewered him with his coral-hued eyes.

"What the hell is going on, Doc?" he asked.

Kane sagged in his chair, as if the wind had gone right out of him.

"Sorry, Kurt. I've spent the last few days with those creeps in a safe house subsisting on pizza and Chinese fast food. I'm starting to get a little loopy."

Austin handed Kane a menu.

"Here's my antidote for fast food. I'd recommend the *psari plaki,* fish Athenian-style. *Tsatziki* and *taramosalata* for appetizers."

When Stavros arrived with glasses of ouzo, Austin ordered two of the succulent fish plates. Then he raised his glass. Looking Kane straight in the eye, he said, "Here's to a discovery that is going to affect every man, woman, and child on the planet."

"Joe must have told you about my near-death confession."

"He said the prospect of a watery grave made you forthcoming, up to a point."

Kane clamped his lips in a smirk.

"I guess I owe you an explanation," he said.

"I guess you do," Austin said.

Kane took a blissful sip of ouzo and put his glass down.

"For a couple of years now, I've been chairman of a scientific advisory group called the Board on Marine Biology . . . BOMB, for short," Kane said. "The board includes some of the most brilliant minds in the field of ocean biomedicine. We work with the National Research Council, and advise the government on promising scientific discoveries."

"And what was *your* promising discovery, Doc?"

"About a year after I had moved the lab to Bonefish Key, we acquired a rare species of jellyfish related to the sea wasp. We named it the blue medusa because it had an amazingly bright luminescence, but the toxin that the thing produced was what really blew our minds."

"How so, Doc?"

"The medusa's toxin didn't kill. It immobilized the prey so that the medusa could dine on food that was still alive. That's not an unknown practice in nature. Spiders and wasps like to keep a fresh snack handy."

Austin nodded in the direction of the restaurant's lobster tank.

"Human beings do the same thing."

"You see my point, then. The steers and hogs that we turn into steaks and pork chops have better medical treatment than many humans. We even load those animals down with antibiotics and other medicines to keep them as healthy as possible until we can eat them."

"Animal husbandry isn't my strong suit, Doc. Where are you going with this?"

"The blue medusa toxin is the most complex naturally produced chemical I've ever seen. It puts up a wall that keeps pathogens at arm's length. The doomed prey enjoys the best of health while it waits to be devoured." Kane leaned across the table and dropped his voice. "Now, just suppose we could put those same protective qualities in a drug for humans."

Austin pondered Kane's words.

"You'd have an all-purpose pill," Austin said. "What the snake oil salesmen used to call a cure-all."

"*Bingo!* Only this was no snake oil. We had found a medical miracle that just might neutralize some of the greatest scourges of mankind, the ailments caused by viruses, from the common cold to cancer."

"So why all the hush-hush?" Austin asked. "If people knew you had discovered a cure-all, the world would build statues in your honor."

"Hell, Kurt, at first we were nominating ourselves for the

Nobel Prize in Medicine. After the initial euphoric thrill, we realized that we were about to open Pandora's box."

"You wouldn't get any love letters from the pharmaceutical and insurance industries," Austin said. "But, in the long term, you'd get a healthier world."

"It's that *long* term that worried us," Kane said. "Say we give this boon to the world, no strings attached. An easily accessible cure-all goes into production. The average life span increases stratospherically. Instead of six billion souls on the planet, we'd have ten or twelve billion. Picture the pressure that would put on land, water, food, and energy resources."

"You could have riots, wars, governments toppled, and starvation."

Kane spread his hands apart as if to say *Voilà!*

"Now imagine what would happen if we kept the discovery secret."

"Nothing is secret forever. Word would leak out. Those who didn't have access to the medicine would resent those who did. People with life-threatening diseases would be pounding down the doors of city hall. Chaos again."

"The scientific board reached the same conclusion," Kane said. "We were in a quandary. So we compiled a report, which we transmitted to the government. Then fate intervened. An epidemic broke out in China, an influenza-type virus with the potential to set off a worldwide pandemic that would kill millions. And guess what? Our crazy little lab held the key to the cure."

"Blue medusa?"

"Yup."

"Is that what you meant when you said your research could impact everyone on the planet?"

Kane nodded.

"Turns out our research held the only hope to fight this thing," he continued. "The government took over the lab, locked the doors, and worked with the Chinese government to keep the research under wraps until we could come up with a synthesized form of the chemical. They put out a cover story suggesting that the new virus was simply an outbreak of SARS and thus controllable. Which it isn't. It's a mutated strain that's even more virulent than the virus that caused the 1918 flu pandemic. In one year, that virus killed millions."

Austin let out a low whistle.

"With the ability people have to globe-hop now," he said, "that 1918 figure would be a drop in the bucket."

"This time, it's the *whole* bucket, Kurt. The feds classified our findings and made all the lab people government employees, so that anyone talking out of turn could be prosecuted for treason. They also added White House and military people to the board. Then they moved most of the research to a secret undersea lab."

"Why not stay at Bonefish Key?" Austin asked.

"Too public, for one thing. But there were practical reasons too. We wanted to be near the resource. The blue medusa once covered a wide area, but now it is found primarily in and around a specific deepwater canyon. And we wanted to quarantine our work. We were developing an enhanced version of the medusa, a sort of superjellyfish, a dangerous predator, not the kind of thing you'd want to find in your swimming pool."

"Are you saying you were working with malignant mutant life-forms, Doc?"

"Essentially, yes."

"What would happen if they got in the wild?"

"Don't worry, there's no danger of them wiping out the ocean's biomass. They can't reproduce and would eventually die out in the open. We took great care during the genetic engineering to prevent the possibility of proliferation."

"That's still playing with dynamite, Doc. Mother Nature doesn't like to be upstaged."

"I know, I know," Kane said, his voice tightening. "But we were under intense pressure from the government. We had to have greater quantities of the toxin to conduct our synthesis experiments, so we simply grew bigger medusae. The enhanced creatures proved to be more aggressive than the original, and the toxin they produced went off the charts."

"Before you came to the *Beebe,* you were in the Pacific Ocean," Austin observed. "Is that where they put the lab?"

"Yes. Micronesia, to be more exact. The government used an undersea observatory under development for the Navy. We call it Davy Jones's Locker. I was working there when I heard I'd been nominated for the B3 dive. The project was about to be wrapped up, so I left my assistant, Lois Mitchell, in charge and took a leave of absence. You know the rest."

"Only up to the point when the Coast Guard snatched you from the deck of the *Beebe.*"

"The call I got on the *Beebe* was to tell me that the secret lab had vanished around the same time as the attack on the B3. The security ship guarding the lab was heavily damaged by a missile that may have been launched from a submarine. The whole undersea complex of labs and living quarters, along with the staff, disappeared from the bottom. The Navy's still searching."

Austin gazed at Kane as if he'd seen the little man who wasn't there.

"You're just full of surprises, Doc." Stavros was coming from the kitchen with plates in his hands. "Why don't you tell me about it over appetizers?"

In between bites of pita bread, Kane told Austin about the attack on the support ship and described the depressions left in the ocean floor. When Kane asked Austin if he had any idea how the lab could have been moved, Austin said he'd run it by Zavala. Then he asked a question of his own.

"How far had the research gone when the lab disappeared?"

"We had identified the microorganism that produced the chemical in the jellyfish. With that done, we were on the verge of being able to produce the synthesized version in quantity. We were going to skip over the clinical trials and rely on lab tests and computer models even as we distributed it. There wasn't time otherwise. We had to have the medicine manufactured and in place if and when the virus broke out of China and spread to other countries."

"Have you thought of who might be behind the lab's disappearance?" Austin said.

"I've been turning the question over in my mind for days. All I've got in return has been a headache."

"You said that a missile was used to knock out the support ship and that it probably was launched from a submarine. Only a government or a big organization would have the resources to attack the bathysphere and move the lab," Austin said.

"My thoughts exactly. It follows that only a government would have the resources to untangle this mess. Without that lab, we have no defense against the pandemic. The virus is spreading in China. Once it hits urban areas there, it will break out beyond her borders."

"The Navy must have ships searching," Austin said.

"They're combing the area. But the people who did this would have expected a Navy search and done something to forestall it. A White House guy at my board meeting said he had heard Vice President Sandecker sing your praises, and I saw what you did when the bathysphere was all but lost. So I put out the word that I wanted to see you. And here we are."

"And here's our dinner," Austin said.

He ordered a dry white Santorini wine to go with the fish. For the next half hour, Austin entertained Kane with accounts of dives he had made in the Greek island's caldera and theories about Santorini being the site of the legendary Atlantis. He then pushed away his empty dinner plate and ordered a custard and thick Greek coffee.

"Well?" Kane asked expectantly.

"I'll do what I can, but you will have to be totally up front with me, Doc. No holding back. And I'll need to be able to get in touch with you at any time."

"You'll have my full cooperation, Kurt." He looked over at his bodyguards. "My babysitters are giving me the eye. I have to leave. They think that there's a whole army of assassins waiting out there to do me in."

"Don't be too tough on them, they're only trying to keep you alive. I'll pick up the tab."

Kane jotted down a number where he could be reached. Austin watched Kane with careful eyes as he left the restaurant trailed by the two men. Then he signaled Stavros for the check.

LIEUTENANT CASEY WAS WAITING outside the restaurant in the navy SUV. Austin got in this time without an invitation.

"Nice to see you again, Lieutenant."

Casey handed him a phone, and Sandecker's voice crackled on the line.

"Dr. Kane fill you in on the situation, Kurt?"

"He told me about the blue medusa research and the missing lab."

"Good. This thing is ready to blow up if we don't find the lab and get hold of that vaccine. You've *got* to find Davy Jones's Locker. I'll put the whole damn U.S. Navy at your disposal."

"How long do we have, Admiral?"

"The CDC computers say the virus will hit the major Chinese cities seventy-two hours from midnight. It will be raging around the world within weeks."

"Then there is still time?"

"Not really. Once the virus goes beyond China's borders, it will become unstoppable. The President is gearing up the National Guard so he can declare a state of emergency."

"In that case, I'll take whatever help you can give me, sir."

"If you need more, give me or Casey a call directly. Don't bother going through intermediaries." His voice softened. "Good luck, Kurt. And keep an eye on that libidinous Mexican pal of yours."

Austin handed the phone back.

"When do we leave, Lieutenant?"

"I'll pick you up and we'll be at the airport at three a.m." He paused, then said, "Just to let you know, I have a wife and two kids, Kurt. I'm told that there will be no way to protect them once this thing spreads to the U.S."

"Those are three good reasons to move quickly, then."

Austin said he would see Casey in a few hours and got out of the SUV in front of the NUMA tower. He called Zavala's number on his way to his office to retrieve the Pyramid file but got no response. He wasn't surprised. His friend could have joined the surveillance team and might be unable to talk. Austin left him a message to call back as soon as he was clear.

Austin picked up the file, then got on the elevator and headed to the fifteenth floor. He followed a corridor to a door marked NUMASAT and stepped into a large, dimly lit space that had a wide, curving wall lined with glowing television screens. The screens displayed information from NUMA's satellite system, a complex network that collected information about oceans from around the world for scientists and universities.

Presiding over the communications network was an eccentric genius named Jack Wilmut, who supervised the system from an elaborate console in the center of the room surrounded by work-stations. From his perch, he could also keep track of every NUMA research project, ship, and staffer working in the field. He saw Austin approaching, and a smile crossed his plumpish face.

"What a surprise to find you here at headquarters, Kurt."

Austin pulled a chair up to the console.

"Don't kid me, Jack, you could figure out exactly where I am in a second. I've got a favor. I've lost contact with Joe. Can you find him?"

Wilmut patted down one side of his double comb-over.

"He's probably in a Washington boudoir," he said. Seeing from Austin's unsmiling face that he was deadly serious, he added, "I'll do my best. What's he got?"

"Transmitter in his Corvette, for one."

"Easy," Wilmut said.

He tapped the keyboard in front of him, and seconds later the screen displayed a blinking red star on a map of Falls Church. The location was displayed in a box next to the star.

"The car is at the Eden Center. He probably stopped in for some Vietnamese food."

The Eden Center was a complex of shops and restaurants that served the Vietnamese population of Falls Church.

"He doesn't like Vietnamese food," Austin said. "Try finding his phone."

Wilmut traced Zavala's cell through its GPS chip.

A second blinking star appeared on the outskirts of the city, several miles from the first. Wilmut enlarged the map and switched to a satellite picture. The star was on one of a couple of dozen rectangles, apparently the roofs of large buildings. He zoomed in.

"Looks like an industrial complex," Wilmut said. "All the buildings look pretty much alike."

"I need an address," Austin said.

Wilmut punched a button and GOOD LUCK FORTUNE COOKIE COMPANY appeared on the screen. He laughed, and said, "Guess he likes *Chinese* food."

Austin thanked Wilmut, and rode the elevator down to the garage to pick up his Jeep Cherokee. As he drove along the Potomac, he found Caitlin's number in his directory. She immediately recognized his voice.

"This must be my lucky week," she said. "The two handsomest men at NUMA calling me. How are you, Kurt?"

"I'm a little worried about Joe. Do you know anything about an FBI Asian gang stakeout involving Charlie Yoo?"

"No such thing, Kurt. Charlie is a guest of the Bureau. He is notified of field ops only at our discretion, and we don't have anything like that going."

"That's what I thought," Austin said. "Thanks for your help, Caitlin."

"What the hell—"

Austin clicked off, and the unfinished question was lost in the ether. Driving with one hand, he quickly programmed the address Wilmut had given him into the dashboard GPS unit.

Next, he reached for a rack under his seat, pulled out the holster containing his Bowen revolver, put it on the seat beside him, then stomped on the gas.

CHAPTER 27

DOOLEY'S VINTAGE SINGLE-WIDE MOBILE HOME ON A PINE Island canal was no five-star hotel, but it had distinct advantages that would not be found at the Four Seasons.

Pine Island was several miles distant from Bonefish Key. The trailer had a water view. And it had Dooley Greene sitting in a deck chair at the end of a dilapidated dock, cigar stub clenched between his teeth, 16-gauge shotgun on his lap, keeping an eye peeled for trouble.

Relying on his deep knowledge of local waters, Dooley had earlier made a fast crossing to the mainland. He had kept his boat's running lights turned off until he headed into a canal lined with mobile homes. As the boat coasted up to the dock and Dooley killed the motor, Gamay confronted Paul.

"Before I burst from curiosity, please tell me how you happened to dash from one coast to the other and arrive just in time to rescue the fair maidens in distress. You weren't scheduled to arrive here for a couple of days."

"Kurt called and said he might have unknowingly sent you

into danger. I couldn't reach you by phone, so I put the seminar on hold and flew standby to Florida."

"How'd you hook up with Dooley?"

"More good luck: he hooked up with *me*," Paul said. "I was at the Pine Island Marina looking for a ride to Bonefish Key, checking out boats and desperately hoping someone had left a key in the ignition, when Dooley saw me and asked what I was doing. When I mentioned your name, he jumped at the chance to take me to Bonefish. He then noticed that two kayaks were missing, and figured out where you might have gone."

"Thanks, Dooley," Gamay said. She gave him a peck on the cheek. "You're probably wondering what all this is about."

"You learn that it's healthier to mind your own business around here, Dr. Gamay, but I'll admit to being a little curious about what's going on."

"You're not the *only* one."

Gamay glanced at Song Lee, who had been huddled on a seat during the trip to the mainland.

Dooley tied up the boat and led the way to the trailer. He extracted a six-pack of Diet Coke from the refrigerator, passed three cans around along with a bag of Goldfish crackers. Without saying a word, he took his shotgun out of a locked cabinet. With the 16-gauge slung over one arm, he ambled out to the dock with the rest of the six-pack.

Song Lee and the Trouts went into the trailer and sat around a Formica-and-chrome kitchen table. She sipped her Coke like an automaton and stared into space.

Gamay sensed that Lee was in shock from the violence she had witnessed.

"It's okay, Dr. Lee," she said. "You're safe now."

Lee turned her head, and Gamay saw tears glistening in her eyes.

"I'm a doctor," Lee said. "I'm supposed to *save* lives, not *take* them."

"You saved *our* lives," Gamay said. "That man and his friends would have killed us both."

"I know that. Still . . ."

"Do you have any idea who they were?" Paul asked.

Lee wiped the tears away with the back of her hand.

"He said he had been watching me for days," she said. "He was waiting for me where I had left the kayak and forced me to go to the house. We were waiting for people coming to take me away. I pleaded with him. We argued. That's when I grabbed the knife and ran."

Gamay put her hand on Lee's forearm.

"I think you had better start at the beginning," Gamay said.

Lee gulped down her Coke like a thirsty longshoreman, then began to tell her story.

She had been born in a rural part of China, excelled in science as a college student, and went to study in the U.S. on a grant from the Chinese government. She had seen firsthand the ravages of disease among the poorer citizens of China and wanted to do something about it. She specialized in immunology at Harvard Medical School, and did her residency at Massachusetts General Hospital.

Returning to China, she found a job with a government program targeting the health of slum dwellers. The work centered on prevention, making sure that people were immunized and eliminating the sources of disease in the water and air. Her success led to a position in a hospital, where she was working at the time the SARS epidemic broke out.

Finally, Lee told Gamay how she had been exiled to the countryside after questioning the government's response to SARS, and about her redemption and assignment to Bonefish Key, to work on a vaccine, based on an ocean organism, for a new virus strain.

"The blue medusa?"

"That's right." She seemed surprised. "It's related to the highly toxic sea wasp. How did you know about it?"

"I badgered Dr. Mayhew, and he showed me the research room."

"I'm amazed that he allowed you to see it," Lee said. She stared at Gamay as if she were seeing her for the first time. "I just realized that I really don't know who you are."

"I'm a marine biologist with NUMA. I came to Bonefish Key because I was interested in ocean biomedicine."

"From the looks of it, you were more interested in *me*," Lee said.

"Sometimes things just happen," Gamay said.

Lee smiled.

"You sound like a Chinese philosopher, Dr. Trout. Anyway, I'm glad you were interested or I might not be here."

"Dr. Mayhew said the blue medusa was a new species."

"That's right. Bigger and more aggressive than the sea wasp. After the work moved to the new lab, they were going to use genetic engineering to produce a more powerful toxin."

"I wasn't aware there *was* another lab," Gamay said.

"It was secret. They called it Davy Jones's Locker. Dr. Kane and Lois Mitchell, his assistant, left Bonefish Key and took a number of scientists and technicians with them. Dr. Mayhew and the remaining staff stayed on to make sure there were no flaws in the original research. I was charting the probable spread of the virus and how best to contain it."

"How effective was the toxin-derived drug?" Paul said.

"It was limited at first," Lee said. "The medusae toxin is incredibly unpredictable. Even a small amount could kill a human, and at first more lab animals died than were cured. Then we made a huge breakthrough in identifying the molecular makeup of the microbe that produces the toxin. We were on the verge of synthesis. And clinical tests would have been the next step."

Song Lee's eyelids had been drooping as she talked, and Gamay suggested she lie down on the sofa. Then she and Paul stepped out of the trailer into the warm Florida night.

"Thanks for coming to our rescue, Galahad," Gamay said.

"Sorry if Sir Dooley and I cut it too close," Paul said. "What's your reaction to Song Lee's story?"

"I know for a fact that she didn't make up the man she killed or his trigger-happy pals, so I assume that everything else she said is true."

"I'll talk to Dooley. Maybe he can fill in the gaps."

As Trout approached the dock, he smelled cigar smoke before he saw Dooley. Trout started to speak but Dooley shushed him. Trout listened, and he heard the murmur of an engine echoing off the canal. Dooley mashed his cigar out with his shoe, grabbed Trout, and pulled him down behind a pile of wooden fish boxes.

The engine sound came closer, and a boat nosed into the canal. It was moving at a crawl, its spotlight sweeping back and forth, until it came to the end of the canal, where it made a U-turn and headed back to open water.

Dooley's 16-gauge followed the boat until the sound of its engine could no longer be heard. He lit up another cigar.

"I'll keep watch, but I think maybe we'd better get Dr. Lee out of here," he said.

"No argument there," Trout agreed.

Trout went back to the trailer. As he was telling Gamay about the suspicious boat, his cell phone buzzed. He checked the caller ID. Austin was calling to check on Gamay.

"I'm in Florida now," Trout said. "Gamay is all right. But we ran into trouble off Bonefish Key."

"What sort of trouble?"

"Gamay was attacked along with a Bonefish Key scientist named Dr. Song Lee, who was working on something called the blue medusa."

"I want to talk to Dr. Lee in person," Austin said. "Call NUMA and have them send a plane down right away to pick you up. Joe and I will be leaving town in a few hours. Meet me at the airport."

"I'll get right on it."

"Thanks. I've got another favor." He gave Trout a phone number. "Call Cate Lyons, Joe's friend at the FBI, and extend my apologies for cutting her off. Tell her I'm heading for the Good Luck Fortune Cookie factory in Falls Church. Got to go."

Moments later, Trout relayed Austin's message to Lyons, who thanked him and hung up. As he tapped out the number to connect him with NUMA's transportation department, he said, "We're flying back to Washington tonight. Kurt wants to talk to Song Lee as soon as possible."

Gamay shook her head.

"Kurt's instincts were right on the mark as usual," she said. "He said to look for something funny on Bonefish Key."

"This is about as funny as it gets," Paul said.

Gamay glanced over at the slumbering Chinese woman, thinking of their close call in the abandoned boat, and then looked at the serious expression on her husband's face.

"If it's so funny," she said, "why isn't anybody laughing?"

CHAPTER 28

A FEW MINUTES BEFORE AUSTIN CALLED THE TROUTS, HE had driven past the Corvette parked near the Eden Center clock tower and thought that Zavala must have had a good reason to leave his pride and joy unattended. He drove onto Wilson Boulevard and joined the traffic that moved at an agonizing crawl. Eventually, the suburban malls and neighborhoods petered out, and he was moving through an industrial-commercial area.

The GPS unit indicated that he was about a block from his goal. Reasoning that a turquoise Cherokee might attract unwanted attention, Austin parked it in an alley between two buildings. He made his way on foot to the front gate of the Good Luck Fortune Cookie Company. The parking lot was empty, and the only light came from above the door to the office.

The gate was locked. Austin walked the perimeter of the chain-link fence to the rear gate. He pushed the gate open and made his way to a rear loading dock lit by a single bulb. He kept to the shadows as much as possible.

He wondered if he had the right address. Those doubts vanished when a figure stepped out from behind a Dumpster and
blinded Austin with a powerful flashlight.

A deep voice said, "Hold it right there, soldier. Put your hands
in the air."

Austin stopped in his tracks and did as he was told. He sensed
rather than saw someone creeping up behind him and felt his
pistol slip from its holster.

"That's better," said the voice. "Turn around ... *real* slow. I'm
giving you friendly warning. These guys call themselves Ghost
Devils, and they mean it. I wouldn't screw with them."

At least a half dozen other figures had materialized from the
shadows.

"Are you a ghost or a devil?" Austin asked.

The man stepped closer.

"Just a guy doing his job. The name is Phelps." He turned the
flashlight beam up to show his face, the angle turning his droopy
smile into a Halloween mask. "This place is loaded with cameras.
A moth couldn't get close without being picked up. We've been
watching you ever since you showed up at the front door. Thanks
for making my work so easy."

"My pleasure. But how do you know I didn't let myself get
caught on purpose?"

"I *don't*, which is why we're being real careful handling you."

"Where's Joe?" Austin asked.

Phelps pointed his flashlight at the loading-dock door.

"*That* way," he said.

The door slid up. Phelps led the way up the stairs to the dock
and herded Austin through the door into the dark warehouse.
Phelps hit a switch, and the interior was flooded with light. The

big space was empty except for a pile of smashed cardboard cartons against one wall and two chairs side by side facing a screen.

"Fortune cookie business must not be very good," Austin said.

"That's a cover," Phelps said. "Place is used mostly to hold smuggled illegal aliens. Besides, you don't want to know *your* fortune. The folks I work for aren't too happy with you."

Austin would have agreed that his prospects for a long and happy life were slim. In addition to Phelps, he was guarded by the tough-faced Asians, all men in their twenties, dressed in black running suits and shoes. They had red bandannas tied around their heads. They looked dangerously unpredictable, but from the cocky way they slouched around with their weapons they appeared undisciplined as well.

Phelps was a tall man in his late forties. He wore jeans, Doc Martens boots, and a black T-shirt that displayed his ropy arms. He wore a U.S. NAVY SEALS baseball cap on his head. And he had Austin's Bowen, which he examined with appraising eyes.

"Nice piece," he said.

"Thanks. When do I get it back?"

Phelps chuckled, and slid the pistol into its holster, which he clipped to his belt. He glanced at his watch and called to a couple of Ghost Devils. They went through a door leading to the front of the building and came back after a minute with Zavala. They shoved him over into one of the chairs and motioned Austin into the other. Both men were then handcuffed to the armrests.

Zavala's face was caked with dried blood, but he still managed to smile when he saw Austin.

"Hi, Kurt, nice of you to crash the party. Time to leave?"

"You'll have to ask Mr. Phelps. Are you okay?"

"Charlie Yoo set me up, and some of these guys used my face for a punching bag, but nothing broken that I know of."

"We'll have to remember to pay them back for their hospitality." Zavala smiled through bloodied lips.

"That's what I like about you, Kurt. The glass is always half full. *Whoops—*"

The warehouse went dark just then, and the two men were enveloped in almost total blackness. After a moment, a spotlight directly overhead blinked on, and they found themselves at the center of a circle of bright white light. A second overhead spot came on about twenty-five feet to the front of where they sat.

The screen was gone, revealing a table covered in green baize. Behind the table sat a woman who seemed to be scrutinizing the two men from NUMA. She was dressed in a dark purple, two-piece outfit, and a cloak the same color was draped around her shoulders. Her dark hair was parted down the middle, and high, arched brows framed a Eurasian face.

Austin stared at the woman in disbelief.

"This is crazy," he whispered, "but I *know* her. She's the *Dragon Lady*."

"I've seen worse-looking dragons. Why don't you introduce me?"

"Not sure I can, Joe. The Dragon Lady wasn't a real person."

Zavala turned and looked at Austin as if his friend had lost his marbles.

"*I'm* the one who got his brain bashed around," Zavala said. "She looks pretty real to me."

"Me too, Joe, but the Dragon Lady was a character in a comic strip. *Terry and the Pirates* . . . Stereotypical femme fatale. My father used to read it to me when I was a kid. She was always causing trouble. Damn. What was her name?"

The woman's lips parted in a smile.

"My name is Lai Choi San," she said in a voice that would have been seductive it if hadn't been drained of all emotion. "Bravo, Mr. Austin. Few people know I even *have* another name. I have been looking forward to this meeting."

"I wish I could say the same," Austin said. "Now that we're good friends, maybe you'd like to tell us why you invited us here."

He could hardly believe he was talking to a comic-strip character. Next, he'd be chatting with Roger Rabbit.

"For a start, I want you to tell me the whereabouts of Dr. Kane," she said.

Austin shrugged.

"Kane is under government protective custody. I can't tell you where they are holding him. Apparently, someone is trying to kill him."

"Really?" she purred. "Who would want to do that to the brilliant doctor?"

"The same people who hijacked the lab that was developing a vaccine from the medusa toxin."

The woman gave him a slow-burn stare, and her face actually seemed to glow with anger. Austin passed it off as a manipulation.

"What you don't know," she said, "is that Pyramid *created* the new virus. Our pharmaceutical company was experimenting with an influenza vaccine for the world market and inadvertently produced the more virulent and adaptable strain. They wanted to destroy it, but wiser heads prevailed."

"Why didn't wiser heads prevent the virus from breaking out?"

"That was an accident, something we would have avoided until we had developed the antidote, which would have gone to members of my organization first. You see, the virus fit in with our larger plan of destabilizing the government. The outbreak of SARS almost toppled China's leaders. Just think how the public would react to their impotence in dealing with an even more lethal virus. They would see Pyramid step in and cure the masses. In return, we would acquire power and fortune. We would replace the Chinese government."

"Do you know that the virus is going to hit your big cities in a couple of days?"

"It was only a matter of time, no matter what the government did. The more, the merrier."

Austin stared at the apparition.

"You're willing to wipe out scores of your countrymen to stir up trouble with your government?" he asked.

"You know a great deal and very little," she said. "What if we killed a few hundred, or even a few million, Chinese? We have a billion people. An epidemic would be far more effective for population control than the one-child-per-couple rule."

"You'll never be able to keep that virus contained, even with the vaccine the lab has been working on. It will move too fast. It will be in every country in a week or so."

"Wouldn't you say that the deaths of millions will be the most convincing reason for people to buy our vaccine?" she said. "Think of it as marketing and promotion."

"You're insane to think a scheme like that will work," he said.

"It is our government leadership that is insane. Pyramid has been in our family for generations. Past governments that have tried to destroy our organization have paid the price. We were here long before those so-called leaders were even born. We won't be thrown into history's dustbin."

The figure at the table seemed to glow incandescently as she launched into a diatribe against the Chinese Communist government for having the audacity to take on an organization that goes back hundreds of years.

Zavala had been staring spellbound at the woman.

"Kurt," he whispered, "I can see through her. Look at her right arm, the one she's waving around."

Austin focused on the moving right arm. Through the material of her loose-fitting silk sleeve, he caught faint glimpses of the brick wall behind her.

"You're right," he said. "She's nothing but a projection, like Max," referring to the name Hiram Yeager gave to the holographic personification generated by his interactive computer.

The Dragon Lady noticed Austin's grin and stopped her tirade.

"You are a strange man, Mr. Austin. Don't you fear the prospect of death?"

"Not from someone who's no more real than a comic strip."

"Enough!" she snarled. "I will show you how real I am. My brother Chang awaits your arrival. He will make sure your death is long and painful."

She issued an order in Chinese, and the guards moved in.

"*Wait* a minute," Austin called out. "What if I can produce Dr. Kane?"

She barked a second order, and the guards froze in their tracks.

"You said that Kane was in protective custody," she said, "and couldn't be reached."

"I was lying . . . I do that a lot."

"That's true," Zavala threw in. "Kurt is one of the biggest liars I know."

Austin gave Zavala a sidelong glance that told him he was laying it on a bit too thick.

"Let me make a phone call," Austin said, looking back at the Dragon Lady, "and I'll set him up."

Austin was trying to buy time, hoping to talk his captors into freeing him from his chair. His immediate plan was to grab a gun. It was a throw of the dice, but was all that he had.

"A futile effort, Mr. Austin," she said. "I no longer care whether Kane lives or dies. His project is near completion and his services are not needed . . . Good-bye."

Austin expected the Ghost Devils to move in again, but they had hoisted their weapons high on their chests and were staring toward the rear of the warehouse.

The hologram shimmered.

"What is that?" she asked.

In answer, an amplified voice came from outside.

"This is the FBI. Throw your weapons aside and come out with your hands up."

It was a woman's voice, speaking through a bullhorn.

Gordon Phelps had been off to the side, watching the exchange between Austin and the hologram. He stepped out of the shadows and into the spotlight. He yelled a command in Chinese to the Ghost Devils, then in English said to Austin and Zavala, "Don't go away, boys."

Then he and the guards ran back toward the loading-dock door.

Austin and Zavala exchanged a glance.

"No time like the present," Austin said.

He jerked his wrist against the cuff, rose from his chair, and dragged it behind him, moving toward the Dragon Lady. After a few steps, he raised the chair to his chest, with the legs sticking out straight in front.

Zavala followed suit and got his chair into a similar position.

Together, they charged the table.

An actual person would have ducked or run for her life. But the system of camera, projectors, microphones, and computers that were the lifeblood of the holographic projection were not endowed with human instinct.

The figure seemed frozen in place. Only the facial features changed, and Austin and Zavala almost hesitated when the Dragon Lady morphed into a fierce-eyed man wearing a scarlet silk hat, then a series of fearsome male and female faces. Then the last face fuzzed at the edges and broke up into a cloud of swirling and sparkling motes.

There was only empty space by the time Austin and Zavala crashed into the table, overturning it. They climbed to their feet and saw Phelps standing under the spotlight where they had been sitting a moment before. He had the Bowen pointed in their direction.

"The boss isn't going to like that," he said in his lazy way.

"No, I suppose she won't," Austin said. "And that's too damned bad."

The corner of Phelps's mouth turned up slightly.

"What were you saying about the lab vaccine and the virus?" he asked.

"The American and Chinese governments have been secretly working to develop the vaccine to head off a deadly virus, but your boss's outfit stole the lab."

"I know all about the lab," Phelps said. "I'm the one who hijacked the damned thing."

"If that's true," Austin said, "then you know where the lab is. Work with us to take it back from these clowns."

"You weren't kidding about the bug spreading to the States, were you?"

Austin looked him straight in the eye.

"What do you think, Phelps? What do you really think?"

"It's not what I think but what I *know*," he said. "I've got family in the States," he added after a pause.

"There's nothing to prevent them from getting sick," Austin said. "You can't let that happen."

"I'm not going to let it. But I've got to do it my own way, and I work alone."

He turned his head at the sound of more shots and shouting in the distance.

He reached in his shirt pocket and pulled out the keys to the handcuffs, which he set on the floor. Then he unclipped the holster from his belt, slipped the Bowen back in it, and, bending low to the floor, sent it skittering across the floor and out of sight. A second later, he disappeared into the shadows.

When the warehouse lights snapped on a moment later, he was gone. Cate Lyons had one hand on the light switch, the other on a pistol. When she saw Austin and Zavala, she came running over to them.

"Are you guys okay? God, Joe, you look like hell. Sorry I'm late. I was waiting for backup. They're searching the building, but I think everybody got away. Will one of you tell me what's going on?"

Austin picked the key off the floor, unlocked his handcuffs, and did the same for Zavala. He stood up and retrieved his Bowen.

"We'll tell you what we know on the way back to Washington," he said. Austin clipped the holster to his belt. "Then we want to talk to a certain Agent Yoo."

CHAPTER 29

AFTER LEADING ZAVALA TO FALLS CHURCH, CHARLIE YOO had headed back to FBI headquarters. He chatted with an agent from the Asian Crime Unit, looking for tidbits of information to pass along to his employers. As a member of one of the world's largest crime organizations, Yoo got a perverse thrill wandering the halls of the world's largest law-enforcement agency. He was still at the Hoover Building when Caitlin Lyons called and asked if they could get together for a drink at a Georgetown bar. Yoo jumped at the invitation. Caitlin was a good source of FBI gossip, and she was attractive as well.

He took the elevator down to the garage and was walking to his car when Lyons stepped out from behind a concrete pillar.

"Hello, Charlie," she said.

Yoo gave her his widest grin.

"Did I misunderstand?" he asked. "I thought we were meeting at the bar."

"I decided to save you the trip. You must be tired after setting up my friends Joe and Kurt for a hit."

Yoo maintained his grin with some effort, and his hand reached inside his jacket.

"Hi, Charlie. How's by *Yoo?*"

Zavala had stepped out behind him.

"Joe!" Yoo said. "Am I glad to see you. What a great surprise . . ."

"That I'm still alive?"

"Huh? Don't know what you're talking about, Joe. Guess we got separated at the warehouse."

Yoo's hand was moving under his jacket in a way that would have seemed casual to the untrained eye.

"Make a bet with you, Charlie," Zavala said. "Five bucks says Lyons drills a hole through the back of your skull before you get that gun out of its holster."

"I'm feeling lucky," she said. "Make it ten."

She held her pistol with both hands, arms extended.

"Take your jacket off slowly and drop it on the floor," Zavala said.

Yoo did as he was told. Zavala stepped forward to relieve him of both his guns, not only the one in the shoulder holster but the one in the belt holster as well. Frisking him, Zavala found a short, double-edged knife in its ankle sheath.

"Let's go for a ride, Charlie," he said.

Zavala held his arm in the air as if hailing a taxi. Headlights snapped on. A car roared out of nowhere with a squeal of tires and screeched to a stop just inches from Yoo. Zavala produced a roll of duct tape, bound Yoo's wrists behind him, put a strip over his eyes, and slapped another over his mouth. Then he shoved Yoo into the backseat and sat next to him, with Lyons on the other side.

They drove in silence for a half hour before stopping. They hustled Yoo out of the back and down a short flight of stairs. He was plunked in a chair, and the tape was removed from his eyes and mouth. He glanced around at the sparsely furnished room.

"Where are we?"

"FBI safe house," Lyons said.

She was sitting on the opposite end of a rectangular table. Zavala sat on one side, staring at Yoo with no humor in his banged-up face. Across from Zavala was a pale-haired man whose eyes were boring into Yoo like blue lasers.

"My name is Kurt Austin," the man said. "Who do you work for?"

"The Chinese state security agency," Yoo said.

Austin sighed and glanced at Lyons.

"Charlie," Lyons said, "do you remember the time we went to the shooting range and I showed you how well I shoot?" She lifted her pistol off her lap and pointed it at Yoo. "Answer Kurt's question or I'll drill you a third eye."

Yoo swallowed hard.

"I also work for the Pyramid Triad," he said.

Austin motioned for her to lower her gun.

"What's your job?" he said.

"I never left the gangs," Yoo said. "I'm a high-level foot soldier. I don't make decisions. I only follow orders."

"Who ordered you to get Joe to the fortune cookie warehouse?"

"After Joe stopped by my office, I reported his visit. I usually just talk to the next in the line of command. That's as high as I go. That way, if I ever got busted, I'd be limited in what I could tell. This time, I talked to the top dog."

Austin thought back to the raid on the *Beebe*.

"You've been with the Triad a long time," he said. "What do you know about a guy in your organization with a shaved head and a bad temper?"

Yoo blinked in surprise.

"Sounds like Chang," he said, "the one I talked to. He's in charge of the gang network worldwide, guys like the Ghost Devils. Do you know him?"

Austin ignored the question.

"Who are the other leaders?" he asked instead.

"C'mon, Charlie," Caitlin Lyons said with impatience when Yoo hesitated, "we know about Wen Lo being the front man for Pyramid."

"Maybe," Yoo said. "Yeah, I guess so."

"Tell me about Phelps," Austin said. "He was in charge of the gang at the warehouse."

"The Ghost Devils are the local D.C. gang. They meet at the fortune cookie place. That's where major orders come through from the boss. You never know whether it's going to be a man or a woman. But, hey, that hologram is pretty cool, isn't it?"

Yoo looked around at the unrelenting stares and his grin faded.

"Okay," he said, squirming in his chair. "Phelps is a mercenary, a hired gun. I don't know much about him, he comes and goes. He does big important jobs for the Triad."

"Is it unusual to have a foreigner at such a high level?" Austin asked.

"The upper leadership doesn't fully trust anyone Chinese. They don't even trust one another, which is why they use the holograms. That way, they can just pop in anywhere around the world and give orders without even being there."

"Why did your bosses want to kidnap Joe and me?"

"They don't like you. I told Phelps we were playing with fire, snatching someone from a big government agency like NUMA. He said that didn't matter, it was orders from the top. They hoped you'd both show at the same time, but Joe worked as bait."

"How could you be certain I'd be able to find Joe?"

"Phelps was going to call, saying he was an FBI agent, to give you Joe's location. Guess you didn't get the message."

"Guess I didn't."

Austin then lobbed a question from left field.

"What do you know about Bonefish Key?"

Yoo gave him a blank look that couldn't be faked.

Austin believed Yoo knew more than he let on and was higher up in the Triad than he admitted, but he ended his questions.

"I'm done for now."

"Can I go home?" Yoo said.

"After we talk some more," Lyons said, "we'll bring you back to D.C. But it doesn't end there."

"I can deal," Yoo said. "Let's talk."

"Good," she said. "You are going to spy on the Triad for us. If we think you're jerking our chain, we'll let it be known through our people in Hong Kong that you are a turncoat."

"That wouldn't be healthy," Yoo said. "I'll do it."

They questioned him further until deciding there was little more to gain. They taped him up again and drove back to the Hoover Building. There, they removed the tape and dropped him off on the sidewalk. Then they drove back to NUMA.

"My head is spinning," Caitlin Lyons said. "What just happened?"

"The Pyramid Triad has developed an influenza virus that they want to use to bring down the Chinese government," Austin said. "They hijacked the lab working on a vaccine for the virus, and, once the Triad topples the government, Pyramid will market the antiviral around the world and make billions."

"Hundreds of thousands of people could die before that happens," she said.

"Do you think anyone at Pyramid gives a damn?" he asked.

"Not from what I've seen. Where do we start?"

"Get the Asian Crime Unit to crack down on the Ghost Devils. While you handle this end, Joe and I will try to find the lab."

"What should I do about Charlie Yoo?"

"Use him, then lose him."

"I like that," she said with an evil smile on her face.

Lyons dropped them off at the NUMA tower. Austin and Zavala headed their separate ways home to pick up their bags and said they would hook up again at the airport.

Austin checked his cell phone while driving home. He had left it in the car when he went to investigate the cookie factory. He listened to the voice mail from Phelps, saying he was an FBI agent. Yoo had told the truth about one thing.

Austin clicked the phone off and nailed the accelerator.

Time, as always, had become the enemy.

CHAPTER 30

AT THREE O'CLOCK IN THE MORNING, THE NAVY BLUE SUV pulled up to a hangar at Reagan National Airport and parked next to a sleek Cessna Citation X jet that had NUMA emblazoned in black on its turquoise fuselage. Austin and Casey emerged from the SUV's backseat, and the lieutenant handed over an eleven-by-sixteen-inch plastic pouch.

"This packet contains the nuts-and-bolts details of the mission we talked about on the drive to the airport," Casey said. "Good luck, Kurt. And keep your eyes peeled for sharks."

"Thank you, Lieutenant," Austin said as they shook hands. "But I'll take a dorsal-finned man-eater any day over the schools of sharp-toothed politicians and government bureaucrats that swarm the Potomac waters."

Casey gave him a knowing smile.

"I'll remember to keep my shark repellant handy, Kurt."

"I was thinking *another* type of repellant might be more appropriate for Washington, but good luck to you in any case."

Austin retrieved his duffel from the SUV and handed it to a

baggage handler who loaded it into the jet's cargo hold. Tucking the pouch under his arm, he stepped up to the open door and paused there. Headlights were bearing down on the Citation and salsa music blared from a car sound system as Zavala's red Corvette raced across the tarmac with its top down.

The car slammed to a stop next to the hangar, and Zavala waved. Austin shook his head. As if to balance out his soft-spoken manner, Zavala never simply arrived at a destination, he made a grand entrance. Austin waved back, then stepped into the jet's plush cabin and dropped the pouch on a coffee table. While Austin went to talk to the pilot and copilot, Zavala raised his convertible's top, grabbed his duffel, tossed it to the handler, and bolted aboard. As he stepped into the cabin, Austin was coming back from the cockpit.

"We're right on schedule," he informed Zavala.

The cabin seating was an arrangement of beige leather chairs and a sofa that all could be made into beds. Zavala stretched out in one of the comfortably padded chairs, yawned, and said, "Any idea where we're going?"

Austin plunked himself down on the sofa and picked the pouch up off the table. He held it up so Zavala could read the TOP SECRET label affixed to the outside.

"Our marching orders," he announced.

He broke the seal with his thumbnail and extracted the thick wad of paper from inside. He unfolded the first page, which was covered with diagrams, and then passed it over to Zavala. Zavala glanced at the diagrams, then read the words printed in large-block type:

U.S. NAVY UNDERSEA HABITAT
AND OBSERVATORY

Zavala looked up from the diagrams.

"These are the blueprints for Davy Jones's Locker," he said, his dark eyes sparkling with excitement.

Austin nodded.

With loving care, Zavala spread the diagrams out on the table. He studied every detail of the spheres and connecting passageways the way some men might savor a naughty pinup. As the brilliant designer of dozens of NUMA submersibles, he paid particular attention to the plans for the cargo shuttle and the lab's specimen-collection submersibles. After a few minutes, he passed judgment from the point of view of a marine engineer who had struggled many times with the thorny challenges posed by currents, depth, pressure, and salt water.

"Brilliant," Zavala said with unabashed admiration. He crinkled his brow. "It's hard to believe anything this size could vanish."

"The lab's design may have made the hijacking possible," Austin said. "As you can see, it was designed as a mobile undersea observatory. Lieutenant Casey said that the Navy built the components on land, towed them out to sea on specially designed barges, then assembled the components and lowered the lab into place. They built in flotation capability, and the spheres and connectors were reinforced structurally so the lab could be moved without breaking apart. The lab also had a stabilization system to keep it level during movement."

Zavala took a ballpoint pen from his shirt pocket and placed it on the diagrams.

"Imagine this pen is a submarine or large submersible," he said. "They hook onto the lab, get it pumped up to neutral buoyancy, and tow it away."

"Great minds think alike," Austin said. "The Russian government has been trying to sell off its fleet of Typhoons for use as cargo carriers in the Arctic. Maybe they found a buyer."

"That solves only part of the mystery," Zavala said. "If this was such a big secret, how did the hijackers know Davy Jones's Locker existed and where it was located?"

"The lab's security was outsourced to a private contractor," Austin said, "and that may have been the weak point. The Navy talked to the support-ship survivors. Lieutenant Casey said the crew got a request from their security company to shuttle a representative down to the lab a short while before the attack. They said he was a friendly guy with a Southern accent. Phelps, of course.

"Phelps admitted he hijacked the lab," Austin continued. "What he didn't say was that the company rep who authorized his visit was killed in a car crash. My guess is, he was coerced into getting Phelps an ID, then was eliminated."

"A convenient coincidence," Zavala said. "What was the lab's last position?"

Austin dug a map out of the pouch and spread it on the coffee table. An area in the Pacific Ocean had been circled in black grease pencil near the island of Pohnpei in Micronesia.

Zavala sat back and laced his hands behind his head.

"Gee, *that* narrows it down," he said with a sour expression on his face. "It could take months to find the lab."

"Sandecker says we have to wrap it up in less than seventy-two hours," Austin said.

"I'm surprised the old sea dog didn't ask us to solve the problem of global hunger and the energy crisis in our spare time."

"Don't give him any ideas," Austin said. "He'll want us to clean up the oceans on our coffee break."

The sound of approaching jet engines broke the early-morning stillness. Austin got up and went to the door. A NUMA jet was taxiing up to the hangar. The engines went silent, and three figures emerged and walked across the tarmac toward the

Citation. Austin recognized Paul Trout's tall, lanky form and Gamay's red hair. The Asian woman walking by the Trouts' side was a stranger to him.

Austin greeted the Trouts, and warned Paul to duck his head entering the cabin. He welcomed the Asian woman with a friendly smile.

"You must be Dr. Song Lee," Austin said, offering his hand. "I'm Kurt Austin. This is Joe Zavala. We're NUMA colleagues of the Trouts. Thank you for coming to Washington."

"And thank you for sending Paul and Gamay to Bonefish Key, Mr. Austin," Lee said. "I'd be dead if they hadn't arrived when they did."

Kurt's eyes drank in Song's flowerlike beauty.

"That would have been a shame, Dr. Lee," he said. "Please have a seat. We don't have much time. You must have many questions."

Song Lee settled into the sofa and looked around in wonderment. With their imposing physical prowess, quiet competence, and easy banter in the face of danger, the Trouts had seemed larger than life. But this pale-haired man, with his broad shoulders and sculpted bronze profile, was even more intriguing. Austin's courtly manner could not disguise the fearlessness and daring that she detected in his remarkable coral-blue eyes. And his dark-complexioned friend Zavala had the swashbuckling air of a pirate prince.

"The Trouts told me about the attack on the bathysphere," Lee said. "Do you know where Dr. Kane is?"

"Safe in protective custody. I spoke to Kane last night, and he filled me in on the work at Bonefish Key and the undersea lab they called Davy Jones's Locker."

Lee's jaw dropped.

"I was aware of the secret facility, of course," she said, "but I had no idea it was under the sea!"

"The Pacific Ocean, to be exact. It was in Micronesian waters, three hundred feet below the surface."

Lee had a dazed expression on her delicate features.

"I would expect Dr. Kane to be unconventional," she said, "but I never dreamed it was anything like *that*."

Austin went on.

"The lab's work and location were tightly held secrets, but somehow it was hijacked along with the staff. Joe and I think that the lab's disappearance, the bathysphere attack, and the attempt to kidnap you are all connected. Dr. Kane told me about the medusa project. What was the exact nature of your work at the Florida lab?"

"I'm a virologist trained in epidemiology," Lee said. "I stayed on Bonefish Key to concentrate on the probable path an epidemic would take and how best to position our resources and the vaccine-production facilities."

"That would make you an integral part of the project."

"I like to think so. The vaccine would be useless without a strategy to deploy it. It would be as if a general sent his troops into battle without a plan."

"What would have happened to the project if you had been kidnapped?"

"Not much," she said with a shrug of the shoulders. "The plans are almost all in place, waiting for the cure to be synthesized into a viable vaccine. With the lab gone, there isn't much chance of that happening."

"Don't give up hope, Dr. Lee. The lab is the object of a massive search. In fact, Joe and I are on our way to Micronesia to see if we can help the searchers."

Lee dropped her gaze to the map lying on the table.

"You're going to Pohnpei?" she asked.

"It looks that way," Austin said. "Have you been there?"

"No, but the island was the epicenter of the deadly epidemic that struck the Pacific whaling fleet in the mid-1800s. This is extremely significant."

"In what way, Dr. Lee?"

"At Harvard Medical School, I did a paper for a Professor Codman that was based on an article I came across in an old medical journal. The doctor who wrote the article had compiled statistics about a group of New Bedford whaling men who had been virtually disease-free for much of their very long lives."

Austin tried to glance at his watch without being obvious. He had little interest in oddball medical phenomena. The whine of the Citation's engines warming up provided a convenient out.

"It has been a great pleasure meeting you," he said. "We're going to be taking off soon . . ."

"Hear me out, Mr. Austin," Lee said, raising her voice above the engines.

Austin smiled at the unexpected firmness.

"Go on, Dr. Lee, but please keep it brief."

She nodded.

"The men in the study group had all crewed aboard the whaling ship *Princess*. They became ill after the ship stopped in Pohnpei."

"I still don't see the connection to the lab . . ."

It was Song Lee's turn to be impatient.

"It's right there in front of you, Mr. Austin. The crew all survived! If that doesn't get your attention, maybe this will. The symptoms of the disease were almost identical to those of this latest epidemic. The crewmen should have died, but instead they enjoyed robust health for the rest of their lives. Somehow, they were cured."

"Are you saying that what cured the whalers might work for the new virus?" Austin asked.

"Precisely."

Austin's mental machinery kicked into gear. A bunch of whalers lived disease-free to a ripe old age after a trip to Micronesia, the same neighborhood where the blue medusa lives. He connected that to what Kane told him about the toxin keeping its prey healthy until the medusa made a meal of it. He glanced around at his colleagues.

"The log of the *Princess* for that expedition *would* make interesting reading," Paul Trout commented.

"I tried to track the 1848 logbook down through Harvard's Widener Library," Lee said. "My research led me to New Bedford. A dealer in antique books named Brimmer said he might be able to locate the book, but I was about to leave for home and had to put the whole thing aside."

The pilot's voice called back from the cockpit.

"We've been cleared for early takeoff. Anytime you're ready . . ."

"Thank you, Dr. Lee," Austin said. "I apologize for cutting you short, but we're really about to leave."

"I want to come with you," she said without thinking.

The statement had leaped from her mouth on its own, but then she punctuated it with a firm set of jaw.

"That's not possible," Austin said. "We'll be on the move, and things could get rough. Joe has uncovered information that suggests a Chinese Triad named Pyramid is involved in all this."

"A *Triad*?" She got over her surprise quickly. "Why would a Triad be interested in the search for an antiviral vaccine?"

Zavala answered the question.

"The Triad developed the virus as part of a scheme to destabilize the Chinese government," he said. "Your vaccine would
have spoiled their plans. They had to take control of the lab to
prevent the antiviral from being used by others."

"This is overwhelming," Song Lee said, "but it makes sense.
My government is deathly afraid of social unrest, which is why
it clamps down so hard at any sign of organized protest. All the
more reason to take me with you. I should be part of any attempt
to stop something started by my countrymen. I'm intimately ac-
quainted with the entire research program, and there may be
something relevant on Pohnpei."

Austin eyed Lee's smoky-smelling T-shirt and shorts, apparently the same clothes she had been wearing on Bonefish Key.

"You'd be traveling pretty light, Dr. Lee. We can give you a
toothbrush but not much else."

"I'll take that toothbrush, and I can buy clothes when we get
there."

Austin sat back and folded his arms. Despite his body language, he was enjoying Song Lee's display of pluckiness.

"Go ahead, Dr. Lee. You've got thirty seconds to make your
case."

She nodded.

"I believe that the blue medusa jellyfish the lab was using in
its research was part of native medicine used to cure the crew of
the *Princess*. And if we can find the place where it happened, it
might lead us to the lab."

"That's a pretty slim premise, Dr. Lee."

"I know that, Mr. Austin. But it's *something*. Right now,
we have nothing. Please don't tell me it's any more dangerous
than the Florida mangroves where I was kidnapped and almost shot."

Zavala chuckled softly.

"Lady's got a point," he said.

Austin turned to the Trouts.

"What do you think?" he asked.

"I was thinking of having Dr. Lee stay with my aunt 'Lizbeth on Cuttyhunk Island until the danger passed," Paul said.

Gamay chortled.

"I *know* your Aunt Lizzy. She'd drive this poor woman crazy with her incessant talk about beach-plum jelly."

"Gamay's right about Lizzy," Paul said. "And Dr. Lee is right when she says her expertise in the lab's work could come in handy. I know how you like insurance."

Austin had a reputation around NUMA for daring that bordered on the reckless. Those he worked with, like the Trouts, knew that his risks were always calculated. He was like the high-stakes riverboat gambler who kept not one but two Derringers up his sleeves.

Austin threw his hands in the air.

"Looks like I'm outgunned, Dr. Lee." He got on the intercom to the cockpit. "Ready to go in five minutes," he told the pilot.

Gamay asked, "What would you like us to do while you're in Micronesia?"

"Get in touch with Lieutenant Casey and tell him that Dr. Lee has joined us. Contact Joe's FBI friend and fill her in." He paused in thought, then said, "See what you can do about tracking down the *Princess*'s logbook."

"We'll start with Perlmutter and let you know," Paul said.

The Trouts wished the others luck and descended to the tarmac. They watched as the Citation X taxied down the runway and leaped into the sky.

Paul gazed at the pink-tinged clouds of dawn.

"Red sky at morning," he said, "sailor take warning."

"That sort of stuff went out when weather satellites went into orbit, Captain Courageous," Gamay said.

Paul was a third-generation fisherman, and weather lore had been passed down in his family from father to son. Gamay was annoyed whenever Paul reverted to his old-salt persona.

He smiled slightly, and said, "Storm is still a storm."

She took him by the arm, and said, "Put on your foul-weather gear. You haven't seen the storm that compares with getting Perlmutter out of bed."

CHAPTER 31

ST. JULIEN PERLMUTTER CUSTOMARILY WORKED INTO THE wee hours and slept until long after the sun had risen. So when the telephone beside his king-size water bed gonged like a ship's bell and awoke the renowned naval historian from a sound slumber, his usually sunny greeting had an edge to it.

His pudgy hand reached to the bedside table, snatched up the antique French telephone's receiver, and stuck it to his ear. Still groggier than a punch-drunk prizefighter, he boomed, "St. Julien Perlmutter here. State your bloody damned business in a brief manner. And you better have a good excuse for calling at this ungodly hour!"

"Good morning, Julien," said a soothing female voice. "Hope I didn't wake you up."

The ruddy features that were almost hidden under a thick gray beard underwent a miraculous Hyde-to-Jekyll transformation. The scowl disappeared, the sky blue eyes suddenly sparkled with good humor, and the pink lips under the small tulip nose widened in a warm smile.

"Good morning, my dear Gamay," Perlmutter purred. "Of *course* you didn't wake me up. I was in that delightful state between sleep and waking, dreaming of breakfast."

Gamay chuckled softly. It was rare when the four-hundred-pound Perlmutter *wasn't* thinking about food.

"I'm glad to hear that, Julien, because Paul and I would like to come over and see you. We'll bring you a treat."

Perlmutter smacked his lips at the prospect.

"I'll get the coffee brewing," he said. "You know where I live."

He replaced the receiver in its cradle and swung his feet out of the bed, which was set into an alcove off a huge combination bedroom, living room, and study. Perlmutter made his home in an N Street carriage house behind two vine-encrusted homes only a few blocks from the Trouts' town house. The floor-to-ceiling shelves that lined every wall sagged under the weight of thousands of books. More books were stacked on tables and chairs, piled on the floor in precariously leaning towers, and even covered the foot of his rippling water bed.

The first thing Perlmutter saw when he blinked his eyes open every morning was what many experts acknowledged to be the finest accumulation of historical ship literature ever assembled. Scholars around the globe were green with envy over his vast collection. Perlmutter constantly fended off museums that wanted him to donate it to their libraries.

Slipping a red-and-gold paisley robe over his purple silk pajamas, Perlmutter eased his small feet into soft leather slippers. He went to the kitchen to put on a pot of Papua New Guinea coffee. Then he washed his face and brushed his teeth. He poured an antique Limoges porcelain cup full of the deep, chocolaty coffee. The heady fragrance almost made him swoon.

One sip of the strong brew snapped him fully awake. He felt

almost human by the time the doorbell rang. He opened the door, and his smile faded as his eyes went to the DUNKIN' DONUTS emblazoned on the flat cardboard box in Paul's hands. Perlmutter recoiled like a vampire being offered garlic, and would have fled into the house if Trout had not lifted the box's lid.

"Just playing a little joke," Paul said with an impish grin.

"We picked up these treats at the deli around the corner," Gamay said. "Smoked Scottish salmon, blini and caviar, and fresh-baked croissants. Not the equal of your culinary skills, but we thought you might not want to cook so early in the morning."

Perlmutter put one hand over his chest and with the other took the box, holding it as if he feared contamination, and led the way into the house.

"You had me going there for a minute," he said, returning to his normal jovial mood. "You've obviously been hanging around too much with that young scalawag Austin. Where are Kurt and Joe these days? Last I knew, they were diving under the sea in the bathysphere replica."

"They're on their way to Micronesia on an assignment," Gamay said.

"Micronesia?" he said. "That's one place I'd like to visit. I hear they mark important occasions with feasts involving enormous amounts of food."

Perlmutter escorted his guests into his kitchen, poured two more cupfuls of New Guinea coffee, and doled out the early brunch on three Limoges plates. They all sat around a polished wooden kitchen table, one of the few flat surfaces in the carriage house not piled high with books.

"Sorry for the early-morning call," Paul began, "but there is some urgency to our search. We're trying to track down the 1848 logbook of a New England whaling vessel named the *Princess*. We hoped you could tell us where to start."

Perlmutter's bushy brows bobbed up and down.

"Caleb Nye's ship!" he exclaimed.

Gamay tossed her head back and laughed in surprise.

"You never cease to amaze, Julien," she said. "We mention a whaling ship, one of hundreds, and you have the name of the captain on the tip of your tongue."

"Only because the young man had an experience that was quite memorable in the annals of whaling. Caleb was not the captain. He was the ship's green hand, the designation given the newest crew member. He claimed to have been swallowed by a sperm whale. The story enjoyed wide circulation in his day."

"Is that even *possible*?" Paul asked.

Perlmutter nibbled thoughtfully on a croissant, then said, "That question has been debated going back to Jonah. Nye wasn't the only one who claimed that a sperm whale had swallowed him. In 1891, some years after Nye's adventure, a whaler named James Bartley, serving aboard the *Star of the East* off the Falkland Islands in the South Atlantic, reportedly disappeared after a sperm whale overturned his whaleboat. When the crew was carving the whale up later for blubber, they found Bartley alive doubled up inside. His skin and hair were bleached white, supposedly from the mammal's gastric juices. He went back to work after a few weeks of rest. Or so the story goes . . ."

"I detect a note of skepticism in your voice," Paul said.

"With sound reason. Bartley's story is one of those tales that never die, like Bigfoot or the Loch Ness Monster. Occasionally, a writer who's resurrecting that old chestnut will contact me. I refer such inquiries to the findings of Edward B. Davis, who thoroughly investigated the story."

"His conclusions?" Paul asked.

"Davis scoured every document he could find on Bartley's story. There really was a ship named the *Star of the East,* but nothing to substantiate the report that Bartley had been checked out at a London hospital for damage to his skin from a whale's gastric juices. Moreover, the wife of the ship's captain said the story was made out of whole cloth. The *Star* was *not* a whaler, and the British did not go whaling off the Falklands at that time. Despite these disclaimers, stories about Bartley's supposed ordeal have persisted through the years."

Paul turned to Gamay.

"You're the marine biologist in the family. Would it be possible for a sperm whale to swallow a man?"

"Sperm whales have been found with giant squids in their stomachs, so, physiologically, it might be possible."

Perlmutter popped a forkful of salmon in his mouth, dabbed his lips, pronouncing the food fit for human consumption.

"Davis theorized that Bartley capitalized on his naturally pale complexion," he said. "He used the name of a real ship, got some stories in the local press, and even may have persuaded a friend to pose as the captain. He eventually joined a circus, billing himself as 'Jonah of the Twentieth Century.'"

Gamay frowned in thought.

"Fascinating," she said, "but what does this have to do with Caleb Nye and the *Princess*?"

Perlmutter pushed his empty plate aside and rose from the table. He knew where every item in his extensive collection could be found. He opened a tall metal storage container, explaining that the box was moistureproof and temperature controlled to preserve his papers, and pulled out a poster two by three feet in size. It announced, in huge circus typeface, that CALEB NYE, A LIVING JONAH, would be giving an ILLUSTRATED PRESENTATION at the FIRST PARISH METHODIST CHURCH in WORCESTER, MASS. The engraving, colored by hand, showed a sperm whale attacking a whaleboat.

"My guess is, Bartley heard about Caleb's show and decided to put one together himself," he said. "After I received yet another query from a tabloid scrivener, I decided to go beyond the Davis research. That's when I discovered that some fifty years before Bartley surfaced, Nye had been the star of a traveling show that featured *him* as a modern-day Jonah."

Gamay said, "Was Caleb's story simply an earlier version of the scam?"

Perlmutter tugged at his beard.

"I think not. In contrast to Bartley, Caleb Nye *did* serve aboard a whaling ship in the Pacific Ocean, and witnesses said he *was* swallowed by a whale. He produced affidavits from the master of the ship, Captain Horatio Dobbs, and fellow crew members saying that the story was true. I think Bartley used Nye's story. Unfortunately, the skepticism over Bartley's claim tainted Nye's claim. You said that you were looking for the 1848 log of the *Princess*?"

"That's right," Paul said. "We're hoping you can help us find it."

"A profoundly wise decision on your part. I suggest that you start with Rachael Dobbs."

"Is Rachael related to the good captain?" Gamay asked.

"A great-great-great-granddaughter. She lives in New Bedford, and is the curator of the Dobbs Museum. I spoke to her when I was researching the subject."

Paul said, "We could be there in a couple of hours."

"Splendid. I'll give her a call."

Perlmutter consulted a Rolodex and dialed the number. He chatted amiably with someone, then hung up and said, "She'll see you at three o'clock, but she had some good news and some bad news. The good news is that the logbook of the 1848 voyage was given to Caleb Nye. The bad news is that a fire destroyed Nye's library."

"I guess we won't be traveling to New Bedford," Paul said with a slow shake of his head.

"Why are you New Englanders such pessimists?" Gamay said.

"Because we're realists," he said. "Without the ship's log, we don't know where the *Princess* stopped after it left Pohnpei."

"True," she said. "But maybe we don't *need* the log if we concentrate on Caleb Nye."

"Of *course,*" Paul said with a snap of his fingers. "Caleb was an eyewitness to the voyage. He told hundreds of people about his experience. We might find something somewhere with the details of his trip."

"It's worth a talk with Ms. Dobbs," Perlmutter said. "By the way, you never said why you were interested in the log."

Paul said, "It's a long story, St. Julien. We can tell you over dinner when we get back. Your choice. Our treat."

The suggestion got Perlmutter off the subject of the logbook, which was what Paul intended.

"There's a new French restaurant near the Watergate I've been meaning to try," Perlmutter said. "But back to business."

He brushed his fingers over a section of shelves and began pulling out books. Minutes later, the Trouts left the carriage house, their arms loaded down with volumes cherry-picked from Perlmutter's whaling collection. The Trouts stacked them in the back of the Mini Cooper Clubman that they used as their in-town car.

On the short drive back to their town house, Paul said, "I hate to be a pessimist again, but Kurt and Joe have set themselves a formidable task. Finding the missing lab may be impossible. We could be doing something more substantial than chasing down a nineteenth-century whaler whose adventures may or may not have a bearing on the case."

Gamay nodded.

"I understand that this trip may turn out to be a waste of valuable time," she said, "but one fact is inescapable."

"What's that?"

"Caleb Nye is all we have."

CHAPTER 32

As the Citation X streaked west over the North American continent at six hundred miles an hour, all was quiet in the cabin, where the passengers slept soundly with forty-three thousand feet of air beneath their pillows.

Song Lee had been the first to turn in, followed by Joe Zavala, who was stretched out on a thickly padded chair. Kurt Austin had read for a short while, then he had set Casey's file aside and glanced at Song, who was sleeping on the sofa. Her bare legs stuck out from under her blanket. Austin adjusted the blanket, then went up to the cockpit and radioed the ground-crew manager at the Los Angeles Airport. He came back, settled into another chair, and within minutes had slipped into a deep slumber.

When the passengers got off at LAX to stretch their legs, the ground-crew manager was waiting to hand Lee a plastic bag. At Austin's request, the manager had contacted his wife, and she had put together a change of clothes to replace the smoky T-shirt and shorts Lee had been wearing since Bonefish Key.

When she opened the bag, she let out a cry of delight, and dashed into the hangar to try them on. She squeezed in a quick shower beforehand, and a brief phone call after dressing, and then the jet leaped into the sky again and set a course for Honolulu. With the California coastline fading behind in the distance, Lee came over and sat next to Austin, who was discussing the maps and charts in Lieutenant Casey's packet with Zavala. She was wearing a pair of conservative black cotton slacks and a sleeveless white cotton blouse that looked stylish on her slim figure.

"I understand you arranged for the delivery of my new wardrobe," she said. "Thank you very much, Kurt. The clothes fit me perfectly."

"Sailors are good at taking measurements with their eyes," Austin said.

He saw Zavala mouthing the word *Smooth,* and realized that he had compared Song Lee's lithe body to a boat keel. Quickly changing the subject, he said, "These are the blueprints for Dr. Kane's undersea lab. From this layout, can you say what was going on there?"

"In general, perhaps." She examined the diagrams. "These spheres labeled LIVING QUARTERS and ADMINISTRATION are self-evident. Those labeled LAB and RESOURCE CULTIVATION tell only part of the story."

"We have lots of time. I'd be interested in hearing the whole story, Song."

She pinched her chin in thought, then said, "Imagine the medusa project as a three-act play. Act 1 was the basic research on the jellyfish toxin at Bonefish Key. Act 2 is the practical application of that research toward synthesizing a vaccine, which was done at Davy Jones's Locker. Act 3 would have been the actual production at centers set up to manufacture the vaccine in large volumes. We were at the second intermission."

"Why were you more successful than other labs working in the area of ocean biotechnology?" Austin asked.

"Because Dr. Kane is a *genius*," Lee declared. "He assembled the foremost experts in a brand-new field known as *systems* biology. The research was a blend of protein study, genomics, and mathematics. The lab used advanced computer technology to pull the research together."

"How did that approach differ from conventional research?" Austin asked.

"It's the difference between squinting through a telescope and taking in a scene with both eyes. The lab had *hundreds* of eyes, absorbing information that was fed into one computer brain for analysis. Even so, it took all our efforts to decipher the medusa toxin's molecular makeup and assay the immune response it provoked in a living organism."

"Dr. Kane mentioned the development of a larger and more poisonous genetically modified version of the medusa," Austin said.

Lee nodded.

"He wanted to produce more toxin and a brighter organism," she said.

"I understand that the bigger the jellyfish, the more toxin to work with," he said. "What about the bioluminescence?"

"The creature's brightness indicates what is happening with its molecular processes. It acts like a biological thermometer. The goal was to produce the vaccine in volume. We transferred the genes that produced the essential compounds to a bacterium that could be quickly cultivated for the vaccine."

"Dr. Kane said that the medusa toxin doesn't kill outright but paralyzes the prey and keeps it healthy and fresh."

"An antiviral has to kill the pathogens without hurting the host. The medusa toxin went beyond that, actually *protecting* its host organism's health . . . for a while, anyway. The process is called hormesis. In small doses, a toxin can trigger repair mechanisms in the body, maybe even retard aging. It works in the same way exercise does, by stressing the body so that it changes the metabolism for the better."

"That which does not kill us makes us strong," Austin said.

"That's an accurate description," Lee said.

"Could hormesis have anything to do with the New Bedford anomaly?"

"It could have *everything* to do with it. Administered in the proper amount, the medusa toxin could have improved subjects' health and prolonged their lives." Lee cocked her head. "Now let me ask *you* a question."

"Be my guest."

"You and Joe and the Trouts have obviously worked together in the past. Who *are* you?"

Austin answered Lee in a way that would satisfy her curiosity without revealing too much about his team's inner workings.

"We're all members of a special NUMA team that investigates ocean mysteries that are out of the normal range of possibility," he said.

"This mystery certainly fits *that* category," she said. "Thank you for being forthright."

"And thanks for enlightening me about the lab's research. Let's talk about the new flu virus. How bad would it be if the epidemic goes beyond China's borders?"

"*Very* bad. SARS hit around eight thousand people, and fewer than a thousand died. If this virus hits your country, it would kill a minimum of more than two hundred thousand people."

"And the maximum?"

"Possibly in the millions. But even in the hundreds of thousands, the epidemic would overwhelm the health system of any country it hits. Many of the people who will die are health providers, widening the disaster even more. The total impact on the industrialized world would be nearly seven hundred thousand deaths and more than two million people hospitalized . . . *minimum*. Developing countries would fare much worse. The total cost could be as much as a trillion dollars."

Austin had been working his jaw muscle as he listened to the grim statistics.

"You've just described a global catastrophe, Song."

"To say the least. The medical community has worried about a mutant flu virus for years. Even without help, the virus can reinvent itself, changing its genetic makeup, hitting people who have no immunity against it."

"Medicine has evolved far beyond what was available in past epidemics," he said.

"So has transportation," she said. "A carrier infected in the U.S. or China can spread the disease anywhere around the world in a matter of hours. Existing vaccines are useless, which is why it was so important to develop the medusa vaccine."

"How does the new virus spread?"

"The old virus spread by contact. The mutant strain may spread that way, but, even more disturbing, it may spread through the water."

"Are you saying that it could seep into the water table?"

"There is that possibility, yes."

"Which means that the virus could be introduced into drinking water."

"That would make its spread even more difficult to control. Everyone drinks water, while personal contact is a hit-or-miss thing. It is extremely contagious either way. It's possible that the whole human race could become infected."

Lee felt emotionally drained by the implications of her dry

recitation and expected Austin to share her pessimism. But, to her surprise, he said, "Thank you for your analysis, Dr. Lee, but we can't let that happen."

"What do you mean to do?"

"Once we find the lab, we'll make sure that the staff is safe. Then we'll retrieve the research and allow vaccine production to move ahead. And then we'll proceed to sink the Triad. How's that sound to you, Joe?"

"Sounds like we'll need some chow to keep us going. I'll see what I can rustle up in the galley."

Austin had summed up his strategy as casually as if he were talking about making a soccer play. Instead of panicking, Zavala was throwing breakfast together. Lee saw no sign of madness or misplaced humor in the face of either man, only calm determination and steely resolve.

For the first time since she had learned that Davy Jones's Locker had vanished, she began to hope.

CHAPTER 33

THE TROUTS HAD TO WAIT UNTIL THE AFTERNOON FOR AN available NUMA executive jet, but New Bedford Regional Airport was only about an hour's flight from Washington. With Gamay navigating, Paul drove their rented SUV past the stately old houses that bordered County Street and swung in to a horseshoe-shaped driveway. A sign in front of the butternut-and-mustard Greek Revival mansion identified the house as the CAPTAIN HORATIO DOBBS MUSEUM AND GARDENS.

The Trouts climbed to the porch, passing between tall Doric columns, and rang the bell. A middle-aged woman opened the door.

"Oh, dear," she said, her smile vanishing. "I thought you were the electrician."

Gamay said, "I'm afraid not. We're from the National Underwater and Marine Agency. We called you earlier today from Washington."

The smile returned.

"Oh, yes, Mr. Perlmutter's friends. St. Julien is a lovely man.

Come in. I'm Rachael Dobbs. Excuse me for being a bit flustered. The Dobbs Foundation rented a patio tent for a jazz concert tonight, and there's a problem with the sound system."

The Trouts stepped into a high-ceilinged vestibule and followed Rachael along a long hallway. The parquet floor had been buffed to a mirror finish. She stopped in front of side-by-side oil paintings. The bearded man in one portrait held a sextant in his big hands. Flinty gray eyes looked out over an eagle nose. The woman in the other portrait wore a dark velvet dress, with a simple lace collar encircling her graceful neck. Large hazel eyes looked out with a steady gaze. There was a slight smile on her thin lips, as if amused by a secret joke.

"These are my great-great-great-grandparents. Captain Horatio and Hepsa Dobbs," Rachael said.

Hepsa and Rachael shared the same carrot-colored hair.

"The resemblance is striking," Paul said.

"I'm pleased with Hepsa's gift of her red hair, but I would have preferred less of a proboscis from the captain," she said. "As you can see, he had plenty to go around."

Rachael Dobbs gave the Trouts a tour of the mansion, introducing the family members in the portraits that covered every wall. The men wore wide-brimmed, Quaker-style hats, the women demure caps.

She pointed to a display case that held a battered top hat.

"That was the captain's lucky chapeau. He wore it on every whaling expedition."

They went out onto a broad deck overlooking a formal English garden bordered with rosebushes. She seated the Trouts at an umbrellaed table on the patio and brought out glasses of iced tea.

"Thank you for the tour," Gamay said. "It's a beautiful house."

"The captain and his wife moved up here from Johnny Cake Hill. The whaling merchants wanted bigger homes and gardens that reflected their status in the community. Now, how may I help you? St. Julien said on the phone that you were interested in one of the captain's logbooks."

"We received a query from a virologist who asked us about an epidemic that struck the Pacific whaling fleet in 1848," Gamay said. "We're surveying logbooks from that time to see if we can find any mention of the event."

Rachael raised an eyebrow.

"The 1848 voyage was the captain's last whaling expedition," she said. "He retired from the sea after that voyage."

"Wasn't that unusual?" Paul asked. "From what we've heard, your ancestor was an extremely successful whaler."

"He was probably the best of his day. And you're right about it being odd that he stopped going to sea at the peak of his career. He had brought in a full hold of sperm oil on his ship's maiden voyage and could have had any command he wanted. He said he wanted to spend more time with Hepsa, whom he had married before he left on that final expedition."

"I don't blame him for wanting to stay home," Paul said. "Your ancestor was a beautiful woman."

Rachael blushed at the indirect compliment.

"Thank you. The captain went to work for the Rotch family. They invented the vertical-integration model still used by multinational corporations and applied it to the whaling industry." She paused in thought, then said, "According to the Dobbs family lore, something happened on that last voyage that changed his views."

"The face in the captain's portrait didn't belong to a man who would scare easily," Paul said.

"No disagreement, Mr. Trout. The captain had been a harpooner before he worked his way up. Anyone who stands in a frail wooden boat and antagonizes a seventy-foot-long sperm whale is not fainthearted."

Gamay leaned forward.

"Could the Caleb Nye incident have had anything to do with the captain's decision?" she asked.

Rachael shook her head.

"Caleb's experience would have been a wonderful story for the captain to tell other ship captains when they got together," she said.

"I believe you told St. Julien that the logbook for the 1848 voyage was destroyed," Gamay said.

"Unfortunately, yes," Rachael said with a sigh. "Caleb's whaling library went up in flames when his house burned to the ground. He must have been heartbroken at losing his beloved library. There's now housing for the elderly on the site of the old Nye mansion in Fairhaven."

"Isn't it curious that the captain would have given his log to a former crewman?" Gamay said.

"Not really. The captain would have known about Caleb's book collection. Also, there was a peculiar bond between the two men. It was said that the captain felt personally responsible for the young man's unfortunate condition. He wrote an affidavit saying that the Jonah story was true. It was read at the traveling show and helped make Caleb a rich man."

"Did Caleb ever write a book about his adventure?"

"Not that I know of. He made the lecture circuit for years under the guidance of a P. T. Barnum type, a promoter named Strater, and they sold pamphlets at the shows, so maybe that was more lucrative than a book would have been. There must have been a great deal written about Caleb. You could dig into old newspaper files, for a start."

Rachael excused herself to answer the doorbell and came back a moment later.

"The electrician is here. We could talk later, if you don't mind waiting."

"We're on a tight schedule," Gamay said. "Do you have any suggestions on how we might find out more about Caleb Nye?"

"You could start in our basement. We have a section of the diorama Nye used in his presentations. He gave it to a library, but they ran out of room and shipped it over here. We didn't have room for it, either. Perhaps I can show it to you when I'm not so busy.

"In the meantime, there is the New Bedford Whaling Museum. And the various local historical societies. But since you're short on time, there is one other avenue, although I hesitate to suggest it."

"We're grasping at straws," Paul said. "Give it a try."

"Well, then," she said with a shrug, "you might want to talk to Harvey Brimmer. He deals in antique documents from a shop near the Seamen's Bethel on Johnny Cake Hill. He unearths some amazing old documents from time to time."

"Why do you hesitate to recommend Mr. Brimmer?" Paul asked.

"Harvey has a reputation for collecting upfront fees, then not locating the documents he was hired to find. There have been rumors of forgeries and dealing in stolen documents, but either the rumors are false or he's too slick to get caught. I believe the latter."

"Thank you for the warning," Paul said. "We'll watch ourselves if we talk to Mr. Brimmer."

"Please don't tell Harvey I mentioned him. He would take that as a license to use the Dobbs name in an advertisement."

The Trouts gave Rachael a sizable contribution to put in the museum's donation box. On the way out, she stopped in front of a print that showed a huge textile mill complex.

"That's the Dobbs mill. The captain became even wealthier when he invested in the textile business. He was apparently robust and would have lived a long life if he hadn't been killed when a loom fell on him. Good luck with your research," she said in parting, then scurried off to meet with the electrician.

"Wasn't Brimmer the guy Song Lee contacted when she was looking for the logbook?" Paul asked.

"I'm sure that was his name," Gamay said. "Maybe we'll have more success than she did."

After leaving the Dobbs mansion, the Trouts drove toward the waterfront. The former heart of the world's whaling industry had dwindled through the centuries to several blocks of historic buildings. Connected by cobblestone streets, the old banks and ship's chandleries that had serviced the sperm-oil industry now overlooked the fishing fleet and processing buildings that lined the Acushnet River.

Brimmer's shop was on the ground floor of a three-story clapboard building. The peeling red paint revealed the gray primer underneath, and the black wooden sign over the door was so faded it was almost impossible to make out H. BRIMMER ANTIQUE BOOKS, MAPS, AND DOCUMENTS.

The Trouts stepped into the shop and adjusted their eyes to the dim light. Several filing cabinets lined walls that were covered with paintings showing various aspects of the whaling trade. At the center of the room were a large wooden table and a couple of green-shaded banker's lamps. Dozens of maps of all sizes covered the top of the table.

A door at the back of the shop opened in response to the jingling of the bell hanging on the front door, and a thinly built man stepped out. He stared at the Trouts from behind thick glasses.

These visitors didn't fit the mold of the scholarly collectors or occasional tourists who were his usual patrons. At six foot eight, Paul was taller than most men, and Gamay had a magnetic presence more striking than beautiful.

"Good afternoon," the man said with a smile. "I'm Harvey Brimmer. May I be of some assistance?"

Brimmer could have played a country druggist in a Frank Capra film. He was of less than average height, and he stooped slightly at the shoulders, as if he spent a long time bending over a desk. His thinning pepper-and-salt hair was parted slightly off the middle. He was dressed conservatively in gray suit pants and a white dress shirt. He wore a whale-motif blue tie knotted in a Windsor.

"I'm Paul Trout, and this is my wife, Gamay. We're looking for any material you might have on Caleb Nye."

Brimmer's watery blue eyes widened behind his wire-rimmed bifocals.

"Caleb Nye! Now, that's a name you don't hear very often. How did you come to know about our local Jonah?"

"My wife and I are whaling-history buffs. We came across Caleb's name in connection with Captain Horatio Dobbs. We were on our way to the Whaling Museum and saw your sign."

"Well, you are in luck. I can put my hands on some brochures from his traveling show. They're in storage at my workshop."

"We wondered if there were any logbooks available for the *Princess* that may have survived the Nye mansion fire," Gamay said.

Brimmer frowned.

"The fire was a tragedy. As an antiquarian, I can only guess at the rare volumes he had in his library. But all is not lost. I may be able to get my hands on a *Princess* logbook. She sailed for many years before she became part of the Stone Fleet, sunk off

Charleston Harbor during the Civil War. The logbooks were dispersed to museums and private collectors. I'd need a finder's fee up front."

"Of course," Gamay said. "Would you be able to find the logbook for 1848?"

Brimmer's eyes narrowed behind his bifocals.

"Why that particular log?"

"It was Captain Dobbs's last whaling voyage," she replied. "We'd be prepared to pay whatever it takes."

Brimmer pinched his chin between his forefinger and thumb.

"I believe I may be able to help you," he said.

"Then the log wasn't destroyed?" Paul asked.

"Possibly not. There's a little-known story about Caleb Nye. He married a Fairhaven girl, but the family was not pleased at her betrothal to someone considered a freak, rich as he was, and they kept the matter quiet. The Nyes even had a daughter who was given some of the books from the library as a dowry. I have contacts I can check with, but I'd need a few hours. Can I call you?"

Paul handed Brimmer a business card with his cell-phone number on it.

Brimmer saw the logo.

"NUMA? *Splendid.* A query from your renowned agency might open doors."

"Please let us know as soon as you hear something," Paul said.

Gamay signed an agreement and wrote out a check for the large finder's fee. They shook hands all around.

HARVEY BRIMMER WATCHED through the window of his shop until the Trouts were out of sight, then he hung a CLOSED sign on the door and went to his office behind the showroom. The documents and maps in his shop were actually overpriced prints of originals or low-end antiques for the tourist trade.

Brimmer picked up the phone and dialed a number from his Rolodex.

"Harvey Brimmer," he said to the person at the other end of the line. "We talked a few days ago about a rare book. I've got some buyers interested in the same property. The price may go up. Yes, I can wait for your call. Don't be too long."

He hung up and sat back in his chair, a smug expression on his face. He remembered the first time someone had asked about the *Princess* logbook of 1848. The call had come in years before from a young woman at Harvard. He told her he would put out the word, but she said she would have to wait because she was going home to China. He hadn't thought about the inquiry again until a few weeks ago when an Asian man dropped by the shop looking for the same item. The man was an unlikely customer, young and tough-looking, and he didn't hide his irritation when he was told the book was not available.

Brimmer could not have known that the visit from the young man had been instigated when Song Lee called Dr. Huang from Bonefish Key and mentioned the story of the New Bedford anomaly. She told her mentor that she was convinced that the medical curiosity had a bearing on her work and she was thinking of going to New Bedford to see an antique book dealer named Brimmer when she had time.

As instructed, Dr. Huang had passed along the details of every conversation he had with the young epidemiologist. Within minutes, a call had gone out to a social club in Boston's Chinatown with orders to visit Brimmer's shop. Soon after that, the leader of the local Ghost Dragons chapter walked into Brimmer's shop and said he was looking for the 1848 logbook of the *Princess*.

Now the couple from NUMA.

Brimmer didn't know what was going on, but there was nothing a dealer liked better than to have collectors bidding against one another. He would go through the motions and make a few calls. He would keep the finder's fees from all three parties and offer them something else. He was a master of bait and switch. Business had been off lately, and this promised to be a profitable day.

What he didn't know was that it would be his *last* day.

THE TROUTS STEPPED FROM the dim shop into the afternoon sunshine and walked up Johnny Cake Hill to the Seamen's Bethel. They tossed a few bills in the donation box and went inside the old whaling men's church. The pulpit had been rebuilt in recent years to resemble a ship's prow, as it had in Herman Melville's time.

Paul waited for a couple of tourists to leave and then turned to Gamay.

"What did you think of Brimmer?" he asked.

"I think he's a slippery old eel," she said. "My advice is not to hold our breath waiting for him to come through. He'll dig out the first logbook he can get his hands on, forge a new date, and try to sell it to us."

"Did you see his expression change when we mentioned Captain Dobbs's 1848 logbook?" he said.

"Couldn't miss it!" she said. "Brimmer forgot his Mr. Friendly impersonation."

Paul let his eye wander to the marble tablets hung on the wall that were inscribed with the names of captains and crews lost in the far corners of the world.

"Those old whalers were tough as nails," he said.

"Some were tougher than others," she said, "if you can believe Song Lee's story about the New Bedford pod."

Paul pursed his lips.

"That medical phenomenon is a link between the past and the present. I'd love to read the paper that Lee wrote at Harvard."

Gamay slipped her BlackBerry out of her handbag. "Do you remember the name of Lee's professor?"

"How could I forget?" Paul said with a smile. "His name was Codman."

"Trout . . . Cod . . . Why are practically all you New England-ers named after fish?"

"Because we didn't have wine connoisseurs for fathers."

"Touché," she said.

She called up the Harvard Medical School on her BlackBerry, thumb-typed Codman's name into a person finder, and called the number shown on the screen. A man who identified himself as Lysander Codman answered the call.

"Hello, Dr. Codman? My name is Dr. Gamay Morgan-Trout. I'm a friend of Dr. Song Lee. I'm hoping that you remember her."

"Dr. Lee? How could I forget that brilliant young woman? How is she these days?"

"We saw her yesterday, and she's fine. She's working with some NUMA colleagues of mine, but she mentioned a paper she had done at Harvard and submitted to you. It has something to do with a medical phenomenon called the New Bedford anomaly."

"Oh, yes," Codman said. Gamay could hear him chuckling. "It was an unusual subject."

"We told Song Lee we'd be in the neighborhod, and she asked if my husband and I could swing by and pick up a copy for her. She's lost the original."

The professor had no reason to have kept a paper from one of hundreds of students who had passed through his classroom, but he said, "Normally, I wouldn't hold on to a student's paper, but the subject was so bizarre I kept it in what I call the *Book of the Dead,* as Charles Fort termed subjects that can be neither proven nor disproven. I'm sure I can put my hands on it."

Gamy gave Paul a thumbs-up.

"Thank you very much, Professor. We'll be there in a little over an hour, if that's convenient."

She jotted down directions to Codman's office in her Black-Berry, and then she and Paul walked from the whaling chapel to the car. Minutes later, they were heading north out of the city.

CHAPTER 34

THE VOICE OF THE PILOT CRACKLED OVER THE CITATION X's cabin intercom.

"Sorry to wake you folks up, but we're making our approach to Pohnpei and will be on the ground in a few minutes. Please make sure your seat belts are buckled."

Austin yawned once and looked over at Zavala, who could sleep through an earthquake. Then he glanced out the window at the landing strip on Deketik Island and the mile-long causeway that connected it to the main island. The sky was clear except for scattered clouds.

"Welcome to Bali Ha'i," Austin said to Song Lee, who was rubbing the sleep from her eyes.

Lee furrowed her brow, confused by Austin's reference to the mystical island that figured in *South Pacific*. She pressed her nose against the Plexiglas window. The island below was roughly circular, surrounded by a thin barrier reef enclosing a vast lagoon of intense blue. Luxuriant green forests laced with waterfalls covered the soaring peak towering over the island.

"It's *beautiful*," she said.

"I stopped here on a NUMA research ship a couple of years ago," Austin said. "The tall volcanic peak is Mount Nahna Laud. It inspired European explorers to call the place Ascension Island. It seemed to to them to rise right up to heaven."

"Is there any place in the world that you *haven't* been to?" Lee asked.

"If it touches an ocean, I've been there," Austin said. "Look, you can see the ruins of the old city at Nan Madol on the southeast coast of the island. They call it the Venice of the Pacific. Maybe we can explore the place after we're through with our other business. Tell you what, I'll take you out to dinner with a water view and introduce you to *sakau*. It's the local firewater that the locals make from pepper plants."

Song gazed with curiosity at Kurt's rugged face. He was as excited as a schoolboy at the prospect of returning to Nan Madol. The fact that he faced a Herculean task and held the lives of hundreds of thousands of people in his hands didn't seem to faze him. *His self-assurance must be catching,* she thought, because she said, "Yes, I'd like that. Perhaps we could make that visit to Nan Madol sooner than later. I've been thinking that it might have a bearing on this other 'business,' as you called it."

"In what way, Dr. Lee?"

"It's a strange little story from the first mate of the *Princess*. The island the ship sailed to when the crew became sick was known to be unfriendly to whalers. So, after dropping anchor, he and the captain went ashore briefly to see if there were any natives there. They didn't see anybody, but they did come across some ruins. The captain remarked on the strange carvings, and said they were similar to those he'd seen on a temple at Nan Madol."

"So if we can find an island that has ruins like Nan Madol," Austin said, "then there's a chance the *Princess* stopped there."

"That's what I was thinking," Lee said.

"How does that help us find the lab? Don't forget, Dr. Lee, that's our primary reason for being in Micronesia."

"Yes, I know. But when I was at Bonefish Key, I heard that the field lab was running short of blue medusae and that a new supply had to be found."

"Kane said that a mutant strain had been developed," Austin said. "Why would they need more of the original species?"

"There was no assurance at the time that the mutant would be the answer," Lee said, "in which case other avenues would have to be explored. There was a plan to collect medusae from a newfound source. If the lab is still working on the vaccine, it would need medusae. Which means that if we find that source, the lab may be nearby."

"Wouldn't Dr. Kane know where this new source was located?"

"Not necessarily. He had pretty much left the day-to-day operations to Dr. Mitchell."

Austin thought about it for a moment, then said, "I know a guide named Jeremiah Whittles who lives in Kolonia, which is the capital of Pohnpei and the biggest town on the island. Whittles took me out to the ruins the last time I was here. He's got an encyclopedic knowledge of Nan Madol. I think it might be worth talking to him to see if he knows anything that might help."

The Citation X circled one last time, then glided in for a perfect landing, hitting the single strip for landings and takeoffs with a soft jounce. Near the end of the strip, the jet made a U-turn, using the strip to taxi up to the terminal.

The moveable staircase thumped against the fuselage. Austin

pushed the door open and stepped out of the plane, filling his lungs with warm air laden with the heavy scent of tropical flowers. It was like stepping into a steam room, but nobody complained about the heat or humidity after being cooped up for so many hours in the temperature-controlled cabin.

The pleasant-mannered customs officer stamped their passports and welcomed them to the Federated States of Micronesia. Lee had left her passport back on Bonefish Key, but a State Department call ahead to Honolulu had produced temporary paperwork that would get her in and out of Micronesia.

The lobby was deserted except for a man holding a square of cardboard with NUMA printed on it. He wore a baseball cap, baggy cargo shorts, sandals, and a white T-shirt emblazoned with an azure blue rectangle enclosing four white stars, Micronesia's flag.

Austin introduced himself and the others in the party.

"Nice to meet you," the man said. "I'm Ensign Frank Daley. Pardon my disguise. The locals are used to seeing Navy personnel around, but we're trying to keep this operation low-key."

Despite his attire, Daley's ramrod-straight bearing, razor-precise crew cut, and chin so close-shaven that it shined all marked him as a military man.

"You're pardoned, Ensign," Austin said. "What do you have planned for us?"

"We've got a chopper waiting to take you to Search Command on my ship, the cruiser *Concord*."

As they walked out to the gray Sikorsky Seahawk that had been awaiting their arrival, Austin asked Daley the status of the search.

"We've covered hundreds of square miles using surface and air," the ensign said. "Nothing so far."

"Have you dropped sonobuoys to listen for underwater movement?"

Daley patted the nose of the Seahawk.

"This bird was built for antisub warfare. It's got the latest in acoustic detection. The info from the sensors is transmitted back to the ship and goes into a network computer system. All negative so far, sir."

"Has the lab site been thoroughly investigated?" Zavala asked.

"As thoroughly as can be done with an ROV," Daley said.

"I heard that there's a NUMA ship helping with the search," Zavala said. "I'll see if I can borrow their submersible and give the lab site a closer look."

Austin had been thinking about his conversation with Lee.

"Dr. Lee has a lead we'd like to pursue on the island," he said. "Could you give Joe a lift out to the ship and pick us up in a few hours?"

"I've been told that the entire Navy is at your beck and call, Mr. Austin," Daley said. "The chopper does two hundred miles an hour. We can be back on the island in no time."

Austin turned to Zavala, who had started to load their bags onto the helicopter.

"Song has unearthed some interesting stuff about Nan Madol," he said, "and it might have a bearing on the lab. Can you ride herd on the search operation while we take a quick look?"

"Hold on, Kurt. You go off with the lovely Dr. Lee and I muck around in the mud. What's wrong with that picture, partner?"

"Nothing as far as I can see, *partner*," Austin said.

"I'll have to admit you've got a point there," Zavala said with an easy grin. "See you in a few hours."

He got into the helicopter with Daley. The ignition fired the twin General Electric engines to life and the spinning rotors gathered speed. The sixty-five-foot-long aircraft lifted off the tarmac, hovered at an altitude of a few hundred feet, pivoted slowly, and flew over the lagoon toward the open sea.

While the chopper carried Joe off to join the search flotilla, Austin and Lee exited the airport terminal to look for the taxi stand. A young man in his twenties who must have weighed three hundred fifty pounds was leaning against a faded maroon Pontiac station wagon paneled with fake wood, KOLONIA TAXI CO. painted on the door. Austin approached the man and asked him if he knew a tour guide named Jeremiah Whittles.

"Old Jerry? For sure. He's retired. If you need a guide, I can hook you up with my cousin."

"Thanks, but I'd like to talk to Jerry," Austin said. "Can you take me to him?"

"No problem," the man said with a bright smile. "He lives in Kolonia town. Hop in."

Austin held the door open for Song Lee, then got in the car beside her. The driver, who said his name was Elwood, shoe-horned his body into the driver's seat, the wagon's springs groaning and its chassis listing to that side. As Elwood pulled away from the curb, a black Chevrolet Silverado pickup that had been parked several car lengths behind the station wagon followed it across the causeway and into Kolonia, a town of about six thousand whose ramshackle Main Street had a frontier air about it. Elwood turned off Main into a residential neighborhood and stopped in front of a neat yellow house trimmed in white.

The Silverado passed the Pontiac wagon and pulled up a short distance ahead where the driver could watch in his rearview mirror as Austin and Lee went up to the front door. Austin rang the bell and heard someone inside say hello. A moment later, a slightly built man who looked to be in his eighties answered the door.

Jeremiah Whittles first smiled at Lee. Then his eyes turned to Austin and widened in surprise.

"Is that Kurt Austin of NUMA? My God, I don't believe it! How long has it been?"

"Too long, Whit. How are you?"

"Older, but not necessarily wiser. What brings you to my beautiful island, Kurt?"

"Some routine NUMA stuff for the Navy. I'm showing Dr. Lee here around. She's interested in Nan Madol, and I couldn't think of anyone more knowledgeable on the subject than Pohnpei's best-known guide."

"Make that best-known *former* guide," Whittles said. "C'mon in."

With his pink-skinned pate, thin aquiline nose, kindly yet inquisitive blue eyes behind wire-rimmed bifocals, and slightly stooped shoulders, Whittles resembled a friendly buzzard.

"I heard you had retired," Austin said.

"My brain was still full of all the facts, like an old stew kettle, but the spine was stiffening up, and I couldn't turn my head without some difficulty, which I need to do to point out features on the tours. Had to swivel at the waist like a wooden soldier. Then my eyesight started to go. Not much call for a half-blind guide, so I thought it best to call it quits."

Whittles led the way through rooms filled with Micronesian folk art. There were masks, totems, and carved grotesque figures on every wall and in every corner. He settled his visitors on a screened-in porch and scuttled off to get them some cold bottled water.

In his travels around the world, Austin had seen clones of Whittles, peripatetic Englishmen who attach themselves as guides to famous cathedrals, ancient palaces, and forgotten temples, absorbing every fact, large and small, and becoming local celebrities in the process.

Austin had met Whittles during a tour of Nan Madol, and the depth and breadth of his historical and cultural knowledge had impressed him. Years before, Whittles had served as a navigator aboard a merchant ship that had stopped at Pohnpei and been entranced by its beauty and history. Retiring early from the merchant marine and relying on his savings, he moved to the island and led a monklike existence centered on the ruins. Nan Madol became not only his livelihood but his whole life.

Whittles came back with the water, settled in a chair, and asked Lee what she knew about Nan Madol.

"Not a lot, I must confess," she said. "Only that it has been called the Venice of the Pacific."

"Nan Madol is a far cry from the city on the Adriatic," he said, "but it is impressive nonetheless. It consists of ninety-two artificial islets dating back to 1100 A.D. The builders rafted hexagonal basalt pillars to the tidal flats and reef off Tenwen, some of the pillars more than twenty feet long, and stacked them horizontally to make artificial, flat-topped islets. A grid of shallow canals connects the islets to one another. Because the city is so remote and mysterious, and located where nothing of this sort should exist, it has given rise to theories that Nan Madol was part of the lost continent of Mu or Lemuria."

"What do you think, Mr. Whittles?" Lee asked.

"I think that the reality is more prosaic but still marvelous. The city was the site of temples, administrative centers, burial vaults, houses for priests and nobles, and a pool said to have been the home of a sacred eel . . . How may I help you, Dr. Lee?"

"Do you know of any ruins engraved with unusual carvings similar to those on another island?"

"Only one instance," Whittles said. "The temple known as the Cult of the Healing Priests. I've heard reports of a similar temple elsewhere but have never been able to verify it."

"What exactly was this cult?" Austin asked.

"It originated on one of the islands near Pohnpei. The priests traveled around the islands tending the sick and became known for their miraculous healing."

Austin exchanged glances with Lee.

"As a doctor," she said, "I'm very interested in the healing part."

"Wish I could tell you more," he said, "but the civilization degenerated from the effects of internecine warfare. And while there is a good chance that the beliefs and ceremonies of the cult survived in some more primitive form, most of what we know today was passed down by word of mouth. There is no written record."

"Wouldn't the carvings be considered a written record?" Austin asked.

"Sure," Whittles said. "But from what I've seen, they're more symbolic and allegorical than historical."

"What do the carvings at Nan Madol represent?" Lee asked.

"I can show you better than I can tell you," Whittles said.

He went into his study and dug through his file cabinets, returning with a brown envelope. He opened the envelope and pulled out a stack of five-by-seven photos. He fanned the photos like a deck of cards, picking out one and handing it to Lee.

"This is the façade of the temple as seen from a canal," he explained. "There's a hollow space under the temple's floor that seems to have been some sort of pool. This picture shows the carvings on the interior."

Lee stared at the photo for a moment, then passed it over to Austin, who studied the bell shapes in it and then looked up.

"Jellyfish?" he asked.

"It appears to be," Whittles said. "Not sure why they decorated the wall of a temple with those creatures. But, as I said, there's a pool dedicated to the sacred eel, so why not one to jellyfish?"

"Why not indeed?" Lee said, her dark eyes sparkling with excitement.

"I'd like to see this place in person," Austin said. "Can you tell us where it is?"

"I can show you exactly, but I hope you brought your bathing suit. The platform the temple rested on got knocked around in an earthquake years ago and sank into the canal. Not too deep. Maybe twelve feet or so."

Austin looked at Lee.

"What's your pleasure, ma'am? Head off to our ship or check out Nan Madol?"

"I think the answer to that question is obvious," she said.

He wasn't surprised by her reply, given what he had seen of her determination.

Austin asked to borrow a local telephone book and within minutes had arranged to rent a boat and some scuba equipment. Whittles marked the temple's location on a tourist map of the ruined city. They thanked him and said their good-byes, then went back out to the waiting Pontiac station wagon. As the taxi headed toward the harbor, the Chevy Silverado pulled away from the curb and followed a few lengths behind.

CHAPTER 35

DR. LYSANDER CODMAN GREETED THE TROUTS IN THE LOBBY of a building that overlooked the grassy square off Longwood Avenue where Harvard Medical School was part of a campus with some of the most prestigious such institutions in the country. The professor was a tall, loose-boned man in his sixties. He had the type of long, big-toothed face that seemed to raise the possibility that some of the old Yankee families had bred with horses.

Codman led the way along a hallway and swept the Trouts into his spacious office. He asked his visitors to make themselves comfortable and poured cups of Earl Grey from an electric kettle. He then plunked himself behind his desk and asked a few questions about their work with NUMA, then held up a bound report so the Trouts could read the title on its dark blue cover:

THE NEW BEDFORD ANOMALY:

A STUDY OF IMMUNE RESPONSE AMONG

CREW FROM THE WHALING SHIP *PRINCESS*

Codman took a noisy slurp from his cup.

"I've had a chance to browse through Dr. Lee's paper," he said. "It's even more curious than I remember."

Paul asked, "Curious in what way, Professor Codman?"

"You'll understand when you get into it. The first section of Dr. Lee's treatise is based mostly on newspaper reports. The reporter was interviewing retired whaling men, looking to chronicle their exploits, and realized that he was onto something. He noticed that a group of whalers in their seventies and eighties had been almost completely disease free for a good part of their very long lives."

"We were in the New Bedford Seamen's Bethel earlier today," Gamay said. "The walls are lined with tablets memorializing whaling crews. Paul remarked at how tough the old-timers must have been."

"It went *beyond* toughness in this case," Codman said. "These men had never suffered a single illness, not even the common cold. They died at an advanced age, usually from some geriatric condition such as congestive heart failure."

"Newspaper writing can be overblown," Gamay said.

"Especially in the nineteenth century," Codman said. "But the stories caught the eye of a doctor in immunology named Fuller here at the medical school. He organized a team of physicians to investigate. They talked to the men and the physicians who had treated them. What they found was even stranger than what newspapers had reported. The men enjoying the most robust health had all served on the whaling ship *Princess* during a single voyage in 1848. They had been infected on that voyage with a tropical illness then making the rounds through the Pacific whaling fleet. While some of those men shipped out again later and died in whaling accidents, fourteen were still living. They were compared to men from other ships, and the statistical differences

healthwise were startling. The doctors backed up their findings
with tables and graphs and so on."

"Yet you expressed doubts over Dr. Lee's findings," Gamay
said.

Professor Codman sat back in his chair, tented his fingers, and
stared into space.

"The preliminary stating of facts didn't bother me as much as
her conclusions," he said after a moment. "The basis for Dr. Lee's
paper was built on empirical evidence that I found hard to swallow: primarily, her observations on the anecdotes told by the men
involved. Unfortunately, the ship's captain died before the interviews took place. His logbook was never found."

"Don't firsthand observations have *some* validity?" Paul
asked.

"Oh, yes, but think of it: these men had been ill at the time,
some even in fever comas, and their recollections were recorded
decades after the event."

"What was the nature of those recollections?" Paul asked.

"They all had the same story: they fell ill after leaving port,
became unconscious, and woke up the next day in good health."

"Was spontaneous remission a possibility?" Gamay asked.

"Dr. Lee presented reports of a flulike plague that rampaged
through the fleet then. Judging by its speed and ferocity, as well
as influenza's high mortality rate, I'd say spontaneous remission
was not likely."

"You said the crewmen all told the same story," Gamay said.
"Wouldn't that strengthen the account of what happened?"

"A whaling vessel was a small community unto itself. I think
they developed a shared story line." He paused. "Only the first
mate had a different version."

"Did he contradict the crew's version?" Gamay asked.

"No. In fact, the first mate *supplemented* it. He recalled the ship dropping anchor at an island, even going ashore with the captain. He also remembered seeing glowing blue lights and feeling a stinging sensation in his chest. He woke up feeling as if he had never been sick."

"That's interesting about the sting," Gamay said. "Do you think he was talking about a primitive version of inoculation?"

"He seemed to have been going in that direction. He said all the surviving crew and officers had a reddish mark on their chests. The lights could have been hallucinations or the electrical phenomenon known as Saint Elmo's fire and the marks insect bites. In any case, inoculation can prevent disease but isn't known to cure it."

"Did the Harvard team take blood samples from the men?" Gamay asked.

"Yes. The samples were subjected to microscopic analysis. There was apparently some unusual antigen activity, but you have to understand that the optical instrumentation then was primitive by today's standards. The science of immunology is comparatively young. Jenner and Pasteur had yet to make their groundbreaking discoveries explaining why people, having survived a disease, rarely caught it again after that."

"Could the blood samples be analyzed today?" Gamay asked

"Sure, if we had them. Apparently, the samples were thrown out or just plain lost." He handed the report to Gamay. "In any event, I'm sure you will find it fascinating reading."

The Trouts were walking back to their car when Paul's cell phone trilled.

He listened for a moment, then said, "Okay." He clicked the phone shut, and said, "Guess we owe our friend Brimmer an apology."

"He's found some papers from Caleb Nye's traveling show?" Gamay asked.

"Better," Paul said. "Brimmer's got the 1848 logbook from the *Princess.* He'll meet us at his workshop to turn it over."

HARVEY BRIMMER PUT THE phone down and eyed the four Asian men in his office. They were in their twenties, dressed identically in black leather jackets and jeans, and all wore black headbands with Chinese characters in red on them. They had arrived in New Bedford not long after Brimmer had made the call about the logbook. Their leader, a thin-faced youth with a scar running down his right cheek, was the one who had visited the bookshop looking for the book. He had told Brimmer to call the Trouts.

"They're on their way," Brimmer said. "Why do you want to see them?"

The leader pulled a gun out of his shirt. He smiled, revealing a tooth inlaid with a gold pyramid.

"We don't want to *see* them, old man," he said. "We want to *kill* them."

He ripped the phone line from the wall, then ordered Brimmer to hand over his cell phone, which he pocketed.

Brimmer's blood ran cold. He was smart enough to figure out that, as witness to a double murder, he would not be allowed to live. As he sat behind his desk, he thought about the spare cell he kept locked in one of its drawers. When he saw his chance, he would make his move.

CHAPTER 36

LIKE MANY OLDER BOATS CONSTRUCTED BEFORE BUILDERS were sure how thick to make a hull with the then-new fiberglass, the battered twelve-foot-long skiff Austin had rented on the Kolonia waterfront was built like a battleship. The wide-beamed craft was powered by a pitted fifteen-horsepower Evinrude outboard that belonged in a museum of nautical artifacts.

Austin was glad to see that the scuba gear he'd rented was in far better shape than the boat or the motor. He inspected the regulator, hoses, and tank and found all the equipment had been well maintained. As an afterthought, he purchased a throwaway underwater camera encased in plastic. Then, after stowing the dive-gear bag, he helped Song Lee into the boat. After a couple of pulls on the starter cord, the Evinrude hiccupped and caught. Once it got going, it proved to have a stout mechanical heart as it powered the heavy boat through the water at a slow but steady pace along the coast.

Nan Madol was about forty-five minutes by boat from Kolonia. As they came up on the city on the southeast shore of Tenwen

Island and caught their first glimpse of the enigmatic islets, Austin reached back into his memory trying to recall what Whittles had told him about the ruins years before. The place had been a ceremonial center going back to the second century A.D., but the megalithic architecture did not start to take shape until the twelfth century.

The city served as a residence for nobility and mortuary priests, and its population never went beyond a thousand. The mortuary spread over fifty-eight islands in the northeast part of the city, a sector called Madol Powe. Whittles had taken Austin there and shown him the islets where the priests lived and worked. Madol Pah was the administrative sector on the southwestern part of Nan Madol. That was where the nobles lived and the warriors were quartered.

Nan Madol's builders had put up seawalls to protect the city from the Pacific's whims. The rectangular islets were all basically the same. Retaining walls, built by stacking heavy, prismatic basalt columns log-cabin style, surrounded cores of coral rubble. Once the walls reached several feet above sea level, platforms were built on top as foundations for living areas, or temples, or even crypts. The more elaborate of these islets, like the spectacular mortuary at Nandauwas, had two twenty-five-foot walls enclosing the royal compound.

In the drawing Whittles had sketched out for Austin, the temple of the Cult of the Healing Priests was in the mortuary sector of Nan Madol. It was a smaller version of Nandauwas, which suggested that the islet had some importance among the inhabitants. The temple was entered through a portal in the outer wall, which enclosed a courtyard, then through another portal in a second wall.

Following Whit's map, Austin steered the boat into the city, cruising past crumbling walls that seemed out of place in the remote location. They waved at the passengers in a couple of open tour boats carrying camera-toting tourists protected from the tropical sun by colorful canopies. Nan Madol had become a popular destination for day trips, and the boat went past a guide leading several kayaks like a row of ducklings.

Consulting the map, Austin left the main area of tourist activity and turned onto a quiet, dead-end canal lined on both sides by basalt walls and palm trees. In bygone days, the temple of the Healing Priests would have presided over the terminus of the canal, but the only sign it had ever existed was a jumbled pile of columns that stuck a foot or so above the surface. Austin killed the engine, let the boat drift to within yards of the debris, and dropped anchor.

Austin had purchased a Hawaiian surf-print bathing suit at the dive shop, flaming orange-red with hula dancers, the only thing that the shop had in his size. He tucked his wallet and phone in the waterproof dive-gear bag and slipped into the buoyancy compensator, weight belt, tank, and fins. He rolled over the gunwale into the tepid water, came up and gave Song Lee a quick wave, then bit down on the regulator mouthpiece and did a surface dive that took him down several feet into the slow-moving brownish green water.

He switched on a waterproof flashlight he had bought at the shop. Visibility was limited in the murky water, but the light picked out the broken basalt that had once been the islet's foundation. Austin swam around the perimeter, then came back up to the rental boat.

Whittles had suggested that the coral core supporting the temple had crumbled when the earthquake throttled the city, causing the building to sink to the bottom of the enclosure and the walls to collapse on top of it.

Austin swam around the pile again, this time at a different

depth, and saw an opening where basalt slabs had fallen down at an angle. He poked his flashlight into the cavity. The light petered out, suggesting that there was open space behind. Austin twisted through the tight space, banging his air tank against the basalt.

Once he was through the passage, Austin swept the flashlight around and saw that he was in a cavelike chamber created when the inner and outer walls collapsed against one another. Even if the temple had not been destroyed, it was hidden behind the wreckage of the inner wall, which had fallen on top of and around it.

Austin thought he had reached the end of his explorations and was preparing to retrace his route when he made another sweep of the chamber with his light. This time, there was something peculiar about the way the shadows fell on the debris to his right. He swam closer, and saw that a slab had fallen and was blocking some columns, thus creating a breach.

Austin slithered through the breach, and, after swimming a few yards, came upon an almost perfectly rectangular entryway. The temple slanted down to the left, and the entry should have been plugged by debris except that its lintel had fallen in such a way that the opening was intact. He made a quick visual check to assure himself that the entryway wouldn't collapse, then swam through it and into the temple itself.

Austin's flashlight immediately fell on the pool that Whittles had described. It was rectangular, about twenty feet long and fifteen feet wide. Debris had fallen in it, but Austin estimated it was around six feet deep. Playing his light against one of the walls, he saw that he was not alone.

Carved on the wall were six male figures dressed in loincloths. They were standing in profile, each holding a basin over his head. Three figures faced one another on either side of a huge bell-shaped jellyfish whose tentacles dropped down to a three-by-six-foot waist-high stone dais built against the wall. Austin flashed the light around the room and saw identical carvings and daises on each wall.

He moved in closer, tracing the contours of one of the jellyfish with his fingers, as if doing so would connect him with the ancient cult of healers. Then he backed off several feet and dug out the throwaway flash camera. He clicked off a dozen shots, then tucked it away.

Eager to tell Lee what he had found, Austin swam out of the temple and wriggled through the outer and inner walls. Looking up to get his bearings, he saw the boat silhouetted against the shimmering surface. As he ascended, his ears picked up the muted buzz of a boat engine. The high-revving noise grew louder. Austin wondered why anyone would be speeding through the peaceful canal. Then an alarm went off in his brain.

He followed the anchor line up. His head broke the surface a few feet from the boat. Pushing his mask up on his forehead, blinking into the bright sunlight, he saw an inflatable pontoon boat coming from the entrance of the canal and speeding his direction. It was too far away for him to see the passengers' faces clearly, but the sun glinted off the shiny bald pate of Chang, the Triad's gang leader who had attacked the *Beebe*. The needle on Austin's danger meter swung into the red zone.

Song Lee was sitting in the rental boat, oblivious to the looming threat. Austin yelled, pointed at the fast-moving inflatable coming in their direction. The smile Lee had greeted his reappearance with became a puzzled frown. Austin glanced back at the inflatable. He was close enough to see the grin on Chang's face as he knelt in the bow with a weapon up to his shoulder. He would have been on them in seconds, but the kayaks seen earlier entered and blocked the way. The inflatable swerved to miss the kayaks, but its wash capsized two of them.

Austin took advantage of the seconds lost in performing the tricky maneuver.

"Jump!" he yelled to Lee.

She put her hands on the boat's gunwale and leaned over the water, not comprehending the danger she was in, until she saw the muzzle flashes and heard the rattle of gunfire. A line of geysers erupted across the water that led directly to her boat as inexorably as a buzz saw. She froze with fear.

Austin pushed himself out of the water as high as he could go, reached up, and grabbed Lee by the front of her blouse and pulled her back down with him. She tumbled over the gunwale into the canal just seconds before Chang's bullets ripped into the boat, sending up a shower of fiberglass splinters.

Lee's additional weight dragged them both down several feet. Austin then expelled air from his buoyancy compensator and they sank even deeper. He put one arm around her waist, as if leading her through a waltz step, and with his free hand pointed the flashlight at his face. She had reflexively taken a gulp of air before hitting the water but now had used up her supply and was flailing in panic. Austin released her, took a deep breath, then removed the regulator from his mouth and pointed to the bubbles streaming from the mouthpiece.

Lee's eyes were wide with fright, but she understood what Austin was trying to convey. She took the mouthpiece and clamped it between her teeth. As she filled her lungs, the panic in her eyes subsided. She then passed the mouthpiece back to Austin.

Buddy-breathing would keep them alive, but there was still Chang and his men to deal with. This became abundantly clear when Austin saw a foamy splash in the water, then another. Chang's men were diving off the boat.

The men easily could have tracked Austin and Lee in the

shallow waters of the canal by following their air bubbles on the surface. Eventually, Chang might get lucky, or he simply could wait until the two used up their air supply. But he was impatient.

Austin drew air into his lungs, passed the mouthpiece back to Lee, and pointed with his index finger.

This way.

Taking Lee by the hand, he swam deeper, toward the entrance of the temple enclosure. Chang's men were at a disadvantage without air and were quickly outdistanced. By the time their prey vanished through the temple wall, the men were swimming back to the surface. Chang's boat moved back and forth, searching for telltale bubbles. Not seeing any, Chang assumed that his targets had slipped past him. He ordered that the inflatable move farther out into the canal. By then, Austin and Lee were inside the temple.

Lee was buddy-breathing like a pro, but she almost gulped down a mouthful of water when Austin showed her the wall carvings. Like Austin, she too put her hand on the jellyfish. She shook her head in frustration at not being able to talk. Austin pointed to the camera clipped to his vest and signaled *OK* with his thumb and index finger.

They perched on the edge of the temple pool, sharing the air supply and taking in the marvelous carvings. Austin checked the supply, then tapped his wristwatch and pointed toward the temple entrance. Buddy-breathing was using up the air in the tank twice as fast. Lee nodded in understanding. They swam side by side, as if joined at the hip, until they came to the outer wall. Austin signaled Lee to wait. He slipped out of his vest and swam out into the canal. All was quiet. He looked up at the surface but saw no sign of Chang or the rental boat.

He heard the sound of a engine, but to his practiced ear it

sounded different from the inflatable's high-revving one. He decided to take a chance. Moving closer to the foundation of the islet, he surfaced and peered out from behind an outcropping where the basalt base had collapsed.

A tour boat was moving along the canal toward the rental boat, which was submerged except for the bow, which stuck out of the water at an angle. More important, Chang and his men had vanished.

Austin waved until someone in the tour boat saw him. When the boat turned his direction, he took a deep breath and went back for Song Lee. He gave her a thumbs-up, then pointed upward. She repeated the *OK,* and together they slowly rose to the surface.

CHAPTER 37

SHORTLY AFTER THE SIKORSKY SEAHAWK LIFTED OFF FROM Pohnpei, Zavala had slipped a chart from the TOP SECRET pouch Austin had put in his safekeeping and matched the specks on it to the islands and atolls he could see from the helicopter. Ensign Daley tapped him on the shoulder and pointed directly ahead, where silhouettes of ships dotted the ocean sheen.

"Looks like we're coming up on an invasion fleet," Zavala said.

"We're entering the search area," Daley replied. "We've got six Navy ships working the waters around the lab site. A research vessel from NUMA has come in to help out. My ship is the command center. We're coming up on her at twelve o'clock."

The Seahawk quickly covered the distance to the *Concord*, hovered over the stern for an instant, then dropped slowly onto the large circle painted on the deck. Zavala slid the helicopter's door open and climbed out. He was greeted by a gray-haired man in a khaki uniform.

"I'm Hank Dixon, Mr. Zavala," the man said, extending his hand. "I'm commander of the guided-missile cruiser *Concord.* Welcome aboard."

"Thanks, Captain. You can call me Joe. My boss, Kurt Austin, is busy in Pohnpei, but he'll be coming along in a couple of hours. Ensign Daley told me that the *Concord* is acting as central control for the search flotilla."

"That's right. C'mon, I'll show you what we've been doing."

The captain led the way to the midship's search-and-rescue center, just off the main deck. A dozen men and women, sitting in front of computer monitors, were processing information that was streaming in from the ships and planes involved in the search.

"How close are we to the actual lab site?" Zavala asked.

Dixon pointed down to the deck at his feet.

"It's approximately three hundred feet directly under the ship's hull. We had been on standby patrol for the lab, acting as backup for the support ship, *Proud Mary.* When we heard the Mayday, we got to the site within hours."

"Where is the support ship now?" Zavala asked.

"A Navy salvage vessel is towing what's left of her to a shipyard, where the forensics folks can take a closer look at her. We were busy taking care of the survivors, so it took some time before we got around to checking on the status of the lab. When we couldn't raise it on the radio, we erroneously assumed at first that the communications buoy got shot out. We carry an ROV for hull inspections, and we got it down." He stepped over to a computer screen. "Those circular depressions you see in the ocean bottom match the feet of the legs supporting the Locker."

"There are no drag marks," Zavala observed. "That indicates the lab was lifted off the site, which would have been possible with the Locker's neutral buoyancy. Can you show me the site on the satellite map?"

Dixon asked a technician to bring up a map-and-satellite-image hybrid of the waters being searched.

"We've been using orbiting spy satellites that can zero in on an area as small as a square yard to look for infrared emissions," Dixon said. "Davy Jones's Locker was west of Pohnpei, between Nukuoro Island on the north and Oroluk Island to the south. We've drawn lines from all three islands and dubbed our main search area the Pohnpei Triangle."

"Those red squares must be the areas that have been searched," Zavala said.

"That's right. The squares designate the territory that's been scoured with sonar. The ships transmit their sonar data to our computer network. We map out a grid of the ocean in squares, the ships move over each square parallel to one another in a line that stretches several miles across, and then they move on to the next square. We can cover a lot of ocean that way in a very short time. We've also got fixed-wing aircraft and helicopters making visual checks."

"These would be the islands circled in red," Zavala said.

"Correct again. They range from midsize islands to atolls not much bigger than a thumbnail. Most are deserted. We've put choppers down on a few of them and talked to the inhabitants, but nobody's reported anything suspicious. The places we can't get to by boat or air we've vetted pretty thoroughly with aerial surveys."

"The ensign said you've deployed sonobuoys," Zavala said.

Dixon nodded.

"It took a while before we figured out the lab was gone and got acoustical sensors down," he said. "We've got three antisub submarines equipped with electronic ears so sensitive they can hear a fish sneeze out patrolling the perimeters of the triangle."

"You might want to tell your subs to use their acoustical detectors to listen for the sound signature of a Russian Typhoon-class submarine. The Typhoons run quiet, but maybe you'll pick something up."

Dixon gave Zavala an odd look.

"You think the *Russians* are involved in this?"

"No," Zavala said, "but one of their old subs might be. Looks like you've got all bases covered. I'd like to go back to square one. I'll contact the NUMA ship to see if I can borrow a submersible so I can get a look firsthand at the site."

"I'll give them a call," Captain Dixon said, then added, "I'm running out of ideas. You got any suggestions?"

Zavala stared at the vast area represented by the satellite image. The Navy faced a daunting, almost impossible task. The Federated States of Micronesia consisted of more than six hundred islands scattered across a million and a half square miles of the Pacific. Actual land covered an area smaller than the state of Rhode Island, but, factoring in the ocean, the FSM was two-thirds the size of the United States.

"The good news is, your search plan is terrific, Captain. Given enough time, I don't doubt you would find the lab."

"Thanks." The captain narrowed his eyes, and said, "What's the bad news?"

Zavala gave him a sad smile.

"We don't *have* time."

CHAPTER 38

PAUL TROUT DROVE THE RENTED SUV INTO THE DESERTED back lot of a four-story mill that had been abandoned decades before when New Bedford's textile business pulled out of the city. Silhouetted against the night sky, the granite building could have been a relic from a bygone civilization if not for the banner-sized sign advertising DISCOUNT FURNITURE. A security light over the front door illuminated a small wooden plaque: BRIMMER'S ANTIQUITIES, 4TH FLOOR.

The mill was otherwise dark, except for the night lights in the showroom and a yellow glow in a fourth-floor window.

"Look familiar?" Gamay asked.

"Yes," Paul said. "It's the old Dobbs mill, the place Rachael showed us in that print back at the mansion."

Gamay pointed to the top floor.

"Either Brimmer is up there," she said, "or the ghost of Captain Dobbs is putting in overtime."

Paul reached for his cell phone and called Brimmer's number.

"Strange," Paul said. "Light's on but Brimmer's not answering. Not even a recording. Are your antennae picking up the same something's-not-right vibes that I'm getting?"

Gamay wrinkled her nose.

"More like a bad smell," she said.

Ticking the points off on her fingers, she said, "Brimmer tells us the logbook is a goner, then calls to say he knows where it is. Then he asks us to meet him at this overgrown haunted house instead of at his shop, or even a public place. Why all the secrecy?"

"I'm getting a picture in my mind of a mousetrap," Paul said. "Only instead of cheese, an old book is the bait. And we're the mice."

"Maybe this creepy old building is making us paranoid," Gamay said. "Brimmer isn't the violent type. What do you want to do?"

"I don't know if the information in the Dobbs logbook will help Kurt and Joe find the missing lab," he said. "But, with lives involved, I say we *go* for it."

"Looking at this from a cost-benefit point of view, I'd have to agree with you. Let's cut the risk factor, though, and scout things out."

Paul parked the SUV in the shadows, and they cautiously approached the main entrance.

"Unlocked," Paul said. "Nothing suspicious there. Brimmer *is* expecting us."

"But he didn't answer the phone," Gamay said. "If he isn't in his office, he wouldn't leave the door unlocked. And that *is* suspicious."

They walked the length of the five-hundred-foot-long building, eventually coming to another door. This one was locked. Continuing on around a corner of the building, they came upon the black cast-iron fire escape that zigzagged up to the top floor.

They climbed it and tried the door at each landing, but all were locked.

Paul jabbed the doorjamb on the top floor with his car key. The wood was soft with rot. He took a step back and threw his shoulder against the door, felt it give, and slammed it a few more times until the latch ripped out of the jamb. Gamay produced a small halogen flashlight from her handbag, and they stepped inside.

Their footfalls echoed as they walked across the dust-layered floor. The vast space where workers once tended hundreds of looms was as still as a tomb. They headed toward the far end of the room, where light was seeping under a door, and eventually came to a drywall partition. Cartons were stacked against it. BRIMMER was written in ink on the boxes.

Paul picked up a two-by-four from a pile of debris, hefting it like a baseball bat, and whispered to Gamay to knock on the door. She did, softly. When there was no answer, she stepped aside, and he did his battering-ram imitation again. The door popped open at first nudge.

The floor was littered with books and papers from the shelves, now empty, that lined the office. Sheets of paper hung from strings stretched across the room. The light visible outside through the window came from a goosenecked desk lamp on a table that also supported a computer, a small artist's drafting board elevated at the back, and Brimmer's body. The antiquities dealer was sprawled facedown, his hand stretched out toward a cell phone several inches from his fingertips. The back of his suit was perforated with a single bullet hole and stained red.

Paul put his fingers to the artery in the dealer's neck.

"Now we know why Brimmer didn't answer the phone," he said.

Gamay bent over the drafting board, which held a half-finished document written in ornate script. Next to it were some antique calligraphy pens and a bottle of ink. She read aloud a handwritten note on a sheet of paper next to an open book:

"Call me Ishmael . . ."

"The opening sentence from *Moby-Dick*?" Paul asked.

Gamay nodded.

"It appears our Mr. Brimmer was forging manuscript pages from Melville," she said.

"Could that type of thing get him killed?" Paul asked.

"Rachael Dobbs would be my first suspect. But it was more likely that someone didn't want him using the phone."

Paul slid a piece of paper under Brimmer's cell and flipped it over so the display screen showed.

"He was calling the police," he said. "He got as far as 91 . . ."

"I think we can conclude that Brimmer was forced to come here," she said. "He would never have let anyone into his forgery workshop otherwise. And, judging from the mess on the floor, I'd say they were looking for something."

"The 1848 logbook?"

"As Holmes would say, eliminate the impossible and you have the possible."

"His body is still warm, Ms. Holmes. What does that tell you?"

"That we had better be on our toes," she said. "And the murderer knew we were coming to see Brimmer."

"Doesn't that seem far-fetched?" he asked.

Gamay pointed to the corpse.

"Tell Mr. Brimmer that it's far-fetched."

"Okay," Paul said with a tight smile. "You've convinced me."

Paul put his finger to his lips and opened a door opposite

the one they had come through. He stepped out onto a landing, edged over to the railing, and looked down the stairs. He saw a tiny orange glow and smelled cigarette smoke rising up the shaft. He backed up into the office, shut the door quietly, and turned the lock.

He picked up Brimmer's cell phone, punched in the second 1 to complete the emergency call. When the police dispatcher answered, Paul said his name was Brimmer, gave the address, and said somebody was prowling around in the building. He suspected they were armed and dangerous.

Paul hung up and put the phone back in Brimmer's lifeless fingers.

He and Gamay slipped out of Brimmer's office and quickly made their way across the wide loom floor. Paul set the two-by-four against the wall, and they stepped out onto the fire escape, only to stop short.

The rickety old fire escape was trembling, and there was the *tunk-tunk* of ascending footfalls on the cast-iron steps. The Trouts ducked back inside, and Paul picked up the two-by-four he'd just left behind. They plastered themselves flat against a wall on either side of the door. He tightened his grip on the board.

Low male voices could be heard, then a quick exclamation of surprise. The men had found the smashed latch. Then the voices ceased.

The door opened slowly. A figure stepped inside, followed by another. There was a spark, as the lead man flicked on a cigarette lighter. Paul calculated that he would have a second to act and brought the two-by-four down on the head of the second figure. The man with the cigarette lighter turned at the *thwack* of wood smacking skull. He was holding a revolver in his other hand. Paul jammed him in the midsection with the end of the two-by-four, and followed up with a blow to the head as the man doubled over.

The Trouts dashed through the door, paused briefly to make sure nobody else was climbing the fire escape, then flew down the steps and raced to their vehicle. As they drove away from the mill, they passed two police cruisers speeding toward it, lights blinking but sirens silent.

Gamay caught her breath, and said, "Where'd you learn to swing a bat like Ted Williams?"

"The Woods Hole summer softball league. I played first base for the institution's oceanography team. Strictly for fun. Didn't even keep score."

"Well, I'm going to put you down for 2 to 0, after that neat double play," Gamay said.

"Thanks. I guess we've reached a dead end on the Dobbs logbook. . . . *Literally,*" Paul said.

Gamay pursed her lips in thought for a moment.

"Captain Dobbs wasn't the *only* one who wrote down his memoirs," she said.

"Caleb Nye?" he said. "All his records went up in flames."

"Rachael Dobbs mentioned the diorama. Isn't that a record of sorts?"

Suddenly energized, he said, "It's worth a try."

Paul pumped the SUV's accelerator and headed across town to the Dobbs mansion.

Rachael Dobbs was saying good night to the cleaning crew that had cleared up after the jazz concert and was about to close down the building. She looked less frazzled than when they saw her earlier.

"I'm afraid you missed the concert," she said. "You found Mr. Brimmer's shop, I trust?"

"Yes, thank you," Gamay said. "He couldn't help us. But then Paul and I remembered the Nye diorama that you mentioned. Do you think it might be possible to see it?"

"If you come by tomorrow, I'd be glad to show it to you," Rachael said.

"We'll be back in Washington by then," Gamay said. "If there is any chance . . ."

"Well, after all, your generous contribution made you members of the Dobbs Society in good standing," Rachael said. "Let's go down to the basement."

The basement of the Dobbs mansion was big and musty. They wove their way through antique odds and ends to a floor-to-ceiling cabinet that Rachael explained was an airtight, temperature-controlled walk-in safe. She opened the safe's double doors to reveal metal shelves stacked with plastic boxes, each labeled. A cylinder-shaped object around six feet long, wrapped in plastic, filled the lowest shelf.

"This is the Nye diorama," Rachael said. "I'm afraid that it's a bit heavy, which is probably why no one has dragged it out to have a look at it."

Paul squatted down and lifted one end of the cylinder up a couple of inches.

"It's doable," he said.

All through college, Paul had helped on his father's fishing boat, and since then he'd spent hours at the gym keeping in shape for the physical demands of his job. Gamay was even more of a fitness nut, and although her long-legged figure could have come out of the pages of *Vogue* she was stronger than many men. Working together, the Trouts easily hefted the package and carried it upstairs.

At Rachael's suggestion, they took the cylinder to the tent, where there was space to unwrap it. The Trouts removed the plastic and undid the ties wrapped around the diorama. It had been tightly coiled, with its blank brownish gray back side facing outward.

Carefully and slowly, they unrolled the diorama.

The first panel became visible. It was an oil painting around five feet high and six feet wide, depicting a whaling ship tied up at a dock. There was a caption under the picture:

JOURNEY'S END.

"We must be looking at the last section of the diorama," Rachael said. "This shows a ship unloading its catch in New Bedford. See the barrels being rolled down a ramp to the dock?"

The colors of sea and sky were still bright, but the other colors were garish, in the style of a circus poster. The brushstrokes were bold, as if the paint had been applied in a hurry. The perspective was wrong, seen through the eyes of an untrained artist.

"Any idea who painted this?" Gamay asked. "The technique is rough, but the artist had a good eye for detail. You can even see the name of the ship on the hull: *Princess.*"

"You're very discerning," Rachael Dobbs said. "Seth Franklin was self-taught, and he sold paintings of ships to their owners or captains. Before he started painting, he was a ship's carpenter. As I understand it, Nye stood in front of the diorama as it was unrolled from panel to panel and fleshed out the details with his own story. The lighting would have been dramatic, and maybe there were even sound effects. You know, someone behind the diorama shouting 'Thar she blows!' "

The next panel showed the *Princess* rounding a point of land that the caption identified as THE TIP OF AFRICA. In another panel, the ship was at anchor against the backdrop of a lush volcanic island. Dark figures that could have been natives were standing on the deck, which was bathed in a blue glow. The caption read:

TROUBLE ISLAND — LAST PACIFIC LANDFALL.

The panel that followed showed another volcanic island, apparently much bigger, with a dozen or so ships at anchor in its harbor. The caption identified the setting as Pohnpei.

Paul continued unrolling the diorama. The next panels depicted, in reverse, the crew cutting up a sperm whale and boiling its blubber down for oil. Particularly interesting was what appeared to be a white-haired man lying on the deck over the caption:

MODERN-DAY JONAH.

"It's the *Ghost,*" Rachael said. "This is marvelous! This shows Caleb Nye as he must have looked after he'd been cut out of the whale's stomach."

The stiff canvas of the diorama was becoming hard to handle, but with Paul unrolling it and Gamay rolling it back on its spindle, the whaling saga continued to unfold in reverse.

The panel before them was the classic depiction of a whaleboat-harpooned sperm whale in the lace-topped waves. Two legs were sticking out of the whale's mouth. The caption identified the scene:

CALEB NYE — SWALLOWED BY A WHALE.

Rachael Dobbs could hardly contain her excitement. She started talking about a fund-raiser to restore the diorama and finding wall space to hang it. Paul and Gamay Trout found the diorama fascinating but of little help. Yet they kept going until they came to the last panel, almost a mirror image of the ship in the first panel, only returning from its long voyage. In this panel, there was a crowd of people on the dock, and the ship's rigging was unfurled. The caption read SETTING SAIL.

Paul stood up to stretch his legs, but Gamay's sharp eye noticed that there were a few more feet of canvas. She asked him to keep unrolling, expecting to see a title panel of some sort. Instead, they were looking at a map of the South Pacific. Lines had been drawn in a crooked pattern across the ocean. There were whales' tails scattered across it. Each tail had a longitude-latitude position inked next to it.

"It's a map of the 1848 voyage of the *Princess*," Rachael said. "Those position notations show where the whales were caught. Captains often illustrated their logbooks to record good whaling areas. The map would have given Caleb's audience an idea of the extent of the voyage and shown where his adventures had occurred."

Gamay got down on her hands and knees and followed a line with her index finger from Pohnpei to a speck called Trouble Island. The island's position had been noted next to it.

The Trouts jotted down the coordinates, rolled the diorama back up, and carried it into the kitchen. Despite Rachael's protest, they gave her a substantial contribution to start the ball rolling on a place for the mural.

While Rachael Dobbs went to close up the museum, the Trouts went out into the garden.

"What do you think?" Gamay asked.

"I'm not sure whether this will help them find the lab," Paul said, "but it's all linked somehow: the present and the past, the blue medusa, the miraculous cure of the men aboard the *Princess*."

"Don't forget that somebody thought the log was important enough to kill Brimmer over," Gamay said. "We should let Kurt and Joe know what we found."

Paul already had his cell phone in hand, scrolling down to a number on his contact list.

CHAPTER 39

LIKE ANY GOOD DETECTIVE, JOE ZAVALA BEGAN HIS SEARCH for Davy Jones's Locker at the crime scene. Using a one-person submersible borrowed from the NUMA ship, he dove to the ocean bottom and made a couple of passes over the circular depressions left by the lab's footings. Seeing nothing new, he broke away from the site and started to explore the surrounding area. The submersible's searchlights suddenly reflected off a piece of metal.

Working the controls of the submersible's mechanical arms, Zavala scooped a twisted piece of steel from the bottom and examined it under the lights before depositing it in a basket slung beneath the submersible.

"I just picked up a chunk of the *Proud Mary*," he called up to the ship's bridge.

"You're sure it's not a piece of the lab?" asked Captain Campbell, skipper of the NUMA ship.

"Reasonably sure. The metal is twisted and melted, the way it would be from a missile strike. It doesn't look at all like the structures I saw in the diagrams. What I've seen fits with our theory that the lab was lifted off its site and towed away."

"Have you checked out the canyon where the lab was prospecting for jellyfish?" asked Campbell.

"Yeah. It's a few hundred yards from the site. I dove down into it a couple hundred feet. The canyon goes down forever. Saw a few blue medusae floating around, but that was it. I could dive deeper, but I've heard that the definition of insanity is repeating the same useless action over and over."

"Come up for air, then," said Campbell. "We'll call the *Concord* and fill Captain Dixon in— Hold on, Joe. Call for you coming through the NUMA net. I'll put it through."

After a moment or two, a female voice came over Zavala's earphones.

"How's your search going, Joe?"

"Hi, Gamay, nice to hear from you. I've picked a piece of the support ship off the bottom, but that's it. How about you?"

"We may have something," she said. "We tried to contact Kurt but the call wouldn't go through, so we tracked you down under the sea. Paul and I came across the coordinates for a place called Trouble Island. It's about a hundred miles from the lab site. It may be where the crew of the *Princess* underwent their miraculous cure. Not sure how it relates to the missing lab, but maybe it will help."

"Give the captain the info," he said, "and I'll come up and check things out."

"We're on our way back to Washington," she said. "Call if you need anything at this end."

Zavala thanked Gamay and Paul, then pointed the nose of the submersible toward the surface and powered the thrusters. A crane was waiting to hoist it from the water onto the deck of the NUMA ship.

Zavala popped the hatch, climbed out, and made his way to the bridge. Captain Campbell was poring over the chart table. He pointed to a speck on a chart of Micronesian waters.

"This is the atoll closest to the position your friends gave me," Campbell said. "Doesn't look like much, and, as you can see, it's within a red rectangle, which means it was searched visually. What do you think?"

Zavala pondered the captain's question, then said, "I think I need to talk to an expert."

A few minutes later, he was on the line with the NUMA navigational unit that supplied the agency's worldwide expeditions with up-to-date navigational information.

"Let me see if I understand," said the map expert, a soft-voiced young woman named Beth. "You're looking for a Pacific island that is no longer on the charts and you don't know if it even existed in the first place."

Zavala chuckled softly.

"Sorry," he said. "This must be like looking for a nonexistent needle in a very big haystack."

"Don't be discouraged, Joe. I like a challenge."

"Any chance the island might have been noted on a British Admiralty chart?"

"It depends," she said. "The Admiralty charts were ahead of their time when it came to accuracy, although the earlier ones were privately produced and had lots of errors. The Admiralty certified some maps that shouldn't have been."

"You're saying that an island could be on some charts but not others?"

"Absolutely! The charts and atlases of the nineteenth century showed more than two hundred islands that never existed."

"How could that happen?"

"Many ways. A land-starved mariner might mistake a cloud

formation for an island and record its position. Figuring longitude was also a problem. Someone might mark a real island in the wrong place. Con men created phony islands to push get-rich-quick schemes. The next guy in the neighborhood looks at his chart and sees empty sea where an island should be . . . Now, tell me what you know about your phantom island."

"I know that it was real," Zavala said. "An American whaling ship stopped there in 1848. But the island is not on any modern map. There's an atoll fairly close by, though."

"I'll start by looking for an 1848 chart or one close to it," she said. "Next, you'll want to compare it to Pacific Chart 2683."

"What is so special about it?"

"It's the gold standard of Admiralty charts. The British Hydrographic Office knew that the Admiralty maps were getting out of whack. Accurate charts were essential for the Navy and commercial interests. So, in 1875, the Admiralty brought in a chief hydrographer named Captain Frederick Evans to purge the phantom islands from all their charts. He got rid of more than a hundred islands in the Pacific alone. The corrected chart was designated with the number 2683."

"Then it's possible that the island never existed?" he asked.

"*Possibly.* But islands can disappear. Your island might have sunk into the sea after a volcanic eruption, an earthquake, or a flood. There is historical precedent: the island Tuanah supposedly sank with its inhabitants. And there are other reported cases on record. It could be a reef or rock below the surface now, and even a satellite wouldn't pick it up. You'd have to get in for a close look."

"Where do we start?" Zavala asked.

"A lot of this stuff is online," Beth replied. "The British Library has the biggest collection of Admiralty charts. I'll go there first, and then I'll take a look at the UK's National Archives. If I have to go to the Royal Geographical Society or the Maritime Museum at Greenwich, it might take a while. When do you need this information?"

"Yesterday," Zavala said. "Lives may depend on what we find."

"Are you joking, Joe?"

"I wish I were."

After a brief pause at the other end of the line, Beth said, "Like I told you, I love a challenge."

Zavala wondered if he had been too dire and tried to lighten the mood.

"Are you married or engaged, Beth?"

"No. Why?'

"In that case I would like to buy you dinner to show my appreciation."

"Wow! Who says you can't meet eligible men in the map division? Gotta go. 'Bye."

Zavala clicked the phone off and made his way to the NUMA helipad. The helicopter was fitted out with pontoons that allowed it to land on water. Zavala gazed at the helicopter lost in thought, then went back to the ship's bridge.

"I've got another favor to ask," he said.

"We'll do whatever we can to help," Captain Campbell said.

"I've got a NUMA map expert looking into the history of the atoll the Trouts found the coordinates for. If she comes up with any leads, I'd like to borrow your helicopter to check them out."

"I'll make sure it's fueled and ready to go whenever you need it."

Zavala thanked Campbell, and went down to the supply shed

on the main deck. He had set aside an emergency life raft and was wondering if he needed additional gear when his phone trilled. Beth was calling back.

"I've *got* it!" she said.

"That was fast," he said.

"Pure luck. I found what I was looking for in the British National Archives. Their stuff is on a database, categorized according to time period. What's your e-mail address?"

Zavala gave Beth the information, and, before hanging up, made sure he had her personal phone number so he could call to set up a dinner date.

Zavala made his way to the ship's communications center and borrowed a computer. He called up his e-mail address and seconds later the British Admiralty chart of 1850 filled the screen. He studied the chart for a moment, especially the dot labeled Trouble Island. Then he clicked the mouse. Pacific Chart 2683 appeared.

He put the earlier chart side by side with the corrected one. The circles on the corrected chart designated the position of nonexistent islands that the Admiralty hydrographers had removed. Trouble Island was not circled, but the name had been removed and the dot designated it as an atoll. Some time between 1850 and 1875, Trouble Island had become an atoll.

Zavala made a phone call to a NUMA colleague who specialized in old sailing ships and got an estimated sailing speed for a fully loaded whaler. Zavala then leaned back in his chair, laced his hands behind his head, and put himself in a ship captain's place.

Song Lee had said that the plague killed within days of infection. The crew would have been in good shape immediately after leaving Pohnpei. He assumed that the ship had a fair wind filling its sails.

Zavala marked an X on the chart west of Pohnpei where the *Princess* would have been at the end of the first day. By day two, the fever would have started taking men down. The ship would have lost time. He marked another X to indicate the ship's position at the end of the second day.

Day three would have been chaotic on board the whaler. Most of the crew and officers would have been out of commission or near death. The ship might have limped along. He marked a third X closer to the second one.

Okay, Captain Zavala, he almost said aloud, you've got a full load of valuable whale oil, your officers and crew are dying, and you're sick. What would you do? I'd want to get to landfall, he thought. Not Pohnpei. It was the source of the plague. And it was out of reach anyhow.

Zavala linked the computer to a surveillance satellite and zeroed in on the atoll of interest. Was it possible this unnamed atoll had once been an island? Beth had said that an island that sank into the sea might leave an atoll in its place. An eruption or earthquake would have been noted by people living on nearby islands, but there was no time to check the historic record.

He zoomed the satellite camera in on the tiny speck. Typical Pacific atoll: a minuscule island with a few palm trees encircled by a lagoon and ringed with a coral reef that was mostly solid and with no opening big enough for a massive Typhoon-class submarine to pass through with the lab in tow. Nothing could be seen in the clear waters of the lagoon.

Zavala called the Search Command ship and reconfirmed that planes had flown over the island and ships had come close for a look, but it was too insignificant to merit further investigation.

Despite his doubts and those pesky facts, he kept coming back to the name: Trouble Island. Someone had designated the island as a source of misfortune. What *kind* of trouble?

Zavala tried Austin's phone number, but there was no reply. He stared into space and contemplated his course of action. He could stay on the NUMA ship and twiddle his thumbs waiting for the search flotilla to hit pay dirt or he could join in the search, well aware that he was probably wasting time and fuel.

He hated inaction. He picked up an intercom phone, called the bridge, and told the captain he would need the helicopter to take a closer look at the atoll.

Crew members helped Zavala haul the emergency raft from the storage shed and load it onto the helicopter. He got into the cockpit and started to work the controls. Moments later, the chopper lifted off the pad, made one circle around the ship, and shot off on a northerly course.

Zavala kept the helicopter at an altitude of five hundred feet and a cruising speed of one hundred fifty miles per hour. Seen from this high up, the ocean was a sun-sparkled blue-green blur. He passed a couple of ships from the search flotilla, but most of them were looking in other areas. The blinding sheen off the water prevented him from seeing the atoll until he was almost on top of it.

He banked the helicopter and looked down at a handkerchief-sized patch of sand with its few palm trees. The atoll looked exactly as he had seen it on the satellite image. He confirmed that there was no break in the reef wide enough to have allowed a boat of any size to pass through. He headed down for a closer look, and brought the helicopter onto a soft pontoon landing a few hundred feet from the atoll's island, which was oddly located at one end of the lagoon rather than at its center.

As the rotors whirled to a stop, Zavala unbuckled himself and stepped out onto one of the pontoons. It was absolutely silent except for the whisper of the waves on the shore. Looking down into the crystal clear water, he saw a crab scuttling along the bottom.

The raft was in an orange-colored plastic container that he muscled out of the cockpit. He set it in the water and yanked an inflation cord. There was a hiss from the carbon dioxide capsule, and the raft writhed into full inflation. Zavala climbed into the raft and paddled to shore.

He pulled the raft up on the blinding white sand and walked around the perimeter of the island. He felt like a shipwreck victim on one of the miniature desert islands that cartoonists like to draw.

The tropical sun beat down like a blowtorch on his uncovered head. He sought shelter in the shade of the few pitiful palm trees. He surveyed his surroundings, absorbing the remote beauty of the atoll, with its otherworldly light and color.

He walked the perimeter of the island again, retracing his own steps. He frowned. This insignificant speck of sand could never have been Trouble Island. It was just a rinky-dink atoll. He walked back to his raft and turned for a last look. A glint of light came from near the top of a palm tree.

Zavala went back and stood under the tree. He craned his neck but couldn't determine the source of the reflection. He clambered onto the palm's trunk, which grew at an angle, and climbed up to where the broad fronds branched out. He found the source of the reflection immediately. Sunlight was glancing off the lens of a miniature video camera attached to the trunk.

Zavala realized, as he looked at the lens, that it was possible the camera was looking back at him. He backed down the palm's trunk only to stop halfway. The tree had a slick, unnatural feel to it. He unsheathed the knife at his belt and dug its point into the trunk, but it went in only so far. He peeled back a section of the trunk and got another shock: it seemed to be made of woven plastic fabric covering a hard metal core.

Zavala reached up and sliced off a section of palm frond. He stuck it between his teeth and bit down: more plastic. He sheathed his knife, and shimmied down the trunk to the sand. He walked several paces to the right, then to the left. The camera swiveled to follow him.

Oh, hell.

Zavala sprinted across the atoll, shoved his raft off the beach, and dug into the water with his paddle. He had to get back to the radio in the helicopter. He looked over his shoulder, expecting all the demons of hell to be after him, but was encouraged that no attempt was being made to stop him. A few more paddle strokes and he'd be in his helicopter.

Then the oddest thing happened. The bottom of the lagoon rose up to meet him, burst from the water in a long, shiny mound directly in front of him. Then the mound parted, and a huge black fin ripped through the bottom of the lagoon, rising until it towered more than forty feet above Zavala's head. He was looking at the conning tower of a giant submarine. Seconds later, the submarine's deck lifted the raft into the air. The helicopter headed skyward at the same time, and it teetered for a moment before sliding off the rounded deck at an angle. When the helicopter hit the foaming water, the water poured into the cockpit.

The raft slid off the rounded sides of the submarine, and water flowed into it. Zavala tried to climb back on the sub's deck from the upended raft, but his fingers slid off the slick, wet metal, and the fast-flowing torrents pushed him back into the lagoon.

He choked on seawater, gasping for breath like a beached fish. Then something like a baseball bat slammed into the side of his head. He saw a brief explosion of brightness before his eyes and then felt a numbing pain. Then someone pulled the shades down, and Zavala was in darkness.

CHAPTER 40

THE TOUR BOAT CAPTAIN WASN'T SURE WHAT TO MAKE OF
the people he had pulled out of the Nan Madol Canal. The half-
drowned young Asian woman seemed harmless enough, but he
wondered about the muscular scuba diver in the wild surfing
trunks.

Checking out Austin with a wary eye, the captain asked,
"What happened, man?"

Austin pointed to the rental boat, which was sinking at a
sharp angle, with only a foot or so of the bullet-riddled bow sticking out of the water.

"Leaky boat," he said.

"I heard a lot of noise," the captain said. "Sounded like
guns."

Austin clamped his hand on the captain's shoulder and turned
him around.

"See that bag floating over there?" Austin said, pointing.
"That's mine. Can we pick it up?"

The doubtful look in the captain's round brown face suggested he was starting to regret his decision to pluck his new passengers from the water, but he sensed that Austin would not be denied. The captain moved the boat closer so Austin could lean over and retrieve the dive-gear bag. Austin unzipped the bag and pulled out his wallet. He peeled off a fifty.

"This is to cover the tickets for the boat ride." He gave the captain another fifty-dollar bill, and said, "This is for asking no more questions." Holding out a third fifty, he wrapped his arm around the captain's shoulders and, speaking low so he wouldn't be heard by the other passengers, Austin said, "How much longer is left in the tour?"

"I dunno . . . half an hour, maybe," the captain said.

"This is yours if you cut that time in half."

The captain grinned, and the third fifty-dollar bill followed the first two into his pocket.

"You just bought the boat, man," he said. "You and the lady, have a seat."

Austin and Song Lee ignored the curious gazes of the other passengers and looked for a place to sit. The boat had a canopy overhead to block the sun, but there were no seats and passengers sat on stacked life preservers. A young Japanese couple on their honeymoon made room for the new passengers.

The tour boat captain was true to his word. Fifteen minutes after Austin and Lee had climbed aboard, he told the passengers to take one last look at the mysterious ruins. Using the housing of one of the twin outboards as a seat, he goosed both engines, and before long the boat was pulling up to the dock at Kolonia.

While Lee went off to the restroom to freshen up, Austin made his way to the dive shop. He returned the scuba gear in good condition but asked the crestfallen owner to come up with a figure to replace the boat and motor. Although the price was exorbitant, Austin produced a NUMA credit card and told him to charge the replacement cost. The bean counters at NUMA who kept an eye on finances had become used to Austin's strange purchases. He asked for a receipt anyhow.

As the boat owner was writing out the purchase order, he said, "Your friend catch up with you?"

"What friend?" Austin asked.

"Asian guy driving a pickup truck. Didn't leave his name. Showed up a few minutes after you took off in the boat. I told him you were going out to the ruins."

Austin did a good job hiding his surprise. He thanked the owner and went into the men's room to change into dry clothes. He stuffed the surfing trunks in a wastebasket and dug his cell phone from the bag. He was glad to see that it was operational. He noticed that the Trouts and, most recently, the captain of the *Concord* had called him. He returned Dixon's call first.

"This is Austin," he said. "I see that you've been trying to get in touch with me, Captain Dixon. I've been away from my phone."

"Glad to hear from you, Kurt. I've got some bad news. Joe has disappeared. He borrowed a NUMA helicopter from the agency's ship and flew to the north of here to take a closer look at an atoll. We lost him on radar."

"Did he send off a Mayday?" Austin asked.

"Not a whisper," Dixon answered. "Whatever happened must have happened fast."

"How soon can you have the chopper pick me up?" Austin asked.

"It's on its way."

Austin clicked off and was about to call the Trouts. But Lee was coming his way, and he put his cell away to hail a taxi.

Austin was only slightly worried about Zavala. The charming young Mexican-American had an amazing talent for survival, and there was little Austin could do at this point anyhow. He was more worried about the fact that Chang had known that Austin was on the island. Someone had tailed him to the harbor, and that meant his comings and goings from the airport had been under surveillance from the time the Citation landed.

He couldn't figure it. Only a few trusted people knew that they were in Pohnpei. He cursed himself for underestimating the Triad.

The taxi dropped them off at the airport, and they went out to the tarmac to await the return of the Seahawk. Austin started to tell Lee about Zavala's disappearance, but she couldn't contain her excitement.

"Do you know what we discovered in that place?" she said. "It was a *hospital* or clinic, where the medusa toxin was administered to cure people! This is the immunology discovery of the century. It proves that ancient men knew the value of inoculation and used it to cure disease. I can't wait to tell Dr. Huang about this. He'll be *thrilled*."

"Who is Dr. Huang?" Austin asked.

"He's my friend and mentor," Lee said. "He's with the Ministry of Health, and was the one who brought me into the medusa project."

"When was the last time you talked to him?"

"He asked me to keep him informed on a daily basis about what I was doing. I climbed the water tower every night at Bonefish Key to get a phone signal."

"Every detail?" Austin asked.

"Yes," Lee said. "I even called him when we stopped at Los Angeles and told him that we were coming to Pohnpei."

"That explains how Chang and his buddies knew we were here."

"Oh, no, you don't think . . ."

Austin shrugged.

"Our mission is top secret," he said. "Only a few trusted people knew we were coming here. But Chang must have had someone on our tail from the second we landed. How well do you know Dr. Huang?" he asked. "Could he be an informant?"

"I met him at Harvard, and he was quite helpful finding me employment." She thought about Huang's failure to fight her exile and his deceptive manner in bringing her into the medusa research. "Dr. Huang is a brilliant but fearful man. It would take only a little threat to bend him to someone's will."

"Someone or something like the Triad."

Her mood darkened.

"Yes," she said. "But it is my fault for letting him deceive me."

"You did a favor for someone you thought was an old friend," he said. "I'd suggest that you keep Dr. Huang in the dark from now on."

The distant *whup-whup* of rotor blades from over the lagoon announced the imminent arrival of the helicopter from the *Concord*. The Seahawk set down moments later. Austin and Lee climbed in, and the chopper lifted off. It was less than an hour, but it seemed like days to Austin, before the helicopter was setting down for a landing on the aft deck of the *Concord*.

Captain Dixon helped Lee off the helicopter, and said, "Welcome to the *Concord,* Dr. Lee. Your government has been trying to get in touch with you."

"We were somewhat delayed in Pohnpei," she said.

"Quite all right," he said. "I told your people that you were on the way. We've got a teleconferencing setup you can use. I'll have my communications officer take you there."

While Dixon stepped off to the side to use his hand radio, Lee turned to Austin.

"You'll have to excuse me, Kurt. Thank you for an interesting day."

"My pleasure," he said. "Perhaps on our next tour of Nan Madol, we can spend more time above water."

"That would certainly be different," she said with a smile.

The communications officer arrived minutes later and led Lee to her teleconference. Dixon welcomed Austin back to the Navy cruiser, and said he would show him on a chart where Zavala had disappeared. On the way to the bridge, the captain said aircraft in the vicinity had made several sweeps around the atoll, but there was no sign of Zavala or the helicopter.

"No debris or oil slick?" Austin asked.

"Nothing," Dixon said. "But we'll keep looking."

"Thanks, Captain, but you can't spend any more time looking for Joe. The lab is our top priority." Noting the frustrated look on the captain's face, he added, "Don't worry about Joe. He pops up when you least expect him."

Austin studied the atoll's location, wondering what had attracted Zavala to the tiny speck of land, and then punched in the Trouts' number on his cell phone. Gamay answered.

"Kurt! Thank goodness you called. We've been worried. What's going on?"

"We had a run-in with one of the Triad leaders in Nan Madol. Guy named Chang. The Triad had an informant. We're back on the *Concord,* but now Joe is missing. Captain Dixon said Joe borrowed a helicopter and went off to check out an atoll."

"We gave him the atoll's coordinates," Gamay said. "It's

located approximately where Trouble Island was, the place
Captain Dobbs stopped at with his whale ship a hundred fifty
years ago."

"You found the logbook?" Austin asked.

"No," she said. "You're not the only one who's discovered that
the Triad has a long reach. We contacted a book dealer who said
he had a lead on the log, but someone killed him and tried to
jump us. We got away by the skin of our teeth."

"Glad to hear that," Austin said with relief. "I'm puzzled,
though. If you didn't find the log, where did you dig up the information about the atoll?"

Gamay told Austin about Perlmutter's lead to Caleb Nye, the
visits to the Dobbs mansion and Brimmer's store, and finding
Brimmer's body in the old mill. Austin fumed as he listened to
the details of Brimmer's murder and the attempt to ambush the
Trouts. Even without Dr. Huang, the vast criminal organization
seemed to have eyes and ears everywhere. He asked for the longitude and latitude coordinates from Nye's diorama and said he
would check them out immediately.

"What do you want us to do in the meantime?" Gamay
asked.

"Call Sandecker and bring him up to speed," Austin said. "I'll
get back to you when I know more."

Austin signed off with a quick thank-you, then sat down in
front of a computer and called up a satellite image on the monitor using Nye's coordinates. Nineteenth-century navigation was
not exactly precise, and the atoll Austin saw on the screen didn't
match the position on the map.

But a radar reading of Joe's trajectory showed that he seemed
to be heading directly for the atoll. Austin zoomed in on the tiny
speck. The monitor showed a palm-studded, handkerchief-sized
patch of sand encircled by a coral reef. Nothing unusual, except

for a dark streak near one side of the lagoon. He ran through the possibilities: school of fish, coral, undersea vegetation, shadows . . . Nothing seemed to fit. He looked up earlier images of the island: the streak was larger then. He kept going back in time, hour by hour.

As he dug back into the satellite photos, he saw that the streak had disappeared. He went further back, and he stopped in his tracks. A cigar-shaped object had taken the place of the streak. The conning tower protruding from the object identified it as a submarine. He enlarged the image, and did a quick Internet search for an Akula-class submarine. He found a series of pictures, extracted one that had the conning tower in roughly the same position, and placed the two images side by side. The subs were identical.

With growing excitement, Austin backed up in the photo file even further. There was no submarine in the lagoon now, not even a black streak. But he saw a dark spot which, upon enlargement, showed the unmistakable outline of a helicopter. Starting with that shot, he rapidly played the pictures forward like images in a nickelodeon: empty lagoon, helicopter, submarine, no helicopter, black streak shrinking in length.

"Thank you, Caleb Nye," Austin said loud enough to be heard by Dixon, who leaned over his shoulder to study the computer monitor.

"Who?" the captain asked.

"He was a nineteenth-century whaler, and he just helped me find Joe."

Austin ran through the series of satellite photos.

"Damn," the captain said. "I think you've *got* something, Kurt."

"We need to get in for a closer look. I'm going to need your help."

Dixon picked up the microphone that connected to the ship's public-address system.

"I'll call the ship's officers together immediately," he said.

Five minutes later, Austin was in the wardroom, running through the satellite series again for the benefit of the cruiser's offers. A gunnery officer suggested surrounding the atoll with every ship in the fleet, then launching an invasion of it.

Austin shook his head.

"A full-fledged naval raid is out of the question, in my opinion," he said. "There simply isn't enough intelligence available on which to base an attack. One miscalculation might result in a massacre of the lab's scientific team."

The officer didn't like being rebuffed.

"Who's calling the shots here, Captain?" he asked. "The U.S. Navy or NUMA? That lab is Navy property."

"That's true," Dixon said, "but I've got orders from the Navy brass to let NUMA take the lead."

"I'm not concerned about competence," the officer said. "It's a question of firepower. NUMA's a research agency, last time I heard."

"We'll back it up as best we can," Dixon said. He was becoming annoyed.

The last thing Austin wanted was an argument over strategy. He intervened to help the gunnery officer save face.

"The officer makes a good point about firepower, Captain," Austin said. "What about putting some ships within hailing distance? You could come to the rescue if I get in a jam."

"Sure," Dixon said. "We could position a few close by, with the rest ready to dash in if needed."

"I'll trust your judgment and that of your officers, Captain," Austin said. "My main concern is getting into the lagoon undetected. Any idea what I'm likely to encounter?"

"We'll have to assume that the atoll is protected by a sensor system," Dixon said. "Night vision devices and radar are a worry, of course, but I'm most concerned about thermal sensors."

"Any way we can get around those security measures?" Austin asked.

"A low-flying helicopter might be able to blend into the sea clutter on a radar screen," Dixon said. "If the insertion was quick, there is a chance you could pull it off."

Austin needed no further encouragement.

"That's settled," he said. "How soon can we leave?"

The captain glanced around at his officers, wanting to give them one last chance to pitch in.

"Gentlemen?" he asked.

Receiving no response, Dixon reached for a phone to pass along his orders. But by that time, Austin had already sprinted for the door.

WHILE KURT AUSTIN WAS debating strategy with Dixon and his men, Song Lee was in another part of the ship, sitting behind a table and staring at a blank screen.

"Just talk to the camera in a normal tone of voice, as if you were having a chat with an old friend," the communications officer said. "The transmission should begin any second."

Lee clipped the tiny microphone to her collar and arranged her hair as best she could. The officer made a call to inform the other participants in the teleconference that all was ready, then he left Lee alone in the room.

The screen fuzzed for a second and then an image appeared of six people sitting at a wooden table in a dark-paneled room. She recognized two people as being from the Ministry of Health, but the others were strangers to her. A silver-haired man wearing the greenish brown uniform of the People's Liberation Army asked Lee if she could see and hear him.

When she replied in the affirmative, he said, "Very good, Dr. Lee. Thank you for this meeting. My name is Colonel Ming. Since time is short, I'll spare the introductions and get right down to business.

"This committee is the counterpart of a similar group that we are working with in the United States. I have been asked to be the spokesman because the Army is at the forefront of the effort to contain the epidemic."

"I have been out of touch," Lee said, "so I know only that quarantine has been imposed around the area where the outbreak began."

"That's correct," Ming said. "The Army was able to contain the epidemic for a time, but this is an enemy we are not equipped to fight. The virus is winning."

"How bad is it, Colonel?"

Ming had expected the question, and a square appeared in the upper-left-hand corner of the screen showing a map of China's northern provinces. Red dots were clustered around one village, with a few stray dots outside its perimeters.

"This shows the outbreak before the quarantine," he said. "The clusters represent virus outbreaks."

Another picture appeared. The dots were centered in one area, but scattered outbreaks were showing up in neighboring towns.

"This too represents outbreaks before the quarantine?" Lee asked.

"No," Ming answered. "The quarantine is in full effect, but the virus has managed to spread despite all that we have been trying to do. I will reserve comment on the next few images."

As the maps were thrown on the screen one after another, the red dots could be seen expanding over a greater part of the Chinese landscape. They clustered and then metastasized like cancer cells. More alarming still, the virus was dangerously close to Beijing in the northeast, and it was sending out spokes toward Shanghai along the southeast coast, Hong Kong to the south, and the sprawling city of Chongqing to the west.

"What is the period of time covered by these projections?" Lee asked, her throat so dry she could barely get the question out.

"One week," Ming said, "ending today. The Ministry of Health projects that the spread of the virus is accelerating. It will hit Beijing first and then spread to the other cities less than two weeks later. You understand better than I what that means."

"Yes, I do, Colonel," she said. "In military terms, it would be like lighting a fuse leading to many different ammunition dumps. The embers thrown out by those explosions will ignite other fuses around the world."

Ming pressed his lips together in a tight smile.

"I understand you were involved in planning for the worst-case scenario, as this appears to be," he said.

"That's correct, Colonel Ming. I drew up the plans to establish vaccine-production centers in locations where it could be best distributed. It's a bit like you and your colleagues planning for a battle."

"Tell me about the vaccine that has been under development in the missing laboratory."

"The last I knew the vaccine was very close to being synthesized from the toxin."

"That is very good news," Ming said.

"True," Lee said. "But the problem from the first was not only isolating the chemical that could kill the virus but producing millions of doses quickly to deal with it. The old method of producing vaccines in eggs was too slow and clumsy: you'd need millions of eggs, and production could take weeks. There was also the problem of a mutating virus. You might have to tailor a vaccine instantly to a different strain of influenza. Tech-based vaccines grown in an animal or human cell could produce three hundred million vaccines in a year."

"The whole population of the planet could be wiped out in less time than that," Ming said.

"That's true," Lee said, "which is why the lab was looking into the genetic engineering of vaccines. You don't manufacture the vaccine but instead produce the molecule that makes it work."

"And what were the results of this research?"

"I don't know. The lab had moved to its new location by then. I didn't have clearance for the final phase."

"Dr. Kane would understand the procedure?"

"Yes, but he wouldn't know the final test results, which he would have been informed of had he been able to return to the lab."

"To put it bluntly, Dr. Lee, even if we find the lab and produce the vaccine, it may be too late?"

"To put it bluntly, yes."

Colonel Ming turned to the others.

"Any questions? No? Well, thank you very much for your time, Dr. Lee. We will be in contact with you again."

The screen went blank. Song Lee was terrified at being alone in the room with her thoughts. She bolted out the door and onto the deck, where she looked around frantically for a glimpse of Kurt Austin's reassuring face. She needed an anchor to keep her from drifting over the edge. She climbed to the bridge, and asked Dixon if he had seen Austin.

"Oh, hello, Dr. Lee," the captain said. "Kurt didn't want to interrupt your meeting. He said to tell you that dinner has been postponed. He left the ship."

"Left? Where?"

Dixon called her over to look at a chart and jabbed his index finger down on the wide expanse of ocean.

"Right now, I'd say that Kurt is just about here."

CHAPTER 41

"WAKE UP, TOVARICH!"

Joe Zavala floated in a netherworld just below consciousness, but he was awake enough to know that the cold liquid being poured on his lips tasted like antifreeze. He spit the liquid out. The roar of laughter that followed his instinctive reaction jerked him into full consciousness.

Hovering over Zavala was a bearded face with a fourteen-karat grin. Zavala saw a bottle again being tilted toward his lips. His hand shot up, and he clamped his fingers in a viselike grip around the man's thick wrist.

A startled expression came to the blue eyes at Zavala's lightning-quick move, but the gold-toothed grin quickly returned.

"You don't like our vodka?" the man said. "I forget. Americans drink whiskey."

Zavala unclenched his fingers. The bearded man pulled the bottle away and took a swig from it. He wiped his lips with the back of his hand.

"Not poison," the man said. "What can I get you?"

"Nothing," Zavala said. "But you can give me a hand sitting up."

The man put the bottle aside and helped Zavala sit on the edge of the bunk. Zavala looked around at the cramped quarters.

"Where am I?" he asked.

"Where *are* you?" the man said.

He turned, and, in a language Zavala recognized as Russian, translated the question for the benefit of three other similarly bearded men who were crammed into the tight space. There was laughter and the vigorous nodding of shaggy heads.

"What's so funny?" Zavala asked.

"I told them what you said, and what my answer will be, that you are in *hell*!"

Zavala managed a slight smile, reaching out his hand.

"In that case," he said, "I'll take that vodka you offered me."

The man handed the bottle over, and Zavala took a tentative sip. He felt the fiery liquor trickle down his throat, but it did little to alleviate the throbbing in his head. He put his hand to his head and felt a bandage wrapped around it like a turban. He still had the bruises on his scalp from his B3 adventure.

"Your head was bleeding," the man said. "It was the best we could do."

"Thanks for the first aid. Who are you guys?" Zavala asked.

"I am Captain Mehdev and these are my officers. You are on a nuclear-powered Akula missile submarine. We are what you Americans know as the Project 941 Typhoon, the biggest class submarine in the world. I am the commander."

"Nice to meet you," Zavala said, shaking the captain's hand. "My name is Joe Zavala. I'm with the American National Underwater and Marine Agency. You've probably heard of it."

Mehdev reached into a pocket of his windbreaker and produced Zavala's laminated NUMA ID with his picture on it.

"Anyone who goes to sea is familiar with the great work of NUMA," Mehdev said. "Your beautiful ships are known around the world."

Zavala took the ID and tucked it into his shirt pocket, grabbed the blanket from the bunk, and wrapped it around him to soak up moisture from his clothes. He took another sip from the bottle and handed it back. One of the officers went over to a sink and got him a glass of water. Zavala washed away the vodka taste with it, and touched his head bandage again.

"No offense, Captain, but you should pay more attention to your driving. Your submarine surfaced right under me and my helicopter."

Mehdev did another translation that his officers found hilarious, but when he turned back to Zavala he had a somber expression on his face.

"My apologies," the captain said. "I was ordered to take the vessel to the surface and bring you aboard. Even for someone with my experience, it is difficult maneuvering a six-hundred-foot-long vessel with any degree of precision. You were floating in the water. We brought you on board. I am sorry too for the loss of your helicopter."

"Who told you to take me prisoner?"

A frown came to Mehdev's genial face.

"The same criminals who hijacked my submarine and have held me and my crew prisoners," he said.

Mehdev launched with angry gusto into his fantastic story. He was a Navy veteran of the Typhoon service who had gone into civilian work. The Rubin Central Design Bureau, which designed the submarine, had come up with the idea to use decommissioned Typhoons to carry freight under the Arctic Ocean. The missile silos were replaced with cargo holds that had a capacity of fifteen thousand tons. A corporate buyer purchased the sub, and it was Mehdev's job to deliver the vessel to its new owner.

The crew of seventy or so was half the normal complement, but without the need for weapons specialists it was large enough to do the job. They were promised big paychecks. The captain's instructions were to surface for an at-sea rendezvous. But a Chinese freighter carrying armed men met them and took over the ship. They were told to sail the ship to the Pacific Ocean. Using a torpedo tube, the kidnappers launched a missile, targeting a surface ship. Then the Typhoon was involved in an operation to move the underwater lab off the ocean floor.

"Where is the lab now?" Zavala asked.

Mehdev pointed downward with his index finger.

"About three hundred feet beneath our hull, at the bottom of a submerged caldera," he said. "There was an eruption many years ago and the volcano collapsed, leaving the caldera in place of the island that was once here. Coral grew on the rim, establishing the reef you came across."

"How did your vessel break through the reef?" Zavala asked.

"We *didn't*. We passed *under* it. The Japanese blasted a tunnel through the caldera, planning to use this place as a submarine base in World War Two. They were going to wait until the American fleet bypassed the atoll and come up behind them with German supersubs to sink their ships. A clever plan. But the Allies bombed the German submarine factories, and then the war ended." Then Mehdev asked, "What do you know of this lab? It must be important."

"*Very* important," Zavala said. "The U.S. Navy has planes and ships out searching. I flew over the lagoon. The water is as clear as crystal. Why didn't I see you?"

"We're below a camouflage net stretched across the lagoon. It's what you Americans call low-tech."

"What about the island I landed on in the lagoon?"

"That is high-tech. An artificial platform on floats, kept in place through a propulsion system geared to a self-correcting navigational system. It provides an observation post to detect intruders. You were seen long before you landed."

"Someone went to a lot of trouble to create a hideaway."

"My understanding is, the people behind this scheme intended to use the atoll for transpacific smuggling."

A pounding on the door interrupted their conversation. Then the door flew open, and an Asian man holding a machine pistol stepped into the cabin. Right behind him was Phelps. Phelps gave Zavala a lopsided grin.

"Hello, soldier," he said. "You're a long way from home."

"I could say the same thing about you, Phelps."

"Yes, you could. I see you've made friends with the captain and his crew."

"Captain Mehdev has been very generous with his liquor cabinet."

"Too bad the party's over," Phelps said. "The captain and his boys have work to do."

Mehdev took the hint and ordered his crew out of the cabin. Phelps told his guard to escort them back to their posts, and then he pulled up a chair and put his boots up on a small writing table.

"How did you find this little hidey-hole?" Phelps asked.

Zavala yawned.

"Dumb luck," he said.

"I don't think so. Next question. Anyone else know about this place?"

"Only the U.S. Navy. You and your pals can expect a visit from an aircraft carrier any minute."

"Nice try," Phelps said with a snort. "The atoll would be swarming with ships and planes by now if the Navy knew about us. The camera on the island sent a picture of your pretty face directly to my boss, Chang. He's the one who ordered Mehdev to grab you, even at the risk of being seen by someone. You've got yourself in a hell of a mess, Joe."

Zavala's lips turned up in a slight smile.

"It only *looks* that way," he said.

Phelps shook his head in disbelief.

"What do they give you NUMA guys to drink?" he asked. "Bull's blood?"

"Something like that," Zavala said. "Now, I've got a question for you: why did you give us the key to the handcuffs and return Kurt's gun after our skirmish with your boss lady?"

Phelps slid his feet off the desk, put them back on the floor, and leaned closer.

"Actually, I've got *three* bosses," he said. "Triplets. Chang is in charge of the rough stuff. He's got a brother named Wen Lo who takes care of business. But the hologram you met back in Virginia is the top dog. Don't know whether it's a he or she."

"What do you mean?"

"Sometimes it's a man image, sometimes it's a woman. You never know."

"What's with the holograms?"

"They don't trust anyone, not even one another. They're crazy too, but you already know that."

"It didn't take a rocket scientist to figure out that they're not playing with a full deck, Phelps. How'd you get hooked up with this bunch of maniacs?"

"I'm an ex-SEAL. Crazy or not, they pay better than the Navy. I was going to retire after this gig." Lowering his voice, he added, "Like I said, I've got family back home. You really think the virus the Triad came up with will hit the U.S.?"

"It's only a matter of a very short time."

"Damnit, Joe, we've got to stop this thing."

"*We?*" Zavala scoffed. "I'm in no position to do much about *anything* right now."

"I'm going to change that. I've been thinking how to work this out. But I'm gonna need your help."

Phelps's cell phone buzzed. He answered the call, listened for a moment, said, "Okay," then hung up. He told Zavala to stay put and slipped out of the cabin.

Zavala pondered his conversation with Phelps. The man was a hired gun and killer, not the type he normally would choose as an ally, but their goals coincided. They would have to smooth out the wrinkles in their relationship later.

Zavala got off the bunk and walked around the cabin. He went over to the sink and splashed water on his face, then walked some more. He was almost feeling normal when Phelps returned.

Phelps was wearing a black neoprene wet suit and carrying a big duffel bag. There was worry in his hound-dog eyes.

"We're going to have to postpone our talk," he said. "That was Chang calling."

"What's going on?" Zavala asked.

"Things just got more complicated," Phelps said. "Feel like going for a swim?"

"I just had one," Zavala said. "Do I have a choice?"

"Nope," Phelps said.

He handed the duffel bag to Zavala, who hefted it.

"Is this part of the complications?" Zavala asked.

Phelps nodded.

He told Zavala to suit up and left him alone in the cabin. Zavala opened the duffel and found a wet suit. He stripped out of his damp clothes and pulled on the neoprene top and bottom, then opened the door and stepped out.

Phelps was waiting in the passageway with two men, also suited up for a dive. He motioned for Zavala to follow and led the way through the labyrinthine innards of the giant submarine. They encountered a number of crewmen who gave Phelps sullen looks. At one point, the guards split off, and Phelps stepped into a compartment at midship.

"Escape chamber," Phelps said, pointing to a hatch over their heads. "There's one on the other side of the conning tower that our two guard dogs will be using."

He opened a bulkhead locker and pulled out two complete sets of scuba gear that included full face masks with wireless-communications capability. When they were ready, Phelps climbed up a ladder into a cylindrical chamber. Zavala followed him up, moving slowly under the weight of the gear.

The escape chamber was a tight fit for two men in full scuba gear. Phelps hit a switch that closed the floor, and water poured in. Once the chamber was flooded, he opened the hatch over their heads.

Phelps let air into his buoyancy regulator and swam up the escape shaft. Zavala followed close behind. They emerged from the submarine at the base of the lofty conning tower. The two guards were waiting for them. Each guard held a gas-powered speargun with a nasty-looking barb on the business end. Zavala ignored them and slipped his feet into his fins.

The greenish light that filtered through the camouflage net bathed the black hull of the submarine in a spectral glow. Zavala had once seen a Typhoon at dock, when the hull was mostly submerged, and had been impressed by its size, but that was nothing compared with seeing the gigantic sub and its massive conning tower in full.

A ducklike voice quacked in his headset, and Phelps waved to get his attention.

"That's enough sightseeing for now, Joe. Follow me. This is a technical dive. Three hundred feet plus, but you've got Trimix in your tank, so you'll be okay."

Phelps switched on a waterproof dive light. With a fluttering kick of his legs, he swam away from the deck, propelling himself through the water using expert form, and then angled downward. Zavala came next, with the two guards following his bubble trail.

They headed toward an amber cluster of sparkling lights. As they descended further, Zavala saw that the lights were on the outside of four large globes attached to each other with tubelike connectors. He immediately recognized the lab from the diagrams he had studied.

"Davy Jones's Locker!" Zavala said.

"Quite the sight, isn't it?" Phelps said.

Zavala noticed something else. Ghostly blue forms were moving slowly in the shadows just beyond the reach of the lab's searchlights.

"Are those blue medusae I see?" he asked.

"Yeah," Phelps said. "You want to stay away from those puppies. They're hot-wired. We can do a nature tour later. We've only got a few minutes to talk. We're the only ones wearing communications gear, so don't worry about those guys on your tail. I was gonna keep you on the sub so we could work out a plan, but Chang said he wanted you in the lab. Didn't say what he's got planned, but, one thing's for sure, he won't be throwing you a welcome party."

"I didn't expect one," Zavala said. "How about *you* throwing me a lifeline?"

"I'll do my best. I'll let you know when I make a move. Meantime, be a good boy and don't give those guys with the spearguns an excuse to use you for target practice."

They were directly above the hemispherical-shaped structure at the hub of the lab complex. Zavala remembered it as the transit module where the airlock for the shuttle vehicle was located. Phelps swam under the transit module, past four minisubmersibles attached to the underside like feeding puppies, then up into a shaft that opened into a round pool at the center of a circular chamber.

Phelps removed his mask and communications unit, and Zavala followed his lead. The guards surfaced seconds later. By then, Phelps and Zavala had used a ladder on the side of the pool to climb out. The guards emerged from the pool, and all four men hung their air tanks and gear on wall hooks. The guards took their masks off to reveal hard Asian faces. They put the spearguns aside and produced machine pistols from their waterproof backpacks.

Phelps pressed a switch and a door slid open. He led the way along a tube-shaped corridor to another door that opened into a small room. Phelps told the guards to wait in the passageway, and then he and Zavala stepped inside.

Half of one wall was made of glass, allowing a view of a laboratory containing several workers dressed in white biohazard suits. The workers looked up when Phelps rapped his knuckles on the glass. All went back to work except one, who waved in acknowledgment and disappeared behind a door labeled DECONTAMINATION.

Minutes later, Lois Mitchell stepped into the room. She was wearing a lab coat and slacks, and her raven hair was still damp

from the decontamination shower. Despite his predicament, Zavala signaled his appreciation of Lois's striking good looks with
a slight smile. Lois saw it, and the corners of her lips turned up.

"*I* know you," she said.

Zavala did a fast mental check of the hundreds of women he
had dated through the years and drew a blank.

"Have we met?" he asked cautiously.

Lois laughed.

"I saw you on TV," she said. "You were the engineer from
NUMA who made the dive with Dr. Kane in the bathysphere."
She furrowed her brow. "What on earth are you doing *here?*"

"I could ask you the same thing," Zavala said.

Phelps said, "Dr. Mitchell, this is Joe Zavala from NUMA."

"*Lois,*" the scientist amended, extending her hand.

"Hate to break up this party," Phelps said, "but things are
moving fast, Dr. Mitchell. My boss is on his way to the lab. My
guess is that he wants to check on your project."

"Actually," she said, "he's coming to get the vaccine."

Phelps narrowed his eyes.

"What do you mean?" he asked.

"While you were away, I told one of those people you have
following me around that we've synthesized the toxin." She
turned and gestured at the glass partition. "This is our fermentation, cell-culture, and analysis lab. Your boss will be able to take
the vaccine culture with him and go into full-bore production
immediately."

Scowling, Phelps said, "That's not good."

"Why?" Lois asked. "Wasn't that the purpose of this whole
project, to produce a vaccine that can be given to the world?"

"You tell her," Phelps said with a shake of his head.

"Once they have the vaccine," Zavala said, "they'll let the
epidemic run until they bring down their government. Then

they'll offer the cure to the rest of the world. Pay or die. You and your lab have become expendable."

The color drained out of Lois Mitchell's already pale features.

"What have I done?" she wailed.

"It's what you're *going* to do that counts," Phelps said.

There was a hard knock on the door. Phelps opened it and one of the guards leaned in close and whispered in his ear. Phelps stepped back inside.

"You haven't said what you want me to do," Lois implored.

"Whatever we do, it better be fast," Phelps said. "Chang's chopper has left Pohnpei for his ship."

Zavala's head was still reeling from its encounter with the six-hundred-foot-long Typhoon, and he was suspicious of Phelps's abrupt change from foe to friend. But the announcement that the Triad's enforcer would soon arrive at the lab had been more effective than having a bucket of cold water thrown in his face.

Since he didn't have many options, Zavala decided to put his money on his former adversary. He grabbed Phelps by the arm, and said, "We need to talk, soldier."

CHAPTER 42

THE SEAHAWK HELICOPTER FLEW WITHOUT ITS RUNNING lights twenty-five feet above the sea, almost skimming the wave tops, as it sped toward the atoll at two hundred miles an hour. Tension in the cockpit mounted as the chopper neared its destination, but Austin remained an island of calm. He sat in the passenger's seat dressed in a lightweight wet suit, his eyes fixed on a satellite-generated hybrid chart spread out on his lap, etching every detail into his brain.

He had marked three Xs on the chart with a grease pencil. The first X showed the position, a quarter mile from the atoll, where the helicopter would drop him off. The second X showed the narrow breach in the coral reef. The third X, from overhead, showed the dark streak in the lagoon.

The pilot's voice came over the headphones.

"Five-minute warning, Kurt."

Austin folded the chart and put it in a waterproof chest pack. He pulled a plastic pouch that protected his Bowen revolver out of the pack, checked the load, and tucked it back inside. Then he unbuckled his seat belt and stood by the Seahawk's open door. The helicopter slowed, then hovered over the predetermined point of insertion.

"Showtime, Kurt!" the pilot said.

"Thanks for the ride," Austin said. "We'll have to do it again sometime when I can stay longer."

The chopper's copilot helped Austin push a six-foot-long inflatable boat out the door, and they lowered it into the sea using a motorized winch. Austin grabbed a two-inch line rigged to the helicopter's hoist bracket and slid down the rope, his hands protected by thick gloves. He then lowered himself into the sea and let go.

The Seahawk moved away from the insertion point, to prevent its rotors from whipping up the water. Austin breaststroked over to the inflatable and climbed aboard. It was stabilized by the weight of the gear pack secured to its makeshift wooden platform between its pontoons. He detached a flashlight from his belt, pointed it at the noisy silhouette hanging over the water, and blinked it several times to signal that he was set.

Its job done, the Seahawk darted off and, within seconds, disappeared into the night.

Austin undid the tie-downs holding the supply pack and pulled out a paddle. He found a waterproof pouch that contained a handheld GPS and pushed the POWER button.

The tiny green screen blinked on, and it showed his position in relation to the island. He tucked the GPS back in its pouch and began to paddle.

It was a gorgeous night. The stars glittered like diamond splinters against the black velvet of the tropical sky, and the sea was on fire, glowing with silvery-green phosphorescence. There was little current and no wind, and he covered the distance in good time. Hearing the whisper of waves washing against the reef, he squinted against the darkness and saw the faint white line of breaking waves.

He checked the GPS again, and followed the course it suggested to take him to the break in the reef. But he ran into trouble as he approached the narrow opening in the coral. The water surged in and out of the break to create a barrier of turbulence that tossed the lightweight boat around like a rubber duck in a bathtub.

Paddling vigorously, Austin brought the bow around and charged into the opening, but again failed to muster the power necessary to overcome the crosscurrents. He made another try. This time, he yelled, "Once more unto the breach," but the inspired words of Shakespeare's Henry V were no match for the power of the sea. All he got for his trouble was a mouthful of seawater.

After his failed attempts, Austin admitted to himself that the sea was just playing with him, and he paddled away from the reef to reconnoiter. As the inflatable rocked in the waves, he caught his breath. Then he extracted a lightweight, electric-powered outboard motor and battery from the pack, clamped the motor to the platform, and punched IGNITION. Except for a soft hum, the motor was almost silent. He goosed the throttle and aimed the inflatable's blunt bow at the creamy surf welling up around the opening in the reef.

The inflatable bounced, fishtailed, and yawed. For a second, Austin gritted his teeth, thinking he was going to be thrown sideways into the jagged coral. Then the outboard's propeller blades caught water, and the inflatable squeezed through the opening and glided into the peaceful lagoon.

Austin quickly killed the motor and waited. Five minutes

passed, and there was nothing to indicate he had been detected.
No blinding searchlights, no hail of bullets, to herald his arrival.

Austin took the lack of a warm reception as an invitation to
stay. He dug his scuba gear out of the pack, buckling on his lightweight air tank and buoyancy compensator. He checked his GPS
and saw that the inflatable had been thrown slightly off course
after passing through the reef.

He began to paddle, until the little black triangle on the GPS's
screen showed he was back on course. A few minutes later, the
triangle merged with the circle marking where the satellite
showed the dark streak in the lagoon. The submarine he had
seen in the satellite image seemed to have sprung from the floor
of the lagoon before it vanished magically from sight. The inex-
plicable disappearance of the Typhoon suggested that there was
more to the lagoon than met the eye. Austin had no logical reason
to assume the lagoon's waters were not as shallow as they looked
from space, but he look no chances, and had borrowed a tank
containing a Trimix mixture from the NUMA research vessel in
the event that he had to make a deeper dive than expected.

Austin pulled on his face mask and fins, chomped on his regulator mouthpiece, hoisted himself belly down onto the inflatable's right pontoon, then rolled off into the lagoon.

Water seeped between the neoprene and his skin and gave
him a momentary chill until it warmed to an insulating body
temperature. He held on to the side of the inflatable for a few
seconds, then he pushed himself away, jackknifed as he dove
under the surface, and descended about twenty feet.

As Austin neared the floor of the lagoon, he reached out with
his gloved right hand. Instead of touching sand, his fingers
pushed against a soft, yielding surface. His coral-blue eyes narrowed behind the lens of the mask. He removed the glove, and

discovered that what he thought was sand overgrown with marine life was a loosely woven net covered with an irregular pattern of colors.

Austin slid his knife from its sheath on his thigh, pressed the point into the fabric, and pushed. With only slight pressure, the blade penetrated the net. He sawed a cut in the net several inches long, withdrew the blade, returned it to its sheath, and glided over the fake ocean botton until he came to where he had seen the streak in the satellite picture.

He saw from a few inches away that the streak was in fact a partially mended tear in the fake bottom. The uneven nylon stitching looked as if it had been done hastily.

Austin unhooked a dive light from his vest.

Holding the light straight out in front of him, Austin squirmed through the opening. He brought his body straight up, paddling with his fins as if he were on a bicycle, and spun around slowly. About midway through his three-sixty pivot, he halted and stared with wonder.

About a hundred feet away was a massive object, faintly illuminated by wavy starlight filtering through the net. No details were clearly visible, but it was obviously an enormous submarine.

Austin instinctively switched the light off, even though it seemed unlikely that anybody aboard the sub was aware of his insignificant presence.

He swam away from the submarine, and saw pinpoints sparkling in the darkness below. He angled his body and dove straight down, only to stop after a few moments to stare at a line of glowing blue objects.

Blue medusae!

About six of them floated across his path of descent. He waited until the deadly jellyfish were out of range, then dove again toward the bottom. As he dove down, he saw that the lights that had first caught his attention were beacons on the tops of four large spheres built around a hemispheric hub. Each rested on four spindly legs with disk-shaped footings that resembled the legs of a spider.

The metal surface of the globes was unbroken with the exception of one sphere which had a transparent dome. Austin swam closer to the sphere and saw two people under the dome. One was a dark-haired woman and the other was Zavala.

The two were sitting in chairs, apparently deep in conversation. Zavala didn't seem to be in any trouble, and, from the look on his face he was enjoying himself. Austin guffawed, the deep laugh coming out as a series of noisy bubbles. Only Joe Zavala could find an attractive woman at the bottom of the sea.

While Austin was trying to make sense of the scene under the dome, the woman looked straight up at him and stared. He peeled off like a fighter plane, swam down to the bottom and under the sphere, then toward the hemispheric hub. He remembered from the diagram that the hub was the transportation module. It had an airlock at the top of it for the cargo shuttle.

He swam under the module past four submersibles hanging from the bottom of the hemisphere, and found the hatch that allowed divers access to the module. He inflated the buoyancy compensator. Air from the tank flowed into the vest and he began a slow rise. At the same time, he removed the waterproof pouch holding the Bowen from his pack. He figured he could have the pistol out and ready to fire within five seconds of surfacing. With the element of surprise, that should give him the edge he needed.

Austin's head broke the surface of the airlock pool inside the hemisphere. He pushed his mask up on his forehead, glanced quickly around, and saw that the Bowen wouldn't be needed and could stay in its pouch for now. The circular room was deserted.

He swam over to a ladder and put the pouch on the edge of the pool, making sure it was within easy reach. Then he slipped out of his weight belt, fins, and tank and set them next to the pouch. He climbed out, retrieved the Bowen from its pouch, and hung his scuba gear on a hook next to four other sets of dry gear. Then he listened for a minute at the only door.

All was quiet. Austin's Bowen filled one hand, and his other pressed the wall switch. The door slid quietly open. Austin set off along a corridor, determined to stir up some trouble.

It didn't take long.

He came to a door marked RESOURCE CULTIVATION SECTION. He opened it and stepped into a twilit chamber that was circular in shape, the walls lined with fish tanks that contained various jellyfish. But it was the larger, chest-high, circular tank at the center of the room that caught his attention.

It contained at least a dozen giant jellyfish. Their bell-shaped bodies were nearly a yard across, and their tentacles were short, thick, and ropy rather than the delicate streaming filaments seen on most jellyfish. They glowed with a pulsating neon blue that provided the sole illumination in the room.

He saw a movement that didn't come from inside the tank. A distorted face was reflected in the curving glass surface. Absorbed by the strange forms in the central tank, Austin had let himself get sloppy.

The Bowen dangled at the end of his arm near his thigh. He whirled and raised the gun, but the powerfully built guard who had been quietly stalking Austin brought the metal stock of his machine pistol down and it hit the flesh inside of Austin's wrist. The Bowen flew from his fingers and clattered on the floor, and a fiery pain shot up to his shoulder.

Austin's right arm was momentarily useless, but with his left hand he reached up and grabbed the machine pistol. As he tried to wrench the weapon from the man's grasp, his assailant pushed him back against the tank. He slammed against the glass wall, but Austin kept a tight grip on the gun, pushed it up and away from his body, and managed to twist the machine pistol away. His fingers lacked the strength to hold on to the weapon, and it splashed into the tank. The giant jellyfish scattered in every direction.

Both men stared at the lost weapon, but Austin was the first to rally. He kept his useless arm close to his side, lowered his head, and butted the man in the chest, driving him back toward the wall. They both slammed against the row of tanks, dislodging a couple that crashed to the floor and broke open.

The gelatinous creatures in the tanks spilled across the floor. Austin lost his footing in the slippery mess and went down on one knee. He struggled to stand again, and the man kicked him in the side of the face.

But the man slipped in the slimy glop in his second attempt to kick Austin's head through the goalposts. The blow glanced off Austin's cheek, rattling his teeth and knocked him over on his right side. The man, regaining his balance, produced a knife from a sheath hanging from his belt and let out a yell. He dove on Austin with knife raised high.

Austin brought his left arm up in what he knew was a futile attempt to block the blade, but at the last second his groping gloved hand snatched up a shard of glass eight inches long and he plunged it into the man's neck. He heard a gargled shriek of pain and felt a shower of warm blood from the severed jugular. The knife dropped from the man's fingers. He tried to get to his feet, only to crumple on rubbery legs as the life drained from his body.

Austin rolled out of the way before the man crashed down on him and got unsteadily to his feet. His right wrist was on fire, and he had to use his left hand to retrieve his Bowen. As he stepped carefully around the spreading pool of blood and dozens of dying jellyfish, he took a quick glance at the big tank. The giant mutant jellyfish glowed even brighter. It was as if they had enjoyed the blood sport.

Austin wasted no time putting the nightmarish scene behind him. He set off down a corridor to search for Zavala, wondering what other delightful surprises Davy Jones's Locker would have to offer.

CHAPTER 43

IT WAS LOIS MITCHELL WHO HAD SUGGESTED A PLACE TO formalize the just-formed alliance with Phelps.

"I've been using Dr. Kane's office," Lois said. "The guards have been ordered not to bother me while I work. We'll be all right there for a while."

"That okay with you, Phelps?" Zavala asked.

"Fine," Phelps said, "but we're going to have to do it my way. The lab is still controlled by Chang's goons, so we can't just take a stroll."

Phelps told Mitchell to take the lead and for Zavala to follow her. He brought up the rear, holding his machine pistol at the ready as if he were escorting the other two under guard.

They passed a few of Chang's men, who gave them a glance and a nod but asked no questions. They avoided the control room, which was off-limits to the staff, and skirted the fermentation lab so as not to arouse curiosity among the scientists.

Despite the direness of the situation, Zavala couldn't help but grin with appreciation when he ascended the spiral staircase to Kane's office and saw the colorful schools of fish nosing around the clear Plexiglas dome that were the ceiling and walls.

"This is fantastic!" he said.

Mitchell smiled, and she said, "I agree. I would spend a lot of time here even if it weren't a refuge from the guards. Please have a seat."

Mitchell turned up the lights to blot out the fishy distraction and sat behind the desk. Zavala and Phelps settled in chairs. Their newborn coalition was still on a shaky foundation, and the initial moment of uncomfortable silence was broken finally by Phelps, who cleared his throat and asked Zavala, "Where's your pal Austin?"

Zavala's instinct to spar went back to his boxing days in college, and he gave Phelps a minimal answer.

"Kurt was on Pohnpei, last I knew."

Phelps twitched his nose.

"Hope Kurt stays out of Chang's sights," he said. "He's been gunning for your friend."

"Don't worry about it, Phelps. Kurt can take care of himself." Then Zavala asked, "How much time do we have before your boss arrives?"

"He's probably just about landing on that freighter he uses as a base," Phelps said. "Ship looks like a rust bucket, but she'll outrun most her size. There's even a moon pool for the lab's shuttle. He'll use the shuttle to get down in the crater. I'm supposed to make sure everything's okay with the airlock. That maniac will be here in under an hour. We won't have a lot of wiggle room once he's on board."

"Where's the staff when they're not working in the lab?" Zavala asked.

"They're confined to quarters," Mitchell said. "They're kept under pretty tight guard, thanks to Mr. Phelps here."

"Just doing my job," Phelps said.

"How do you *undo* your job?" Zavala asked.

"I'll try my best, Joe, but it won't be easy."

"Don't worry," Zavala said, "there will be lots of opportunities here to redeem yourself. For a start, do you have any idea how we can get the staff away from the lab?"

"I've been thinking about that," Phelps said. "We can use the minisubs under the transit hub. They'll each take four people. We've got fifteen scientists down here plus the cargo-shuttle pilot."

Zavala forgot his throbbing head in his eagerness to go on the offensive.

"You and I can go out the way we came in," he said. "We've got to neutralize those guys on the Typhoon. How many will we have to deal with on the sub?"

"The Triad triplets like to do things in threes," Phelps said. "Something to do with lucky numbers. They got three squads of three on the sub, which makes nine, minus the two that came down here with us. They're all armed and meaner than rattlesnakes."

"They've had it easy up until now," said Zavala, "so they've lost their edge and won't be expecting anything. They won't have a chance."

Phelps let out a deep chuckle.

"Like Chesty Puller said when they told him he was surrounded: 'They won't get away this time.'"

"That's right," Zavala said. His mind raced ahead. "Okay, we get the people on the minisubs and they leave the lab . . . Where do they go?"

"Through the big tunnel in the side of the crater," Phelps said. "They've got enough power to get well beyond the reef, past Chang's freighter, to where they can surface and send out a Mayday."

"We've got to get to the staff and let them know what's up," Zavala said.

"I can do it," Lois Mitchell said. "The guards are used to seeing me around the lab."

Phelps glanced at his watch.

"That will have to wait until I get back. I've got to get things ready for Chang's arrival. Why don't you two get to know each other better?"

"Ladies first," Zavala said after Phelps had closed the door behind him.

Mitchell gave Zavala a brief overview of her work with Dr. Kane and the medusa project, going back to Bonefish Key.

"You're to be congratulated for the success of the project," he said.

"I never dreamed it would come to this," she said. "And you, Mr. Zavala, how did you come to be in this awful place?"

"I'm an engineer with NUMA. My boss, Kurt Austin, and I were asked by the Navy to help search for the lab. So here I am."

He was surprised when Lois Mitchell didn't question him further. She seemed distracted, with a far-off look in her eyes that said her thoughts were elsewhere. He had the feeling that she was holding something back. But then she blinked and focused behind Zavala.

"What was that?" she asked.

He turned and saw only the schools of curious fish caught in the light from the office interior.

"Did you see something?" he asked.

"I thought I saw somebody swimming." She smiled. "Sorry, I've been down here too long. Probably a big fish."

The incident seemed to bring her back to reality. Joe's charm and soft-spoken manner penetrated Lois's shell, and she began to relax. She was actually smiling until Phelps returned with the news that his boss was bringing along someone named Dr. Wu.

Mitchell stiffened when she heard the name.

"He's no doctor," she said, "he's a monster!"

"Maybe it's time you showed Joe the video," Phelps suggested.

Mitchell was stone-faced as she took a key on a chain hung from around her neck and unlocked a drawer in her desk She reached in and pulled out a box holding a number of CD-ROM discs. She picked out one labeled COMPUTER PROGRAM BACKUP. Her fingers trembled as she slipped the disc into her computer and turned the monitor around so that it was facing the two men. The disc's narrator spoke Chinese.

"No subtitles?" Zavala asked.

"You won't need them once this thing gets going," Phelps said. "I've seen it before."

"Wu is Chang's creature," Mitchell said. "His job is to check on our progress. When he's here, he kicks me out of my office. Luckily, he doesn't like being on the lab.

"I found this disc in the computer after his last visit. He must have been reviewing its contents. I made a copy, then left the disc in the computer. He eventually realized he had left the disc behind and sent one of his thugs to retrieve it."

A picture had come up on the screen. The camera showed Wu talking to a man in a suit, then switched to a view of some people lying in beds encased in transparent cylinders. Figures in protective suits moved among the cylinders. The camera zoomed in to show close-ups of the people in them. Some appeared to be asleep or possibly dead. Others had faces mottled with mahogany splotches and contorted in agony.

"Is this a hospital?" Zavala asked.

"Far from it," Mitchell said in a tense voice. "That's Dr. Wu narrating. From what I can determine, the video was shot at a lab in China where they were experimenting with vaccines the Triad created. I don't know the man in the suit. They used human subjects, and of course they had to infect their subjects with the virus. You can see the results on the screen. He's worse than that Nazi Mengele, the concentration-camp doctor."

"Dr. Mitchell showed me this stuff a while ago," Phelps said. "Now you see why I've come over to your side."

A rage began to build in Zavala's chest, and when the video had ended he said, "Someone is going to pay for this."

"Funny to hear you say that," a familiar voice said. "I was thinking the same thing."

Three heads turned simultaneously. And three pairs of eyes widened at the sight of Austin, who stood in the doorway, leaning against the jamb. He held his Bowen loosely in his left hand.

Zavala stared at his friend. He wasn't totally surprised to see him: Austin had a way of popping up when you least expected him. But Austin's wet suit was covered with blood and jellyfish slime.

"You look like you've been wrestling in raspberry Jell-O," Zavala said. "Are you okay?"

"My right arm is feeling a little useless right now, but the blood isn't mine. On the way here, I stopped in a room with a big round tank. A guy jumped me, and we were waltzing around when some of the smaller tanks in the room broke and spilled their insides all over the floor."

"The small tanks contained organisms in various stages of

mutation," Mitchell said. "You're lucky the big tank didn't break. Those creatures were the final mutant phase, the one used to make the vaccine. Each tentacle contains thousands of nematocysts, tiny harpoons that inject the toxin into prey."

"My apologies for the damage, but it couldn't be helped," Austin said. He introduced himself to Lois Mitchell. "When I saw you from outside the dome, I thought that only Joe Zavala could find a lovely woman at the bottom of the ocean."

Her eyes widened.

"That was *you* I saw?"

Austin nodded.

"I was watching you and Joe and got careless."

He turned to Phelps.

"From the conversation I overheard a few minutes ago, it sounds like you've come over from the Dark Side."

"That video nailed it for me," Phelps said. "Joe seems to be okay with the deal."

Austin didn't have time to subject Phelps to a lie-detector test. He glanced at Zavala, who gave him a nod, then came back to Phelps.

"Welcome aboard, soldier," Austin said. "What's our status?"

"Chang is on his way to the lab to pick up the vaccine," Phelps said.

"He'll be here any minute," Mitchell added.

"That's good," Austin said unexpectedly. "Chang and the people responsible for the scenes on that video are walking dead."

Unexpectedly, Lois began to sob.

"*I'm* one of those people," she said. "I collaborated on the vaccine work."

"You can't beat yourself up, Dr. Mitchell," Austin said, trying to cushion the force of his words. "You were forced to work on the vaccine. You and the other scientists would have been killed if you hadn't."

"I know that," she said. "But I went *overboard* to make sure the project was a success. It was as if I were trying to show them we could meet the challenge."

"Rock and a hard place," Phelps said. "Now that the vaccine's a fact, they won't need the staff or the lab. Joe and I have come up with a plan to get everyone off the Locker."

Austin didn't answer right away. He squinted through the dome where he had seen a flicker of light. Recalling the high visibility of the globe's interior to outside eyes, Austin hit the light switch, throwing the office into darkness.

"Your plan had better be a good one," Austin said. *"Look."*

All eyes turned to see the shuttle carrying Chang and Dr. Wu as it descended toward the lab like a star falling in slow motion.

CHAPTER 44

MINUTES LATER, THE SHUTTLE SETTLED ON THE LANDING pad and the open roof over it closed again like two halves of a clamshell. Powerful pumps kicked into action and rapidly cleared the airlock of water, but Chang nonetheless was seething with impatience. He finally burst from the shuttle like a moray eel springing from its den and slogged toward the exit door as the last few inches of water gurgled down the drains. The weasel-faced Dr. Wu followed a couple of paces behind.

When the door to the airlock hissed open, Phelps was standing in the adjacent chamber next to the control console. He stepped up to Chang and greeted him with a lopsided grin.

"You got here fast, boss. Musta put the pedal to the metal."

Chang stared at Phelps with barely concealed contempt. American jargon was lost on him, and it annoyed him when Phelps used it. He had never fully trusted Phelps and suspected his loyalty extended only to the next paycheck.

"Enough talk!" Chang snarled. "Where is the vaccine?"

"Dr. Mitchell has it," Phelps said. "She's been waiting in the mess hall for you to arrive. The NUMA guy is with her."

"And the laboratory staff? Where are they?"

"They're all tucked away in their quarters."

"Make sure they *stay* there. You have disabled the minisubs, as I ordered?"

Phelps dug out four flat, rectangular boxes tucked in his belt.

"These circuits control the subs' power supplies," he said.

Chang snatched the circuit boards from Phelps, dropped them on the metal floor, and ground them to pieces with his heel. He barked an order to his men, who had emerged from the shuttle carrying wooden boxes in their arms. They stacked the boxes near the console and then returned to the cargo hold for more.

Printed on the boxes in big bold red letters was

HANDLE WITH CARE

EXPLOSIVES

Phelps rapped the top of a box with his knuckles.

"What's going on with the firecrackers, Chang?" he asked.

"It's fairly obvious," Chang said. "You're going to use your expertise with explosives to blow up the lab. It has fulfilled its function."

Phelps poked at the smashed electrical circuits with the toe of his boot.

"One problem," he said. "How are the scientists going to get off the lab with the minisubs disabled?"

"The scientists have fulfilled their function. They'll stay with the lab."

Phelps stepped in front of Chang and faced off.

"You hired me to hijack the lab," Phelps said. "Killing a bunch of innocent people wasn't in my job description."

"Then you won't prepare the explosives?" Chang asked.

Phelps wagged his head.

"That's right," he said. "You can count me out of this deal."

Chang stretched his liverish lips in a death's-head grin.

"Very well then, Mr. Phelps. You're *fired.*"

Chang's hand reached down to his holster and, in a lightning move, drew his pistol and shot Phelps point-blank in the chest. The impact at such close range threw Phelps backward, and he crashed to the floor. Chang gazed at Phelps's twitching body with the expression of a craftsman who considered his job well done. He ordered one of his men to prepare the explosives, and then he charged off. Dr. Wu followed a few paces behind.

Chang burst into the mess hall, and his jade-green gaze fell on Joe Zavala and Lois Mitchell, who were tied to their chairs and sat back-to-back under the watchful eye of the same hard-faced guards who had come down with Phelps. Chang leaned close to Zavala.

"Who are you?" he demanded.

"You've got a short memory," Zavala said. "We met on the *Beebe.* You left with your tail between your legs while Kurt Austin and I entertained your friends."

"Of *course,*" Chang said. "You're the NUMA engineer. My men deserved their fate. We won't be so careless next time. How did you find us?"

"One of our planes flew over the atoll and saw something suspicious."

"You're lying!" Chang grabbed the front of Zavala's shirt. "I don't like being taken for a fool. If that were the case, planes and ships would be swarming around the atoll. My observers report that all is peaceful."

"Maybe it's what you *don't* see that you should worry about," Zavala said.

"Tell me how you found us."

"Okay, I confess. A little bird told me."

Chang backhanded Zavala across the jaw.

"What *else* did your little bird tell you?" Chang asked.

"He told me that you are going to die," Zavala burbled through bloody lips.

"No, my friend, it is *you* who are going to die."

Chang let go of Zavala's shirt and turned to Lois Mitchell, who was staring in horror at Joe's bloodied face.

"Where is my vaccine?" Chang demanded.

She glared at Chang, and said, "In a safe place. Untie me and I'll get it for you."

At a nod from Chang, his men untied her. She stood and rubbed her wrists, then went over and opened the door to the walk-in refrigerator used to store food for the mess. Stepping inside, she came out carrying a large plastic cooler, which she placed on the floor. Dr. Wu unlatched the lid of the cooler.

"The cooler holds the microbial cultures that will allow you to synthesize the vaccine in quantity," she said.

Packed in foam were a number of the shallow, wide petri dishes. Wu smiled.

"This is a miracle," he said.

"Actually," she said, "it's nothing more than very innovative genetic engineering."

She bent down and removed the top rack of petri dishes. Underneath were three stainless-steel containers, also packed in foam.

"These are the three vials of the vaccine that you requested," she said. "You will be able to make more with the cultures." She replaced the rack, closed the lid, and stood up. "Our job here is done. Mr. Phelps said that we would be free to go once we completed the project."

"Phelps is no longer in our employ," Chang said.

Her face went ashen at the ominous tone of the announcement.

"What do you mean?" she asked.

He ignored the question, and ordered his men to tie her up again.

"Your friend Austin escaped me again," Chang said to Zavala, "but it will only be a matter of time before we meet. And when we do, I will take great pleasure in describing your last moments to him."

Chang took the cooler from Wu's hand and ordered the doctor and his guards to return with him to the shuttle. Austin stepped out of the walk-in refrigerator seconds later after they left, holding the Bowen in his left hand.

"Good thing old bullethead left when he did," Austin said. "I was starting to feel like a side of beef in there."

He tucked the revolver under his right arm. Using a kitchen knife, he sliced the bindings holding Zavala, who reached for a napkin to staunch his bleeding lips. Despite the cuts and bruises, he was in good humor.

"Chang isn't going to be happy when he finds out that the vaccine cultures you gave him are bogus," he said to Lois Mitchell.

She gave Zavala a knowing smile, and went back into the freezer. She came out with another cooler, almost identical to the first.

"Wait until he learns that we've got the *real* thing," she said.

CHANG WAS ALREADY far from happy. He uttered an angry curse as he entered the airlock chamber and saw that Phelps's body was gone. A trail of blood led off toward a corridor. Phelps must have survived the gunshot and dragged himself down one of the passageways.

No matter. Phelps would die when the lab blew into a million pieces. Chang inspected his sapper's handiwork and ordered him to set the timer. Then he herded his men into the shuttle, and the pilot used a remote control to activate the pumps. The airlock quickly filled with water. As the shuttle rose through the opening halves of the clamshell roof, Austin stood in the airlock control room watching the ascent on the instrument console's television monitor. He spun around at the sound of a footfall, only to lower the Bowen a second later.

Phelps stood at the entrance to the passageway with his lips contorted into a strained grin. He was stripped to the waist, and a makeshift bandage soaked with blood covered the upper left part of his chest. His face was pale, but his dark eyes were defiant.

"You look like crap," Austin said.

"Feel like it too," Phelps said.

"What happened to you?"

"I figured Chang was going to be on hair trigger, thanks to you NUMA boys, so on my trip back to Kane's office I grabbed a soft body-armor vest. It only covered my vitals, and I didn't ac-count for Chang's bad aim. Bastard nicked me in the shoulder."

"Why did he shoot you?"

"He got testy when I told him I wouldn't rig the C-4 he and his boys brought down in the shuttle."

"He planned to destroy the lab with people in it?"

"Oh, hell, they put down enough explosives to wreck the Great Wall of China. Sloppy work, though. Lucky they didn't blow themselves up."

Phelps tossed a bundle of colored wires on the floor in an expert's gesture of disdain for amateurish work.

"What's Chang going to do when he discovers that his explosives didn't go off?" Austin asked.

"My guess is, he'll send somebody down to check it out." Phelps cocked his head. "On second thought, he'll probably come back to shoot your friends so he can tell you about it." He gingerly touched the bandage. "Chang's kinda bad-tempered that way."

"I've noticed," Austin said. "We've got to get everyone off the lab in the minisubs."

Phelps pointed at the black discs that had been pulverized under Chang's heel.

"These are circuits for the subs' controls," he said. "Chang stomped them."

"Damn!" Austin said. "The subs were our only hope."

"Still are," Phelps said. "I gave Chang some other discs for his temper tantrum. The originals are still in the subs."

Austin gazed at Phelps, thinking that he still had a lot to learn about human nature.

"What say you get the subs ready while I round up the scientists," Austin said.

Phelps gave a quick salute and headed for the transit hub while Austin hurried back to the mess hall. Zavala had already rounded up the entire staff. The expressions on their faces ran the gamut from joy that they'd been freed to fear about what would happen next.

Austin introduced himself, asked everyone to be quiet for a minute, then announced: "We're abandoning the Locker." He shushed the group again and warned them to move as quickly as possible. Questions would be allowed later.

The weary and frightened scientists climbed down to the minisub hatches. A few hesitated, and there were angry shouts when they saw Phelps, but Austin told them to pipe down and get into the subs. With some grumbling, they did as they were told.

"Are the subs likely to encounter Chang on their way out of the crater?" he asked Phelps.

"Not if they move fast. Chang would have gone back to his freighter to wait for the big boom. If the subs stay submerged as long as they can, they'll be well past Chang's ship, and can put out a Mayday."

Austin passed Phelps's advice along to the pilot of each sub. He delegated the shuttle pilot to take the lead vehicle. Mitchell got in one of them and held the cooler with the real vaccine cultures in it tightly on her lap. Then, one by one, the subs detached from the underside of the hemispheric hub and followed the leader across the bottom of the crater and through the tunnel.

With the staff on its way, Austin turned to the next order of business: the Typhoon. As they got back in their wet suits, Zavala filled Austin in on the situation aboard the Russian submarine. Austin's view of the situation was less optimistic than Zavala's. Feeling was returning to Austin's right arm, but he still wouldn't be able to raise and fire the heavy Bowen revolver with any degree of accuracy. Phelps would be of limited help.

When Phelps tried to get into his wet suit, the snug neoprene top pressed painfully against his wound. Zavala used Austin's knife to cut the arm of the suit off and part of the chest area to relieve the pressure.

Phelps noticed that two sets of scuba gear were missing and surmised that the pair of guards who had escorted Zavala from the sub had gone back to join their comrades. More bad news: the guards were now back to their full complement.

Zavala helped Austin lower Phelps into the pool and guide him down the shaft to open water. With Austin on one side of Phelps and Zavala on the other, all three slowly rose from the bottom up toward the Typhoon, whose gigantic shadow loomed near the surface.

By prearrangement, Austin and Phelps entered the hatch on the starboard deck of the giant sail and Zavala used the port hatch. Once inside the escape chambers they closed the hatch, pumped out the water, then opened the lower watertight door and descended the ladder. They whipped their masks off to see Captain Mehdev standing there with a curious look on his face.

The captain had been in the control room when an alarm went off signifying the airlocks were in use. The two guards had returned earlier from the lab, so he went to see who had entered his submarine. He wasn't surprised to see Phelps and Zavala, but he raised a bushy eyebrow when he saw the broad-shouldered stranger.

Zavala said, "Kurt, this is Captain Mehdev, the commander of this incredible boat and keeper of the vodka cabinet."

Austin extended his uninjured left arm for a handshake.

"Kurt Austin. I'm Joe's friend and colleague at NUMA." Noticing the hostile glance Mehdev shot in Phelps's direction, he added, "Mr. Phelps is no longer working for the people who hijacked your sub. He is helping us now."

"Yes, but for how long?" Mehdev asked, making no secret of his skepticism.

"Good question," Phelps said. "Sorry, can't answer that. But I'm going to help you guys take your sub back."

Mehdev shrugged.

"What can my men and I do?" the captain said. "We are sailors, not Marines."

"Start by telling us where the guards are and what they are doing," Austin said.

"Three are asleep in the officers' quarters in the starboard hull," Mehdev said, "and the others are gambling in the wardroom or they're in the mess hall. They like to be close to the gym and the sauna, which were made off-limits to my men."

"I think it's time we end their little sojourn at Club Med," Austin said. "Let's take care of the snoozers first."

Phelps pretended to be guarding Zavala and Austin in case the four encountered a wandering guard. They filed through the control room, where Mehdev, who had been in the lead, whispered in Russian to the crewmen, who passed the word on to others, that it would be a good idea to stay out of sight. The captain then picked up some rolls of duct tape from the machine shop and continued through the labyrinth of pressurized compartments until they came to the first of the officers' staterooms.

Three off-duty guards awoke in the first room to find themselves looking down the barrel of Austin's revolver. They were trussed up by Zavala, had their mouths taped, and were tucked back in their bunks.

The raiding party headed toward the smell of cooking food. Mehdev entered the mess hall alone and smiled at two guards who sat at a table drinking tea while watching Jackie Chan on DVD. They glanced at the captain only briefly, then went back to their DVD.

Mehdev spoke in Russian to the quartermaster, who was tending the steam table. He nodded in understanding and slipped out of the mess hall. Then Austin and Zavala stepped into the room, brandishing their weapons. The stunned guards were pushed, belly down, to the floor, then given the duct-tape treatment to keep them immobile and quiet.

With Mehdev again in the lead, Austin and Zavala kept moving through the sub until they came to the wardroom. The captain poked his face through the doorway and asked with a smile if anyone needed anything. One guard looked up from his cards and answered with a growl that needed no translation. Still smiling, the captain withdrew.

"Four places but only three players," Mehdev whispered to Austin and Zavala. "Half a bottle of vodka gone."

Austin didn't like having a stray guard wandering around the submarine, but he wanted to press his advantage. He nodded to Zavala, and they stepped into the wardroom with guns leveled. The slightly drunk guards were slow to react. Minutes later, they were facedown on the floor bound with duct tape. Then the hunt was on for the missing guard.

They found him a few minutes after that. Or, rather, he found them. As the men entered the compartment that housed the sauna, the door opened and the guard stepped out wearing only a bathing suit. This time, it was Austin and Zavala who were slow to react. The guard was young and fast, and he reached into a nearby locker, grabbed a holster with a handgun in it, and bolted through the hatch into the next compartment. Austin gave chase, but he tripped on some pipes and went down on one knee. He was up in an instant, but by then the guard had disappeared into the innards of the submarine.

Austin would have lost his prey if not for the crewmen who pointed him in the direction of the fleeing guard. With Zavala right behind him, he kept moving until he came to a closed door. He and Zavala were pondering their next move when Mehdev caught up to them.

"What's on the other side of that door?" Austin asked.

Huffing and puffing, the portly captain said, "The missile battery was replaced with a cargo hold. A freight elevator goes up to a loading hatch on the deck. A catwalk from the elevator crosses over the bays to another elevator on the forward side of the hold, which is filled with empty containers that were supposed to be used for cargo. You'll never find him in there. Just secure the door."

"Could he still cause trouble if we let him alone?" Austin asked.

"Well, yes," the captain answered. "There are electrical and other conduits that run through the hull. He could disable the sub."

"Then I think we should disable him," Austin said.

He asked the captain to have his men keep watch over the guards who had been neutralized, then plucked a flashlight off the bulkhead wall, turned the compartment lights off, and slowly opened the door. He stepped into the next compartment, flicked the flashlight on, and played the beam over the open elevator shaft. The elevator cables were thrumming inside the shaft. The elevator car then clanged softly to a halt at the top.

Austin went over and pressed the elevator's DOWN button. He and Zavala stood to either side of the doors with their weapons ready, but when the elevator car returned it was empty. Zavala took a fire extinguisher from the wall and stuck it between the doors to keep the car in place.

After a quick conference, Zavala climbed the stairs to the catwalk to drive the guard toward Austin, who then would cut him off at the other end of the hold. Austin had spent a lot of time at the shooting range using both hands and was confident that he could get off a reasonably accurate left-handed shot if he had to.

The vast interior hold, which had once housed missile silos and twenty city busters, took up almost a third of the sub's length. When the silos were removed, large loading-dock doors had been installed in the deck overhead and partitions installed to separate one cargo from another in their own bays.

Austin stepped into the first bay and found a light switch. Floodlights hanging from the catwalk turned night into day. He made his way along a corridor between the metal containers until he came to a partition. He stepped through an opening into the next bay and repeated his search.

As Austin made his way through the hold bay by bay, Zavala kept pace along the catwalk. Austin had crossed the hold without incident until he came to the last bay. Haste made him careless.

Austin assumed that the guard was still ahead of him, caught in the pincers of their maneuver. But the prey had figured out the intention of the maneuver and had hidden in a narrow space between container stacks. He waited for Austin to pass and then silently emerged behind him. Moving quietly on bare feet, the guard lifted his gun with both hands and carefully took aim between Austin's shoulder blades.

"*Kurt!*"

The shout came from Zavala, who was peering over the rail of the catwalk. Austin glanced up and saw his friend's pointing finger. Without a backward glance, he ducked around a big metal container as a bullet twanged off its corner. Then another gunshot rang out, this one from above. A moment later, Zavala called down.

"You can come out, Kurt, I think I got him."

Austin peered around the corner of the container, then he waved up at Zavala. The guard lay dead in his bathing suit on the floor. Even shooting down at such a difficult angle, Zavala had drilled him through his chest.

Austin remembered then what Phelps had said about the Chinese fetish for numbers. He shook his head. When your number was up, your number was up.

CHAPTER 45

CHANG WAS A CLASSIC PSYCHOPATH. HE DIDN'T HAVE A drop of human empathy or remorse in his squat, ugly body, and for him killing was as easy as crossing the street. The other Triad triplets had channeled his murderous impulses to their own ends. He displayed a real talent for organization, so they gave him responsibility for the network of gangs that operated in the world's big cities. The job slaked his blood thirst by allowing him to participate in assassinations for commercial advantage, retribution, or just plain punishment.

The job also had restrained Chang from tumbling into the abyss of sheer madness, as long as the other two triplets provided balance. But now he was on his own, far from the familial reins that had kept his barely restrained violence in check. The voices that sometimes whispered in his head were now shouting for his attention.

After leaving the lab, Chang had delivered the vaccine cultures to the freighter lying in wait near the atoll and then waited for a report from the submarine. The failure of the explosives to detonate, to destroy the lab and staff, had finally pushed him over the edge.

When the appointed time had passed, Chang got back in the shuttle with his most cold-blooded killers, and ordered the pilot to head back into the crater. As the shuttle emerged from the tunnel, the undimmed lights at the bottom seemed to mock Chang. A vein pulsed in his forehead.

Dr. Wu, sitting at Chang's side, had sensed his employer's growing fury, and he tried to will himself into invisibility. Even more disconcerting was Chang's sudden lightness of mood when he turned and said in an almost cheerful tone more frightening than his anger:

"Tell me, my friend, what would happen if someone were to fall, quite by accident, into the tank with the mutant jellyfish?"

"That person would be stung immediately."

"Death would be instant?"

"No. The nature of the toxin is to paralyze."

"Would it be agonizing?"

Dr. Wu shifted his weight uncomfortably.

"Yes," he said. "If the person didn't drown, he would be aware of every sensation in his body. In time, the jellyfish would begin to absorb him."

"*Splendid!*" Chang clapped Dr. Wu on the back. "Why didn't I think of this earlier?"

He announced that, since the lab hadn't blown up, they were going back for some "sport." Once they were aboard, they were to round up the scientists and kill them any way they wanted. The men he brought in the shuttle were his most cold-blooded killers. They were to spare Zavala, who would be thrown into the medusa tank. Dr. Wu would record his death on video so his final moments could be transmitted to Austin.

Carrying its cargo of murderers, the shuttle descended to the transit hub. The pilot activated the shuttle's airlock. Minutes later, Chang and his followers burst out of the airlock and almost stumbled over a box of C-4. A length of colored wires had been tied in a bow and placed on top of the carton. And resting against the bow was a white envelope with CHANG on it in big block letters.

The man who had set up the explosives picked up the cluster of wires.

"Nothing to worry about," he said. "These wires aren't connected to anything."

He handed the envelope to Chang, who ripped it open. Inside was a piece of stationery with a Davy Jones's Locker logo on it. The paper had been folded in three. Printed on the first panel was

BANG!

Chang quickly unfolded the paper. There was a smiley face on the next panel and

JUST KIDDING!

The last panel read

I'M IN THE CONTROL ROOM.

Chang crumpled the paper and ordered his men to search the complex. They came back a few minutes later and reported that the complex appeared deserted and that wires had been torn from all the C-4.

Chang stormed off to the control room, only to pause at the door. Suspecting that the room had been booby-trapped, he sent his men in first.

They scoured the room and reported back to Chang that it

too was deserted and that nothing was amiss. He stepped in to see for himself. He glanced around, his scowl deepening. He wanted somebody to take his fury out on. He saw Dr. Wu filming the room.

"Not now, you fool!" Chang shouted. "Can't you see there's nobody here?"

A metallic voice issued from the wall speakers.

"You're right, Chang. You and your pals are the only ones on the lab."

Chang wheeled around, the stock of the machine pistol tight against his chest.

"Who's that?"

"SpongeBob SquarePants," the voice said.

"Austin!"

"Okay, I confess, Chang. You got me. It's Kurt Austin."

Chang's eyes narrowed to slits.

"What happened to the scientists?" he asked.

"They are no longer on the lab, Chang. They left in the mini-subs."

"Don't toy with me, Austin. I destroyed the subs' power circuits."

A different voice came on the speaker: Phelps.

"Those were backup circuits you stomped on," he said. "The subs were fully operable, boss."

"Phelps?" Chang exclaimed. "I thought you were dead."

"Sorry to disappoint you, Chang. Austin ain't jerking you around. Dr. Mitchell and all the other scientists are long gone."

"I'll find them," Chang shouted. "I'll find you and Austin and kill you!"

"That's not very likely," Austin said. "By the way, the vaccine cultures they gave you are useless. The real ones are with the staff."

✦ ✦ ✦

THE VOICES IN CHANG'S HEAD began to rise in volume and number, reaching an evil cacophony. A white hate flowed through his bull-like body like a power surge. He ordered his men back to the shuttle. As it rose from the lab, he radioed the freighter, giving orders to start scouring the depths with sonar. A minute later, he got a reply. Sonar had picked up four shapes moving away from the atoll. Chang ordered the freighter to be on hand when the minisubs surfaced.

The shuttle went full speed toward the tunnel. Chang allowed a smile to cross his face, anticipating the looks on the scientists' faces when they saw the freighter bearing down on them. He was savoring the scene, imagining how they would react when he rose from the deep like Neptune, when he heard the pilot call out. Chang leaned forward in his seat and stared out the cockpit window.

A huge black shadow was bearing down on the shuttle.

The pilot recognized the massive blunt bow of the Typhoon hurtling right at them and he yelped like a frightened puppy. Chang yelled at him to turn, but the pilot's hands were frozen on the controls. Uttering a feral snarl, Chang grabbed the pilot by the shoulders, pulled him out of his chair, and took his place. He yanked the wheel hard to starboard.

The shuttle's turbines continued to drive it forward, but after a few seconds the front came around to the right, narrowly edging the shuttle out of the way of a head-on collision with the six-hundred-foot torpedo hurtling its way. But the Typhoon was moving at twenty-five knots, and it clipped the tail end of the shuttle, demolishing its rudder and sending the shuttle into a wild spin. The violent impact caused the cargo door to fly open, and water began flowing in.

The weight of the inrushing sea dragged the shuttle's tail down, and the front of the shuttle angled upward like a dying fish. Chang's men grabbed onto the seats and pulled themselves up the slanting deck toward the cockpit.

Dr. Wu struggled to join the pack, but the stronger guards pushed him under the water and his flailing arms soon grew still. Chang was not about to share the pocket of air with anyone. He turned around, leaned his pistol over the back of the seat, and shot any man who tried to encroach on his space. Within seconds, he had killed all his guards and was alone in the cabin.

By then the weight of the water in the shuttle had shifted forward. Its nose leveled out, and the shuttle began to sink to the bottom of the crater. The cabin was plunged into complete darkness. Chang fought to keep his head up in the diminishing pocket of air, but the bodies swashing around in the blood-stained water made it difficult. As soon as he pushed one body out of the way, another body came along to take its place. At one point, he was eye-to-eye with dead Dr. Wu.

More water came in, diminishing the pocket of life-giving air even more. Chang pressed against the ceiling of the shuttle with only a few inches left. As water filled his mouth and nostrils, he looked up, saw the monstrous shadow of the Typhoon gliding overhead, and, with his last, soggy gasp uttered:

"Austin!"

THE OWNER OF THAT NAME sat next to the Russian helmsman in the Typhoon's control room. Zavala was on the other side of the man, a young Ukrainian who had a natural talent for his job. The captain stood by Austin's side, relaying orders in Russian to the helmsman.

Minutes earlier, the helmsman had backed the sub into the

tunnel, facing into the crater. The sonar operator watched for the shuttle and alerted Austin when he picked up its moving blip. A monitor connected to a camera in the sub's sail picked out the shuttle's twin searchlights approaching. Austin gave the order for a full-speed ram. The helmsman gripped the wheel as the submarine began to move forward. The ambush was under way.

After glancing off the shuttle, the Typhoon had continued into the crater and made a wide turn. As the sub headed back toward the tunnel to finish the job, the camera picked up the shuttle once again. Austin watched with pitiless eyes as it plunged to the bottom. He felt no sense of triumph. Not yet. He was all too well aware that the Triad was a *three*-headed monster.

CHAPTER 46

WHEN THE *CONCORD* FAILED TO HEAR FROM AUSTIN, CAPtain Dixon had moved the Navy ships under his command in closer to surround the atoll. He stood on the foredeck with Song Lee, who had stayed by his side since Austin had set off on his mission hours before.

The captain was watching the atoll through binoculars in the dawn light, unaware of the drama that had transpired under the calm waters of the lagoon. He was pondering what his next course of action should be when Lee pointed toward a boiling patch of water. She grabbed him by the arm.

"Captain Dixon, look!"

As they were looking, the massive conning tower and high vertical rudder of the Typhoon broke the surface several hundred yards east of the atoll. After a few minutes, two figures appeared in the lofty tower and waved their arms. Dixon brought his binoculars to his eyes.

"I'll be damned," he said.

He handed the binoculars to Lee.

She raised them to her eyes, and blurted, "It's Kurt! And Joe!"

Dixon laughed out loud. Only Kurt Austin could go fishing in a remote lagoon and catch the world's biggest submarine.

After another wave, the two men disappeared from the tower and emerged moments later from a hatch in the deck. With the help of some crewmen, they pulled an inflatable boat up on deck, lowered it over the sub's rounded hull into the water, then climbed in and came skimming over the waves toward the cruiser.

Song Lee was waiting on deck to throw her arms around Austin, then Zavala. Then Austin again. She gave him a kiss full on the lips.

Austin would have liked to prolong the pleasant experience, but he gently disentangled himself from her arms and turned to Captain Dixon.

"Have you seen any sign of the lab's staff?" he asked. "They should have surfaced in the minisubs by now."

Dixon shook his head. He called his first officer on the bridge and asked him to ask the other ships in the vicinity to be on the lookout for the surfacing minisubs. Moments later, a call came in from the NUMA ship. The first minisub had surfaced. Dixon issued an order to get the *Concord* under way. It rounded the atoll just in time to see a second sub popping out of the water, then a third. Each had an identification number painted on its side.

Austin scanned the sea for the fourth minisub carrying Lois Mitchell and the vaccine. After a few anxious moments, it too popped out of the water.

He let out the breath he had been holding.

"We need to bring the scientists from the last sub on board immediately," he told the captain.

Dixon ordered a boat in the water. The rescue crew pulled Lois Mitchell and the other scientists out of their minisub and brought them back to the cruiser. As the boat came close, Lois saw Austin leaning over the railing. She waved, then pointed to the cooler in her lap. When she climbed aboard, she handed the cooler off to Lee.

"Here's our vaccine," Mitchell said, "safe and sound."

The joyful smile on Lee's face dissolved. She looked crestfallen as she held the cooler, like someone just told her it was radioactive.

"It's too late, Lois," she said. "The epidemic will explode throughout China within twenty-four hours and spread to the rest of the world within days. There is no time to produce the vaccine in the massive quantities we need."

Mitchell took the cooler back, set it on the deck, and pushed the top back to expose a rack with dozens of aluminum cylinders in it. She pulled one out and showed it to Lee.

"You weren't in on the last phase of the research," Mitchell said, "so you don't know how far we have gone."

"I was aware that you had integrated the antiviral molecule into microbes in an attempt to speed up the synthesis process," Lee said.

"We decided that was too slow," Mitchell said. "So we incorporated the toxin's curative protein in fast-growing saltwater algae."

Lee's expression of dismay turned to laughter.

She picked up a cylinder and said, "This is wonderful."

Seeing the puzzled expressions on the faces of the three men, she explained.

"Algae grow at an incredible speed," she said. "Once we get these cultures to the production facilities, they can extract enough vaccine for hundreds of people in a short time. We can do the same for thousands, then hundreds of thousands within a few days."

She handed the cylinder to Austin, who held it gingerly as if he expected to feel some sort of magical emanations. He carefully placed it back in the cooler and closed the lid, then turned to Dixon.

"This has to get to China as soon as possible," he said.

The captain picked the cooler off the deck.

"It's on its way," he said.

Ten minutes later, the Seahawk carrying the cooler lifted off the deck and headed toward its rendezvous with a fast jet waiting at Pohnpei Airport. Within hours of landing in China, its cargo would be distributed to vaccine-production facilities that Lee had set up during her time on Bonefish Key.

Austin stood on the deck, watching the helicopter shrink to a speck. Lee had volunteered to escort the vaccine back to China. Austin was sad to see her go, but the evil smile of the Dragon Lady was already starting to overshadow his thoughts of Song's lovely face.

THE GIANT RUSSIAN SUBMARINE led the way into Pohnpei's harbor like a proud leviathan. Next was Chang's freighter, now manned by a Navy crew that had taken over after a destroyer had chased her down. Without orders from Chang, his crew had surrendered to the no-nonsense Navy SEALs without a shot.

Phelps had come over from the submarine and was giving Austin and Zavala a tour of the deceptively decrepit-looking vessel, showing them the moon pool, the high-powered engine room, and the state-of-the-art communications center with its hologram-projection booth that Chang used to communicate with his other two triplets.

The last stop was the ship's salon. Austin made himself immediately at home in the oversize room. He passed out three

Havana-wrapped cigars from a humidor and lit them with a silver-plated lighter. He, Zavala, and Phelps sat in plush red-velvet chairs and puffed on their cigars.

"Chang had a good nose for smokes," Zavala said, "but his taste in decorating stinks."

Austin blew out a smoke ring and glanced around the spacious salon.

"I dunno," he said, looking at the purple drapes and dark wood paneling, "the Castle Dracula look is all the rage in Transylvania."

"Kinda reminds me more of a Nevada whorehouse," said Phelps, who had been studying the ash on his cigar. He flicked the ash onto the maroon carpet, and added, "I stopped there one time to ask for directions."

Austin smiled and took a few more puffs, then snuffed his cigar out in an ashtray.

"We've got to talk," he said to Phelps.

"Talk away," Phelps said.

"Joe and I are grateful for your help," Austin said, "but we've got to discuss what comes next. We've got that issue about the scientist you killed on board the lab."

"It was an accident," Phelps said. "Lois will vouch for that."

"I thought she didn't like you," Zavala said.

"We've gotten to know each other better. She's a beautiful woman. I like them big-boned."

Austin stared at Phelps, thinking that the man was full of surprises.

"Tell me, Phelps," he said, "do you have a first name?"

"Don't believe in them," Phelps said.

"Well, here's the problem," Austin said with a heavy smile. "You killed that man in the commission of a crime, the hijacking of U.S. property and the missile attack on the support ship. You're lucky no one died on the *Proud Mary.* Then there's the death of the security-company man who got your ID."

"The missile attack was meant to distract the guards long enough to steal the lab," Phelps said. "I'll admit someone could have been killed, but I'm glad that didn't happen. I had no part in the security man's death . . . But I see what you mean."

"Glad to hear that you understand the situation," Austin said. "I'm going to have to turn you over to the authorities when we land. I'll tell them the whole story, and that's sure to mitigate your punishment."

"Ten years in the brig instead of twenty?" Phelps grinned. "Well, sometimes you gotta do what you gotta do. Mind if I go tell Lois what's happening?"

Austin couldn't help admiring the man's calm. He nodded, then rose from his chair. They left the salon, and a few minutes later were in a pontoon boat headed back to the *Concord.*

Lois Mitchell was waiting there for them. Phelps peeled Lois away from the others, and they went off to talk while Austin and Zavala went to the wardroom to meet with the captain and the scientists from the lab.

Dixon brought everyone up to date on the progress of the jet flying to China. It would be close, but the vaccine would make it there in time.

Austin glanced at his watch. He excused himself and went out on the deck. He asked several crewmen if they had seen Phelps and Mitchell, and he finally got an answer when one of them pointed toward shore.

"They took the inflatable into port," the crewman informed Austin. "They said they would be back in a couple of hours. Guy said to give this to you."

Austin unfolded the sheet of lined notebook paper and read the short, scrawled message:

"Gotta do what you gotta do. P."

An annoyed smile came to Austin's lips. Phelps had out-foxed him.

Austin walked over to the railing and looked toward Pohnpei. Kolonia was small town on a small island, but the local police department wasn't exactly Interpol. Phelps would be far away by the time local police mobilized.

Austin climbed to the bridge at a very leisurely pace, and asked a crewman to call the police, report a stolen launch, and give them a description of Mitchell and Phelps.

He took solace in the fact that Chang was dead. His attempt to spread the virus had been foiled. The vaccine would soon be made available.

One Triad triplet had been eliminated, but that still left Wen Lo and the mysterious Dragon Lady.

Austin was still pondering his course of action when his cell phone rang. It was Lieutenant Casey.

"Congratulations, Kurt," Casey said, "the admiral just called and gave me the good news."

"Thanks, Lieutenant, but our work isn't done as long as the other Triad triplets are on the loose."

"We're well aware of that, Kurt. I have someone on the line who would like to talk to you."

Austin told Casey to transfer him. A few seconds later, a man's voice came on the line.

"Good day, Mr. Austin," he said in a silken tone. "Let me introduce myself. I am Colonel Ming of the People's Liberation Army."

"Good day, Colonel Ming. How can I help you?"

"That is not why I called, Mr. Austin. The question is, how can I help *you*?"

CHAPTER 47

WEN LO EMERGED FROM HIS FAVORITE NIGHTCLUB WITH A gorgeous prostitute clinging to each arm. His walk was unsteady, but the Triad triplet wasn't too drunk to see that something was very wrong. His guards were gone. The two SUVs that escorted his armor-plated Mercedes everywhere were gone. His Mercedes was gone, and a black Roewe sedan had taken its place at the curb.

Standing on the sidewalk next to the car was a husky, granite-faced man in a dark blue suit. He opened the Roewe's rear door and motioned for Wen Lo to get in.

Wen Lo looked up and down the street, as if he could make his guards and car reappear through sheer willpower. No pedestrians or traffic moved in either direction. The street obviously had been cordoned off.

Wen Lo dispensed the prostitutes with a shove and a brusque word and got in the Roewe. The husky man shut the door and slid in front next to the driver. As the car pulled away from the curb, a slender man in an Army uniform sitting in the backseat, said, "Good evening, Wen Lo. My apologies for spoiling your night out on the town."

"Good evening, Colonel Ming. No apologies necessary. It is always a pleasure to see you, my friend."

In this case, it was more of a relief than a pleasure. Colonel Ming was the liaison between the Army and the Triad, and both organizations profited handsomely from the hundreds of brothels that they jointly operated around the country.

"The feeling is mutual, of course," said the colonel, a soft-spoken man whose patrician air seemed more suited to the diplomatic corps than the Army.

Wen Lo always trod carefully around Ming. He was not unmindful of the fact that the colonel's comrades had nicknamed him Colonel Cobra.

"I must say that I was concerned when I saw my men were not at their posts and my car was gone," Wen Lo said.

"Rest assured, they are in a safe place," Ming said. "I thought it best not to have any distractions while we talked over a serious problem that has arisen."

"Of course," Wen Lo said. "What sort of problem? Are you looking for a more luxurious apartment . . . or car? . . . Or is there someone that you would like removed from the scene?"

"This is not personal," Ming said. "This is business. The problem is in Pyramid's pharmaceutical division."

"That puzzles me, Colonel. The contaminated drugs have been destroyed. The poisoned infant formula killed only a few hundred children."

"Perhaps this will explain the problem better than I can," Ming said.

Colonel Ming stretched his hand out to a DVD player built into the back of the driver's seat and pushed the ON button.

Wen Lo's face appeared on the screen. He watched himself taking a tour of the secret lab with Dr. Wu, whose voice was narrating, and close-ups of the subjects and their disease-ravaged faces.

"Where did you get this?" Wen Lo asked as the video came to its end.

"That is of no importance," Ming said. "But I am puzzled as to the nature of this facility your organization is operating."

The colonel was being disingenuous. The video was quite detailed in its presentation.

Wen Lo glanced at the men in the front seat. Speaking in a conspiratorial whisper, he said, "I am taking you into my confidence, Colonel. The secret I am about to reveal is held by me and a few of the most powerful people in the government. The laboratory has been working on a revolutionary new vaccine that will not only contain a new outbreak of SARS but will cure dozens of other diseases caused by viruses."

Colonel Ming lightly clapped his hands.

"That is *wonderful* news, Wen Lo! Congratulations."

"Thank you, Colonel. It has been a long, hard road, but our work will put China in the medical history books. This will be a boon to mankind. And to the Army, I might add. You and your comrades will derive great benefits from our endeavors."

"Excellent!" The colonel paused for a moment, then said, "I am not a medical person, but, since you mentioned mankind, I wondered if it is customary to use human beings as lab animals."

"Pardon me, sir, but they would be very upset to be described in that fashion. They are all volunteers from the slums. They faced miserable lives, in any case."

The colonel nodded.

"Yes, I see your logic, Wen Lo. Your lab served to shorten their misery. I applaud your humanity and your genius."

"I do nothing solely for myself, Colonel Ming. I am always thinking about the good of my country."

"And your country would like to reward your hard work and sacrifice," Ming said. "But this video raises some concerns. It is easily copied and transmitted. I fear that it will surface in quarters where people will not be as enlightened as you and me. You see the potential for disorder?"

Wen Lo was well aware of the government's aversion to disorder. Through intimidation and assassination, he and his thugs often had stifled dissent when the government choose to pursue a hands-off policy.

"Yes, of course," Wen Lo said. "But the government controls the media and the Internet. We can claim that the video is a fake. My organization can deal with those who choose to make an issue of this matter."

"All true," Ming said. "But we cannot control the foreign media, and the government has no wish to be associated even by implication with what the video shows. Since you are the public face of Pyramid, we feel it best if you disappear."

"Disappear?" Wen Lo croaked.

Ming patted Wen Lo's knee.

"Don't be alarmed," the colonel said. "We are old friends as well as colleagues. We have arranged for you to quietly leave China. The government is prepared to work with Pyramid while you are out of the country."

"I suppose that may work," Wen Lo said with reluctance.

"We will need to know where and how to reach the number one person in your company," Ming said.

"Impossible! We never meet face-to-face. We communicate electronically through holograms."

A sad look came to the colonel's face.

"That is a shame," Ming said. "I'm afraid the onus will fall entirely on your shoulders. You will be brought to trial, and the outcome is a foregone conclusion. An example will be made of you."

Wen Lo was well aware of the consequences of being made an example of in China. He knew a number of the men who had been tried and executed for corrupt business practices.

"Very well," Wen Lo said with a deep sigh. "We use a simple telephone number to set up our hologram meetings."

The colonel reached into his pocket and pulled out a pen and a small notepad, which he gave to Wen Lo. After a few seconds of hesitation, Wen Lo jotted down a number and handed back the pad and pen.

"Thank you," Ming said, inspecting the number to make sure it was legible. He tucked the pad and pen back in his pocket. "Now we can deal with your future. How does London sound, for a start? We can move you around, to Paris and New York, as need be. And, when it's safe, we can bring you home again."

Wen Lo's mood brightened.

"London is fine. I have a town house in Soho."

"Too public. The government will find you a less obvious place to live. Do you still play tennis?"

"Every day. It's my passion."

"Splendid. You will have endless time to work on your back-hand."

Ming lit a cigarette, took a drag, and tapped on the window separating the backseat from the driver. The car pulled over to the curb, and the colonel said to Wen Lo, "See you in Paris."

The husky man got out of the front, opened the door, and escorted Ming to a second Roewe sedan that had pulled up behind the first one. As Ming got into the second car, he said to the man, "Make sure it's neat."

As the colonel's car pulled away from the curb, he tapped out a number on his cell phone. After a few rings, a man's voice answered.

"Mr. Austin?" Ming said.

"That's right," Austin replied.

"I have the information you are looking for."

WHILE THE COLONEL WAS talking on the phone in his car, the husky man walked back to the first car and got in next to the driver. He tapped on the glass behind him and slid the partition open. Wen Lo looked right at him. This gave the man a perfect target when he shot Wen Lo directly in the right eye with a .22 caliber pistol.

The shooter slid the glass partition closed and grunted an order to the driver. They drove Wen Lo's warm body to a mortuary that was waiting to embalm it. A glass eye replaced the one the bullet had vaporized. The embalmed corpse was turned over to the Bureau of Police. A tag attached to the big toe there certified that he had died while being incarcerated in a Chinese prison.

The police noted the death on records that were promptly destroyed. The body was shipped to a warehouse where the receiver complained about the quality of the merchandise. The corpse was dissected, immersed in acetone to eliminate all traces of moisture, and then given a bath of polymers. The muscles and bones were touched up with paint, and the body bent into a standing position, the arm cocked and ready to smash a tennis ball.

When the transformed corpse arrived in London to join other bodies in an exhibition that would take it to Paris and New York, a tennis racket was placed in the boney hand.

In time, Wen Lo's skinned body would adorn T-shirts, key chains, refrigerator magnets, even the cover of the catalog sold at the traveling exhibition.

And, as Colonel Ming had promised, Wen Lo had endless time to work on his backhand.

CHAPTER 48

WHEN JOE ZAVALA WASN'T DATING HALF THE FEMALE POPulation of Washington or tinkering with his Corvette's engine, he loved figuring out how things worked. To Zavala, the hologram projection room adjacent to Chang's garishly appointed ship's salon was nothing but an elaborate engine whose purpose was to send and receive lifelike images.

Zavala prowled through the intricate arrangement of microphones, lenses, lasers, projectors, and computers that surrounded the circular table and three chairs under the hanging cones. Austin was standing by, connected by cell phone to Hiram Yeager back at NUMA headquarters. Yeager was an expert on holograms, having developed a lovely young holographic woman named Max as the personification of the NUMA computer system, which he presided over. Austin relayed questions to Yeager and sent him photos of electronic or optic devices that Zavala was unable to describe.

After an hour of analyzing the ingenious setup, Zavala stepped back and brushed his palms together.

"She's all set and ready to go, Kurt. You can project yourself with a push of that button."

Austin peered up into one of the cones overhead.

"This isn't going to reassemble my molecules so that I end up with the head of a fly, is it?" he asked.

"Nothing to worry about, Kurt. This is all high-tech illusion, smoke and mirrors."

"Keep a flyswatter handy, just in case," Austin said, settling into the padded, contoured chair.

Zavala stood off to the side ready to intervene if something went wrong. Austin glanced across the table at the two empty chairs, studied the control panel for a moment, and then punched in the code number Wen Lo had given Colonel Ming before the Triad triplet met his premature demise.

Lights blinked and machinery hummed as a complex set of optics scanned every square inch of Austin's body and transmitted the information via electronic pulses to a computer that digested the information and sent it to another computer to be reassembled in a 3-D projector. The scan was all smoke and mirrors, as Zavala had said, but Austin tensed his shoulders, expecting to feel an electrical tingle that never came.

Instead, the air under a cone across from Austin shimmered as if heated. A cloud of whirling motes began to form with no distinct outline at first, then materialized into the rough image of a human head and shoulders, transparent at first, becoming translucent, then solid, as the facial features filled in. Austin knew from his encounter with the Dragon Lady that the hologram was mutable and could be changed at a whim. But the face across the table was stranger than anything he could have imagined.

The eyes below the gracefully arched brows were the same jade-green as Chang's hate-filled orbs. The fleshy lips were feminine, but the soft-featured face was at odds with stubble on the

chin and the professional wrestler's body with shoulders strain-
ing the seams of the black collarless shirt. The third Triad triplet
seemed to be neither man nor woman but a freakish combination
of both, a hermaphrodite.

The hologram remained as still as a marble statue. The small,
delicate hands remained on the table. The features were frozen,
eyes staring straight ahead. Then the lips moved, and a mellow
voice, neither male nor female, came through the surrounding
speakers.

"We meet again, Mr. Austin," the hologram said.

"Should I call you Dragon Lady or Lai Choi San?" Austin
asked.

"I am known as *One* to my followers. I was the first of my
siblings to come into this world, by a few minutes. We Chinese
are superstitious when it comes to numbers and believe a low
number denotes good fortune."

"From the way your luck has been going lately," Austin said,
"you'd better look for a new number. Your holographic image is
all out of whack too. Nothing is moving except for your mouth."

"That's because I can't move my limbs. I have limited movement of my eyes and full movement of my lips only."

"What happened?"

"I was hoping you could tell me that, Mr. Austin."

Austin paused, recalling Kane's revelations about the paralyzing effects of the medusa toxin.

"We wondered what happened to the vaccine," he said. "The
ship's helicopter was gone, so we concluded that the cooler with
the vaccine and cultures was no longer on Chang's freighter."

"The serum was transported directly to me. Upon the assurance of my brother Chang, I orally vaccinated myself. I knew
that the virus would spread to my city in a matter of hours and I
wanted to be the first to be made immune. I became paralyzed

as I sat here trying to contact my brothers." The thin lips spread in a grotesque parody of a smile. "It seems that the chemical was flawed."

"The cylinder Chang sent you contained a transitional vaccine that was going to be discarded. It could kill the virus, but it still paralyzed the host."

"Then the research was a failure?"

"Not at all, One. The real vaccine is rapidly being produced throughout China and around the world in quantities that will stop the epidemic you started."

The lips snapped back to a thin line.

"The fact that you are on Chang's ship tells me that my brother is no longer in the picture. He would never allow you to live if he were alive."

"I'm afraid Chang became a victim of his own violent impulses."

"Too bad," the hologram said without sadness. "Chang was brilliant in many ways but too often impetuous."

Austin's jaw hardened.

"The murder of scores of innocent people," he said, "is not what most people would describe as impetuous."

"That's because our family has always looked at the world in a different way from others. Pyramid Triad was in existence centuries before your rabble chased the British back to England. We have not survived all this time by being sentimental when it comes to the deaths of others, or even deaths in our own family."

"Glad to hear that," Austin said, "because you won't shed any tears over the loss of your brother Wen Lo."

"Wen Lo is dead too?"

"He ran afoul of the Chinese Army . . . another casualty of your insane scheme."

"There was nothing insane about it. Our country's leadership is extremely fragile. The government would have reacted violently to protests in the streets. We would have encouraged the mob rule that would have followed and then stepped in to end the epidemic and take over the reins of government. With the vaccine, we would have held the power of life and death over a billion of our countrymen. We would have offered the same choice to the rest of the world in exchange for money and power. The plan was well thought out. We didn't anticipate the interference from you and your NUMA friends."

"NUMA doesn't deserve all the credit," Austin said. "You planted the seeds of your own destruction when you decided to play at being a three-headed god. You're not the first ones to appoint yourselves immortals, and you won't be the last, which is why I will always have job security."

"Did you say the same thing when your CIA unit was dissolved?"

"I'm happy to say that my work became no longer necessary with the end of the Cold War, but, from the sound of it, you've been digging into my past."

"I know more about you than your closest friends, Zavala and the Trouts. I have studied your house on the Potomac via satellite. I know what kind of music you listen to, what kind of philosophy books you read. But some of your life is hidden in the shadows, which gives me hope."

"Hope for what, One? You're almost completely immobile. The best you can look forward to is being hired as a hat rack."

"But you could change that, Austin." The voice had become as soft as a snake rustling through grass. "My pharmaceutical company developed the virus, and, given some time and direction, they can work on an antidote to neutralize the effects of the toxin. I would reward you beyond your wildest dreams."

"Seeing your Triad wiped off the face of the earth is the only reward I want."

A flash of anger came to the staring holographic eyes.

"I could squash you like an ant, Austin."

"You could, if you could lift a finger. So long, One. The toxin will keep you alive for a long time. Have a good life."

Austin's finger was poised over the button that would have ended the transmission.

"*Wait!* Where are you going?"

"After dealing with you and your brothers," Austin said, "I need a long, hot shower."

"You can't leave me all alone like this."

The plea could have been genuine, but it made no difference to Austin. He felt only revulsion toward the freakish figure.

"Then I'll make a deal with you," he said. "Tell me where you are and I'll relay the information to the Chinese government. You can take your chances with them."

After a moment, the triplet reeled off an address in Hong Kong.

"Thanks, One. Now I'll give you some good advice. Forget any thoughts about bribing your way out of this. The government is appropriating all your assets. You have nothing to offer them."

"I will kill you, Austin. Somehow, I will find a way."

"Good-bye, Dragon Lady."

"*Wait!*"

Austin pushed the button to halt the projection. The words came out of a formless cloud of dancing motes. It was a woman's voice.

"*Come back!*"

Zavala, who was standing off to the side, muttered something in Spanish.

Austin realized that he was soaked with sweat. Even separated at a distance of thousands of miles, he had never been so close to pure evil.

"I am become Death, the destroyer of worlds," he murmured.

Zavala overheard him.

"What was that, Kurt?"

As if awakening from a dream, Austin said, "It's a quote from the Bhagavad Gita. It popped into my mind just now. Did you jot down the address that thing gave me?"

Zavala held up a sheet of paper.

"What do you want to do with it?" he asked.

"When we get back to the *Concord,* call Colonel Ming and give him the information. It's his party from now on. Then fill in Paul and Gamay on what's happened. Then go pour yourself a stiff shot of tequila, followed by another one, saving some cactus juice for me."

"Aye, aye, sir. What are you going to do in the meantime?"

Austin rose from his chair and headed for the door.

"Take that long, hot shower I talked about."

CHAPTER 49

BONEFISH KEY, FIVE WEEKS LATER

SONG LEE WAS SITTING ON THE SUNLIT PATIO IN FRONT OF the lodge going over some notes when she heard the drone of an outboard motor echoing through the mangroves. Recognizing the sound of Dooley's boat, she looked up and smiled at his impending arrival.

Dooley had been her main contact with the outside world since she had returned to the island to work on her medical text on ocean biomedicine. Returning to Bonefish Key had required determination. But the lab had been at the forefront of a science whose roots went back to the ancient culture of Nan Madol and the Micronesian islands, and it was the most compelling place for her to write.

Lee could not yet muster the courage to visit the barrier beach. She had no desire to see the cove where she had killed a man or to revisit the burned-out hulk of the cabin cruiser that had nearly been her funeral pyre. She still kayaked but stayed closer to the island. She went to bed early and was up with the sun, tapping at her laptop computer in the lab's research library for hours on end.

The island was practically deserted. With the project at an end, Dr. Mayhew had returned to academia, and his team had scattered to the four winds. A small cadre stayed behind to tend to the specimen tanks, but the guards who had put in double duty as support staff had left. Dr. Lee enjoyed the camaraderie of a handful of technicians as they prepared their own meals.

Dr. Kane had visited the lab once. He had breezed in with a camera crew to film the lodge and lab buildings before he swept out again as if carried on the wind.

Although the governments of China and the United States were still nervous about telling the whole story of their secretive collaboration in stopping the near pandemic, the Herculean effort to stop the virus was big news around the world. Kane basked in his celebrity, flying from interview to interview, consulting with health experts and politicians around the globe. He was using his status as pandemic guru to pry money from Congress to support the type of ocean biomedicine research that had saved the world.

Song Lee had been content to labor in anonymity, but the remoteness of the island had started to get to her and she had been thinking of finishing her book back in China. She often thought of the NUMA people who had swooped in to save her and the world. She missed the Trouts and Joe Zavala, but most of all she missed Kurt Austin. A few weeks after she had arrived on the island, he had called her on one of the lab's radiophones. He was on Pohnpei, still helping with the recovery of Davy Jones's Locker, and would be in Micronesia longer than anticipated.

The drone of the marine motor grew louder, and seconds later Dooley's double-hulled boat rounded the corner of a mangrove island and coasted up to the dock. There were two people in the boat: Dooley, who was at the wheel, and, beside him, a broad-shouldered man wearing a Hawaiian shirt. As they approached the dock, the broad-shouldered man removed the baseball hat from his head, revealing a thick mane of steel-gray hair. Song was already up and running down to the dock by the time Kurt Austin had started to wave his cap in the air. She and the boat got to the end of the dock at the same time.

Dooley tossed her the bow line as the boat bumped up against a piling.

"Brought you some company, Dr. Lee," he said.

Song barely heard him. Her eyes were fixed on Kurt, who had a wide grin on his bronzed face. The grin grew even wider when he climbed out of the boat and Song threw her arms around him. He returned her embrace with enthusiasm. She planted a kiss on his lips that was warm and long, and might have gone on forever if Dooley hadn't cleared his throat.

"Pardon me, folks, but I've got to get back to the mainland." He extended his hand. "Nice to meet you, Kurt. Call when you want to go back to Pine Island."

"Thanks for the ride, Dooley," Austin said. He asked Dooley to toss him his small rucksack.

As the boat disappeared into mangroves, Austin said, "I got back to Washington a few days ago and thought I would hop down here to say hello."

Lee hooked her arm in Austin's and led the way toward the lodge.

"I'm glad you did," she said. "How are Joe and the Trouts?"

"They're fine. Zavala has found true love with a NUMA cartographer, and the Trouts just got back from New Bedford. The city's whaling museum was dedicating a room for Caleb Nye's diorama. It's part of a special exhibition on the strange voyage of the *Princess*."

"And a very strange voyage it was," Lee said. "I start off my book with their experience on Trouble Island."

"How is the book coming?"

"I've finished the outline and I'm doing supplemental research. I think the findings will revolutionize our understanding of viral immunology, particularly inoculation. But we have just scratched the surface of wonder drugs that will come from the ocean. It's ironic that the vaccine might never have been developed without the threat of the Triad's epidemic."

"A classic case of yin and yang?" he asked.

"I hate to think that the opposing forces of good and evil were bound together in this case," she said, "but without one, the other would not have produced a benefit to the world."

"More than one," he said. "China and U.S. relations have never been warmer. And the Triad is no longer with us. Yin and yang on hormones."

They had climbed the hill to the patio and settled into a couple of chairs that faced the waterfront and the mangroves beyond.

"I have a tough question to ask," Austin said. "Dr. Huang's role as an informant enabled the Triad to pursue its evil goals. After he tipped off the Triad about the lab, they eavesdropped on Doc Kane and pinpointed its location. What should we do about him?"

"I don't know," Lee said. "He is a mouse and frightens easily, but he's a brilliant doctor. I would hate to turn him over to the government. They would execute him." She looked off at a snowy egret gliding over the water, and when she turned back to Austin a smile lit up her face. "*This* is what I propose for Dr. Huang."

She explained her idea to send Huang to take her place as a country doctor. Austin threw his head back and let out a hearty laugh.

"A solution that is perfect in its symmetry. Now it's my turn to make a proposal."

He zipped open his rucksack and pulled out a bottle and two shot glasses. He poured each glass half full and offered one to Song.

"This is the Micronesian *sakau* I promised you. It's made from a pepper plant and is slightly narcotic, so it is best taken in small doses."

They raised their glasses, and, after a moment of thought, Song said, "Here's to warm relations between China and America."

They clinked glasses. She made a sour face and put her glass down on the table.

"It's an acquired taste, which is probably a good thing," Austin said with a smile. "As I recall, I also promised you a dinner with a water view." He swept his hand in the air. "Here's the water view. Dinner may have to wait until your work here is done."

"Maybe not," Song said. "One of the lab techs caught some fresh redfish this morning, and we will be grilling them for dinner. Please join us."

Austin accepted the invitation, and they sat on the patio talking until the dinner bell clanged. They ate in the dining room with a half dozen staffers, then retired to the patio to enjoy an after-dinner drink as the island became enveloped by a liquid darkness. Austin had repacked the *sakau,* and they were drinking a less lethal port.

Kurt and Song talked for hours, with the sensuous sounds and smells of the semitropic night in the background, and it was late when they realized that the rest of the staff had drifted off and they were all alone.

Austin glanced at his watch, and said, "It's almost midnight. I had better call Dooley to have him pick me up."

Song laughed softly, and said, "Dooley is in bed by now. And you would have to climb the water tower to pick up a signal. Why don't you stay the night with me in my cottage? It's quite snug and comfortable."

"Never let it be said that Kurt Austin stood in the way of warm Chinese-American relations," he said. "But these clothes are all I have. I left my pajamas at home."

Song reached out and touched Kurt's hand.

"You won't need them," she said with a smile in her voice.

THEY AWOKE EARLY THE next day to a waterbird symphony. Austin had to get back to Washington for a meeting. While he climbed the tower to call Dooley, Song and the lab technicians produced a send-off breakfast that was heavy on fresh fruit. As they dined on the patio, Austin savored the peace and quiet of the island.

"It's going to be tough to leave paradise," he said.

"Do you really have to go so soon?" she asked.

"Unfortunately, yes. I'm sorry to rush off."

"Maybe you can rush back just as quickly."

"I have the feeling we'll be seeing each other sooner than we think. How's your research going on the New Bedford anomaly?"

"I've been going over what material I have. But so much is missing." She frowned, and said, "I think I hear Dooley."

Song walked Kurt to the end of the dock. They embraced and kissed good-bye. Before Austin got in the boat, he reached into his rucksack and pulled out a package wrapped in plain paper. He handed it to Lee.

"You might find this of interest," he said.

Lee took the wrapping off and stared at the book in her hand.

The blue leather cover was crinkled with age and weathered from the time it had spent at sea. She turned to the first page and read aloud:

"November 20, 1847. Wind northwest at ten knots. Good ship Princess *departs New Bedford on maiden voyage. Adventure and prosperity beckon. H. Dobbs."*

"It's the missing logbook!" she said. "Where did you find it?"

"The Trouts picked it up when they went to New Bedford for the dedication. Seems Harvey Brimmer's story about Caleb Nye's secret marriage was true. The book was part of a dowry he gave his daughter. It's been in her family since then. They'd like it back after you're done with it."

Kurt gave Song a peck on the cheek, then got in the boat with Dooley. As the boat headed toward the mangroves, Song finally seemed to realize that Kurt was leaving. She waved her hand and shouted a thank-you.

"Too bad you got to leave Dr. Lee so soon," Dooley said.

"That's okay," Austin said. "She's got a young guy to keep her company."

"Sorry to hear that," Dooley said with real concern. "Anybody I know?"

"Probably not. His name is Caleb Nye."

"Women," Dooley muttered with a sad shake of his head.

Minutes later, they broke out of the mangroves into open water. Dooley goosed the throttle, and the boat raced across the blue-green waters of the bay to the distant mainland.